Lincolnshire
COUNTY COUNCIL

discover libraries

This book should be returned on or before the due date.

NBl

To renew or order library books please telephone 01522 782010
or visit https://lincolnshire.spydus.co.uk

You will require a Personal Identification Number.
Ask any member of staff for this.

The above does not apply to Reader's Group Collection Stock.

City so vividly, it feels like only yesterday'   *Weekly*

THE
LAST DAYS
OF NIGHT

GRAHAM
MOORE

SCRIBNER

LONDON NEW YORK TORONTO SYDNEY NEW DELHI

Published in Great Britain by Scribner, an imprint of Simon & Schuster UK Ltd, 2016
This paperback edition published by Scribner, 2017
A CBS COMPANY

1 3 5 7 9 10 8 6 4 2

Simon & Schuster UK Ltd
1st Floor
222 Gray's Inn Road
London WC1X 8HB

www.simonandschuster.co.uk

Simon & Schuster Australia, Sydney
Simon & Schuster India, New Delhi

A CIP catalogue record for this book
is available from the British Library

Paperback ISBN: 978-1-4711-5668-7
eBook ISBN: 978-1-4711-5669-4

The Last Days of Night is a work of historical fiction.
Apart from the well-known actual people, events, and locales that
figure into the narrative, all names, characters, places, and incidents
are products of the author's imagination or are used fictitiously.

Printed and bound by CPI Group (UK) Ltd, Croydon, CR0 4YY

Simon & Schuster UK Ltd are committed to sourcing paper
that is made from wood grown in sustainable forests and support the Forest
Stewardship Council, the leading international forest certification organisation.
Our books displaying the FSC logo are printed on FSC certified paper.

FOR MY GRANDFATHER, DR. CHARLIE STEINER,
who first taught me to revere science on a trip to
Bell Laboratories when I was nine years old. He set an
example of intelligence, kindness, and decency to which
I aspire every day.

CONTENTS

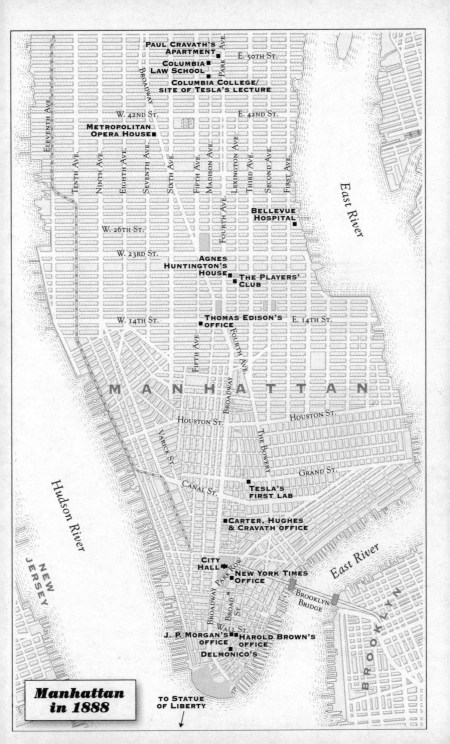

Manhattan in 1888

PAUL CRAVATH'S APARTMENT
E. 50TH ST.
COLUMBIA LAW SCHOOL
COLUMBIA COLLEGE/ SITE OF TESLA'S LECTURE
E. 42ND ST.
W. 42ND ST.
METROPOLITAN OPERA HOUSE
ELEVENTH AVE.
TENTH AVE.
NINTH AVE.
EIGHTH AVE.
SEVENTH AVE.
SIXTH AVE.
BROADWAY
FIFTH AVE.
MADISON AVE.
FOURTH AVE.
PARK AVE.
LEXINGTON AVE.
THIRD AVE.
SECOND AVE.
FIRST AVE.
East River
BELLEVUE HOSPITAL
W. 26TH ST.
W. 23RD ST.
AGNES HUNTINGTON'S HOUSE
THE PLAYERS' CLUB
W. 14TH ST.
THOMAS EDISON'S OFFICE
E. 14TH ST.
FIFTH AVE.
FOURTH AVE.
BROADWAY
M A N H A T T A N
HOUSTON ST.
HOUSTON ST.
VARICK ST.
THE BOWERY
GRAND ST.
CANAL ST.
TESLA'S FIRST LAB
CARTER, HUGHES & CRAVATH OFFICE
Hudson River
NEW JERSEY
CITY HALL
PARK ROW
NEW YORK TIMES OFFICE
BROADWAY
BROAD ST.
East River
Brooklyn Bridge
BROOKLYN
WALL ST.
J. P. MORGAN'S OFFICE
HAROLD BROWN'S OFFICE
DELMONICO'S
TO STATUE OF LIBERTY

THE
LAST DAYS
OF NIGHT

PART I

Salients

Don't you understand that Steve doesn't know anything
about technology? He's just a super salesman. . . . He doesn't
know anything about engineering, and 99 percent of what
he says and thinks is wrong.   —BILL GATES

CHAPTER 1

The Last Days of Night

People don't know what they want until you show it to
them.   —STEVE JOBS

MAY 11, 1888

O N THE DAY that he would first meet Thomas Edison, Paul
watched a man burn alive in the sky above Broadway.

The immolation occurred late on a Friday morning. The
lunchtime bustle was picking up as Paul descended from his office
building onto the crowded street. He cut an imposing figure against
the flow of pedestrians: six feet four inches, broad shouldered, clean-
shaven, clothed in the matching black coat, vest, and long tie that
was to be expected of New York's young professional men. His hair,
perfectly parted on the left, had just begun to recede into a gentle
widow's peak. He looked older than his twenty-six years.

As Paul joined the throng along Broadway, he briefly noticed a
young man in a Western Union uniform standing on a ladder. The
workman was fiddling with electrical wires, the thick black cables
that had recently begun to streak the skies of the city. They criss-
crossed the thinner, older telegraph wires, and the spring winds had
gusted them into a knotty bundle. The Western Union man was attempting to untangle the two sets of wires. He looked like a child
flummoxed by enormous shoelaces.

Paul's mind was on coffee. He was still new to the financial district, new to his law firm's offices on the third floor of 346 Broadway. He hadn't determined which of the local coffeehouses he preferred. There was the one to the north, along Walker. And the slower-serving but more fashionable one, on Baxter, with the rooster on the door. Paul was tired. The air felt good against his cheeks. He hadn't been outside yet that day. He'd slept in his office the night before.

When he saw the first spark, he didn't immediately realize what was happening. The workman grabbed hold of a wire and tugged. Paul heard a pop—just a quick, strange pop—as the man shuddered. Paul would later remember seeing a flash, even if at the time he wasn't sure what it was. The workman reached out for support, grasping another wire with his free hand. This, Paul would come to understand, was the man's mistake. He'd created a connection. He'd become a live conductor.

And then both of the workman's arms jolted with orange sparks.

There had to be two hundred people crowding the street that morning, and every head seemed to turn at the same time. Financiers parading in their wide-brimmed top hats; stock traders' assistants sprinting down to Wall Street clutching secret messages; social secretaries in teal skirts and sharp matching jackets; accountants out hunting for sandwiches; ladies in Doucet dresses visiting from Washington Square; local politicians eager for their duck lunches; a fleet of horses dragging thick-wheeled cabs over the uneven cobblestones. Broadway was the artery that fueled lower Manhattan. A wealth heretofore unknown on the face of the earth was burbling up from beneath these very streets. In the morning's paper Paul had read that John Jacob Astor had just become officially richer than the Queen of England.

All eyes fixed on the man in the air. A blue flame shot from his mouth. The flame set fire to his hair. His clothes burned off instantly. He fell forward, his arms still wrapped around the wires. His feet dangled against the ladder. His body assumed the position of Jesus upon the cross. The blue flame fired through his mouth and melted the skin from his bones.

No one had screamed yet. Paul still wasn't even sure what he was watching. He had seen violence before. He'd grown up on a Tennessee farm. Death and the dying were unspectacular sights along the Cumberland River. But he'd never seen anything like this.

Epochal seconds later, as the man's blood poured onto the teenage newsboys below, the screaming began. A stampede of bodies fled the scene. Grown men knocked into women. The newsboys ran through the crowd, not heading anywhere in particular, simply running. Trying to pull the charred flesh from their hair.

The horses reared on their haunches, kicking their legs into the sky. Their hooves flew at the faces of their panicked owners. Paul was frozen in place until he saw a newsboy fall in front of the wheels of a two-horse carriage. The stallions shook at their reins, lurching forward and drawing the wheels toward the boy's chest. Paul was not aware of making the decision to lunge—he simply did it. He grabbed the boy by the shoulder, pulling him out of the road.

Paul used his coat sleeve to brush the dirt and blood from the child's face. But before Paul could check him for injuries, the boy fled into the crowd again.

Paul sat down against a nearby telegraph pole. His stomach churned. He realized he was panting and tried to steady his breath as he rested in the dirt.

It was another ten minutes before the ringing of bells announced the arrival of the firemen. Three horses pulled a water truck to a stop beside the grim scene. A half dozen firemen in black-buttoned uniforms lifted their disbelieving eyes to the sky. One reached instinctively for his steam-powered hose, but the rest simply gazed in horror. This was like no fire they'd ever witnessed. This was electricity. And the dark marvel of man-made lightning was as mysterious and incomprehensible as an Old Testament plague.

Paul sat transfixed for the forty-five minutes it took the fearful firemen to cut down the blackened body. He took in every detail of what he saw, not to remember, but to forget.

Paul was an attorney. And this was what his as yet brief career in the law had done to his brain. He was comforted by minutiae. His mortal fears could be assuaged only by an encyclopedic command of detail.

Paul was a professional builder of narratives. He was a teller of concise tales. His work was to take a series of isolated events and, shearing from them their dross, craft from them a progression. The morning's discrete images—a routine labor, a clumsy error, a grasping arm, a crowded street, a spark of fire, a blood-speckled child, a dripping corpse—could be assembled into a story. There would be a beginning, a middle, and an end. Stories reach conclusions, and then they go away. Such is their desperately needed magic. That day's story, once told in his mind, could be wrapped up, put aside, and recalled only when necessary. The properly assembled narrative would guard his mind from the terror of raw memory.

Even a true story is a fiction, Paul knew. It is the comforting tool we use to organize the chaotic world around us into something comprehensible. It is the cognitive machine that separates the wheat of emotion from the chaff of sensation. The real world is overfull with incidents, brimming over with occurrences. In our stories, we disregard most of them until clear reason and motivation emerge. Every story is an invention, a technological device not unlike the very one that on that morning had seared a man's skin from his bones. A good story could be put to no less dangerous a purpose.

As an attorney, the tales that Paul told were moral ones. There existed, in his narratives, only the injured and their abusers. The slandered and the liars. The swindled and the thieves. Paul constructed these characters painstakingly until the righteousness of his plaintiff—or his defendant—became overwhelming. It was not the job of a litigator to determine facts; it was his job to construct a story from those facts by which a clear moral conclusion would be unavoidable. That was the business of Paul's stories: to present an undeniable view of the world. And then to vanish, once the world had been so organized and a profit fairly earned. A bold beginning, a thrilling middle, a satisfying end, perhaps one last little twist, and then . . . gone. Catalogued and boxed, stored for safekeeping.

All Paul had to do was to tell today's story to himself and it would disappear. To revisit the images over and over in his head. Salvation through repetition.

But as it turned out, a flaming corpse over Broadway was only the second most terrifying thing that Paul Cravath would see that day.

Later that evening—after his secretary had departed to her York-ville apartment, after his senior partners had retired to their upper Fifth Avenue three-stories, long after Paul had failed to leave for his Fiftieth Street bachelor's flat and instead penned so many notes with his rubber Waterman that the blister popped on his right middle finger—a boy arrived at the office door. He bore a telegram.

"Your presence is desired immediately," read the message. "Much to discuss in strictest confidence."

It was signed "T. Edison."

CHAPTER 2

The Wizard of Menlo Park

Hell, there are no rules here—we're trying to accomplish
something.

—THOMAS EDISON, *HARPER'S MAGAZINE*, SEPTEMBER 1932

PAUL GRABBED FOR his jacket and refastened his necktie before
making his way to the door. He had been engaged in litigation
against Thomas Edison for almost six months, but still hadn't
met the world's most famous inventor.

Edison must have heard about the accident. The very public death
by electricity of a man on a city street. He would surely be preparing
a response. But what would he want with Paul?

Before leaving, Paul removed a folder from a drawer. He placed
some documents into the inside pocket of his wool overcoat. Whatever Edison was planning, Paul would have his own surprise in store.

Broadway was dim at such a late hour. The few gas lamps that lit
the street painted the cobblestones with a thin yellow glow. Only one
point sparkled in the distance. Wall Street, to the south, was a citadel
of bright electrical light amid the murky smoke and gas of Manhattan.

Paul turned to the dark north and quickly hailed a four-wheeled
carriage.

"Sixty-five Fifth Avenue," he instructed the cabby. While the Edison General Electric Company still kept his famous laboratory in New Jersey, the company's main office had assumed a much more fashionable address.

The man turned around to look at Paul. "You're going to see the Wizard?"

"I can't imagine that's what his mother calls him."

"His mother died a long time ago," replied the cabby. "Don't you know?"

The mythmaking that surrounded Edison's story never ceased to amaze Paul. In less than a decade of public life, Edison had made himself into a modern-day Johnny Appleseed. It was infuriating, though one had to appreciate the skill involved.

"He's just a man," said Paul. "No matter what *The Sun* says about him."

"He makes miracles. Lightning in a glass bottle. Voices in a copper wire. What kind of a man can do that?"

"A rich one."

The trotting horses carried them up Broadway, past quiet Houston and the fashionable row houses of Fourteenth Street. The island was dark until they made the turn onto Fifth. Suddenly the electric lamps that lit the avenue became visible. The vast majority of New York streets were lit at night by coal gas, the same flickering light that had illuminated the city for a hundred years. But recently a handful of wealthy business owners had been able to outfit their buildings with these new electrical bulbs. Just a few streets contained something like 99 percent of the electricity in America, and their names were well known: Wall Street, Madison Avenue, Thirty-fourth Street. Every day these blocks grew a shade brighter as another building was wired for current. The high-strung cables formed a fortress around each block. Paul looked up Fifth Avenue and saw progress.

And yet if he was successful, he would see Edison's illuminated empire torn down.

Paul entered 65 Fifth at eleven in the evening. The bulky men behind the glass windows carried their firearms casually. There was no need for bellicose posturing. Only a very stupid person would have walked into that building unafraid.

A bearded man of middle age met Paul by the building's central staircase. He didn't smile as he extended his hand. "Charles Batch-elor."

"I know who you are," said Paul. Batchelor was Edison's right-hand man: the head of his laboratory and his chief goon as well. If Edison required dirt be dug up, it was Batchelor who would till the soil. The newspapers said the two were never far apart. But unlike his employer, Batchelor granted no interviews. His face never joined Edison's on the front page.

"He's been waiting for you" was all that Batchelor said. He led Paul up the stairs. Edison's private office was on the fourth floor. Batchelor opened the oak double doors and ushered Paul inside before hovering silently in the entryway. It was as if he were invisible when not in receipt of further instruction.

The office was richly adorned. Chairs upholstered in Spanish leather. A glazed mahogany desk, covered in electrical devices. A sleeping cot tucked into the far corner. The rumor was that Edison slept only three hours a night. As with most rumors concerning Thomas Edison, Paul wasn't sure whether to believe it.

Along the patterned walls, beautiful electric bulbs, shaped like roses, had been affixed every few feet. And dear Lord, were they ever bright.

Paul looked down at his hands. He realized that he had never actu-ally seen his own hands under electric lights before. He could see the blue veins running underneath his skin. Freckles, pockmarks, scars, dirt, the ugly creases a man accumulates by the time he's twenty-six. His telltale middle finger, always twitching when he was nervous. Paul felt not only that the lights were new, but that he was. A spark of the filament, and he had been revealed as something he never thought he might be.

Behind the deep mahogany desk, smoking a cigar, sat Thomas Edi-son.

He was more handsome than Paul had expected, thinner than he seemed in photographs, boasting a strong midwestern jaw. Even in his forties, his hair remained unkempt as a schoolboy's. It would make a lesser man look old; it made Edison look like he had more important things about which to care. In the harsh light, Paul could even make out the gray of his eyes.

"Good evening."

"Why am I here, Mr. Edison?"

"Straight to the point. I appreciate that quality in a lawyer."

"I'm not your lawyer."

Edison raised his eyebrows curiously, then slid a sheet of paper across the desk. Paul hesitated before coming forward. He didn't want to cede position. But he also wanted to see what Edison was showing him.

It was a mock-up of the front page of *The New York Times*. MET DEATH IN THE WIRES, screamed the headline. HORRIFYING SPECTACLE— A LINEMAN ROASTED ON A NETWORK OF WIRES. Down the column ran a fevered article denouncing the dangers of electrical power. The editors were questioning the safety of running cables stuffed with raw and poorly understood energy across the city.

"This is tomorrow's paper," said Paul. "How did you get this?"

Edison ignored the question. "Your little firm, what's the name? Housed right near there, aren't you?"

"I saw it happen."

"You did?"

"I saw the man lit up and I was there when the firemen cut his corpse from the wires. But the cables on lower Broadway aren't yours. And they're not my client's either. They're U.S. Illuminating Company wires. And since I'm not Mr. Lynch's lawyer, thank heaven, this has nothing to do with me. Or the dispute between yourself and George Westinghouse."

"Do you really believe that?"

"What am I doing here?"

Edison paused before he spoke again. "Mr. Cravath, there's a war on, in case you haven't noticed. Within the next few years, someone is going to build an electrical system that lights this entire nation. It could be me. It could be Mr. Westinghouse. But after today, it's not going to be Mr. Lynch. The press will have him chewed to a nub by morning."

"Sounds like a good day for my side."

Edison flicked ashes from his cigar onto a gold tray.

"In the past year," he said, "I have had many opponents to whom I might direct my attention. After today I will have only one. Your client. Either I will win, or Mr. Westinghouse will win. It's that simple. My company is ten times the size of his. I have a seven-year head start on manufacturing this technology. J. P. Morgan himself has promised us bottomless coffers for our expansion. And me . . . Well. I think you know who I am."

Edison took a deep puff from his cigar before blowing a plume into the air. "I brought you here to ask you this: Do you really think you have a chance?"

He regarded Paul as a dogcatcher might look upon a soon-to-be-euthanized stray.

"Mr. Cravath, I invented the light bulb. George Westinghouse did not. So I'm suing him for everything he's got. He's a rich man, and you're about to squander his fortune trying to beat me at a game I've already won. By the time this is over, I will own Westinghouse's company. I will own your law firm. So stop. The line is drawn. Whoever is in my way is going to get hurt. For your sake, I am asking that you not be one of them."

There was a strange crinkle at the corners of Edison's gray eyes. It took Paul a long moment to recognize it. Thomas Edison was regarding him with . . . concern.

This was what stirred Paul's anger.

"I'm glad you asked me here tonight," said Paul. "You've saved me the trouble of having to make an appointment."

"Oh? And what was it you'd wanted to speak with me about?"

"To deliver some bad news. You're being sued."

"I am?" said Edison, the slightest of smiles forming on his lips. "By whom?"

"By George Westinghouse."

"My boy, I think you've gotten it the wrong way around."

"We're countersuing you."

Edison laughed. "For what?"

"For violating *our* patent on the light bulb."

"I invented the light bulb."

"So said the patent office. Only . . . weren't there existing light bulb patents before yours? Hadn't anyone else filed claims on any similar designs?"

Edison quickly determined what Paul was getting at. "Sawyer and Man? But that's a joke. Their designs were an ocean apart from my own. If they want to sue me, they're welcome to."

"They can't, I'm afraid. Because they don't own their patents anymore." Paul held up the folder he'd pocketed before leaving his office and slid its contents across Edison's mahogany desk. "We do."

Edison examined the papers before him. His fingers drummed a quiet orchestration on the thick desktop as he read that the Westinghouse Electric Company had entered into a licensing arrangement with William Sawyer and Albon Man. Westinghouse now owned the exclusive rights to manufacture, sell, and distribute electrical lamps employing the design those men had patented.

"That is exceptionally clever, Mr. Cravath," said Edison at last. "Really. I can see why George likes you."

The familiar use of Westinghouse's first name was a calculated move. Edison slid the papers back across the desk. He reclined in his deep chair before he spoke again. "I've looked you up. I hope you don't mind."

"Can't imagine there's much to find."

"Graduated first in your class from Columbia Law School two years ago. At which point you were given a tutorship by Walter Carter personally. Terribly impressive. A year and a half later, Carter leaves and you follow him to his new firm. You're made partner, instantly. At twenty-six years of age."

"I'm precocious."

"You're ambitious. Six months ago you were the junior partner at a new firm. You had never tried a case. And then, somehow, you managed to acquire your very first client: Mr. George Westinghouse, the man I had just sued for more money than you, your children, and your grandchildren will ever see in the total of their pedestrian lives."

"Mr. Westinghouse has an eye for talent."

"You are a child hired to be the lead litigator in the largest patent suit in this nation's history."

"I'm very good at what I do."

Edison's laugh was a deep rumble. "Oh, come on, Mr. Cravath. No one is *that* good. How did you get George to hire you?"

"Mr. Edison," Paul said, "why are you pretending to be impressed by me?"

"What makes you think that my admiration isn't genuine?"

"Because I'm standing on the fourth floor of the Fifth Avenue offices of the most successful inventor in the history of God or man, who registered his first patent at twenty-one and made his first million by thirty, whose every utterance is printed in thirty-eight-point type across the front page of *The New York Times* as if he were the Oracle at Delphi, and whom the president of the United States—and most of its citizens—believes literally to be a wizard, whose name instills awe in the heart of every child with a wrench and a dream, and fear in the heart of every banker on Wall Street, and he thinks that *I'm* ambitious."

Edison nodded calmly. Then he turned for the first time to his associate by the door. "Mr. Batchelor, might you do me a kindness and bring in those files on Maryanne's desk?"

Batchelor returned bearing a stack of documents almost three feet high.

"Just on the desk here would be lovely, thank you," said Edison. "Now, Mr. Cravath, you don't need me to tell you that these things here are lawsuits."

"A great many of them, by the look of it," said Paul with the briefest glance at the pages.

"Three hundred and ten," said Edison. "There are, I believe, three hundred and ten lawsuits in that pile. And they are all against Westinghouse subsidiaries."

"Three hundred and twelve," corrected Batchelor. "The Rhode Island and Maine suits were completed this evening."

"Quite right. Three hundred and twelve. You see, I'm not only suing you. I'm suing everyone you do business with. I'm suing everyone you've ever *done* business with. Every Westinghouse subsidiary, every local and state manufacturer, every factory, every sales office. The thing is, I don't have to win all of these suits. Or even most. I only have to win one. You're countersuing me? Best of luck. Because you won't need simply to beat me once. What you'll need to do is to beat me three hundred and ten—I'm sorry, three hundred and twelve—times. Straight."

Edison ran his fingers across the mahogany desk, past the mysterious boxes and sealed glass tubes and thin copper strips to a black button at the far edge.

"Do you like the view?" Edison turned to the windows. Beyond the glass, lower Manhattan rose from the ocean. The city shimmered in a glow of burning oil and gas, punctuated by the occasional flicker of an electrical bulb. "You can see the statue from here."

There it was: Lady Liberty, just visible all the way from Bedloe's Island. Paul thought back to his first visits to the city, when the arm was still on display in Madison Square Park, before the city had raised enough funds to build the rest. Paul and his friends would picnic under the shade of her elbow.

The light from the statue was dim this far away. But its source was unmistakable: electricity. The statue's torch was powered by an electrical generator on Pearl Street, on the southern tip of the island. It was Edison's generator. It was Edison's light.

"We've been having trouble with the Pearl Street station recently," said Edison. "Some instabilities." He tapped his black button.

And suddenly the light went out. One tap of Thomas Edison's finger, and the torch on the Statue of Liberty five miles away went dark.

"Power can be such an uncertain thing. Gas was so predictable. You take a heap of coal. You heat it, filter it, pressurize it, strike a match, and voilà—a flame that will light a room. Electricity is trickier. So many different kinds of bulbs—different filaments, casings, generators, vacuums. One malfunction and we're all thrown back into darkness. And yet the old system of power is becoming obsolete. A new one rises to take its place. Once it becomes stable—once it is perfected and ubiquitous—there won't be a going back. Do you know, the police tell me that all manner of horrid violence decreases in public places when my lights go up? Blessed with my brightness, men's working days are no longer bound by the setting sun. Factories double their production. Midnight and noon lose their distinction. The nighttime of our ancestors is ending. Electric light is our future. The man who controls it will not simply make an unimaginable fortune. He will not simply dictate politics. He will not merely control Wall Street, or Washington, or the newspapers, or the telegraph companies, or the million household electrical devices we can't even dream of just yet. No, no, no. The man who controls electricity will control the very sun in the sky." And with that, Thomas Edison pressed his black button again and the statue's torch burst back to life.

"The question that should concern you," he said as he reclined in his chair, "is not how far I'm willing to go to win. The question is how far you'll go before you lose."

A good attorney could not scare easily. A great attorney could not scare at all. But as he stared at the brilliance of the distant Statue of Liberty, at the dark devices on Edison's desk, at the 312 lawsuits that he had to win, at the pale face of a man who could do with one finger what generations of Newtons and Hookes and Franklins could not even conceive, Paul was scared. Because in that moment Paul saw what real power was.

Need. Power was the need for something so great that absolutely nothing could stop the getting of it. With a need like that, victory was not a matter of will. It was a matter of time. And Thomas Edison needed to win more than any man he had ever met.

All stories are love stories. Paul remembered someone famous saying that. Thomas Edison's would be no exception. All men get the things they love. The tragedy of some men is not that they are denied, but that they wish they'd loved something else.

"If you think you can stop me," Edison said softly, "go ahead and try. But you'll have to do it in the dark."

CHAPTER 3

Prodigies

It's necessary to be slightly underemployed if you are to do
something significant.

—JAMES WATSON, CO-DISCOVERER OF DNA

A YEAR EARLIER, PAUL had been an eager young prodigy with one of the most coveted positions in New York law and not a single client to his name.

In the spring of '86, weeks before his graduation from Columbia Law School, Paul had been personally recruited by the venerable Walter Carter. Paul accepted a clerkship at Carter, Hornblower & Byrne, to apprentice with Mr. Carter himself. If there existed a law student in the city who was not after such a position, Paul hadn't met him.

Which is why it felt like the whole world was collapsing when, only months later, the firm began to dissolve. Suddenly Carter and Byrne wouldn't even speak to each other. Paul never learned the substance of their disagreement; at that point it didn't matter. The two split off into different firms, and Paul needed to pick a side.

Byrne took Hornblower, as well as the majority of the clients and virtually all of the prestige. If Paul followed Byrne, he'd be a clerk at arguably the best-known firm in the city.

Carter's new firm, by contrast, was to be a two-person operation.

Three, if Paul joined. Carter had partnered with an untested attorney named Charles Hughes, actually even younger than Paul but also engaged to marry Carter's daughter. Their family firm would have no clerks. It would boast no significant clients. It would trade only on Carter's name, which had been recently sullied by the rift with Byrne.

And yet, because his new firm was so small, Carter was able to offer Paul something that Byrne could not: partnership. To be sure, the split Carter suggested was far from generous—60/24/16, with Paul in the minority share. And yet . . . at no other firm in the world would Paul have his name on the door.

Did Paul want to be Byrne's clerk? Or Carter's partner?

The firm of Carter, Hughes & Cravath opened its doors on January 1, 1888.

Of paramount importance in those early days was the matter of attracting clients. Carter mined his decades of business connections. Hughes had been helpfully engaged in some minor but long-standing litigation for the Rome, Watertown, and Ogdensburg Railroad. But Paul had nothing more to work with than a handful of school chums and a decent sales pitch. By the close of the sixth week, having failed to bring in a single dollar to the practice, Paul felt his confidence give way to disappointment. Every hour that he spent alone at that desk, in the quiet of his uselessness, revealed him to be a fraud.

His former schoolmates turned out to be neither helpful nor sympathetic. "Oh, that's so very Paul," they would say as he met them at their clubs for Scotch. "It must be terribly hard to get everything you want."

In point of fact it was. But how could he illuminate the pressures and uncertainties of a position for which they would all gladly stab one another in the back? They wanted what he had. To tell someone jealous of his success that that very success was not what he might hope it to be, and was instead just another series of ever-more-demanding pressures and concerns, would be to sully his dreams. To dismiss his ambitions with what he would take, mistakenly, to be false modesty.

Paul had always wanted to be a prodigy. But what no one ever told him was that prodigies don't feel like prodigies; they feel old. They feel like has-beens just at the moment that they're said to be blossoming. When they are praised for their precociousness or their youthful ingenuity, they will shrug it off, because in their hearts they know themselves to be ancient and decaying. It is only later, after years of achievement have freed them of insecurity, that they will be informed that they are no longer prodigies but rather merely brilliant successes. And they will cringe. Because they know themselves, only then in the waning of their prodigiousness, to be true prodigies.

Paul had wished sometimes, very privately, to be a clerk again.

And then, quite out of the blue, he'd been invited to a dinner at the estate of George Westinghouse.

It turned out that years before, Paul's distant uncle Caleb had taken a job at a Westinghouse subsidiary in Ohio. When Caleb had overheard a senior member of the company's staff despairing about their uncreative legal representation, he'd made a suggestion. Caleb had a nephew in New York. A brilliant young man, Caleb had explained. An absolute wunderkind who just partnered with the esteemed Walter Carter at the astounding age of twenty-six. Mr. Westinghouse should share a meal with him. The kid might have an idea or two.

When Caleb first sent word through Paul's father that he'd recommended his nephew to the Westinghouse Electric Company, Paul felt faintly embarrassed. He was mortifyingly unqualified for such a position. He could just imagine the polite dismissal with which Westinghouse must have greeted the mention of his name.

Paul even wrote to his father to say that while the familial support was certainly well meaning, it was a bit naïve. This was New York, not Tennessee. Erastus Cravath responded with a brief message containing two quotes from Proverbs and a reminder of Jesus's warm embrace. It was not the first exchange of letters in which Paul felt that his father did not really understand the depth of the waters in which he swam.

And yet to Paul's surprise a letter arrived two weeks later. "Mr. George Westinghouse of Pittsburgh, Pennsylvania, requests the pleasure of your company tomorrow evening at dinner."

On the way to Pittsburgh, Paul rode in a first-class train car for the first time in his life. For the entirety of the daylong trip, he kept his only good dinner jacket laid carefully across his knees. Paul's greatest fear was that the jacket, hand pressed the previous night, would wrinkle. He had no replacement. He'd learned in law school that if you could keep a black dinner jacket crisp enough, you could wear it to every formal dinner without anyone noticing that it was the only one you owned.

At Pittsburgh's Union Station, Paul was ushered onto the *Glen Eyre*—Westinghouse's private train. It carried Paul—and Paul alone—the six miles to Homewood, the leafy suburb where the Westinghouse family kept their white-brick villa. *A man designs enough trains*, Paul thought, *and they'll give him his own locomotive.* Westinghouse got his own *line.*

Dinner was set for sixteen. A few engineers from Westinghouse's lab, a visiting professor from Yale, some bigwigs from the railroad industry, a German financier whose name Paul never quite caught. Marguerite Westinghouse sat them all at a table of Sèvres china and solid-gold silverware while her husband tended to his salad dressing. Marguerite explained that such was George's way—no army of hired chefs would ever deter him from making the dressing, his mother's recipe. Twenty years of marriage and she'd never once prepared a salad for her husband. Marguerite's smile indicated a routine frequently repeated and still enjoyed.

George Westinghouse greeted Paul with a firm handshake and a long look in the eye. And then utterly ignored him. Westinghouse was an imposing presence. He had a bearlike frame, burly muttonchops, and a grizzled mustache so large that it completely hid both his upper lip and the majority of the lower one. He was a few inches shorter than Paul, and yet when they stood near each other, the young attorney felt dwarfed.

The dinner conversation was technical. Paul quickly gave up trying to follow along. The railroad men were old friends of Westinghouse's from the seventies, when they'd all become millionaires together. They asked endless questions about air brakes. One of them even attempted to enlist Paul.

"Don't you agree with Mr. Jenson's supposition, Mr. Cravath?"

"I'm sure I would if I had the least idea what any of that meant," replied Paul with what he hoped was witty nonchalance. "Afraid I missed the natural sciences at school. And the mathematical ones to boot."

From the other end of the table, the look on Westinghouse's face made it clear that Paul's quip had been the wrong tactic.

"The death of mathematical education will be the death of this country," proclaimed the inventor. "A generation of young men who have never even heard of the calculus, much less possess the ability to determine instantaneous rates of change. What will you lot invent?"

"Well, nothing," replied Paul. "If you'll do the inventing, my lot will see to defending your rights in court."

Westinghouse shrugged. He returned his attention to the crème fraîche that decorated his roasted-pumpkin soup.

Such was the sum total of Paul's contribution to the conversation. His one chance to impress Westinghouse and he'd squandered it. Paul took his embarrassment out on the Bordeaux. Who knew if he'd ever taste such an expensive bottle again?

His despondent fixation on his wineglass was diverted only by an offhand comment from the professor. Just a few words half heard across the long table. Something about the physics department at Yale. A grumbling about a new PhD candidate. The usual grumpy gossip of academia, except for the one word that stuck out. "A Negro in the physics department?" said the professor with a weary shake of his head. "It's one thing to have a few in the college. But teaching? And teaching science at that?"

"Would you have the man lecture somewhere else?" It was only after speaking that Paul realized he'd said it rather loudly.

"Pardon?" said the professor, clearly surprised.

"I—well—" Paul stammered. To go on would be insane, not to mention rude. And yet the wine did the talking for him. "You'd prefer the man taught physics elsewhere, I suppose? That he drag down those useless mutts at MIT instead?"

"Met more than a few useless mutts from MIT myself," said Westinghouse. He was trying to defuse the situation with all due haste.

"Perhaps he might lecture in one of his own damned universities," said the professor.

"Unfortunately, there is no physics program at any of the Negro colleges. Though I'm told there will be soon at Fisk. A generation that could have been lost to the fields will instead understand more about your air brakes and electrical wiring than I ever could."

"And how would you know that?" asked the professor.

"Because my father founded Fisk."

A silence crept across the table. Paul had taken an awkward situation and magnified its power with the force of one of Mr. Westinghouse's steam engines.

"Your father founded a Negro college?" came the curious voice of their host.

"The family tradition, Mr. Westinghouse," said Paul.

Ordinarily, Paul took no particular pride in telling this story. He agreed with his parents' political proclivities, but he didn't go parading them around. Perhaps it was the wine. Perhaps it was the shame at being so out of place at a dinner of this elegance. Or perhaps it was simply the fond thoughts of the family who would gladly take him in to their Tennessee farmhouse when he failed in New York. "My grandfather was an early supporter of a small college in Ohio called Oberlin. He'd been an advocate of women's education, and the school became his great experiment. Men and women in lecture halls together. I studied there myself. My parents met at Oberlin Seminary, married, and my father became a deacon. He served as a chaplain in the war, which led him to a cause that meant as much to him as women's education had to my grandfather: the educational difficulties facing Negroes in the South. He's a deeply devout man, and he felt—still feels—that God put him on this earth for a reason. And he'd found out what it was. A college that would do for the southern Negro what Yale has done for the rich New Yorker."

There was no applause at the close of Paul's speech. Only the awkward clink of soup spoons against Sèvres. He hadn't made any brilliant intellectual argument. He'd simply made an ass of himself.

The meal wore on. The tinge of embarrassment kept Paul's face red all the way through the cheese course. And then Westinghouse said something that surprised not only Paul, but every other guest at the table.

"Care to join me in the study, Mr. Cravath?"

Still not sure that Westinghouse hadn't misspoken, Paul followed the inventor into his study. The desk alone seemed larger than Paul's entire Manhattan apartment. Thick Persian rugs padded the floor, while a bookcase stocked with engineering journals rose to the ceiling. Westinghouse shut the door behind them.

"Cigar?" he offered.

"No, thank you," said Paul. "Afraid I don't smoke."

"Neither do I. Can't stand the smell. But Marguerite says it's impolite not to keep them around for guests." He poured two tumblers of an ancient Scotch. "Kid, I am getting the impression that you might be an honest man."

"I'm flattered, sir. Though I'm not sure that's a desirable reputation in my line of work."

"I've recently found myself in need of a man of conviction." He paused as if trying to determine how most aptly to broach the coming subject. "I am being sued."

Paul was well aware. In the time since his invitation to dinner, he'd devoured all the newspaper accounts of Westinghouse's legal troubles. The dispute was highly public. "Thomas Edison has sued you for infringing on his patent on the incandescent light bulb."

"Edison's bulbs are terrible—poor-quality designs, two generations behind mine. There are a dozen companies across this country making bulbs of more advanced design than Edison's. Mine just happen to be by far the best."

"Yours are better. But Edison's were first. It's the latter issue that is of legal concern. Your difficulty is that he's the one with the patent."

"I did not copy Edison's design for the light bulb. I improved upon it. Tremendously. My light bulb is to his as a motorwagon is to a horse-drawn carriage. Would there be justice in forbidding Mr. Benz from selling the former because of the existence of the latter? Of course not. Edison is not suing me—he is suing progress itself because he lacks the ability to invent it."

"It sounds," suggested Paul, "as if you're in need of a very good attorney."

"I need a very good attorney who is not afraid of Thomas Edison."

Westinghouse folded his wide body into a leather armchair. He sipped at his Scotch. "If you're committed to the cause of justice, I can promise you that you will find no more just cause than our defense against Edison. Your firm is small, which is good. When I hire someone, I expect his full attention. I've done my research too. No need to look surprised. Anyone can hire a lawyer, Mr. Cravath. I need a partner. I need a man of honor who will not be afraid to tell me difficult truths. I am the most technically adept inventor of this age. That intimidates some people. Will it intimidate you?"

"You impress me," said Paul. "But you do not and will not intimidate me. Neither, for that matter, will Thomas Edison."

Westinghouse gave a small laugh. "Everyone thinks that at first. Then they find out what they've gotten into."

"And what would I be getting into?"

"It's this lawsuit. . . . It's substantial."

"Of course."

"My accountants are still going through the numbers, trying to approximate the scope of the thing. It's rather impossible to place an exact value on indoor electrical light, you see."

"At my previous firm with Mr. Carter, I worked on one of the Kuhn and Loeb bulge-bracket suits." Paul was exaggerating. He was barely involved in the case. But Westinghouse would have no way of knowing that. "It was $275,000 in damages. Quite unprecedented. And we succeeded."

Westinghouse raised an eyebrow. "That's a lot of money."

"Yes."

"Thomas Edison is suing me for one billion dollars."

Westinghouse examined the look on Paul's face, and then, for the first time that evening, gave a big, wide smile.

"So then," said Westinghouse. "Do you still want the job?"

CHAPTER 4

A Suggestion of Compromise

One could not be a successful scientist without realizing that, in contrast to the popular conception supported by newspapers and mothers of scientists, a goodly number of scientists are not only narrow-minded and dull, but also just stupid. —JAMES WATSON, CO-DISCOVERER OF DNA

T HE REQUISITE DOCUMENTS were sent to New York, the contracts exchanged and signed. Coffers filled with money. Westinghouse did not merely pay on time—he paid in advance. Carter, the elder partner, was overjoyed, while Hughes, the younger one, was nakedly jealous. Their junior partner had just signed one of the plummiest clients in the country. But the terms of their partnership had been drawn up plainly: Paul had been the one to sign Westinghouse, which meant that it was Paul's case. The elder partners could take their 84 percent of the fees, but they could not take the credit.

In the following three months, Paul heard little from his sole client. He received nothing in the way of guidance. Westinghouse seemed indifferent to the specifics of the law. When Paul requested technical schematics of the various machines in question, they arrived promptly and without comment. When Paul sent copies of the briefs he wrote, no response came. Westinghouse spent their infrequent meetings in Pittsburgh largely in silence. As if expecting something from Paul, something Paul hadn't yet said. Paul's response to his client's silence was to keep talking. Verbosity was Paul's best approximation of friendliness.

It was only when some scientific point would come up that Westinghouse would grow animated and speak, at length, in stentorian tones. Westinghouse seemed to have only two modes of interaction: silent or lecturing. Often Paul felt that Westinghouse wasn't listening to a word he said. Paul would ask a question and Westinghouse would silently ponder some paper upon his desk before responding on another matter entirely.

Sometimes Paul felt as if he might as well be polishing his client's silver instead of attempting to save his company.

The only nonscientific topic that could get a rise out of the older man was Edison. Westinghouse sneered at any mention of the name. At the suggestion—made at length by Edison's attorneys—that Edison had invented the light bulb and Westinghouse had illegally piggybacked off his work, Westinghouse would sputter with indignation.

Who was right? Paul was neither a scientist nor an engineer. He had no idea. His job was to zealously defend his client, and that he would do. His own future depended upon his success. If only Westinghouse would be any kind of help.

The day after the burning of the workman above Broadway and the midnight meeting with Edison, Paul immediately left for Pittsburgh. He did not do his client the courtesy of requesting an audience; he simply telegraphed that he'd be there that evening.

Paul arrived to find Westinghouse in the laboratory. Sleeves rolled up, topcoat off. Contemplating a steel disc on the worktable before him.

As Paul recited the events that had transpired in Edison's office, Westinghouse caressed the device in front of him, running his fingers over its rough contours. It was as if his touch might be enough to bring the unfinished mechanism to life.

"Edison was trying to scare me," explained Paul. "Which is not necessarily a bad thing. It means he's afraid of something himself."

Westinghouse waved a hand in the air. "You say he had a switch on his desk that controlled the statue's torch? That's not possible."

Paul was unsure how to respond.

"What's the distance from Fifth Avenue to the Statue of Liberty?" wondered Westinghouse aloud. "Must be four miles. Five? There's no way Edison's electricity could cover that much land. His current can extend but a few hundred feet from its generator. What did it look like?"

"It looks like a gigantic statue of a lady holding a torch—"

"No, no, the switch. What did the switch look like?"

Paul stared at his client. He tightened the Windsor knot on his long black necktie as he gathered himself. "I'm afraid I don't recall, sir."

"It's the problem of distance," lectured Westinghouse. "My own men go sleepless trying to solve it. Electrical current, of the voltage required to power a light bulb, cannot travel more than a few hundred feet before withering. Edison must have been sending a telegraph signal—yes, that's it. Morse code to a man at the Pearl Street station, who could then turn the torch on and off for him. It's the only explanation. There is no way Edison's team has solved the distance problem. I don't believe it."

Paul refrained from reacting visibly. Westinghouse, an engineer to the bone, had the tendency to maniacally fixate on minuscule technical details while ignoring larger, more-pressing concerns. There was a billion dollars on the line, and he cared only about the shape of Edison's switches. What Paul needed to explain to his client was that it didn't matter whose switches were more elegantly constructed; if Edison succeeded in suing him into oblivion, Westinghouse would be designing dynamos from a Bowery stockyard.

"Unless," continued Westinghouse, "this was a display meant for me, not for you. He knew you would report back to me, and he wanted me to think he'd solved the distance problem. He wanted to scare me. Well. It has not worked, has it?"

"You don't much like lawyers, do you, sir?" said Paul.

A curious expression overtook Westinghouse's face. Paul had gotten his attention.

"I don't blame you. Yet right now you are very much in need of one. And I need you to help me do my job."

"Very well."

"It is among my jobs to identify any course of action that might serve your interests. Especially if you might not previously have been aware of it."

Westinghouse sat back in his chair. Paul couldn't tell whether he'd impressed his client with his speech or simply his gall.

"I would like us to begin to ponder a compromise," suggested Paul.

"A compromise?"

"That serves you, and that best serves your products. Fair or not, this is the world in which we live."

"What precisely do you mean by a compromise?"

"That's not for me to say," said Paul diplomatically. "There are any number of different ways that some sort of compromise might be arranged. We can take some time to determine which might be most beneficial to you."

"Such as?"

"A merger, for instance. The Westinghouse and Edison Electrical Company. Or call it the American Electrical Company, maybe; take both of your names off it for simplicity's sake. Or—how about this? A licensing arrangement, such as we've made with Sawyer and Man. You sell Edison's generators and pay him a royalty, while he sells your far-superior bulbs and pays you a royalty. Or you each sell each other's bulbs *and* each other's generators, under a similar royalty scheme, and the consumers decide which they prefer."

"Mine are better." Westinghouse's simple, earnest statement tore a hole in their conversation.

"All right." What else could Paul possibly say?

"Edison's bulbs break constantly. His generators need repair even more often than his shoddy telegraphs. Do you know, the light bulbs he sells last half as long as mine? And produce three-quarters the brightness? A product inferior in all ways. And yet people buy them by the cartload. He outsells me four to one, despite the poverty of his constructions. Who knows why? Can't people tell that Edison is without the patience, not to mention the skill, the craft, to build quality products? EGE makes so very many things, of such unprecedented breadth, and yet each one is, pardon, shit. They're shit. Edison makes shit and he sells so much shit that no one notices that it's all shit. *Shit* is what Thomas Edison invented. I invented the light bulb. I perfected it, built it. It is the best in the world and it is only getting better."

Paul's client reminded him of no one so much as Edison. The two men were perversely alike. Each was so confident of his own genius as to be disdainful of the other's.

Westinghouse's ego was no smaller than his enemy's. Paul's first task, he realized, would not be to negotiate with Edison. It would be to negotiate with his own client.

"I know, sir," said Paul. "But what does it gain you to be the best if doing so drives you into bankruptcy? You run a business. It is one of the largest in this nation. And this business is presently facing a great variety of possible futures. You have options. It is my professional duty to see that you're aware of them."

Westinghouse's charcoal coat had been hung by the door. Without looking at Paul, he went to it and removed a folded piece of paper from the inside pocket. Gingerly, as if it were an object far more delicate than one of his machines, he carried it back and handed it over.

"Six months ago," said Westinghouse, "I wrote to Edison. This was before you came on board. I suggested to him just such a 'compromise.' I harbor no romantic dream of playing David to his Goliath. I know the odds against us. Everyone loves an underdog, but that doesn't mean he's a sound investment. So I wrote, and I attempted conciliation. This was his response."

Paul looked down at the letter. It was from Thomas Edison himself, and it consisted of one word: "Never."

"So, kid," said Westinghouse after Paul had spent a few moments taking this all in. "You're supposed to be some kind of legal virtuoso. Prove it."

CHAPTER 5

The Curious Case of
U.S. Letters Patent No. 223,898

> I have not failed. I've just found ten thousand ways that
> don't work. —THOMAS EDISON

WHO INVENTED THE light bulb?

This was the topic at hand. Technically, the litigation was between the Edison Electric Light Company and the Mount Morris Electric Light Company, but everyone knew that these were subsidiaries and legal proxies for their parent companies. Even the attorneys litigating this $1 billion case called it simply *Edison v. Westinghouse*. The issue before them: U.S. Letters Patent No. 223,898, granted to Thomas Edison on January 27, 1880, which described the invention of an "incandescent electric lamp." Quickly nicknamed the Light Bulb Patent by the press, it was without question the most valuable patent ever granted in the history of the United States. And George Westinghouse was accused of infringing on it.

Yet, as Paul pointed out to his client, even a problem so simply put might yet admit to many layers of unraveling. In fact, the question hinged on one's precise definition of the terms involved—"who," "invented," "the," and, most importantly, "light bulb."

The first electric lamps had actually been invented almost a century before, Paul had learned when he'd first begun to research the case. Sir Humphry Davy had publicly demonstrated early "arc lights" in 1809. By attaching a battery to two charcoal sticks, he'd caused a U-shaped thread of electricity to "arc" across the gap between the sticks. The explosion of light was blindingly bright; perfect for lighting dark outdoor areas, if it could be tamed into safety and reliability.

And over the following decades, tamed it was. Michael Faraday created the first hand-cranked electrical generators in the 1830s by moving magnets through fields of coiled wire. The improbably named Belgian inventor Zénobe-Théophile Gramme improved upon Faraday's generators and then created the first electrical motor—by simply building the generator's inverse—in the 1870s. By 1878, the American Charles Brush was selling massive outdoor arc-lighting systems to cities and towns all around the nation. Across the globe, a Russian named Paul Jablochkoff was selling what he called electrical "candles." Much smaller than Davy's original arc lights, but constructed on the same principle, these "candles" were almost suitable for indoor use . . .

. . . Almost. None of these early iterations were fit for the home—no wife in America would sanction the installation of a lamp that was confusing to use, expensive to repair, and more likely than not to set the drapes on fire. Plus, there was the quality of the light itself. It was horrific. Ugly. Displeasing to the human eye at close quarters. The electricity that arced between the sticks remained too elemental. The heat seared too violently. Gas lamps remained far safer and far more beautiful.

That's when Thomas Edison, already the most celebrated inventor in the world for his work on the telegraph and the telephone, entered the scene. On September 16, 1878, Edison took to the pages of The New York Sun to proclaim that he had solved the problem of creating a reliable, safe, and, most importantly, pleasing indoor illumination. He had invented an "incandescent electric lamp." He told the adoring press that he would have all of lower Manhattan wired for indoor electrical light within months.

The day that Edison announced this discovery, the stocks of all the major gas companies in the United States and Britain plunged more than 20 percent. The scientific community was less impressed: Academics responded from their university perches first with skepticism and then with outright derision. It was impossible, they claimed. There was no way to steady an even current through a filament to create a gentle and constant glow. Electricity was unruly. It was not like kerosene or shale oil, natural elements created by God and crafted by man for his purposes. Electricity was a *force*. Taming electrical current would be like bending gravity to man's will. Like traveling through time. There were some things in this world with which not even science could mess about. Edison's "soft glow" violated all the accepted laws of physics.

And so, Paul learned from the old newspapers he'd pored over in his office, Edison had held a series of private demonstrations. Only a select few reporters and potential investors were invited. The men who would fund this enterprise—to be called the Edison General Electric Company—were let in to see the lit bulbs for only a few minutes at a time. They were never shown the blueprints. And yet these men were stunned by what they saw in a guarded back room. For the first time in their lives, they witnessed a new kind of light. They described it breathlessly in their papers, their magazines, their journals, their stockholder reports. Paul had read them all that spring, ten years later. The men wrote as if they'd discovered a new color. And they had named it Edison.

On November 4, 1879, over a year after announcing his device in the press, Thomas Edison finally filed his patent for the incandescent light bulb. Paul kept a copy of that patent application atop his desk and stared at it every day. Within it rested the fate of his whole case. If the patent held, no one but Edison could manufacture and sell incandescent bulbs within the United States. If Paul could not break the patent claim, Thomas Edison would have a monopoly on light itself.

The story of Edison's invention had been laid out plainly and the patent awarded easily. But in Paul's profession, no story was ever this simple. With only the slightest change of perspective, the subtlest of reframings, Edison's story might be made to yield the most contrary of impressions.

So, who invented the light bulb?

First: "who." Edison was far from a lone wolf in his lab. How many others helped him? If the work of others had been used to create Edison's lamp, was their work his property? Or might another man lay claim to part of Edison's supposed breakthrough? Moreover, a thousand other laboratories across the United States and Europe had been at work on this very problem—might Edison have used ideas that were first developed elsewhere and published in one of the many popular engineering journals? Theft was theft, whether it was intentional or not.

Second: "invented." Was Edison's incandescent lamp a fundamentally new invention, or was it simply an improved version of an earlier device? The law stated that for a patent to be valid, the invention described must constitute a major breakthrough. A man can't simply tweak another's device and call the resulting machine his own. It must be a truly new thing. Hadn't Joseph Swan already taken out patents on incandescent lamps? Hadn't Sawyer and Man? What made Edison's incandescent bulb different from the others? What made it an invention?

Third: "the." Perhaps the trickiest word of them all. Even if Edison was the one who did the inventing, and even if inventing is what occurred, did he actually invent "the" light bulb—or just "a" light bulb? Why the definite article? There could be as many varietals of light bulb as roses blooming in the gardens of Central Park. What made Edison's preeminent? The lawyers for the Edison General Electric Company were not claiming that Edison held a patent on one specific design of one light bulb; they claimed that the patent covered all designs of all light bulbs. They argued that no other company had a legal right to manufacture incandescent bulbs, because incandescent light itself was covered by Edison's patent.

This was the very heart of the matter. George Westinghouse and Eugene Lynch and Elihu Thomson and the dozens of other competitors were each selling different lamps. Westinghouse's were shorter and featured straight, unwound filaments, not coiled ones. Eugene Lynch's had featured a wider base, before the unfortunate incident of the flaming workman had lurched his company toward insolvency. Were not all these things members of the infinite and diverse variety of objects we might refer to as "light bulbs"? Paul could suggest, carefully and with great logic, that Thomas Edison might have patented a specific light bulb, but he could not patent the entire *idea* of a light bulb. He might be able to prevent Westinghouse from selling one particular design of bulb, but he could not stop his competitors from manufacturing any kind of bulb at all.

And finally that magical new term itself: "light bulb." No one even knew where it came from, or who had coined it. "Light" had only been coming from "bulbs" for a few years now, since . . . well, since Thomas Edison. The term had caught on and become commonplace. Yet a lawyer in Paul's position was duty-bound to ask: To what did the words truly refer? What made something a light bulb? The law stated that for a device to be patentable, it must be "non-obvious." A man couldn't take out a patent on something that already existed—a turkey sandwich, for instance. Hungry Americans had been lunching on such sandwiches for generations. But more important, you also couldn't patent a turkey sandwich with sauerkraut on top, even if you might in fact be the first person in America to put together a combination that disgusting. Any drunken chef might have done it by accident.

And so the question needed to be asked: If Thomas Edison and his phalanx of attorneys claimed that his patent covered the whole idea of a light bulb, well, wasn't the idea of a light bulb in the air already? Had men not been frantically working to build such a thing for decades? Hadn't engineers and scientists been discussing the possibility of this light bulb concept since 1809? The idea of a light bulb was hardly "non-obvious"—only Edison's one particular schematic, admittedly quite clever, was. Paul was simply offering that Edison's work on the light bulb was the tallest evergreen in the Appalachian Mountains. Magnificent and noteworthy, laudable even, but also a single sprout amid a much larger growth.

So who had invented the light bulb? The answer, according to Paul's reasoning, was that it depended. And that it was not the place of the federal government to suffocate innovation in its cradle while the field was so new. To say that Thomas Edison had invented the light bulb was bad for free enterprise. It was bad for scientific progress.

It was bad for business. It was bad for consumers. And it was bad for the United States of America.

"You know," said Westinghouse finally after Paul had spent some hours largely in monologue, laying out this strategy for his client. "You were right about me before. I don't like lawyers."

Westinghouse looked at the sun setting outside the squat laboratory windows.

"But as lawyers go, you might be halfway decent."

CHAPTER 6

Locusts

I can always hire mathematicians, but they can't hire me.

—THOMAS EDISON

THAT SPRING, THE light-bulb lawsuits descended like locusts upon the land. The filings swarmed on the coast—New York, Washington, Philadelphia—before sweeping west across the plains. The assault was biblical, the mood among the attorneys apocalyptic.

Paul had never seen anything like it, because no one had. He was aware of previous patent disputes. Skirmishes over various aspects of the telegraph had been popping up for decades. The sewing machine— now a common appliance in any decent home—had produced a thunderous volley of claims and counterclaims. But those were small beer to this. Not only were there now 312 separate lawsuits between Thomas Edison and George Westinghouse, but there were dozens of other smaller electrical companies who were suing and being sued by one another with equal vigor.

Carter would check in on Paul periodically from his adjacent office, feigning helpfulness, inquiring as to whether Paul could use any advice. Paul declined the offers of his onetime mentor easily. Hughes was sneakier, though, approaching Paul obsequiously in *search* of advice. Paul had to give the man credit both for persistence and for being so transparently phony that it barely counted as subterfuge. Inept lying was almost as good as honesty. "My clients at National Steel would sure be tickled pink if they knew their contracts were getting a second look by the genius who represents George Westinghouse." Paul couldn't refuse, but he also knew enough of Hughes's competitive ambitions to keep the man as far away from the files as possible.

"Say, Cravath," began Hughes one spring afternoon as he entered Paul's office. His square face and prematurely thinned hair gave him a look of thoughtfulness. "There's been something gnawing at me of late. It seems to me that if Edison is out there plotting against us, we might want to think a bit about just what he's got in store."

Paul took note of Hughes's unsubtle use of "us" and "we," but did not comment on it.

Hughes shut the door behind him conspiratorially. "Have you thought about acquiring a spy?"

Paul set down his straight-capped Waterman. The pen had by that point left a permanent scar on his finger. Even a brief respite felt pleasant.

"A spy?" he asked.

"In Edison's shop. Someone to leak his plans. His strategy."

"A spy sounds melodramatic."

"I can help us find one." Hughes slapped a newspaper upon Paul's desk. Looking down, Paul saw that it was the morning's *New York Times*—not the city's most egregious Edison sycophants, but far from the least either. The story to which Hughes gestured was buried behind a dozen columns of financial news and agony pages. The headline read: EDISON FIRES SENIOR STAFF. And the article went on to describe a bloodbath of spring firings—a dozen engineers who'd been let go from Edison's laboratory.

"Thomas Edison cannot sneeze without it becoming national news," said Hughes. "The papers have him under closer scrutiny than we ever could."

"Why is he firing his top people?"

"Because he's in need of someone to blame. What if something in Edison's laboratory isn't working the way he wants it to, so he's going through engineers until he finds someone who can get whatever it is to function?"

This was an intriguing possibility. Paul hadn't been thinking the matter through from Edison's perspective. What troubled the great man, perched high in his Fifth Avenue office? What remained unaccomplished by the man who could light up the Statue of Liberty with a touch of a button?

"It's the distance," Paul realized. "He still can't get the distance to work. Like the statue."

"What statue?"

"Lady Liberty. Westinghouse explained it to me once. Or he tried, at any rate. Electrical current, of the sort Edison and Westinghouse are both manufacturing, cannot travel more than a few hundred feet. It can't go from Edison's office on Fifth Avenue all the way down to— it doesn't matter. But Westinghouse was positive on the point: It does not matter how large a generator you build; electrical current can't venture more than the length of a city block."

"Why?"

"I have no idea. But Westinghouse suggested that it's a terrible problem. His own men go sleepless failing to solve it. Installing generators every few blocks, as both companies are forced to, is extremely expensive, not to mention inefficient."

Hughes pointed down at the names of Edison's now-former employees. "This man right here, mentioned in the article. Reginald Fessenden."

"He's one of Edison's top engineers. Worked directly beneath Charles Batchelor."

"Which means that he'd most certainly have been engaged on this distance problem. And even better: *The Times* says he's been with EGE for four years."

"So?"

"So if I spent four years working for a man, giving him my very best every day, and then was unceremoniously fired one morning because I'd failed—and my entire team had failed—to solve a problem that no one else could solve either, I'd have a bit of an axe to grind."

CHAPTER 7

Rivalries

[In any] machine, the failure of one part to cooperate
properly with the other part disorganizes the whole and
renders it inoperative for the purpose intended.

—THOMAS EDISON

REGINALD FESSENDEN WAS even younger than Paul. Neither his thick beard nor the long handlebar mustache that bridged it helped him to look any older. Yet when Fessenden spoke, he adopted a professorial air. His chin would rise high as he peered beneath his spherical bifocals, and his words would flow slowly. He lectured like an old man.

Paul reasoned that Fessenden had every reason to play the professor, since he'd recently found employment as one. After his sudden departure from EGE, he'd been offered a position teaching electrical engineering at Indiana's Purdue University. In no time at all, he'd found himself going from designing vacuumed glass tubes on Fifth Avenue to teaching basic motors amid the Indiana cornfields. When Paul visited him in his undecorated office on the Purdue campus, two weeks after the conversation with Hughes, Fessenden didn't seem pleased about this unexpected course his career had taken.

"Thomas Edison can burn in hell."

The blue midwestern morning poured through the muntin-sashed windows. The air felt clean, though Paul did not. He had barely slept on the night train in. He hadn't had time to change clothes. He hid the wrinkles in his white shirt under his black overcoat.

"So you didn't leave Edison's employ willingly?" Paul asked, playing dumb.

"I well should have. He's a fool if he thinks he can get along without me. Us. Without all of us. It was a massacre in there. Something about the price of his stock—his war against your client is costing him quite a bit of capital. It's not my damned job to care about his stock, I'll tell you. It was my job to design his machines, and I was doing quite exceptionally fine at it."

"What about the distance problem?"

Fessenden's eyes narrowed. "Why do you ask?"

Paul explained that he was in need of help. That to win Westinghouse's case against the man who'd done them both wrong—who'd kneecapped Fessenden's career just as he'd poisoned Westinghouse's with libelous charges of intellectual theft—he would need to know as much as he could about the inner workings of Edison's laboratory. He wanted to know about its operation today, as well as some years back when Edison had first patented the light bulb. Fessenden possessed information, Paul explained, that could do a lot more good in Paul's hands than his own.

Fessenden took this in quietly. His face betrayed nothing. It was only when Paul had finished that he raised an eyebrow and asked a very telling question.

"And what exactly, Mr. Cravath, is it that you're offering me?"

Paul wanted to smile. These scientists were all businessmen in their hearts.

"I get the impression," said Paul, "that you might be in need of a new job." He gestured out the window toward the open expanse of Indiana fields. In the distance, a pair of old workhorses carried pails of water across the arid dirt.

He'd prepared the offer days before: Pittsburgh. Westinghouse's laboratory. Head of engineering. When Paul described the position, Fessenden's lips quivered. Would George Westinghouse, Fessenden asked, really offer such a senior position to someone so young?

"Well," Paul answered, "I might be able to think of another fairly senior position in his organization that he offered to someone a good deal younger than expected."

When Fessenden leaned back, the rusty wheels of his chair squeaked. "You enjoy it there?"

Paul shrugged. "If you can find a better position somewhere else, do let me know."

Fessenden grinned. "Okay," he said. "I'm in."

They signed the paperwork then and there. The terms were generous enough that Fessenden did not bother to consult his own attorney. He would be extremely well compensated.

"So what do you want to know?" Fessenden asked as Paul slipped his fountain pen back in his pocket. The answer was: quite a bit. How did Edison's laboratory function? What was its organizational structure? Though Fessenden hadn't been there when Edison filed for the light-bulb patent, what had he heard from the men who had?

"Edison dictated the problems," Fessenden explained. "We solved them. Experimentation, that's how he did it. Endless, tedious experimentation. Invention, you know, it isn't like the way the press describes it. It's not Edison in a dark room with a box full of wires. It's a system. It's industry. It's the man at the top, Thomas, saying, *We're going to build a light bulb. Here are all the ways people have tried to build light bulbs before. They don't work. Now, let's you lot find a way that does.* And then he'd set fifty of us on that task, for a year. And eventually . . . a light bulb."

"So," said Paul, excited, "Edison was in fact making use of existing technologies in his light-bulb design?"

"Well, of course."

"Did he look at any of the preexisting patents? Sawyer and Man? Houston?"

"I wasn't there, of course, but based on what I know, he must have."

Paul's heart sped. This was everything he'd hoped to hear. "Which ones?"

"I'm sure he looked at all the previous patents, Mr. Cravath. But not in the way you're thinking. Thomas wasn't using them to see how he should solve a problem. He used them to see how he *shouldn't*."

Paul's heart sank as Fessenden continued. "That's how Thomas works. It's not *What's the right answer?* It's *Let's try every answer until we find one that isn't wrong.* And the intellectual property that your client owns—Thomas was very pleased by how wrong those answers were."

Paul was dejected. He pressed on for some hours, but Fessenden gave him nothing that helped. According to everything Fessenden had learned, Edison truly had developed his light-bulb design in his own laboratory.

Paul had never heard of anything quite like Edison's factory full of geniuses. Westinghouse was responsible for tremendous feats of manufacturing—extremely well-built devices made by a factory of hundreds, each one supplying a part. A chain of construction. Edison, on the other hand, had built himself a factory that did not produce machines, but rather ideas. An industrial process of invention. Hundreds of engineers set to work on a great problem from the top down, each man in charge of his own small part. In this way they could tackle problems more difficult than anyone else's.

It was ingenious. It was annoyingly, confoundingly, disastrously ingenious.

The sun was just starting to descend toward the cornfields by the time Paul finished. It had been a long and unproductive interview. Fessenden would head to Pittsburgh the following week, to begin work in Westinghouse's laboratory. He'd be questioned again by the engineers, but Paul did not hold out much hope that this would produce much of use. Perhaps there was a spare technical detail that might benefit the lab. But he had found nothing that could help the legal case on which that lab's existence depended.

"I'm sorry," said Fessenden as Paul rose to his feet. "I fear this wasn't as helpful as you'd hoped."

"Mr. Westinghouse will have his own questions, no doubt, but I'm quite satisfied." There was no point in making Fessenden feel dejected. Westinghouse would need him at full enthusiasm when he arrived.

"You know," said Fessenden offhandedly as Paul shook awake his legs, "if you're interested in finding another former engineer of Edison's who might toss you more dirt than I have, there's a man you might look up."

"I'd be grateful. Who is he?"

"An awful jerk, but that might come in handy, given your present needs. He's an engineer's engineer, if you catch my meaning. Conversation is not his strong suit. Speaks with this impenetrable accent—Serbia, I think? Fresh from the South Street docks, still smelling of sea salt, he got a job at EGE a few years ago. Roundly hated by everyone from the very minute he arrived, which was likely the only accomplishment he managed during his tenure. You couldn't deny that he was smart, but it wasn't much use. He couldn't work with anyone, always off on his own projects. Finally he and Edison got in some terrific row—nobody ever found out what it was about, but we could hear the yelling. Charles Batchelor had to escort the poor man from the building. That was the last we saw of him. Three years ago, perhaps it was? But if you're looking for somebody who'd be eager to speak ill of Edison—he might be the man for you." Fessenden looked to the ceiling as he muttered, "If you can manage to understand a word out of his mouth."

"His name?" asked Paul, removing his fountain pen.

CHAPTER 8

The Ghost of Nikola Tesla

> I don't mind being, in the public context, referred to as the inventor of the World Wide Web. What I like is that image to be separate from private life, because celebrity damages private life.
>
> —TIM BERNERS-LEE

NIKOLA TESLA WAS dead. Or, if he wasn't, Paul felt he might as well be.

Not a soul had heard from him since his sudden and angry departure from Edison's lab three years previous.

The community of electrical engineers, so Paul was learning, was tight-knit. They talked, they gossiped. Trading between firms—such as Fessenden had just done in coming to work for Westinghouse—was not uncommon. Which made it all the more remarkable that Tesla had not been heard from at all.

No one had spoken to him. No one had seen him, no one had received a letter from him, no one had gotten a telegram from him. Perhaps, Paul reasoned, he'd returned to Europe. Perhaps he'd gone into another line of work entirely. Or perhaps he'd fallen to tuberculosis. It was as if, having jettisoned the coils of Edison's lab, Tesla had jettisoned the mortal one as well.

He was a ghost. An amusing anecdote passed from engineer to engineer. *Do you remember that tall fellow? Funny accent? What a loon! Whatever became of him, do you think?*

Nothing at all, apparently.

On Paul's next trip to Westinghouse's estate, he sought to mention the missing engineer to his employer along with updates on his recent courtroom appearances. His strategy, thus far, amounted to little more than stalling for time. And yet time, if it could be acquired, might prove quite valuable. Edison's patent on the light bulb expired in six years. If Paul could argue his way against any definitive rulings against them for such a length of time, they'd be in the clear. Losing very slowly was almost as good as winning.

When Paul arrived, the butler informed him that the main house's portico was being repainted. Would Mr. Cravath mind coming around to the back?

Paul tried to shake the thought that this might be a sign of something. He sat on a small chair that had been placed in a back hallway, and the minutes drew on.

Paul waited for over an hour in the quiet hall. He had papers to read in his briefcase, but he didn't take them out. If Westinghouse was proving a point, then so would Paul. He would not appear bored or distracted when Westinghouse arrived.

When Paul finally heard his name, he turned to see Marguerite Westinghouse regarding him with concern. Her arms were crossed in front of her. The lady of the house's white hair was done up stylishly. If Marguerite had ever committed an inelegant act in her life, Paul had seen no signs of it.

"Paul," she said familiarly, "don't tell me my husband has kept you waiting."

"It's been no trouble, ma'am."

Marguerite smiled. Of course it had. "You are an exceedingly polite young man. Come with me."

Paul followed Marguerite through the house all the way to the large white kitchen. Standing before the threshold, Marguerite paused.

"George likes to do this with all of the young men," she said as she turned to Paul.

"Oh." The words that echoed through Paul's head were "all of the young men." He was simply the latest in a line of protégés for the great George Westinghouse. Marguerite's gesture of sympathy had the unintended effect of making Paul feel even less secure in his position.

"You're doing well," she said, seemingly predicting his thoughts. "But would you mind some advice? George spends most of his days in the factory. Not the laboratory. He loves to watch his things as they're built."

Paul was unsure of her point.

"The factory floor is quite loud, you see," she continued, as Paul clearly failed to catch her meaning. "Speak up when you talk to him. Sometimes it may seem like he's being rude, but actually he's just having a hard time hearing you."

Paul smiled. He thought back on the many unprompted and disorientating turns into which Westinghouse had pivoted their conversations. This went far toward explaining them.

He was impressed yet again by Marguerite. She hadn't told him this to betray her husband's confidences; rather, she'd done so because she knew that Paul's help was the very thing her husband needed.

When she led Paul into the kitchen, they found George Westinghouse seated on a stool. He was hunched over a bowl of what Paul quickly determined was salad dressing.

"I found your attorney in the hallway, darling," she said. "If you leave him there too long, we'll have to invite him to dinner."

Westinghouse looked up, registering the gentle rebuke from his wife. "Come in, come in," he said simply.

Marguerite seemed to take that as her cue to leave them alone.

Paul spoke loudly as he updated Westinghouse on the 312 lawsuits against them. Continuances, delays, postponements—these were Paul's best tools. His argument that Westinghouse's light bulb was not in violation of Edison's patent would come next, though as slowly as he could manage. Westinghouse gave a few grunts of acknowledgment. It was only when Paul got to the small matter of a former Edison employee that Westinghouse perked up.

"Tesla?"

"Yes, sir. He's vanished into the breeze."

"Nikola Tesla?"

"Yes, sir," said Paul even louder. Marguerite's advice was not proving as helpful as he'd hoped.

"Where have I heard that name before?"

"I'm afraid I don't know."

"Strange name." Westinghouse seemed to be rolling it around on his tongue, as if its incantation would help him place its origin.

Suddenly he stood and led Paul to the mansion's book-lined study. Paul realized that he hadn't been back in this room since his first visit to this house, those long months before.

"Tesla . . . Tesla . . . ," said Westinghouse as he flipped through a large pile of letters on his desk. It looked like overdue correspondence awaiting replies; Paul found it hard to imagine that Westinghouse kept current in his letter writing.

"Here it is!" said Westinghouse with satisfaction. "A letter from Thomas Martin. He's a scientist, sometime journalist. He edits a technical journal, name of *Electrical World*."

"I can't claim to be a subscriber."

"Pity." Westinghouse handed the letter to Paul, revealing beneath its cover note another sheet, on which was depicted a very detailed mechanical schematic. Paul could not make either heads or tails of the design, but he could attest to its complexity.

Paul looked the letter over. "Your friend Mr. Martin claims that he received these schematics from a stranger named Nikola Tesla, who requested that he publish them?"

"And Martin, his interest piqued by the daring nature of the designs, asked if I'd be so kind as to give them a look. To determine if they were at all manufacturable."

"Manufacturable?"

"It's one thing to design something, kid. Even Thomas Edison designs all manner of junk. It's another thing entirely to design something that can be practically built. A thing that will work. That is what a real inventor does. He designs manufacturable devices."

"Is Tesla's design manufacturable?"

Westinghouse took the letter back before answering. "I had some of the boys look into it—it's interesting, I'll give your ghost that. But it's decidedly half formed. Would take months of work to hone it into something that might be built."

"Does the letter come with Tesla's address? With a way for me to find him?"

"No," answered Westinghouse. "But it comes with a way for me to do so."

He gestured again to the schematics. "Mr. Martin has agreed to publish the schematics. He's also asked that Tesla prove the efficacy of his design with a public demonstration. Martin has gotten Tesla to agree to present his work before the American Institute of Electrical Engineers. An organization of which I am, you may have reasoned, a member."

The demonstration would be in New York in only a few weeks. If Paul wanted to interrogate Tesla about his work in Edison's lab, he was welcome to be Westinghouse's guest.

As they returned to the laboratory to discuss other matters, Paul was encouraged. He had no idea what he was to make of this mysterious Mr. Tesla. But any enemy of Edison's was bound to be a friend of Westinghouse's.

CHAPTER 9

Mr. Tesla Has Something He Would Not Like to Show You

> Science may be described as the art of systematic
> oversimplification—the art of discerning what we may with
> advantage omit.
> —KARL POPPER

THREE WEEKS LATER Paul led George Westinghouse through the evening crowds along Forty-seventh Street. Westinghouse was clearly no admirer of New York. The commotion, the bustle, and most likely even the noise overwhelmed him. He told Paul with pride that he hadn't been to Manhattan in over two years. This Mr. Tesla would need to put on quite a show to justify breaking such a successful streak.

The two men arrived at the corner of Madison Avenue, where before them rose the blocks-long campus of Columbia College. They entered onto the grassy lawns to the echoing St. Thomas Church. Paul had not been back to his alma mater in some time. The sensation, as he stepped between the gray slabs of Greek Revival buildings, was one of time travel. He walked past the former Institution for the Deaf and Dumb. The property had been bought by the savvy trustees of Columbia years earlier. New wings were being added to nearly every building as the college expanded. The law school lay closer to Forty-ninth Street, on the north end of the campus. As Paul gazed at the unkempt students on the lawn, he felt impossibly old. Was it only a few years before that he had been this young?

To be a stranger in the place of your coming-of-age, to be an old man to your peers but a young man to your partners—these were the signs of generational displacement endemic to the young and successful. Paul felt an instinctive desire to be back here, to be a student again with so much to prove. And yet he remembered how tense and unhappy those years had been. He had found himself the poor Tennessee boy among the moneyed children of New York royalty. He'd thought he'd met a well-to-do crowd—sons of merchants and railroad men—at Oberlin, but that was only because he'd never met the truly affluent. He had never felt poor before Columbia.

As Paul led Westinghouse into the engineering school, he noticed he was far from the only postgraduate walking under the new stone archway. Clearly the publication of Tesla's designs had served as some advertisement that tonight's lecture would be far from ordinary. Whatever "ordinary" might mean in an organization so young as the American Institute of Electrical Engineers, and in a field so untested.

As he and Westinghouse settled into two empty seats near the back of the long hall, Paul saw a familiar face several rows closer to the podium. Charles Batchelor winked as their eyes met. And then Batchelor turned away, lost in the sea of engineers.

So Thomas Edison was tracking Tesla too. Of course he was.

The schematics that Thomas Martin had published in *Electrical World* a week before were incomplete. They suggested the beginnings of some new device, but gave little indication as to its function. Yet evidently whatever Tesla had sketched had the potential to be quite revolutionary.

No one knew precisely what Tesla was to unveil. Westinghouse had said that, based on the schematics, it could be one of a hundred different electrical devices. The mystery only served to increase the potential.

They waited for half an hour. The longer the delay, the greater the expectations became. The chattering of the tightly packed crowd grew louder and more insistent with every minute in which Tesla failed to appear. The seats creaked under the weight of their gossip.

Finally the main doors opened to reveal Thomas Martin—identified by Westinghouse—leading a man who could only be Nikola Tesla into the hall. Tesla was shockingly thin, easily six and a half feet tall, with a delicately curled mustache and a part dead in the center of his slick black hair. Paul's first thought was that he must be on loan from P. T. Barnum's circus. Tesla appeared immaculate in his stiffly pressed suit and thickly greased hair, and yet utterly uncomfortable as he was literally yanked to the stage by his host. Martin deposited Tesla awkwardly into a reserved seat in the front row before immediately stepping up to the podium.

Everyone settled in for the evening's performance.

"I will begin by stating the obvious," said Martin with a commanding voice. "Our guest of honor does not want to be here."

The joke was greeted by a warm chuckle from the crowd. Martin was as close to an éminence grise as New York's engineering community possessed. Science was becoming a young man's game, if the composition of this audience was any indication, and the white of Martin's beard made clear that he no longer was one.

"Nikola Tesla is a genius," continued Martin. "And like many geniuses, he is a deeply private man. However, he has allowed himself to be convinced that on this one night, he should share his particular genius with us. Discoveries such as his, I am sure you will shortly realize, were never meant to remain in the dark." Paul could read the satisfaction in Martin's slight smile. Ownership, that's what Martin was imparting upon the crowd. Tesla was his discovery. By extension, whatever it was that Tesla would bring into the world, Martin was laying a claim to as well.

"Gentlemen," continued Martin, "if you'll permit me one last unorthodoxy, I will not bore you with further introduction of your guest of honor. He has requested that the details of his life before this moment go unmentioned, as they have little bearing on tonight's proceedings. So I will honor his wish, and without further ado, I present to you my friend and colleague Nikola Tesla. He has something he would *not* like to show you."

It took a moment for the applause to catch up with the speech. Martin had already bounded away from the podium. Tesla ascended toward the great chalkboard at the front of the room, then turned to face the crowd. He kept his hands in his pockets as he stared off into the distance. The applause died down, but Tesla seemed not to notice. He placed no notes before him on the lectern. He did not reach for the chalk, or do anything else that might convey to an observer that he was in fact about to deliver a lecture.

Tesla continued staring into a vague and uncertain distance. Whatever world this man occupied, he was its only inhabitant. He seemed completely unaware of the existence of the hundreds assembled before him, prepared to hang on his every word if only he'd be so kind as to utter a few.

"Please pardon my face," came Tesla's high-pitched and thickly accented voice. "My pallor is white as pale. My health is in a condition dishabille."

Between the muddle of his Serbian accent and the bizarre nature of his syntax, it took Paul a few moments to determine that Tesla was in fact speaking in English. It was soon clear that his command of the raw materials of the language—words, short phrases—was deep, and yet his use of its intricacies—grammar, sentence construction—was haphazard. It was as if Tesla tossed up into the air all the words he knew on a given subject, and then walked away before he could see where they landed.

"Laboratories are better-fit places for machines than personages," continued Tesla. "But I am digressed. The notice I received for tonight's lecture was rather small, and I have not been able to treat the subject so extensively as desired. My health, I have said. I ask your kind indulgence, and my gratification shall be in your minor approvals."

And with that, Nikola Tesla marched out of the room.

CHAPTER 10

Alternating Current

> Always remember that it is impossible to speak in such a
> way that you cannot be misunderstood: There will always
> be some who misunderstand you. —KARL POPPER

THOMAS MARTIN DID his best to calm the crowd. From the aggrieved look on Martin's face, it seemed to Paul that this stunt was but the latest in a long line of Tesla's rebellions.

If Martin's intent had been to claim Tesla as his own, this disaster in progress served to convey precisely the opposite impression. Tesla belonged to no one.

And then, quite suddenly, Tesla burst back through the wide double doors. He entered as quickly as he'd departed. But this time he pulled behind him a four-wheeled cart, atop which hung a long black cloth. From the uneven protrusions along the surface of the cloth, it was clear that something strange lay underneath. Something that Tesla intended to display at the right moment. Paul couldn't help but be reminded of a magician setting up a trick.

"The subject on which I have the pleasure of carrying to your notices is a novel system of electrical distribution and power transmission." Tesla's words were delivered at a volume more suited to luncheon with an old friend than to a lecture hall of hundreds. The audience members hushed one another as they struggled to make out what he was saying. Paul looked to Westinghouse. Could the old man even hear a word?

"Alternating currents are the basis of my system's use, as they afford advantages particular over the direct currents common to the terrain in this age and day. I am confident that I will at once establish the superior adaptability of these currents to both the transmission of power and to the ways of motors."

The recently won quiet of the audience broke instantly. Shouts of disbelief came from all corners of the lecture hall. "*Alternating* current?" came the first cry of many. Whatever Tesla was saying seemed deeply controversial.

Tesla yanked away the black cloth, revealing three metal devices underneath. To Paul's eye, these devices, each about twice the size of a typewriter, looked to be collections of wire coils, hollow tubes, and strange wheels.

"Forgiveness for me," said Tesla. As he'd failed to raise his voice, his gentle insistence was lost on most of the audience. "It would seem that explanations are ordered."

Tesla finally went to the chalkboard and began scribbling equations. It looked to Paul like chicken scratch, but whatever he was writing had a hypnotic effect on the engineers. When Tesla would reach the end of one line and had to pause as he slid the ten feet leftward to begin writing a new one, there were audible gasps. Paul quickly turned his attention from Tesla to the faces of the crowd. He saw their wrinkling brows as they struggled to piece together what Tesla was showing them. More than a few took out pencil and pad. The product of their own scribblings seemed only to confuse them further. They would look back up at the board and squint their eyes, as if to make sure they weren't hallucinating.

"Do you know what this all means?" asked Paul of Westinghouse. Paul turned and saw that his client's mouth was literally agape. "Sir?"

"I'm not sure anyone does," replied Westinghouse, entranced by the display of mathematical acumen at the front of the hall. "Is he multiplying 'K' by the cosine of—what is that? A 'U'?"

"Afraid you're asking the one man here who doesn't know what a cosine is."

At the front of the room, Tesla scribbled on, giving what appeared to be a very animated lecture into the chalkboard as he did so.

"Look," said Paul, "can you give me the big picture here? What are those machines? Generally speaking."

"For God's sake—that one is a generator. Over there is a motor. And the middle is a stepping-down transformer, looks like."

"Why such a fuss, then?" Paul was relatively certain he'd heard of all these things before.

"It's the current," said Westinghouse. "He's made—well, he's saying he's made, I can't tell right now—a closed system of currents in alternation."

Westinghouse furiously scribbled in his notebook. Around the lecture hall, dozens of other engineers were engaged in similar conversations, trying to make sense of the demonstration.

"What's alternating current?" inquired Paul.

"There is a part of me that almost feels some measure of satisfaction at your finally asking me for a scientific education. But most of me just wants you to hush."

Westinghouse tore the top page from his notebook and began to sketch a simple diagram. "There are essentially two varieties of electrical current. Continuous, sometimes called direct, which has been the standard in use since Faraday. And alternating, which is actually just as old but isn't to be found anywhere outside of a laboratory. Because it's useless."

"Useless?"

"Do you know how electricity is generated?"

"Yes!" answered Paul enthusiastically. "A generator."

"Dear God . . . I mean do you know how a generator *works*? How it generates current?"

"Oh . . . No."

Westinghouse gestured to his diagram as he explained the components he'd sketched. "Simply, and do understand that I'm excising a number of salient details in the name of brevity, there is a magnet, and then a coil of wire rotating around that magnet. One moves the coil with a hand crank, typically, or a steam engine in bigger systems, and as the coil moves through the magnetic field, current is generated. Got it?"

"I suppose. But why? Why does spinning a wire coil through a magnetic field create electrical current?"

"Nobody knows."

"What do you mean 'nobody knows'?"

"I mean that no one knows. Electrical energy is a force. It just happens. Only God himself knows where it comes from. For us mere mortals, and for us particularly bright mortals who call ourselves scientists, all we know is how to make the stuff. Would you like me to continue?"

"Very much." While Paul hoped that Westinghouse would not get impenetrably technical, any explanation he provided would still be more comprehensible than the buckshot of white chalk lines Tesla continued to spread across the blackboard.

"Every time the coil passes around the magnet, it creates a burst of electricity. Zoop! Zoop! Like rifle fire with every spin. Though please note: It's actually nothing like rifle fire; I'm employing a metaphor so you'll understand. Now, in order to properly power a device, these bursts are fed into something called a commutator. The commutator smooths these bursts of energy out into an even stream. Like a dam in a river."

"That makes sense."

"I'm thrilled to hear it. Because now it gets more complicated. All electric systems must be closed loops, correct? Part and parcel of the strange force. Electricity will only flow in a complete circuit; a partial one will not do. So a generator, as I said, summons the energy from God knows where and then sends it to a commutator for smoothing out—think of turning a series of distinct water droplets into a gentle flow. The commutator then sends this flow to whatever device it's powering, let's say a motor, or a lamp. Then, to complete the loop, the lamp is connected back to the commutator, then back to the generator."

Westinghouse showed Paul his hastily sketched diagram. It depicted a circle, with a box marked "generator" on one side, a box marked "commutator" connecting in the middle, and a box marked "motor" on the far side. Westinghouse moved his finger clockwise around the circle to indicate the path of the electricity. "The current flows continuously, constantly, *directly* around this loop. Like a circular river. Clear enough? D/C, we call it."

"I'm following," said Paul with moderate confidence.

Westinghouse gave a short humph, seemingly unconvinced. "There's another way to build this circuit. It's the same circuit, only a different type of generator. Remove the commutator. Now, instead of sending current around constantly like before, it's sending it in bursts, yes? Bap! Bap! Bap! And due to an oddity of generator design that's too subtle for you to understand, instead of sending current around the circle only clockwise"—Westinghouse traced his fingers around the circle to further elucidate his point—"these bursts of current switch directions. A burst goes clockwise, then stops, then reverses itself and goes around counterclockwise. Then stops, reverses again, et cetera. It makes these reversals hundreds of times every second. The current 'alternates,' you see. A/C. And I hope you realize that when I say clockwise and counterclockwise, I'm again speaking in metaphor, since electricity is not strictly speaking directional. You appreciate the use of metaphor?"

"So who cares? Direct, alternating—D/C, A/C—why does it matter?"

"It doesn't. Unless of course you wanted to run your home on electrical current. Then it would matter very much indeed. Alternating current runs at considerably higher voltages than direct because it doesn't have a commutator smoothing it out, compressing, so to speak, its power. It's more efficient."

"So why don't we use it?"

"Because it doesn't work. Think of one of my light bulbs. It's powered with direct, continuous current. That's what makes the light so smooth, so even. Now imagine if it were fed with alternating current. The light would flicker on and off, on and off, a hundred times per second. It would be horrible. Moreover, imagine trying to power a motor with the thing. On and off, on and off, on and off. Terrible, right?"

"Right."

"The only thing is that an alternating current would be stronger. So if you could somehow make the thing work . . . well, your lights would last longer. Your motors would spin faster. Oh, and, by the by, the distance you could send this electricity would be far greater."

Paul looked up from the diagram. "The distance problem? Alternating current is the solution."

"Alternating current *might* be the solution. It's hard to tell just yet, because I'm teaching you basic physics instead of listening to Tesla."

An engineer from the row in front hushed them. Rather than take offense at the man's rudeness, Westinghouse appeared too engrossed in Tesla's demonstration to respond. Paul turned to the front of the room in silence as Tesla finished with his equations and, at last, activated his machines. He turned a wheel on one of the devices and a mechanical hum spread forth into the room. He then turned a wheel on an adjacent machine, releasing a hum of a lower pitch. They sounded to Paul like the groans of distant beasts.

The machines whirred steadily. Their smooth hums were almost pleasing to the ear. The wheels of the motor spun without pause. "Tesla's figured out how to make this alternating current work, hasn't he?"

Westinghouse did not respond. He didn't need to.

Paul leapt to his feet. The war between Thomas Edison and George Westinghouse was about to take a decisive turn. A new weapon had just made an appearance on the battlefield. And Paul knew that Westinghouse must have him on his side.

CHAPTER 11

A Dash to the Door

I do not care so much for a great fortune as I do for getting
ahead of the other fellows.   —THOMAS EDISON

BEFORE WESTINGHOUSE COULD ask him what he was doing, Paul had shuffled across the row of seats. Engineers scowled as his coat dragged against their scribbling pencils. Reaching the aisle, Paul climbed the steps toward the rear, where, he knew from his student days, a service entrance awaited. The service door led Paul to a back staircase, which he took in three-step strides.

Within minutes Tesla was going to be the most in-demand inventor in the country. Charles Batchelor would assuredly attempt to rehire him instantly. Paul hadn't a clue whether Tesla's machines could be made to help Westinghouse. But he knew that he could not let Edison have them. And he knew that he did not have much time.

Paul burst out of the building into the cool night. The evening breeze washed over his face as he ran to the other side of the engineering school. He stopped on the long stone steps. And he waited.

If he had things figured correctly, Tesla was not the type to relish the spotlight. Martin would shield him from the horde of eager engineers and lead him out of the school, by way of the very door where Paul was waiting. What could he say in only a few short seconds that would attract Tesla to his cause? He'd never before had to craft such a concise argument.

Half a minute later, out walked Tesla and Martin.

"Mr. Tesla!" Paul called out.

Seeing Paul, Martin grabbed at Tesla's coat sleeve, pulling him along.

"Mr. Tesla," continued Paul, approaching the pair. Up close, Tesla was inches taller than Paul, who was unaccustomed to being without a height advantage.

"Pardon . . . apologies . . . ," mumbled Tesla. Martin continued to lead him away.

"Mr. Tesla," said Paul, "I work for George Westinghouse. And we'd like to offer you a very special partnership." At the name "Westinghouse," both Tesla and Martin turned their heads. Paul had his target before him.

"I'm told you've had some unpleasant experiences with Thomas Edison in the past," continued Paul. "How would you feel about the opportunity for revenge?"

As Tesla's lip began to curl into a curious smile, Paul knew he had him.

CHAPTER 12

A Lobster Dinner at Delmonico's

> No rational argument will have a rational effect on a man
> who does not want to adopt a rational attitude.
>
> —KARL POPPER

A N ARRAY OF silver knives glittered on the table. The gaslight
threw shadows against the white tablecloth. Oil paintings
hung from the walls: placid landscapes, quaint rural scenes.
Every man in the smoky chamber beneath William Street was there
for battle of one kind or another, taking their places behind the sharp-
ened cutlery with which they would joust. Paul Cravath, stiffly shifting in his dinner jacket, peered down at his crustaceous second: the
softest, most butter-soaked lobster upon which he'd ever laid eyes.

The lobster on Paul's plate had been caught off the coast of
Maine—possibly that very morning—before it had been shipped in a
densely packed smack to the Fulton Street fish markets. Purchased
personally by the chef, Charles Ranhofer, this lobster was then
dropped alive into a pot of hot water and boiled for a full twenty-five
minutes. The claws had been cracked, the tail sliced open, and all the
wet meat had been removed from the shell and fried in a cast-iron
pan of clarified butter. Fresh cream had been poured over the brown-
ing flesh, and then, after the liquid had been reduced by half, a cup of
Madeira had been added to the mixture. The flame had been rein-

forced beneath the pan as the liquid had been brought to boil a second time, burning off the fortified wine. A tablespoon of cognac had been mixed in, along with four large egg yolks. Chef Ranhofer had sprinkled the faintest snow of cayenne pepper over the top before a retinue of servers delivered the tender meat to Paul's plate. This was lobster à la Newburg, the *spécialité de la maison*.

Three courses into dinner, and they were still only on the lobster. He had no idea how he was going to get all of this food into his already bloated belly. The buttons of his trousers, newly purchased at R. H. Macy's, felt ready to rip. His never-worn white shirt was growing damp with sweat. His bow tie pressed his wing-tipped shirt collar into his neck as if to pop his head clean off, like a boiled shrimp. Business dinners such as this were pure blood sport: How much meat and wine could a man pour down his gullet while still managing to conduct himself in even a slightly professional manner?

At Delmonico's, the most elegant and fashionable restaurant for New York's ruling class, delicacy of cuisine was defined not as much by complexity as by volume. Too much? There was no such thing. Quails, cakes, cardamom, and coins—there would never be enough to go around. If Paul could be blamed for any of this, it was only that he was a man of his time. It was with a tinge of longing on his wet tongue that he had to admit, if only to himself, that he genuinely loved the taste of *sauce béarnaise*.

Paul took a sip from his port and gestured to the identical plate of lobster à la Newburg that lay before his dinner companion.

"Have you had this lobster before, Mr. Tesla?" said Paul. "It's the best in New York."

This was not a lie per se. It might very well be the best lobster in the city, even though Paul had never eaten it before. Carter and Hughes had taken clients here frequently, but Paul had never been invited along.

Paul's goal this evening was to make an impression. The night before, after Tesla had quickly accepted his offer to dine, Paul had found Westinghouse at his hotel and they had hatched their plan: Westinghouse and his team would analyze Tesla's newly acquired A/C patents. If they could modify the bulbs that the company was selling to work on alternating current, they would gain an undeniable technological advantage over Edison. Their lights would not only be powered more efficiently, but they could be powered over far greater distances as well. At the same time, Paul would let Nikola Tesla know on which side his bread might be buttered, rather literally speaking.

"I have not tasted this crustacean," replied Tesla. "Fish is not welcomed by my palate." Tracing his finger in a circle around the plate, Tesla continued with an odd question: "How many centimeters do you think? Thirty?"

"Excuse me?"

"The plate. Thirty-five centimeters? Yes, I think thirty-five. And four centimeters deep."

"I suppose so . . ."

"Quite a bit, is it not? One hundred and forty cubic centimeters of this smelling-sweet broth, minus the broth dispositioned by the tail of lobster. So only . . ." Tesla paused as he measured the length of the lobster meat with his finger, counting the knuckles. "Yes, one hundred five cubic centimeters."

"You've a good head for figures," replied Paul. He could not tell precisely what the topic of conversation was, so this seemed as good a shot as any at remaining on it. "I'd imagine that's a valuable trait in your line of work."

"It is the unevenness of the shape, that is what makes difficulty in calculation. I could be otherwise greater in precision." Tesla stared at his food.

"Might you like to try eating it?"

"I cannot."

"Because you don't enjoy shellfish?"

"Because it is *not* one hundred five cubic centimeters, Mr. Paul Cravath; I think that we both know. And approximations are worthwhile only to the degree of their precision. That is saying not at all."

"You can only eat the lobster once you've accurately measured its cubic dimensions?"

"Well, of course not; please do not mistake me for a crazy. I can only ingest a dinner the cubic volume of which adds to a number divisible by three."

To think that Paul had once found Westinghouse difficult to talk to.

Four waiters worked in tandem to slide *ris de veau* onto the table as Paul launched in. "What my client can provide you is a laboratory and a staff in which to pursue your devices. You have built some marvelous inventions, but you've not yet developed them into products for the marketplace, have you? Westinghouse possesses the resources to do just that. It sounds like a beautiful marriage. And as its humble clergyman, I'd advocate a spring wedding."

Tesla gave no indication of being either moved or unmoved by what Paul had said. He seemed in a different place entirely.

"Products?" said Tesla, as if even pronouncing the word felt wrong.

"Yes. Your designs. The wonders you've theorized. George Westinghouse is in a position to build them. To make them real. To bring them to life."

Tesla frowned. "It matters not at all whether these things are built. I have seen them in my mind. And I know that they work. Whether they are products in your markets—what concern is that to me?"

Paul wasn't sure how to respond. What creator did not live to see his creations brought to life?

Paul had to change tactics. Whatever animated Tesla, whatever spirit moved him, was a force unknown. But no matter how otherworldly Tesla might be, Paul hoped that he might at least possess some of the baser instincts known to all men.

"And Thomas Edison?" asked Paul. "Would you like for him to see your designs brought to life?"

"Mr. Thomas Edison would be unable to understand the designs I have done if even they were built before his eyeballs. He is not inventing. He is not science. He is a face for the photographs. An actor on the boards."

"What happened? Between the two of you?"

The expression on Tesla's face was one that he might make tasting rancid milk. That is, if Tesla even drank milk.

"I ventured Europe as a young man, after departing Serbia. By '82, I'd journeyed to Paris, France, where I made the meeting of Mr. Charles Batchelor. He'd been delivered to oversee Edison's manufacturing in Paris, France; the gentleman gave me a hiring there. He remained for a few of months, and as he looked over my still humble tinkerings, told me to look up to him if I ever made it to New York City, America."

"So you did."

"So I did. I moved to New York City, America, with a nickel inside my pocket. I marched right to Edison's offices. My first meeting with the great Mr. Thomas Edison. It was . . . Have you ever met Mr. Thomas Edison?"

"I have. It's not an experience I'd recommend to the faint of heart."

"He laughed at me. 'Who is this Parisian tramp and what is he saying?' That's what Mr. Thomas Edison said. My accent is wide. Perhaps you have been noticing. Mr. Charles Batchelor told him I was a clever one, but he did not believe. So I offered him a demonstration. They had a ship in the harbor of New York City, America—failure of its engines. It had been supposed to bring materials to London, England, but couldn't leave port. Their fixing person was in Boston, America, but would not be down to repair it for two days. So I said I would take it in my care."

Tesla gazed at his veal rounds. With his silver knife, he sliced the *ris* into halves. And then quarters. And then, with infinitesimal precision, further into eighths.

"Engines are not complicated things, Mr. Paul Cravath. People seem so fearful of them. A fear of digging one's hands inside. 'Too many moving parts!' I am quite brilliant, you know, and yet while I would wish for this tale to illustrate my brilliance, it doesn't. Because any one of persons can fix an engine. All you do, you see, is you take the first part. You study: What is this piece doing? To what is it connected? And then you follow along: What is this next piece? To what is *it* connected? An engine is a chain, and all chains are made of linkings. Mr. Charles Batchelor could have done the same himself if he'd possessed the patience."

"But he didn't," replied Paul. "You did."

"Edison was . . . impressed, perhaps. I went to work for him the next day, at his laboratory in New Jersey, America. It was filthy."

"Filthy?"

"Not only would he have the laboratory cleaned unoften, but Edison's men worked as pigs in a pool of slop. Commutators here, gears there, all the screws in one big pile in the center of the table so that to find two matched ones, God forbid, would be as if finding two needles simultaneously in the same haystack. Edison is a slob. He is a bull in a shop. What is it?"

"China."

"Pardon?"

"It's a china shop," said Paul. "With the bull. Harder to explain than would be worth your time."

"I appreciate your honesty. That laboratory is a place I will not return to, do you understand? It's not only the filth. It's the absence of vision. Let's say you want to do something . . . say, all right, say you wanted to build a table. So you would set out the top, and then Edison would say, *Let us try building it with two legs!* And a reasonable man would respond, *But a table clearly should have on it four legs. Let us build that.* And Edison would say, *But we must experiment.* That was the word he loved—'experiment.' He was experimenting always. Every possibility, every variation, every useless, no-point, waste-of-time modification he could devise. So the two-legged table, it would not work. And I would say, *Might we now build our four-legged table?* And Edison would say, *No, let us try a three-legged table!* And he would build it. And then, at long length, six months later, you would finally be granted permission from Lord Sir Thomas Edison to build a table of four legs. You have wasted half a year on a task that should have cost you but a day. Edison General Electric's lab is not designed to foster invention. It is designed to foster tedium."

"So you left," said Paul, as a waiter refilled his glass of Montrachet.

"At the end of that year, one thousand eight hundred and eighty-four, I requested of him for a raise. Another seven dollars a week. It would have brought my salary to a princely twenty-five dollars per week."

"And Edison said no to such a reasonable request?" soothed Paul. To be sure, twenty-five dollars a week was a very decent salary—and yet it was nothing compared to what Edison had made from the patents created at that lab.

"He laughed at me. Again. I will never forget his laughter. 'The woods are full of men like you, Tesla.' That is what he said to me. Those were his very words. 'The woods are full of men like you, Tesla. And I can have any number of them for eighteen dollars a week.' I walked out of the door to his office on that day and I have not seen him since."

"It sounds like the time is right for getting even."

"So it is that you have suggested, Mr. Cravath. But how is that to become occurrence?"

"Why don't I show you?" said Paul as he reached, with some flourish, for his billfold. He removed a check, drawn from Westinghouse's bank.

It was, of course, not Paul's own money that he slid across the table. And yet he felt a thrill at the ability to command such a fortune with his fingertips.

"That's fifty thousand dollars." His dinner companion glanced down at the check. "Do you know what the best revenge is, Mr. Tesla?"

Paul motioned for the waiter to bring two glasses of champagne and settled back into his armchair.

"Success."

CHAPTER 13

Money

> Bill likes to portray himself as a man of the product, but he's
> really not. He's a businessperson. . . . He ended up the
> wealthiest guy around, and if that was his goal, then he
> achieved it. But it's never been my goal.　　—STEVE JOBS

TESLA FORGOT TO take the money.

That's what bothered Paul most as he stirred fitfully beneath the sheets in his two-room apartment on East Fiftieth Street. Tesla had left the money on the table. The servers had delivered his overcoat and Tesla had made it halfway through the front door before Paul saw the promissory note on the table. Sitting there under a knife, the slightest stain of red wine grazing its top edge.

Paul had run to return it. He'd been thanked halfheartedly.

Tesla had come to New York with five cents in his pocket, and now, four years later, he'd absentmindedly left a check for fifty thousand dollars on a restaurant table.

Paul had come to New York with a bit more than a nickel, though not much more. He could recite the precise contents of his account at First National to the penny. He had earned each of those pennies, and he was proud of them. Granted, people never spoke of such things. This was difficult for him, sometimes, with his friends. He made a good living, and he wanted to shout to his closest allies,

Look at what I've accomplished! But the word "dollar" itself seemed rude.

Paul did not understand people who did not like money. What motivated their dreams? What comprised their desires? Could happiness be "purchased," as they say? Well, of course not. But it was not as if it were free either.

It seemed to Paul that the people who did not care about money came in one of two varieties. The first were the blithely wealthy. Born to privilege, they had been so rich for so long that the question of money had honestly never occurred to them. They might be aware of their good luck, but the concept was purely theoretical. They knew in the abstract that they had things that others didn't, but—or perhaps because of this—they seemed always to be conjuring up purely hypothetical desires that remained abstractly unfulfilled. They imagined other people far richer, and took great care to delineate their differences from such genuine excess. *If only one could make the trip to Europe every year*, they might say, *like the So-and-So's*. That sort of thing. Then they weighted themselves with their humdrum family dramas, with the tragic intrigue of wastrel brothers and unmarried sisters. The daily slights and indignities of familial melodrama allowed them the freedom to imagine themselves burdened. Such people could afford to choose for themselves what to be miserable about.

The second variety was, ironically, the unknowing poor. They hadn't a dime, they'd never had a dime, they weren't likely to have a dime, and while they liked the notion of dimes in principle, they had no idea quite how much pleasure a dime could purchase. They were not happily poor—that would be a condescending caricature. Being poor did not make anyone happy. It was only that some people managed to be both.

Paul's father was closer to this second type. He wasn't after money. He wasn't after a station, an appointment, a jeweled career. He was after justice, and he'd tell you about it plain as day. He wanted to build a more just world because the God he worshipped had taught him to love laboring for it. Sometimes Paul envied the simplicity of his father's perspective. To seek only the light of the Lord's grace was a far simpler thing, or so Paul thought, than his own demands. Paul wished that he might share his father's beliefs. And yet try as he might, the God of Erastus Cravath could not be forced by act of mental will into his son's heart.

Tesla's relationship with money was spookier. It wasn't exactly that he didn't care for money. He'd accepted Paul's offer. Yet money was clearly not the thing that he wanted. Which suggested the question that kept Paul up that night, as the spring air grew warm enough that he'd flung the heavy sheets from his bed:

What did Nikola Tesla want?

CHAPTER 14

A Difficult Negotiation

Show me a thoroughly satisfied man and I will show you a
failure.   —THOMAS EDISON

LEMUEL SERRELL, TESLA's attorney, made it quite clear he shared
little of his client's ambivalence toward money—he wanted an
additional forty thousand dollars to make a deal. Just for a start.

Serrell's office looked as if it had been there for a hundred years,
rather longer than the fifteen it had actually occupied the space.
Serrell was a legend, if such a thing existed, in the relatively recent
class of patent attorneys. His father had likely been America's very
first patent lawyer, establishing his own firm immediately following
the Patent Act of 1836. The act had created for the first time in the
history of the world a "patent office" of a government. No longer
would any patent applied for be granted, with the merits to be weighed
if and only if a lawsuit was later filed. The office was staffed with scientific experts to evaluate every application. Serrell's father had clev-
erly realized that if there were government experts managing the
half-legal, half-scientific realm of the patent, there would necessarily
be a market for private experts as well. Scientists were not known for
their legal expertise; nor, for that matter, were lawyers known for
their scientific fluency. The elder Serrell, and then his son, had developed invaluable experience in both.

The younger Serrell had cut his teeth on Edison's own early patent work. Boasting a keen eye for talent, Serrell had signed up the twenty-three-year-old Edison and composed all of the prodigy's early telegraph and telephone patents. Not long after, Edison had decamped for Grosvenor Lowrey's more prestigious firm.

The summer sun warmed the black-dyed maple of Serrell's desk. Serrell and Paul took seats directly across from each other in high-backed leather chairs. Serrell removed his jacket in a sign of familiarity. Despite the heat, Paul kept his on.

"I spent two years working on the A/C patents with Nikola," said Serrell in a genial tone. "They were sent back at first with a demand for more specificity, if you can believe it. But of course, dear Nikola wouldn't give up, so we refined both his device and the language of the claim. You'll see they're quite airtight."

"That's why my client would like to purchase them."

"Yes, yes," said Serrell. "Purchase . . ."

Serrell turned in his chair to gaze out the window. This was not Paul's first negotiation, and he knew the move well. He'd guessed, when he'd received Serrell's note, that as the more experienced attorney, he would elect to play the bully in negotiations, all bluster and ballast. An Edisonian strategy. But Serrell had adopted the role of the thoughtful moderate. A kind of disinterested third party who wanted only for Tesla and Westinghouse to reach a fair arrangement. So much the better for Paul's afternoon, he reasoned, though he would certainly appreciate it if Serrell would get on with things.

"So you're Westinghouse's young prodigy," said Serrell as the light from the grand window framed his bearded face. "Such responsibility on such young shoulders. You know he approached me about your position, before he offered it to you."

Paul could not afford to show his surprise. To allow that Serrell knew more than he on the subject of Paul's own client would be a disaster.

"Well, of course," lied Paul coolly. "I assumed he'd discussed the job with many men in town. You know George. He never likes to make a decision without examining all the possible choices."

"Have you ever asked him about it?"

"About what?"

"About why he chose you."

Paul looked Serrell dead in the eye. Politeness was not going to work.

"Sir," said Paul, "not to be indelicate, but I've been intimidated a lot recently. And quite a bit more forcefully than this. If you're trying to scare me, get on with it. If you're not, you might want to tell me how much more money you'd like my client to pay your client in exchange for his patents and then we can both find other ways to spend the remainder of our afternoons."

Lemuel Serrell smiled.

"My goodness, Mr. Cravath. You really haven't been long at this, have you? There's this lawyerly code of conduct—well, we just prefer our threats unspoken, if we can help it. You understand. Needling each other under cover of pleasantry, that sort of business."

"Apologies."

"You're a better fit for Westinghouse than I would have been." Serrell took a piece of paper and wrote down a relatively simple financial formula. "Mr. Tesla is not going to sell you his patents. Calm down, calm down, don't give me that look. He's not going to *sell* them. But he will license them to you. A combination of cash, stock, and per-unit fee. Look over these numbers, talk through them with Westinghouse, and then let's chat again. I'd tell you I need an answer within twenty-four hours, or some such ticking-clock tactic, but I suspect you wouldn't respond well to it."

Paul glanced down at the paper as Serrell handed it to him. The numbers were exceedingly generous to Tesla. But certainly negotiable.

"A pleasure to meet you," said Paul as he placed the folded paper into his jacket pocket and rose from his seat.

"My best to Mr. Carter and Mr. Hughes," said Serrell. "Oh, and . . . I hope you don't think it impolite, but if you've ever a mind to leave your firm, we have quite a few clients here who would love to know that they're cared for by the same hands that handle George Westinghouse's business."

"I'm happy with my position. And Mr. Westinghouse is content at our firm. But thank you." Paul stood in the doorway. There was a thought he couldn't shake.

"Out of curiosity," said Paul, "why did you turn it down?"

"Hmm?"

"The job that Mr. Westinghouse offered you."

"Oh." Serrell looked down, tapping his fingers together as if their rhythm might instruct him how best to phrase his answer.

"More-experienced attorneys, like myself, we're done no good by taking on a losing case. But someone like you . . . a young man, starting out. Your career will still benefit from having your name in the papers. And I'm sure you won't be blamed personally for losing a case that no one could win."

CHAPTER 15

Networks

We're not going to be the first to this party, but we're going
to be the best.   —STEVE JOBS

THE DEAL WAS finalized by July. Tesla would get a total of
$70,000 up front, two-thirds of which would be in Westing-
house stock and one-third of which would be in cash, as well
as $2.50 per horsepower sold on all machines utilizing Tesla's
alternating-current technology. However, Tesla would work for his
money: He would join the Westinghouse Electric Company as a
consultant, moving his own laboratory to Pittsburgh. Westinghouse
had concerns about Tesla's ability to work in the more rigid con-
fines of his corporate environment. He expressed these to Paul as
the two entered his study on a sweltering morning in the first week
of July.

"It still says 'Westinghouse' on the front door," Paul reassured him.
"You're in charge. If he wants to work, he'll have to work for you. Unless Mr. Tesla is as handy with a chisel as he is with a rotor, you haven't
much to worry about."

Paul couldn't tell if Westinghouse had even heard him. Speaking
louder, he decided to broach a delicate topic.

"Why did you hire me?"

Westinghouse was as surprised by the question as Paul was by his own nerve in asking it. Each man looked away from the other.

"Serrell said you offered him the job first. Before me."

Westinghouse took a moment to answer. "That's true."

"So why me? Not just my own partners, but fifty attorneys I could name have more experience than I do."

"Would you like me to see if any of them are available to take your place?"

"No. I want you to tell me why you chose me."

Westinghouse looked Paul in the eyes. He was gauging something.

"You are correct that I did not hire you for your experience. In fact, I hired you for your lack of it. Between EGE and the dozen financiers on Wall Street who have an interest in its success, there isn't a law firm in New York that's not in one way or another bound up in Edison's web. I looked, believe me. Every one of them had financial arrangements with either Edison or one of Edison's supporters. J. P. Morgan owns sixty percent of EGE *personally*. Can you imagine the difficulty—the impossibility—of finding a firm that isn't in business with Morgan?"

"While I hadn't a client to my name."

"No clients. No conflicts. No ambiguous allegiances."

Westinghouse's logic was very good. Funny, to think that all this time he thought he'd been valued for what he had accomplished—instead, it turned out that his value lay in his very lack of accomplishments.

"Don't make a sour face," suggested Westinghouse. "With a little luck we just might make something out of you yet."

Paul felt that this was as close to a fatherly pat on the back as he was going to get from his client. It was certainly more than he'd gotten from his actual father.

"Your friend Tesla," said Westinghouse, "may have provided just that good fortune. My men have much refining to do, but we're changing almost everything about our electrical system: generators, dynamos, even the width of the wires. By the time we're done, our A/C system will not only be the best method for producing and delivering electrical light in the world, but it will be so different from Edison's D/C system as to render moot practically all of his three hundred twelve lawsuits."

Westinghouse was correct in his legal analysis. But there was a crucial detail that the inventor had left unaddressed.

"You're changing *everything*?"

Westinghouse knew to what Paul was referring. "I said almost everything."

"The light bulb."

"That goddamned light bulb."

"The biggest suit of them all. You can change every element of your electrical system, but if the light bulb that system powers is still similar to Edison's, it'll all be for nothing."

"This is how I will put Mr. Tesla to use. If he was able to theorize a new kind of electrical system, then it's possible he can theorize a new kind of light bulb as well. A better one, one that takes full advantage of alternating current's efficiencies."

"It doesn't have to be better," said Paul. "It only has to be different. From a legal perspective, if you and Tesla can together create a fundamentally new design of light bulb, then, sir . . . well, then you won't have to worry about Edison in court."

"Kid . . . your courts, your lawsuits . . . If you only understood. The promise of A/C is so much greater than that."

Paul had never before seen such enthusiasm from Westinghouse. It occurred to him that this was the side of the inventor that only the men in his laboratory got to see: the childlike response of the man who chose to make his living inventing things for the joy of it.

"Fessenden and I, we've been going over the A/C ideas, and by solving the distance problem, well, it suggests to us an even greater advantage." Westinghouse walked to his desk. Taking a key from his pocket, he unlocked the bottom drawer and removed a set of large paper sheets. Paul expected to see engineering schematics. But as he drew closer, he realized that they were maps. Maps of the United States.

"Edison's D/C current may only travel a few hundred feet at a time, so he is forced to sell his generators one by one. He has done a damnably good job of convincing wealthy men across this nation to wire their homes with his current, but he still must sell a generator to every single one of them. By utilizing A/C, we will no longer be so encumbered."

Westinghouse gestured for Paul to come closer. Paul read the legends on the corners of the maps. "Grand Rapids, Michigan." "Jefferson, Iowa."

"Alternating current will allow us to build one great generator at the center of every community. After which we can simply attach as many homes to this single generator as wish to be. It doesn't take much work to attach a new home to the system once it's built. We can put up our generator, have a few homes take us up on our current . . . then their neighbors will see how brilliant our light really is . . . and soon enough the entire town will be lit by Westinghouse lamps."

Here, between the bent and soiled gear bits, lay the framework for the electrification of the United States.

"You'll be able to sell to whole municipalities at once," said Paul. "Entire towns will become Westinghouse towns."

"Precisely. Alternating current isn't just better technology. It's better business."

Paul thumbed through the maps. Red dots blotted what was clearly already Edison territory—New York, Boston, Philadelphia, Chicago, Washington. Only Pittsburgh among the large cities was unmarred by a crimson spot.

Yet Westinghouse had also placed tiny blue dots throughout the land, marking off receptive townships: Lincoln, Nebraska; Oshkosh, Wisconsin; Duluth, Minnesota.

Westinghouse's electrical revolution would not hail from the steel towers of America's moneyed metropolises. Instead, his insurgence would come from a thousand sleepy villages. Together, these hamlets would form a network of power that would stretch from Ithaca, New York, to Portland, Oregon.

Edison had taken Broadway. So Westinghouse would take Broad Street, Ohio.

The lines were drawn. Everyone would have to choose a side. Everyone would join a network. Networks of light. Networks of people. Networks of power. Networks of money.

"We can begin selling immediately," said Westinghouse. "And we should be able to install our first system by the autumn." He took in the wonder on Paul's face. "If you can keep the courts off our backs, then Nikola Tesla and I will stop Thomas Edison."

CHAPTER 16

One Step Forward, Two Steps Back

> What I do has to be a function of what I can do, not a
> function of what people ask me to do. —TIM BERNERS-LEE

ON THE NIGHT Tesla moved into his new laboratory on the Westinghouse estate, there was to be, at Paul's suggestion, a welcome dinner in the inventor's honor. A friendly meal at the central mansion, attended by Tesla, Westinghouse, and the more garrulous members of the senior staff, Fessenden and his lieutenants. Would Tesla do something strange at Westinghouse's dinner table? Likely. But Marguerite would be there to soothe, and the engineers would be there if Tesla launched into one of his impenetrable monologues. The conversational bases were manned.

While the household staff helped Tesla move into his newly furnished apartment, Marguerite supervised the preparation of the rosemary-roasted chickens. George Westinghouse whipped up his traditional salad dressing. White ties were knotted across the gentlemen's necks, and Paul's lone dinner jacket was pressed yet again.

Everyone gathered at the door as the servants ushered Tesla into the mansion for the first time. The gentlemen bowed in a line, right to left. Tesla approached Marguerite, bending to take her hand, and then he emitted a high-pitched yelp.

Paul—and everyone else—was too startled to speak. Tesla retreated slowly to the door. Marguerite strained what looked to be every muscle upon her face to keep a smile in place. It was the butler, finally, who inquired of Tesla as to whether he was all right.

"It is the hair," said Tesla gravely. He looked in horror to his sleeve. Paul peered. Sure enough, there on Tesla's shirtsleeve was a long white hair. It could only have belonged to Marguerite.

"I cannot stand to its touch," said Tesla. "My apologies, Mrs. Marguerite Westinghouse."

With that, Tesla walked out the front door. The dinner that followed at the Westinghouse table was mercifully brief.

As it turned out, Tesla would never set foot in the main house again. His laboratory space was only a short walk down the dirt road, but the engineers tasked with assisting him reported that he almost never left.

His meals consisted solely of water and saltine crackers, brought to his apartment above the lab at odd hours of the night upon an urgent ringing of his bell. Any attempt to get a bit of meat into his belly met with disastrous results, as the cubic contents of the braised pork shoulder presented to him on a polished silver plate were deemed to be a multiple of seven, and hence toxic to his bloodstream.

Weekly meetings were set to inform Westinghouse of the inventor's progress at designing a light bulb that would elude the reach of Edison's patents. The meeting times came and went without an appearance from Tesla himself. In fairness to him, there was no progress to report, so his decision not to attend such meetings was in some sense perfectly rational.

For all these eccentricities Westinghouse had little patience. This was a place of business, in which men conducted themselves in a manner commensurate with the seriousness of their task. Westinghouse seemed to think of himself as the father to a large clan of eager children; he would famously grace them with presents at holidays, and had in fact been the first employer in America to reduce his employees' workweek to six days. Every soul in his company, from the head of his accounting division to the lowest assembler in his factories, received at least a day of rest per week. For Westinghouse, such gifts were signs of respect. All hands in the Westinghouse Electric

Company were in this mess together. There was a clear enemy not so far away in New York, a rival army dwarfing theirs in number and resources and power.

Westinghouse found himself impotent in the face of Tesla's willful insubordination for the simple reason that he needed Tesla, while Tesla only found Westinghouse to be vaguely useful. Westinghouse could not dock Tesla's pay, because Lemuel Serrell had ensured its inviolability. He could not forbid access to any tools of the lab, because he needed Tesla to make as much of their resources as possible. And any social pressures he might place on Tesla were equally pointless: Isolation was no punishment for a man who sought, above all else, to be left alone.

CHAPTER 17

A Famous Visitor

> High achievement always takes place in the framework of
> high expectation.
>
> —CHARLES F. KETTERING, INVENTOR
> OF THE ELECTRICAL STARTER

O N A HUMID morning that August, Paul was startled by a rap on his office door. He looked up from his correspondence to see the stunned face of the firm's secretary, Martha.

"You have a visitor," she said. "Well, actually . . . two of them."

The calling card she handed him contained a name familiar from the society pages.

"Agnes Huntington is in the waiting area?"

"Yes."

"The real Agnes Huntington?"

"If a girl that lovely isn't the real Agnes Huntington," answered Martha, "then I can't imagine what a light the original must be."

Why was he being visited by one of the leading young singers of the New York stage?

Of course he knew all about her. He read the papers. She was American by birth, but she'd come to fame in London, selling out a run of *Paul Jones* at the Prince of Wales, where, in a brilliant spark of casting, she'd performed the male title role. The glowing notices she'd received for such a bravura comedic feat had traveled across the Atlantic. Agnes had followed them soon enough, singing for a long run in the Boston Ideals and then making a tour of the East Coast. The Metropolitan Opera had finally courted her away at what the papers suggested had been a considerable expense. The summer season was consumed with talk that she would reprise her famed role. Paul hadn't seen it, of course. An evening's box at the Met would likely cost him a month's salary, if he was even able to purchase a ticket. Lawyers were day laborers to the truly rich. That attorneys labored with pens rather than shovels did not dignify their position in the eyes of Rockefellers and Morgans and Roosevelts. It only made their attempts at society life all the more quaint.

And yet Agnes Huntington, the brightest star to shine under the glow of Broadway's footlights, was waiting patiently in Paul's front room.

"You said there were two visitors?" inquired Paul. "Who is the other one?"

"Oh," replied Martha. "It's her mother."

"Luminous" had been among the words the London papers had chosen to describe the twenty-four-year-old star. Paul might have gone even further in his choice of adjectives. Agnes's curly ash-blond hair was perfectly done up in a halo around her face. Her skin was the same milky shade as her teeth. Her eyes were a winter gray, and they were impossible to read. Blue lace hung from the bottom of her green dress. The lace alone was likely more expensive than Paul's entire suit. And yet as pristine as she appeared, her demeanor was not delicate. She was no porcelain doll. She was a distant glacier. Remote, quiet, and yet possessed of great and unknowable activity beneath the surface.

Paul found the effect unnerving. Luckily, her mother, Fannie, did enough talking for the three of them.

Yes, tea would be welcome. No, sugar would not. The matter that they had come to discuss was quite a delicate one. Paul's discretion would be appreciated. They were in need of an attorney who could see to it that the present situation did not find its way to *The Sun*'s society page. Paul, Fannie Huntington had gathered, represented George Westinghouse against Thomas Edison. He had, perhaps, some experience with underdogs. He was unafraid of an unfair fight.

The mention of Thomas Edison reminded Paul of his professional capacity. "I can assure you," he said, "that whoever it is who's giving you trouble, he could not possibly be as powerful a foe as Thomas Edison."

This was precisely what Fannie Huntington wanted to hear. Paul did not get the impression that she was a woman frequently disappointed. She was among the smallest women Paul had ever seen, but fit a double-sized personality into a squat bullet of a frame. She was a rifle shell. Hardened and cooled, packed and loaded, ever ready to explode. How this mother had bred this daughter was a question for Mr. Darwin.

The problem, Fannie explained, had begun in Boston, when Miss Agnes was singing with the Ideals. Was Paul aware of this group, she asked, and of Agnes's previous position therein?

"Mr. Cravath is quite aware of who I am, Mother," said Agnes more sharply than he would have imagined. Her speaking voice had a hard edge. It gave no indication of the marvel that had made her famous. "He knows that I sang with the Ideals. He knows that I'm singing at the Met now. I'd wager he's likely been to a matinee."

"I'm afraid I haven't been so lucky." Paul supposed this confession would lower him a peg in her estimation.

"Well, then we must invite you to a performance," suggested Agnes graciously, without hint of condescension.

Paul had met but two strains of celebrity. The first laboriously upheld the pretense of being unaware of their own fame; they feigned humble surprise when you knew who they were. *Golly!* The second were experienced enough in their position not to bother. Agnes, having fit more than a few years of fame into her brief life, was of this latter type.

That she felt no need to prove anything to him, while he felt such desire to prove much to her, only accentuated the continent of social distance between them.

"So what is it that befell you in Boston?" he asked formally.

"Oh, it began in Boston," answered Fannie. "But the difficulty occurred in Peoria."

The Ideals, she explained, had traveled on their first tour of the Midwest. Indiana, Ohio, Illinois, Missouri. Of course, Agnes had never before sung in such places, Fannie was quick to note. But W. H. Foster, the owner of the Ideals, had been motivated by pecuniary gain to attempt a tour of places that did not have exposure to the higher arts. Tickets had been discounted for farmers and the like. What the Ideals might lose in the quality of their patrons they could make up for in quantity.

Single-night engagements were the standard for the tour. An evening in Gary, Indiana, for example, before two thousand theatergoers who were, as Fannie put it, "inexperienced attendees of a fine performance." Then on to Dayton for another show the next night. Her daughter had begun to feel like she'd joined up with P. T. Barnum.

In Peoria, Illinois, this conflict came to a head: Mr. Foster told Agnes that to save money, she'd have to travel with the chorus. Naturally, such a thing wouldn't do. Agnes complained politely. But Mr. Foster had not met Agnes's arguments with reason. Instead, he'd met them with undeserved punishment.

First, he forbade Fannie from traveling with her daughter. Then he began to skim from Agnes's salary. They had a contract, one that made very plain that Agnes was to receive two hundred dollars per week while on tour. First, ten dollars went missing from her weekly check. Mr. Foster said it was a mistake of his accountant's and he'd see to fixing it. He did not. A few weeks later the deficit was fifty dollars. Then one hundred dollars. And soon enough Agnes was receiving less than half of her agreed-upon salary.

So, at the advice of her concerned mother, Agnes quit the Ideals. She packed her bags, got on a train in Chicago, and two days later was home in Boston. Within a few months' time, the Met had happily moved Agnes and her mother to New York. Her career proceeded apace.

However, their wish to put this whole miserable ordeal behind them had gone unfulfilled. Mr. Foster had threatened suit against Agnes for her sudden departure. She told him that he could keep the money that he'd stolen, but that wasn't enough for Mr. Foster. He was demanding that Agnes return to Boston, to sing again with the Ideals.

"And if Miss Huntington does not do as he asks?" asked Paul.

"Mr. Foster claims to have many friends among the newspapermen of Chicago. He says that with only a letter, he could cause quite a stir. He could tell horrid lies to the paper about the reasons for Agnes's departure from the Midwest. He might even intimate . . . I cannot even say it."

Paul waved his hand in the air, indicating that she need not continue. "A scandal. Something of that nature."

He looked to Agnes, attempting to gauge her response to this unpleasant tale. There was none. Agnes maintained an expression of utter implacability. Her eyes simply shone their February gray. Her lips betrayed neither frown nor smile.

"We need this to go away," said Fannie. "And we need it to go away quietly. Might you be able to assist us?"

What Paul was forced to say next was difficult. But it was unavoidable.

"I would be happy to introduce you to my partners. They are excellent attorneys, and you'd be in extremely capable hands."

There was a moment of silence from the women. Neither appeared particularly accustomed to being turned down. It was as if they did not quite know how to respond to such a thing.

"I'm afraid it's simply an issue of time," continued Paul. "I don't have any. George Westinghouse's defense requires my full and unfettered attention."

"It is some lawyer," said Fannie, "who is uninterested in a new client."

"Right now, I have one client. I have one case. I must win it."

Agnes seemed faintly amused by Paul's earnestness. If she was offended, she didn't show it. She looked rather like she had already forgotten about Paul's existence and was readying for her return to the great world of concerts and parties from which she had dropped in. Paul faced the unpleasant thought that she would go away so soon. When was the last time he had even spoken to a woman his age? But he knew what he had to do.

"Come along, darling," said Fannie. "There are a hundred other attorneys on this block who would take your case with a moment's notice."

Paul's further apologies were dismissed. No sooner had they arrived than they were gone, Agnes leaving in her wake the faintest scent of some exotic perfume he would never smell again.

He looked to the impossible stack of papers on his desk. *This is what is required of the victorious,* he reminded himself. He remained at the office late that night, till his writing hand was useless, and he didn't sleep well.

CHAPTER 18

Fathers and Sons

A man, as a general rule, owes very little to what he is born
with. A man is what he makes of himself.

—ALEXANDER GRAHAM BELL

ERASTUS CRAVATH WAS not impressed. Of this he made his son
well aware over the course of his visit to New York at the end
of August.

Erastus was not impressed with Paul's client. Coal lamps were good
enough for the family home in Nashville.

He was not bowled over by Paul's Fiftieth Street apartment. Erastus
didn't much like New York in the first place. He couldn't imagine
why Paul would want to live there. Erastus found the summer in Manhattan to be stifling. He found the city noisy, filthy, unpleasant. He
found the conditions of the Jews, confined as they were to their Lower
East Side tenements, to be appalling. He found the treatment of the
Negroes in the Tenderloin to be even worse. Wasn't typhoid a concern?

Erastus didn't know why his son's apartment still hadn't been properly decorated after two years of habitation. He was reticent to ask at
which church Paul spent his Sundays, because he knew what the answer would be.

He found Central Park overly manicured, like the fussy gardens of some ancient English lord. He hadn't a taste for lobster, but if Paul wanted to spend the money gorging on shellfish, he wasn't going to tell a twenty-seven-year-old how to feed himself.

Paul had been informed by letter of his father's intention to visit. It would be his first trip to the city since Paul had lived there. He had business in the city. A meeting with some of the Fisk College donors— the few men in New York who possessed both strong moral convictions and the bank accounts necessary to support them. The old man had not even said that he was looking forward to seeing his son.

Paul in turn wrote Erastus that while he'd be happy to host him, the case was keeping him exceedingly busy of late. He wouldn't have much time for entertaining. Erastus responded that he wasn't sure what New York had to offer in the way of entertainment, but he didn't think it would be much that he'd like anyhow.

When Erastus arrived, he lugged his baggage up the four flights to Paul's apartment, huffing up the stairs while refusing help along the way. He was almost as tall as Paul, but he carried considerably more weight around the middle. His white beard, Paul noted, had grown so long that the fraying tips touched his shirtfront three buttons down.

Paul had cleared his afternoon of work, but Erastus said the journey had been exhausting and he'd be grateful for a few hours on Paul's daybed. Paul did not have a daybed, he told his father, but the elder Cravath was welcome to Paul's own bed for both the afternoon and the duration of his stay. So Erastus took to the mattress at two o'clock, while Paul puttered around the apartment idly. He pined for his office.

When Erastus awoke, Paul offered to take him out for a decent meal. But Erastus pointed out that that was a waste of money. He'd be more than content to make a stew. Where was the local butcher, so that he could get a good cut of flank steak?

Paul made the stupid mistake of admitting that he didn't know. This allowed Erastus the invitation he required to comment that if only Paul had a wife, he might have some help with his shopping. The topic of Paul's ceaseless bachelorhood had thus been broached.

Paul assured his father that he wanted a wife, that marriage wouldn't be far off, but that at the present moment work had been rather consuming. Wouldn't it be best to make a name for himself before he married?

"But you cannot," his father said as he boiled onions in the kitchen, "be after the love of a woman who loves you for your name. You want one who loves you for the man behind it."

Paul's goal in this conversation was to see it ended as swiftly as possible. Receiving romantic advice from his father was like receiving financial advice from a junior Rockefeller: If one has never suffered for want of a thing, one has no conception of the trade-offs required in getting it.

Paul's parents had a beautiful marriage. Of this he was convinced, although it confounded him. They'd met young and married instantly. His father could be irascible, his mother had a tendency to be even more judgmental than her husband, but together they were happy. And they excused each other's faults. Their rigid moralism stopped at the foot of their Tennessee two-story. They granted each other a forgiving kindness they granted few others. It was only as he'd grown older, as he'd seen his friends fall into their own uninhabitable and desolate unions, that he'd realized that his parents enjoyed a rare privilege. It was a privilege that Paul had not yet been afforded.

In twenty-seven years, Paul had kissed four girls. He never spoke of this, of course. But he thought about it sometimes, and the memories gave him pleasure to recall. Since his passing encounter with Agnes Huntington two weeks earlier, he found these memories both more insistent and more bygone.

The first girl he'd kissed was Evelyn Atkinson, back in Nashville. Her papa ran a shipping company down by the docks. Paul took his schooling at home, but every afternoon he'd run to the riverside to meet up with teenagers his own age. He had kissed Evelyn late one night, as the wispy light from the cloud-shrouded Tennessee moon illuminated the dimples on her smiling cheeks. She was always smiling, that's what he remembered most about her. Even while they kissed, the corners of her mouth remained raised.

By the time he'd kissed Gloria Robinson at the autumn tobacco festival, his taste for kissing was undeniable. He told no one. Other boys teased him out of jealousy, but only for what they imagined he'd done. For what they imagined girls had let him do.

Gloria's younger sister Emily he'd kissed three times. Which he'd felt bad about, but as he was sure Gloria hadn't told Emily, and Emily hadn't told Gloria, and he'd told no one, there had been no harm committed. Still, it had probably not been his finest hour.

He met Molly Thompson at Oberlin. She was quiet and redheaded, prone to fits of ticklishness in the Ohio grass. They'd kissed regularly. His classmates were certain that more than kissing had gone on— rumors spread quickly in a school that small—but Paul and Molly knew the truth. They'd taken walks along Plum Creek, danced to the fiddlers in Allencroft Hall, and whispered the whole histories of their brief lives behind the sandstone houses along Lorain Street. She'd asked him to return with her to her family in Cincinnati after they'd graduated. Paul had informed Molly that he was going to New York. And that was that.

He'd received a letter from her once, while he'd been in law school. Her son was six months old and her husband was a senior clerk handling finances in the mayor's office. She wondered, sometimes, how Paul was doing. He'd responded by sending her a clipping from the Columbia law journal. His article had won the annual third-year prize. He told her he'd soon be graduating first in his class.

She didn't write a second time.

And that had been the extent of his wet-lipped career. Law school afforded little time for making the acquaintance of women, and his professional life even less. His bachelorhood had for some years been total.

Paul knew that he was old, at twenty-seven, to be still unmarried. Not impossibly old, but older than most women of marrying age would like. He was a young attorney but an old bachelor. Paul had made good choices in his life, and they were paying off. That he sometimes wondered what it would be like if he'd made other ones did not mean that he'd ever dream of taking any of them back.

He could not quite say any of this to his father. Paul's gift with language did not extend to meaningful communication with the man who'd taught him to read. What would he gain by immodestly telling his father that he was by most accounts the most successful attorney of his generation, the lead litigator on the largest patent suit in the history of the United States? No matter what dragons Paul slayed, they would never be the kind to impress.

Erastus was never going to change. He wasn't going to suddenly develop an interest in his son's views of the world. He wasn't going to start appreciating either Paul's ambitions or his accomplishments. Nothing would be gained by exposing to his father the fraying nerves of his heart. He was content to maintain cordial relations with the old man. The push for anything more would upset the fragile equilibrium they'd finally reached.

Erastus saw no path to righteousness other than faith. He prayed to a Lord and Savior in whose existence Paul did not even believe. But to confess that to his father would be unthinkable. Whatever secrets he might imagine admitting, his university-bred atheism was not among them.

And so they quadrilled genteelly through their conversation. Paul asked about his sister. She was well. He asked about his mother. She was also well. She'd suffered through the winter with a terrible cough, but the spring seemed to banish it, thank goodness. Erastus opined about the election—he was campaigning aggressively for Harrison, having seen firsthand what economic devastation Cleveland had wreaked. Paul wondered aloud whether Harrison would be able to convince the Mugwumps to rejoin the Republicans in the fall. By eleven Erastus was ready, again, for bed. Paul lay on the floor of his sitting room, half wrapped in a blue cotton sheet. The apartment was hot in the summer, and Paul stayed up for some time, unable to sleep. Only after much tossing and turning was he treated to a series of dreams, one of which indelicately concerned a woman with the face of Agnes Huntington.

Paul woke with a start at five-thirty in the morning to find that his father was already boiling coffee on the stove. Looking over the morning papers, Erastus grunted as his son got up and made his way to the sink for a shave.

As soon as Paul sat, Erastus slid a page from the previous night's *Evening Post* in his direction.

"Something in the paper there you might want to look at," said Erastus. "The editorial—it's on your line of work, isn't it?"

By the time he'd gotten through the editorial's first sentence, Paul was apologizing to his father. His presence was required in Pittsburgh immediately. He needed to make haste to the Grand Central Station for the next train.

Erastus said that he understood. He said that he could take care of himself just fine over the coming days; he'd leave the key for Paul at the coffeehouse on Fifty-fourth Street. There were donors to be seen, the future of the college to be secured. Erastus had never seen the spires of Trinity Church, so he would be grateful for the chance to take a stroll.

Paul was out the door, overnight valise in hand, by the time he realized that he'd forgotten to give his father a farewell embrace. He knocked at the closed door of his own apartment, the keys safely inside with Erastus.

Yet Paul's father did not come to the door. Perhaps he'd gone back to sleep, or was unable to hear the knocking over the clatter of plates as he cleaned up the previous evening's meal. Paul turned away, down the four flights and off to Pittsburgh.

CHAPTER 19

Death in the Wires

America is a country of inventors, and the greatest of
inventors are the newspaper men.

—ALEXANDER GRAHAM BELL

BOARD A FIRST-CLASS car of the Pennsylvania Railroad, Paul
reread the *New-York Evening Post* editorial yet again.

DEATH IN THE WIRES, blared the headline. THE PERILS OF AL-
TERNATING CURRENT. The article was attributed to "Harold P. Brown,
electrical engineer." Paul's first question concerned who in the world
Harold P. Brown was. Paul's second concerned why he had been given
such a prominent space to proclaim his absurd opinions.

"Every day brings the news of more lives cut short by the menace
of electrical wiring that now dangles above our city. Never in the history of this nation has such a dangerous, poorly understood, and crim-
inally untested technology been thrust so haphazardly into the homes
of our families and the playrooms of our children, with no regard for
their safety." The paper went on to mention the tragedy Paul had
witnessed on Broadway, as well as other deaths at the hands of faulty
electrical wiring. "Several companies who have more regard for the
almighty dollar than for the safety of the public have even adopted
the new 'alternating current' for incandescent light service," continued the paper. "If arc current is potentially dangerous, then alternat-

ing current can be described by no adjective less forcible than 'damnable.' That the public must submit to constant danger from sudden death in order that a corporation may pay a slightly larger dividend is simply evil."

The paper went on to suggest, in language of unvarying vehemence, that alternating current was likely to fry the bones of any child within a hundred feet of its use. Because it ran at twice the voltage of direct current, it was, so Harold P. Brown argued, twice as deadly. There was, moreover, no legitimate scientific reason to prefer alternating current to direct; only the marketplace had caused these devious merchants of death to adopt this crooked technology. And, finally, the paper named the main proponent of this deadly system: George Westinghouse. "A villain who apparently will stoop to new lows to make an extra dollar off the naïve and gullible.

"To prevent the wholesale loss of human life," concluded Harold Brown's editorial, "all alternating current, such as that offered by George Westinghouse, must be banned immediately by the legislature of this state."

That evening Paul watched George Westinghouse pace across his laboratory. Gas lamps hung along the walls and washed the cavernous space with a pale orange light. Westinghouse's engineers feared that electric lights might interfere with their tests on new light-bulb designs. The newest colors on the market—the softest yellows, the wispiest fading whites, the lightest bursting sun flares—were developed here. The colors of the future had to be examined in the dim past.

Identical editorials from Brown had appeared in four other East Coast papers. Westinghouse's first commercial A/C system, based on Tesla's ideas, was set to be installed in only a few weeks' time in Buffalo. The department store Adam, Meldrum, and Anderson had already taken out advertisements touting the 498 A/C-powered bulbs that were soon to shine from its Italianate ceilings. Unless, that is, Harold Brown succeeded in having such a system banned.

"It isn't true," said Westinghouse. "A/C is *not* more dangerous than

D/C. Just the opposite. Why would the *Evening Post* print such a bald-faced falsehood?"

"Do you know who owns the *Evening Post*?" said Paul.

"I do not."

"Henry Villard."

"Who is . . ."

"Some middling newspaper tycoon. But a middling newspaper tycoon who happens to have quite recently come into possession of some two thousand shares of stock in Edison General Electric."

Westinghouse stopped his pacing. "Edison gave him shares in exchange for denouncing me on his paper's front page?"

"We'll never be able to prove it," said Paul.

"Can he do this? Can he really get the state legislature to ban my current?"

"It depends."

"Damned lawyers," grumbled Westinghouse. "Just give me a straight answer: Can he do this or can he not?"

"I sent inquiries to Albany from the station. It appears that Edison has already gotten a friendly New York state senator to submit just such a bill."

"I'll hazard a guess that Edison has found a way to compensate his state senator as well?"

"Having failed to produce a better product than you, he's now going to use the law to make your product illegal. I've already sent a message to my state senator. I'll argue your case before the legislature myself. He can't bribe *all* of them."

Westinghouse lowered his gaze to the floor. "A/C is better," he said quietly. "My work is better than his." Whoever he was talking to, it was not Paul.

"Can you help me to understand it? I'm a layman. Talk to me like a layman. Your alternating current runs at twice the voltage of his direct current. You told me so yourself. Well, to a layman: twice the current, twice the danger. It sounds like common sense."

When Westinghouse next spoke, his voice was low. "But this is the very thing about electricity. Nothing about it makes any common sense at all."

Westinghouse summoned Reginald Fessenden for help with a dem-onstration. After only a few months here, Fessenden appeared to have aged a few years. He seemed exhausted. Whatever work he was doing, and whatever stresses were being placed on him, was quickly graying his temples.

A smallish generator was attached to something Westinghouse called a capacitor. The thing was about six inches long, shaped like a cylinder, encased in a material—rubber?—that was smooth and per-fectly black. It looked, to Paul, something like a French dessert.

At Westinghouse's request, Fessenden gave a few spins to a hand crank at the machine's side. It whirled with a soft hum.

"And now," Westinghouse said, turning to Paul, "I'd like you to place each of your hands on one of those leads there. Yes. Those are the ones."

Paul looked at these "leads"—open-ended strips of cable—with trepidation. He remembered the flaming workman above Broadway.

"Sir . . . won't that electrocute me?"

"Yes. When you put your hands on those leads, one hundred ten volts of alternating current will shoot right through your body."

Paul blinked. This sounded like a certain death.

Westinghouse registered Paul's fear. "You don't trust me?"

"It's not that, but . . ." Paul looked at the machines. These deathly, futuristic things. Paul took a long, slow breath, and grabbed as hard as he could at the wire leads.

A popping sound.

A sharp yell from deep within Paul's throat.

And in under a second, it was over.

Paul waved his hands in the air, wriggling his fingers to shake off the sting. The pain was akin to that of catching a baseball without a mitt.

There'd been no flash of light. No spark. No caged lightning un-leashed upon his flesh.

"Oww," said Paul finally, when he remembered to speak.

"So," said Westinghouse patiently, "what have we learned?"

Paul turned to Fessenden for an answer.

"Voltage," supplied Fessenden dutifully, "is not the same as power.

A/C may run at higher voltages than D/C, but it does so with a variable amplitude. I can show you a notebook full of equations to explain this if you're curious."

"Aha!" said Westinghouse. "We're teaching Paul some science, at long last. Now: What is it about the very *nature* of alternating current that makes it less dangerous?"

Paul again turned to Fessenden.

"Right," said Fessenden. "So, it's called *alternating* current, you'll remember, because it literally *alternates* direction hundreds of times per second. While direct current remains constant. Now, in response to electrical current, the muscles of the human body contract. As yours just did. This is why people are electrocuted to death. They grasp the current, and they can't let go, because the current contracts the very muscles that are holding on."

"The brain wants to let go," said Westinghouse, "but the muscles won't comply. Just now, as soon as you felt the shock, what happened?"

"I let go."

"You were able to let go because as the A/C changes its direction each of those hundreds of times per second, there is actually an infinitesimal pause in the current. Think of it like a carriage: It goes in a circle clockwise as fast as it can, then to turn around it has to slow, and then stop, and then speed up again in the other direction. Such is the case with alternating current."

"Except for the slowing-down part," corrected Fessenden.

Westinghouse agreed. "Electricity lends itself poorly to metaphor. Gravity, centripetal motion—much easier phenomena to explain by way of literary analogy. If Newton worked in poetry, we're left to toil in prose. I have pondered this on occasion."

Paul took in all that he'd been told. How could they explain all of this to potential customers without demanding that each of them try sticking their hands inside an A/C generator to see for themselves?

Having a better system than Edison's would do no good if they couldn't explain to the public why it was better. Reality mattered not at all; perception was the whole of business. Edison had realized this before they had. While Westinghouse was using Tesla's discoveries to develop a superior product, Edison had skipped straight to developing a superior story.

And stories were supposed to be Paul's expertise.

As if he'd been reading Paul's train of thought, Westinghouse spoke again. The professorial tenor was gone from his voice.

"Paul," said Westinghouse quietly, "I rely on you to see this kind of thing coming."

Westinghouse's words were a cold breeze. They were so soft as to be almost inaudible, and yet they froze Paul in his place.

"I'm sorry, Mr. Westinghouse," said Paul. "I knew that Edison was going to respond to our hiring of Tesla and our adoption of A/C. But I didn't know how. I didn't think he'd go this far."

"This is your job," continued Westinghouse. "You are not, if this situation is to be any indication, doing it as well as I might hope."

Embarrassed, Paul looked to Fessenden. But the engineer was busying himself with the documents in his hands, conspicuously avoiding eye contact.

"You've made the mistake," said Westinghouse, "of underestimating the villainy of Thomas Edison."

"I have. And what I can promise you today is that I will never do so again."

Paul was dismissed a few minutes later. He and Fessenden left the inventor to the quiet of his dark and empty laboratory.

"He'll get over it," said Fessenden as they walked side by side toward the mansion, across the moonlit lawns of the estate. The muggy air threatened to burst into a summer storm above the country oaks. "I've been on the receiving end of that same look. He has a way of making you feel six inches tall. But don't worry: He'll be on to someone else's failures tomorrow."

"How's Tesla doing?" Paul hadn't heard any complaints about Tesla in a few weeks, which he'd taken as a positive development.

At the mention of Tesla's name, Fessenden grimaced. "Well . . . I'm afraid that's going to be a bit difficult to explain."

CHAPTER 20

The Difference of Opinion Between Mr. Tesla and Mr. Westinghouse

> Only when they must choose between competing theories
> do scientists behave like philosophers.
> —THOMAS KUHN, *THE STRUCTURE OF SCIENTIFIC REVOLUTIONS*

I T TURNED OUT that Tesla had presented Westinghouse with a sketch. Something concerning the airless vacuum that filled the light bulbs. Westinghouse had suggested making a few tweaks and then testing both versions to see which operated better, and in response Tesla had gone up to his office and shut the door in protest.

Four days later, Fessenden and his men had still not heard a word from Tesla. He had been scribbling nearly illegible demands for saltine crackers on the backs of Machinery Department requisition forms and then slipping them without ceremony under his door. It had taken a full day for a passing char girl to notice them. The girl brought the papers to the attention of the butler, who then had to figure out some way of bringing the incident to Westinghouse's attention without causing the old man to break something glass-carved and expensive.

At least they'd been able to fit the saltines under Tesla's door.

Paul asked Fessenden to lead him to Tesla's apartment above the private laboratory. Tesla was apparently still locked inside, having reneged on his promise to come out once he'd been delivered his saltines.

Tesla did not answer the door. Paul's pleas for a brief audience fell against the mute wooden doorway.

As he turned down the hall, Paul saw a slip of white paper flit out from under Tesla's door. He bent over to pick it up.

"Mr. Paul Cravath" were the first words he read on the Machinery Department requisition form. "It is imperative of me that I am quitting the employ of Mr. George Westinghouse. He is not of an inventing person. I take my leave and will see you in Manhattan, New York, New York.—Nikola Tesla."

The problems before Paul had just doubled. Not only would he have to manage the public war in print between Edison and Westinghouse, but he would now have to manage the private one between Westinghouse and Tesla.

Unexpectedly, it was Tesla who selected the venue for the peace negotiations. Even though he seemed to have no taste for the food, nor the slightest interest in the wine, he appeared to have developed an affinity for Delmonico's. Not even Tesla was immune to the fragrance of exclusivity. He was merely immune to the expectations of politeness.

So in the same week that Edison's lawyers trapped Paul into nuisance court appearances in three states over the differences between A/C and D/C, and the New York State Legislature held bloviating sessions about banning A/C altogether, Paul had to beg his own client to travel to New York to share *canard aux olives* with the man most likely to get them free of it all.

"This gentleman knows neither morsel nor iota of what it means to invent," sniped Tesla. The Bordeaux that had been generously poured into his glass went unsipped. "He has never so done, and never will he."

"This is the malarkey I've been dealing with for *months*," said Westinghouse.

"What I'd like to suggest," offered Paul impartially, "is that the language we all employ in this conversation take a more soothing tone."

Tesla was having none of this. "It is Mr. George Westinghouse whose language is sorely incapable of expressing the varied wonders in which I am conversant."

"My point precisely! Does anyone have even the faintest idea of what he is talking about? He sounds like the only English he's ever learned is from Chaucer."

"I have not any such acquaintance," explained Tesla. "Is he another of your idiotic laboratory mammals?"

"Stop," pleaded Paul. "Both of you. Stop."

Paul had not thought this was going to be easy, but he had also not been aware of how personal their disagreement had become. "This is about more than the vacuum-bulb issue, isn't it?"

"You are in the right," said Tesla. "The problem I have faced is that Mr. George Westinghouse is not an inventor."

"The problem I have faced is that Mr. Nikola Tesla is an ass."

"Mr. Tesla," said Paul, "Mr. Westinghouse is one of the most accomplished inventors in American history. This is not me speaking as his attorney, mind you, but as a man whose every day is graced by the products of his work."

"Air brakes," said Tesla. "You, sir, conjured a few bright notions on the halting of heavy objects traveling at speeds very fast. Twenty years in the past, you made a quite big train stop. Bravo. The orchestra stands and every patron shall bow."

"Please," said Paul, "we would all be helped by rather more clarity and rather fewer insults."

"What manner of electrical system have you invented, Mr. Westinghouse?"

Seeing Paul's look, Westinghouse answered with great patience. "The alternating-current system that my company is perfecting—and has already begun selling—is a product of both your recent breakthroughs, for which I give you full credit, and the Sawyer–Man patents, which we acquired some time ago. You, sir, had a good idea. I built a system that put it to use."

"Yes indeed, precisely true," snapped Tesla. "But you have not invented a thing, do you see? Misters Sawyer and Man, they are my peers. They had most brilliant ideas. You signed a check."

"They registered patents. I bought the rights to those patents. And then I combined their work with yours and my own and created—am in the process of refining—an electrical system that will change the nature of human life. That's how business works."

"The workings of your business," said Tesla, "are not to be found listed in the catalogues of my concerns."

"What are your concerns?" asked Paul, hoping this might provide some clarity as to the root of the men's disagreement.

"Alternating current works. It can power motors. It can power lamps. It can power cities. I know this to be true."

"And I as well," said Westinghouse.

"All right," said Paul. "We find ourselves on common ground."

"And so we should travel elsewhere," said Tesla. "You wish for the building of an alternating-current lamp, something different from that of Edison. But why? For your legal problems. Not for scientific discovery. You are wanting a new product. I am wanting a new invention."

At this both Westinghouse and Paul were momentarily at a loss for words. The waiters took the opportunity to slip between the men fresh pours of Bordeaux and three sautéed duck breasts.

"I make things, Tesla. I make wonderful things. My company manufactures triple-valve automatic air brakes and steam engines and ampere meters and Rotair valves. We make these things better than anyone else in the country. Better than Eli Janney. Better than George Pullman. Most certainly better than Thomas Edison."

"I will grant the factual veracity of that statement," offered Tesla.

"In Edison you two have a common foe," said Paul.

But even Westinghouse ignored this. "What do you make?" he asked Tesla.

"Thoughts," answered Tesla, as if speaking to a child. "I have thoughts. And my imaginings, they will last longer and drive deeper into the next centuries than shall your fragile toys."

"The many things that I have built will last for ages."

"No, Mr. George Westinghouse. Buildings are ephemeral. It is ideas that last forever."

Tesla stood and gestured to the server for his long coat.

Paul mediated the wars of men who devoted their lives to creating things from thin air. But such different things! Westinghouse created objects. Tesla created ideas. While Edison, a few miles away, was busy creating an empire.

Paul did not have a creative mind. He knew that men like Edison, Tesla, and Westinghouse possessed something he did not. An extra organ, an extra region of the brain, a God-lit candle such as the one that gave Saint Augustine faith—there was a creative *thing,* and Paul knew he didn't have it.

What would it feel like to be a creative man? To experience their eurekas, to thrill at their inventive madnesses? Paul tried to imagine what an Edison, a Tesla, a Westinghouse might feel in the moment of pure inspiration . . . but he couldn't do it. Paul did not invent; he solved. Problems came across his desk, and he solved them. Questions answered, mistakes corrected. The way Paul thought of it, if you asked him a question, he was exceptionally good at providing the right answer. But he wasn't the sort of person who came up with the questions.

In the strangest sense, Paul felt that he saw these men more clearly than they would ever see one another. Because he was not of them, he could peer at them remotely, three great giants in the misty distance. Three entirely incompatible ways of approaching science, industry, and business.

"Farewell," said Tesla before turning away and walking out the door. "You may consider me no longer any part of your Westinghouse Company."

CHAPTER 21

Intrigue at Carter, Hughes & Cravath

Everything comes to him who hustles while he waits.

—THOMAS EDISON

"**W**E'RE HERE TO help," lied Charles Hughes. He was leaning against the frame of Paul's office door in an attempt to appear casual. It wasn't working.

Carter stood behind him. The elder partner's scowl disarmed the younger partner's imitation of friendliness.

"I appreciate that," lied Paul in return.

"I doubt it," said Carter. He made no effort to conceal his condescension toward his onetime protégé.

"Where are you with Tesla?" asked Hughes. It was two weeks after Westinghouse and Tesla's ill-fated dinner. Paul had sent a few letters care of Lemuel Serrell, but had heard nothing back.

"I've received no response. But he's been seen in Manhattan a few times—dining with high society, if you can believe it. My theory is that he's seeking financiers for his own company. Setting up shop somewhere in New York, but Serrell either won't tell me exactly where he is, or doesn't know himself." Why were his partners so focused on Tesla? Of all the crises before them, the loss of Tesla seemed the most manageable.

"We must convince him to go back to Westinghouse," said Carter.

"Or find someone else to help Westinghouse create a non-infringing A/C lamp." Paul knew that geniuses of Tesla's caliber did not grow on trees. But they had to grow somewhere. "The loss of Tesla's expertise is a problem, to be sure, but it's a scientific one, not a legal one. The patents remain firmly in Mr. Westinghouse's hands."

"Yes," said Hughes. "That's what concerns us."

It seemed that Paul's partners knew something he did not.

"We looked over the contracts," said Carter.

"Two dollars and fifty cents per horsepower on every unit sold?" asked Hughes.

"I don't have the papers in front of me, but yes, I believe that's the royalty Westinghouse is paying."

"And he's paying them whether or not Tesla is working with him to make the patents useful."

"Yes," said Paul. "Westinghouse keeps the patents even if Tesla leaves, no change in conditions. This is a good thing."

"Well," said Hughes with a carefully feigned humility, "the thing of it is, it's not."

". . . How do you mean?"

"Oh my," said Carter. "He genuinely doesn't understand."

"Walter," said Hughes, "we don't need to make Mr. Cravath feel any worse about this, do we?"

"Make me feel worse about what?" asked Paul.

"When you negotiated with Mr. Serrell," said Hughes, "on your own, without our guidance, you negotiated a flat fee and a royalty structure that covered both Mr. Tesla's patents and his future work. And of course this structure was quite generous, wasn't it?"

"Well worth it, I believe," said Paul. "So does Westinghouse."

"Well worth it if it covered both the patents and their future refinement. But now that same fee only covers the patents. Mr. Westinghouse will have to bring on new men to replace Tesla, but he's still paying Tesla his full rate. In perpetuity."

"You thought you were negotiating a patent deal, Paul," interrupted Hughes, "but you were actually negotiating a labor contract. And now your client—a client of this firm—is paying a usurious royalty rate for work that the other party is not obligated to perform."

"But . . ." Paul tried to think of a response, his cheeks flaming with shame. "How else could I have—"

"You could have put another goddamned clause into the deal," barked Carter. "'If and when Tesla leaves, the royalty rate cuts to fifty cents,' or twenty-five cents—who knows what you could have gotten."

"We employ such clauses frequently in these sorts of deals," said Hughes. "American Steel has them with Benjamin Marc. I've worked on similar deals with Serrell before. He was expecting the ask. But you didn't think of it. And you didn't consult us. He must be laughing himself silly."

How could Serrell have manipulated him so thoroughly? As Paul replayed the negotiation in his head, Serrell's wicked ingenuity at last revealed itself.

Carter came to the same realization. "He offered you a position, didn't he?" Carter crossed his arms with the worn exasperation of looking at someone who might once have been so promising but had turned out to be so very, very dim.

Hughes put the matter more sympathetically than his father-in-law. "He offered you a position at his firm so that you wouldn't confer with us. He knew you were inexperienced. And he knew you were ambitious, eager to take all the credit yourself. So by offering some simple conspiracy against us, he drove a wedge between you and your more experienced partners."

Paul's shame curdled in his stomach. "I did not know that such a clause was an option," he said with all the control he could muster.

"You did not know," said Carter, "because you are twenty-seven years old. You are buried over your head in dirt and you are too stupid to realize it's quicksand."

"Walter," ventured Hughes. "There's no need."

"I do not require your false pity," said Paul with a force he hadn't intended. "You're to play the angel on one shoulder while Mr. Carter is the devil on the other? Spare me the penny theater."

"This is hundreds of thousands of dollars Westinghouse will lose because of your arrogance," said Carter. "Millions, possibly."

"The patents only last six more years," pleaded Paul lamely. "It's a lot of money, to be sure, but in six years the damage will be done, and once we prevail over Edison it won't matter."

"Prevail?" said Carter. "How in the hell is Westinghouse supposed to beat Edison when he's locked into paying a two-fifty-per-unit royalty that Edison is not? Westinghouse will either have to make his units more expensive than Edison's, which will be death in the marketplace, or sell them for a price such that he's barely making a profit, and then the whole corporation will sink. A fine position you've put him in."

It was the "you" that stung the most. This disaster was of Paul's making.

"I made a mistake."

"You made a mistake," repeated Hughes. "But you won't again. That's all we ask."

Paul looked to Hughes for a rope of any kind with which to pull himself up.

"What do you want?" asked Paul. But as soon as he said it, he realized what was coming. And he realized that he was powerless to fight it.

They wanted to share the client. And if Paul refused, they would tell Westinghouse not only about the full implications of the expensive royalty he was obligated to pay, but that such payments might have been avoided had it not been for Paul's error. The bad news could be delivered in one of two ways: either with a tone of gentle inevitability, with which attorneys typically mollified their clients, or with the attachment of blame that Paul could not deny. The whole firm would likely be fired. Yet only Paul was without additional clients. Only he could not recover from the loss of this one.

Perhaps he had been too young for a case of this magnitude, Paul admitted to himself. Perhaps Westinghouse's faith in him had been misplaced.

He accepted their proposal without argument.

"Well then," said Carter. "We'll send word to Westinghouse. We'll tell him it's firm policy, the size of this lawsuit being bigger and more important than any one man. Three attorneys for the price of one—he can't be too upset."

Paul watched as Carter and Hughes left the room. He did not turn away from the slight smiles on their faces. He wanted to remember their looks. If ever again he was tempted into overconfidence, he would have those smiles to chasten him.

A beginning. A middle. An end. And then gone, to be recalled when necessary.

A resolution firmed his spine as the door shut. There was, Paul knew, only one way to win. And that was to win Tesla back. He didn't leave that night until he'd figured out how.

CHAPTER 22

A Visit to Number 4 Gramercy Park

No experiments are wasted.

—THOMAS EDISON

AGNES AND FANNIE Huntington lived in a two-story brownstone at Number 4 Gramercy Park. The block lacked Fifth Avenue's old-money hauteur, and it boasted none of Washington Square's ancestral mansions. Yet it made up for both by way of its high-art fashionableness. This was a street of a discerning, popular class: a group of people who'd worked for a living, but whose work had paid off handsomely. All in all, the collection of artists, writers, actors, and singers that lived within just this half-mile square was arguably the most impressive in America. The writer John Bigelow and the wallpaper dealer James Pinchot lived just down the street. The railroad man Stuyvesant Fish had recently bought a four-story at the corner and had the place remodeled, at considerable expense, by the architect Stanford White. The fourth-floor ballroom of the new Fish mansion and the marble staircase that led up to it were already the stuff of society-page legend.

The Huntingtons' was the smallest house on the block. Its eight white window frames projected a classical simplicity, while the black iron railing that led Paul up the six front steps hinted, tastefully, at just the right amount of wealth.

Paul waited for the ladies in the tea room. His new hat, purchased only the day before, hung uselessly by the front door. The brightly patterned couch on which he sat was small, so he struggled to perch his oversized body upon it in a dignified manner. He crossed and uncrossed his legs as he waited, trying to find a position that didn't make him look like a top about to tip over.

"Perhaps you'd prefer the armchair?"

Fannie Huntington was a small spear of black silk arcing across the Oriental rug. Agnes entered quietly behind her mother, the same impenetrably polite smile on her face as the last time he'd seen her. Paul tried to stop wondering what might lie behind it.

After they were seated, Paul thanked them again for agreeing to see him so promptly. As he had mentioned in his letter of the day before, he had changed his mind. He would be delighted to take on their case, if they could forgive his initial resistance, and if they still hadn't found a suitable attorney. In Fannie's curious look, he could tell that they hadn't. Paul wasn't sure why, but did not want to ask. Perhaps what they needed most from a lawyer was total discretion. In New York, that might be the only thing women of their class couldn't purchase with ease.

He told them that his strategy on their behalf would be a simple one. He would write to W. H. Foster, manager of the Boston Ideals, informing him that the firm Carter, Hughes & Cravath now represented Miss Huntington in all matters. Paul would mention no other specifics. His role would be to cool tempers. Surely whatever unpleasantness had passed between Miss Huntington and Mr. Foster, he would politely suggest, would be better left a memory. No one had anything to gain by digging up skeletons.

Paul would issue no warnings. Those would come later, and only if absolutely necessary. "Only an amateur begins with a threat," he said. He attempted to muster as much authority as he could while Agnes's gray eyes seemingly searched his face for weakness. "One appears hysterical, and has nowhere to go from there. The most powerful threats are always left unspoken, as both parties know well the stakes of whatever it is in which they are engaged.

"One very helpful thing you have on your side is that you seek only to maintain the present state of affairs. He seeks to change them. As such, no action is, for us, victory." It was not lost on Paul that this was essentially true of his other client as well. His expertise was to be in creative delays. He felt this was reasonable. Who had ever hired an attorney in the hopes of speeding a matter along?

When Paul was finished, Fannie poured milk into her tea. "And what compensation will you require for this change of heart?"

She was no fool. Paul named a sum that was less than half the typical rate. This seemed both to satisfy Fannie's business sense and to arouse her suspicions.

"Additionally, I would like to ask one small favor in return."

"What sort of favor might I do for you?" said Fannie.

"Not from you, Mrs. Huntington. From your daughter. And it's not for me. It's for George Westinghouse."

Agnes gave a world-weary laugh. "I'm afraid I don't perform privately anymore," she said. "Part of my contract with the Met."

"Actually," said Paul, "it's not that. . . . I'd . . . well . . . I'd like you to take me to a party."

CHAPTER 23

The Players' Club

There is nothing in a caterpillar that tells you it's going to be
a butterfly.
                                    —BUCKMINSTER FULLER

J UST A FEW houses down from Agnes Huntington's sat a four-
story stone mansion that had, a few months before, been purchased by the actor Edwin Booth. Booth's plan was not to make
the whole of this Gramercy palace his home, however. Fitting himself
into a small apartment on the top floor, he dedicated the rest of the
space to the creation of a private club. A club for artists, he'd told the
society pages of *The Sun* and *The Times*. A club more fashionable than
the ones that served the haughty residents of Washington Square.
The Players' Club, he called it. All the leading lights of the Broadway
stage and the New York literary beau monde had been invited to join.
The weekly parties, it was well reported, were spectacular.

What went conspicuously unspoken in the press reports, but was
frequently discussed by the gossiping New Yorkers who read them,
was that Booth had clearly opened the club as a ploy to resuscitate his
family's good name, which his brother John Wilkes had sullied rather
spectacularly two decades back. His plan was to present the court of
public opinion with a new topic of conversation. His club would be
exclusive. The fewer people he invited, the more would yearn to be.
What went on inside would be the subject of tea-table gossip every

week. The Booth name, then, might become synonymous with something—anything—other than the unseemly assassination.

There was to be a party at the Players' in a week's time, Paul informed Agnes and Fannie Huntington. Women weren't allowed to be members of the club, but Agnes's stature in the theater granted inclusion on its guest list.

"Those parties," said Fannie politely. "They have a certain reputation."

"So I've read," said Paul.

"I can't imagine that my daughter would find herself comfortable in such company." At her mother's comment, Agnes looked away.

"I had not planned to attend," she said demurely.

"Miss Huntington, if you were willing to attend and bring me as your guest, it would be of tremendous help to me."

"I'm afraid I don't understand," said Fannie, preempting any response from her daughter. She crossed her hands in her lap. "How will attending a party at this Players' Club help you win a victory for Mr. Westinghouse?"

"This particular party," said Paul, "is to be thrown by Stanford White."

Fannie blinked. Stanford White was the most famous architect in New York, having designed the Villard houses and Madison Square Garden. His design for the arch that would rest at the top of Washington Square was at that moment under construction. But renowned as he was for his work on the Manhattan skyline, his professional reputation was largely becoming eclipsed by his personal one. A lifelong bachelor, White had long been the subject of rumors about the many young women with whom he spent his time.

The look on Fannie Huntington's face made plain that she was well aware of this sordidness. And that she did not like one bit the idea of her daughter becoming party to it.

"The thing is," said Paul, "that Mr. White appears to have made himself a new friend. And next week's party is to be thrown in this friend's honor. To introduce the distinguished guest to the most fashionable of Manhattan society."

Paul leaned forward in his chair. "The guest of honor is a very odd scientist whose name you will likely not recognize. But it's terribly important that I speak to him."

One week later, on a crisp September evening, Paul collected Agnes from her home at Number 4, to walk her across Gramercy Park to Number 16, where the Players' was located.

Agnes said almost nothing during her mother's brief lecture to both of them on the dangers inherent at any party Stanford White was attending. Then, miraculously, Fannie showed them out and they were alone together outside Number 4.

Paul knew enough to offer her his arm for the short trip across the park. But before he could even discuss the pleasantness of the evening, Agnes spoke first.

"Oh my dear Lord, do I need a drink." Agnes had spoken so little in their previous meetings that Paul was surprised at both the timbre of her voice and its sudden gaiety.

"You are a consecrated saint," she continued, "for getting me out of that house. I did not move to Gramercy to spend every night playing Hearts with Mother."

Paul found himself on uncertain ground. He thought of Fannie's admonitions. "I hope the environment won't be too unruly. If you feel uncomfortable at any point, you may take your leave of—"

"Are you kidding? Stanford's parties are heaven. The last one I went to lasted until two hours past dawn. When I finally got home, Mother was up in the sitting room, just waiting to catch me. Somehow I convinced her that I'd woken early for a fresh-air stroll. I thought she bought it, but I've barely been able to get away from her for a month. Which means you, Mr. Cravath, are my guardian angel."

The Agnes Huntington in whose company Paul found himself was evidently quite different from the vision of respectability he'd signed on to represent. That perfectly crafted smile was suddenly replaced with a devilish grin.

"You're friendly with Mr. White?" he asked as they approached the club. He didn't know how to feel about the prospect of that, and instantly worried that the question was impolite.

For the first time in his presence, she gave a great roaring laugh. "Any girl who's trod the boards is *friendly* with Stanford White. The only reason I haven't had to worry about getting even friendlier is my age. Thank goodness."

Paul tried to appear at ease with this line of conversation. "I'm glad to hear that your youth is . . . a welcome deterrent to such men."

Agnes looked at him disappointedly. "Quite the contrary. I'm far too old for him." Paul looked to his shoes so she couldn't see his surprise. "That little Astor girl whose trip to the family doctor—I'm sure you can guess why—started his recent mess? She was fourteen."

"Oh" was all Paul could think to say.

"Sort of ironic, don't you think? He gets caught swelling the belly of the one girl he consorts with who's old enough to swell."

Paul felt himself at the precipice of a world whose rules he did not know.

"Now," said Agnes brightly as they ascended the concrete steps to the Players' entrance, "my mother has gone to sleep, the night is waking, and I think it's high time that we got low-down drunk."

Inside, Paul was greeted by more champagne than he'd ever seen in his life. It was everywhere, and the flowing torrents from every open bottle matched the golden frames along the walls. Even the alcohol in this place was the color of money.

Agnes requested a glass with two fresh raspberries dropped inside. "A present for getting to the bottom," she said.

She introduced Paul around. He was good with names, good with noting the telltale details that might accumulate into memories. Mr. Honeyrose with the salt-and-pepper muttonchops, Mrs. Sheldon with the Spanish accent, Mr. Farnham with the short stance and silver walking stick. Paul clocked them all as he shook their hands.

Agnes seemed to know everyone. At each kiss of her hand, she deployed a joke; with each curtsy came a story she'd been simply dying to share. She took to the party as if she'd been born into it.

In a way, she had. From what Paul knew, the Huntingtons were an old family. They'd settled into America at the roots. They'd flourished in the western industries, in California gold and Colorado trains, as well as the eastern halls of the House and Senate. The Huntingtons had bloomed so colorfully across the vista of American money and power that, Paul realized, he didn't know from which branch of Huntingtons she had descended. Her family connections had gone unmentioned in the newspaper accounts of her career.

Yet she'd come to him for representation, not to someone older or more well known. Agnes and Fannie must have lacked the protection, then, of someone more powerful than Paul. As Paul was not particularly powerful, this must mean that they came from some lesser tributary of Huntingtons. But wherever they were from, the young woman Paul watched charm her way through the Players' Club seemed happy to be here.

"Tesla," said Paul after what felt like the thousandth handshake. "I need to find Tesla."

"He'll be with Stanford, I'm sure. Grab us two more flutes and then let's pop upstairs."

The second floor was thick with cigar smoke. A quartet of musicians was cramped into one corner, the fiddlers sweating as they sawed their horsehair bows. The clomp of hard leather shoes against the floorboards threatened to drown out the music. Agnes led Paul across a floor of tipsy dancers stumbling to the rhythm of the fast waltz.

On the third floor Paul saw a clump of partygoers assembled around a pair of couches. The guests had organized themselves into a half circle. All eyes seemed to be focused on the thin man whose head poked up in the center.

Tesla. By the crooked grin spread across the inventor's face, Paul saw he was enjoying the scene. Paul could not believe that someone who took so little delight in other people seemed to find such pleasure in other people's delights.

"A magnet and a coil," said Tesla to the crowd. "These are the tools you need. Think of it thusly: The magnetic force we have been knowing for some time. The coil is to be found in each of your mattresses." The assembled snickered gaily at the mention of bedding. Tesla seemed not to know what had caused their laughter, but appreciated it nonetheless.

"But where does it *come* from?" asked the man standing next to Tesla. Considerably shorter, he wore a bushy, unkempt mustache and a trail of gold buttons up his starched white wing-collared shirt. Paul looked to Agnes for confirmation. This was Stanford White.

"Electricity arises from nowhere," said Tesla. "Everywhere. The air everywhere and all around. It is not created. It is harnessed."

"Like a horse?" asked White as the crowd laughed.

"Like the strength of steam," said Tesla. "From where does water come? It does not. It is. Then men learned to heat it. And to direct the clouds of air that flew up above the hot water . . ." He clapped his hands. "There you have it! Power."

Paul watched the ladies turn to each other and smile while the men shared approving looks. They all strove to indicate both that they were impressed by what Tesla was saying and that they understood it.

As Tesla continued to speak, Paul noticed that he kept his body carefully removed from the others. He swayed stiffly to avoid the well-coiffed hair dangling precariously from the women. His various insanities read, to the assembled, as fascinating eccentricities.

White turned to the crowd with a wink. *You don't hear this every day*, he seemed to be saying to his friends. Tesla was the party's resident curio.

"Your friend seems less like a guest," said Agnes quietly, "and more like the entertainment."

Of all the roles he had imagined that Tesla might play, that of court jester to Manhattan's artistic royalty had never been among them.

"He loves a good novelty, Stanford," Agnes continued. "He was dragging around a Chinese magician, last I was here. Sleight of hand for the slight of mind. This is the first time I've seen him make a show of a scientist, though."

Tesla, still monologuing colorfully on the nature of electricity, finally caught sight of Paul. He stopped in his speech. "Mr. Paul Cravath," said Tesla. His eyebrows rose in wonder.

The crowd, confused, turned to see to whom Tesla was speaking. Their confusion was in no way ameliorated when they realized it was Paul.

Stanford White spoke before Paul could. "Does Mr. Tesla have a friend?"

"He does," answered Agnes. "This is Mr. Paul Cravath. He's my lawyer."

White regarded Agnes warily.

"Might we give the old boys a minute to talk?" suggested Agnes.

"Only," said White, "if you'll honor us with a song."

Agnes smiled. "If you're very lucky, perhaps." She drew White back into the crowd, tactfully giving Paul his chance.

"What is it that you are doing here, Mr. Paul Cravath?" said Tesla after Paul had sidled up to him.

"I've been trying to reach you." Remembering the inventor's dislike of physical contact, Paul held his palms inches away, guiding by gesture rather than by touch. He led Tesla to a spot where they could speak without being overheard. "We should talk."

Tesla's tone grew light. "Oh! Indeed. If you will come tomorrow night, there are magnificent things to be seen."

"Come where?" asked Paul.

"To my new laboratory." Tesla grinned at Paul's evident surprise. "You do not think that I have in idleness been passing these days."

"You've invented something new?" Paul tried to imagine what Tesla, left to his own devices, might have devised. But such things were quite literally beyond Paul's imagination.

Tesla leaned in to whisper his next words.

"It is a wireless telephone."

Paul stared dumbly. Telephones had existed for only a decade; almost no one owned one, on account of their tremendous cost. Paul himself had never used one. Who would want a wireless one? What would a "wireless telephone" even be?

Tesla laughed a high cackle. Paul's disbelief seemed to thrill him. He named an address on Grand Street. "Come tomorrow evening," he whispered, "and I will show you something that so few men ever can claim to be seeing. That is: something that they have never seen before." He handed Paul a plain card on which was written no name, but simply the Grand Street address.

Before Paul could ask for a clarification, he was distracted by a sound from across the party. A song rose high above the din and rested gently in the air on its own sweet plaintiveness. The voice was forceful but tender, a bright twinkle through the smoke-darkened room.

Paul couldn't see the singer, but he didn't need to. He knew in an instant that it could come from only one person, and that her reputation had been well deserved.

Agnes hadn't brought one of her arias to the Players'—instead she sang "Where Did You Get That Hat?," a ditty that had found itself unexpectedly in vogue that summer. Only she'd slowed the tempo, singing it with a strangely mournful air. She'd somehow made the song both more amusing and at the same time oddly haunting.

Even Tesla was transfixed. The inventor abruptly passed Paul by, moving toward the source of the song. Tesla's shoulder grazed Paul's as he walked, yet he didn't seem to notice a contact that would typically horrify him. Paul followed until they came to a knot of partygoers surrounding Agnes, who was just letting go of the song's final notes.

Paul tried to catch Agnes's eye amid the applause. She really was something.

As the applause dwindled, Stanford White had clearly had enough singing for one night.

"What a delight!" he bellowed. "Mr. Tesla, was not this performance *electrifying?*" Amid the laughter, he began plying Tesla with more questions about this electricity business. The crowd enveloped Tesla. Paul could see only his head poking out above the smoky dinner jackets and pearl-laden necklines.

Paul watched at the outskirts of the circle for a few minutes as Tesla spoke. He heard the petty giggles of the revelers, the snickering at Tesla's impenetrable accent and impossible syntax. The genius had become their pet. Their strange new toy.

But Paul knew that someone as singular as Nikola Tesla would be left to wither in the cold when a change in season called these revelers to some other well-appointed magic. Not even Tesla would be immune to the passing of their whims.

It was then that Paul, for the very first time, felt something like kinship with Tesla. They were both cogs in the machines of their betters. They both served as their functionaries. At least Tesla was a genius. How would a merely smart person like Paul survive these people?

Or had he become, in the past year, one of them? He was using Tesla too. The only difference was that while they were conniving for a laugh, Paul was conniving for a leg up. He strained to preserve a sense of his own moral superiority.

It was time to leave. He slunk through the party in search of Agnes. He finally located her in an alcove on the floor below, deep in conversation with a man Paul did not recognize. He turned away, leaving her to frolic in the gardens into which at least one of them had been planted.

The breeze outside felt cleansing. He hoped that if it blew hard enough, it might wash off the smell of cigars and perfume.

He stood on the street for a moment, taking in the sight of Gramercy Park. The yellow gaslight painted the fruit trees in wide smudges of color. Was that the New York that he aspired to? Was that the show to which winning his case would afford a ticket? Paul felt as if he'd been the victim of some sort of trick. Proud as he was of his accomplishments, he was prouder still of his ambitions. If the world inside that building was not what he should aspire to, then what on earth was?

"I don't think you liked the party." Paul turned to see Agnes coming down the steps behind him. She reached into her purse, removing a polished silver case. She lit herself a thin cigarette without offering one to Paul.

He wasn't sure what to say. He didn't smoke.

"Perhaps it wasn't the party," she continued. "Perhaps it was the guests."

"They're horrid." He blurted it out suddenly, without intending to. "I'm sorry. I didn't mean that. Just too much champagne. Thank you ever so much for bringing me."

Agnes puffed a plume of smoke into the night.

"Stop being polite," she said. "I get quite enough of that at home. Did you get what you needed from your odd friend?"

Her bluntness was bracing.

"They're going to devour him," Paul said. "He's too naïve. Too innocent. And they are wolves, batting a piece of meat between their paws."

Her agreement was matter-of-fact and unsentimental. "Stanford

White is using Tesla for a laugh. Edwin Booth is using Stanford for rehabilitation. I'm using Edwin for a night away from my mother. And you're using me to get in the door. It's the transactional circle on which the whole world spins."

Paul watched as she puffed at her long cigarette. This was yet another side of Agnes he had not seen. A serrated edge behind her smooth smile. A dark shadow beneath the genteel flower of high society.

She raised an eyebrow. "Or don't you like it here, amongst us wolves?"

Paul thought before answering. "I'd like to help him."

"I thought your client was George Westinghouse."

"I actually have two clients now, Miss Huntington."

She smiled at this. Maybe he'd managed to say something witty.

"Cravath," said Agnes as she dropped what was left of her cigarette on the stone, "naïveté does not become you. You can play their game and you can beat them at it. Or you can let them banish you from New York in tatters. Just as Mr. Foster is trying to do to me. But do you know something? Nobody ever won a game they didn't play."

She slipped her cigarette case back inside her purse, then inhaled the night air one last time. "I'm not going back to goddamned *Boston*. You want to go back to . . . where is it, Tennessee? Be my guest. But if you want to stay here, if you want to earn your place in Manhattan, remember: You chose to go to this party. There's no leaving early."

She turned away, headed back inside. He wasn't sure which shocked him more—her profanity or the fact that she knew he was from Tennessee.

"Miss Huntington," he said as he watched her ascend the stone steps, "I'm not going to lose."

She turned back to face him, the curls of her hair framed by the arch of the doorway. She made a face that was extremely serious—a comical caricature of a grave frown, as if she were trying to peer deep into his soul. And then her frown instantly splintered into a great grin. Her laugh mocked Paul's earnestness.

"Yes," she said, turning back in to the house. "I wouldn't have followed you out here if I thought you were."

CHAPTER 24

Nikola Tesla's Laboratory of Wonders

> Be alone—that is the secret of invention: be alone, that is
> when ideas are born. —NIKOLA TESLA, FROM HIS DIARY

A T SEVEN O'CLOCK the following evening, Paul walked from his office to an address on Grand Street, near the corner of Lafayette. He gazed up at the five-story factory building, wide as a city block, that stood there. The nameplates on the front door indicated that each floor housed a different small enterprise. MASTERS & SONS CARPENTRY on the first floor. JEFFERS LEAD on the second.

This building housed Tesla's laboratory. Yet the neighborhood was all sweatshops of seamstresses and woodworkers, endless emporiums of buttons and freshly blown glass. The most futuristic scientific thinking in the country was being done amid the rickety wood of America's jury-rigged past.

Paul pressed the bell for the fourth floor. It was the only blank nameplate in the building. He waited. Again Paul was impressed by Tesla's ability to disappear.

He had telegrammed Westinghouse that afternoon to report that he'd been granted an audience with Tesla at the latter's new laboratory near the Italian Quarter. It was an opportunity to see the man's newest work. "Take him to Delmonico's," Westinghouse had responded instantly. "Buy him a very expensive dinner that he won't eat. And get him back on our side." There had been no interest, Paul had noted, in what Tesla's new inventions might actually be.

Paul hadn't told his partners that he'd made contact with Tesla. He'd caused the royalty problem on his own. He'd fix it in the same manner.

He waited in front of the door for a few slowly ticking minutes before it opened. The man revealed was not, as Paul had hoped, Tesla. It was a workman from another company in the building, whose departure gave Paul a chance to enter through the door.

Paul climbed a set of sagging wooden steps to the fourth floor. The stairs creaked under his weight. It seemed as if they'd been built as primitive scaffolding and had never been replaced.

Paul arrived at a heavily fortified door. It looked both as secure and as uninviting to visitors as was possible. He knocked.

"Mr. Tesla?" he called. "Are you in there? It's Paul Cravath." He wondered if Tesla had forgotten their appointment.

But then Paul heard something. Straining to listen, he realized that it was a series of metallic clacks coming from the other side of the door. The sound of locks being unbolted. And then silence once again.

He reached for the doorknob and found that it now turned easily. The door yielded to his push. A puff of musky air greeted him from inside, blowing dust across the landing. Behind the threshold was pitch black. Paul stared ahead into an expanse of nothingness.

"Mr. Tesla?" called Paul. "I cannot see you, I'm afraid."

Footsteps in the distance. Paul heard what sounded like a hurried shuffling from inside. "Is that you?"

Still nothing in response. Paul took a hesitant step into the black room. Tesla's laboratory could contain quite literally anything. This was not a place one wanted to wander blind.

"Nikola? Is there a light in here?"

There were a few more creaks in the distance before Paul heard Tesla's nasal voice.

"I shall not illuminate you with mere light, Mr. Paul Cravath. I shall instead do so by electrical *storm*."

Suddenly the heavens themselves split open and a divine lightning cleaved the room. Or so it seemed to Paul as he employed his coat sleeve to shield his eyes. He shut them to find scars of bright reds and purples imprinted on his vision.

A horrible noise accompanied the display. A spitting and sizzling, violently loud; it was as if the air were being ripped apart by elemental forces.

After a moment, he was able to blink his eyes open. What he saw in front of him, in the center of a huge room, was an electrical device the size of a trolley car. A glass shaft, shaped something like a light bulb, only many multiples the size, extended at least twenty feet above it. From its exterior there extended throughout the room what Paul could only describe as enormous tentacles of electrical energy. They grasped at the ceiling, the walls, the far corners of the cavernous space. They snapped out into the room like the grasping arms of a gigantic electrical beast.

Paul flinched from an instinctual fear that this beast might descend and devour him whole. But the maniacal tentacles of energy were somehow avoiding him. They avoided the scattered desks around the room, and they avoided the tall Serbian in a black suit who sat calmly in a wooden chair mere feet from the glass shaft. Nikola Tesla's hands rested comfortably in his lap as all around him the air sizzled with energy.

"So then," he said as he crossed his long legs and gave Paul a smile. "How goes the work in Mr. *Westinghouse's* laboratory?"

It was something called a resonant transformer, Tesla explained after he shut it off. A coil that produced a rapidly alternating current of very high voltage and very low amperage. Quite safe, despite the spectacle. And though spectacle was the most obvious use for the device, its inner workings might be applied to telegraph machines, radio transmitters, medical devices . . . and possibly even the "wireless telephone" that Tesla was designing. Tesla confided all of this to Paul as the two men walked around the laboratory. Paul understood little of what Tesla showed him, and less still of what Tesla attempted to explain. Edison and a few others had been working on improvements to Alexander Bell's initial "telephone" device. Tesla was attempting to make the devices work without the aid of any wires at all. One didn't have to be much of a scientist to know that this was absurd. Even if by some miracle Tesla managed to make them function, who in the world would have any use for them?

Among the many differences between this lab and Westinghouse's, two things most struck Paul. The first was an absence of even the smallest particle of dust. The second was an absence of even the barest trace of another human being. This was Tesla's own private world, and he would keep it free from the impurities and irritations that marred his experiences outside it. He was alone, finally, with his wonders.

There was something Tesla called a Crookes tube on a table toward the back. It looked rather like an electric lamp, though about double the size. It was an eighteen-inch tube of glass, from which most of the air had been removed. One wire was connected to the base, while another poked into the sealed tube about three-quarters of the way toward the head. The device rested carefully on its side, above a glass base. Tesla turned a knob on the base, and instantly a ray of energy shot from one of the wire ends to the other. The ray was a sparkling blue, and yet the wide far end of the tube glowed a ghastly green. It gave the impression of a witch's bubbling cauldron.

"Cathode rays," explained Tesla. "Firing particles of a negative charge from one lead to the other."

"What does it do?" asked Paul as he admired the pulsing colors.

Tesla looked at Paul curiously. "That is what it is doing. Tell me it is not a beautiful thing."

"You should share these devices with the world. Tell people what you're working on. Tell *someone*."

"Am I not telling you, Mr. Paul Cravath?"

"You are. But I'm no scientist."

"Perhaps that is the very reason I can be telling you," said Tesla with a smile. "You could not steal my ideas even if you wanted to."

"I suppose that counts as trust in our business," said Paul.

Tesla laughed his high-pitched bark.

"I want to talk to you about rejoining Westinghouse," ventured Paul.

"I had imagined that you would do so," said Tesla coyly. "But for this conversation I do not share your enthusiasms."

As Paul prepared to begin his argument, he found himself suddenly interrupted.

The sound of a commotion from the building's central staircase caught both men's attention. Boots were clomping against the steps outside. The footsteps sounded as if they were coming from at least a dozen people, and the commotion seemed only to be growing. Paul instinctively moved to the door to see what was going on.

As Paul pulled open the steel door, he saw that the central staircase, all five stories of old wood, was awash with flame.

CHAPTER 25

Instability in the System

A scientific revolution is not fully reducible to a reinterpre-
tation of . . . stable data. In the first place, the data are not
unequivocally stable.

—THOMAS KUHN, *THE STRUCTURE OF SCIENTIFIC REVOLUTIONS*

P AUL'S DISBELIEF MOMENTARILY immobilized him. This felt like a
horrific hallucination, a deathly trompe l'oeil that had been
hung before his eyes.

Men working on the floor above sprinted down the steps. Chunks
of burning wood fell from beside them. Paul watched as one man
placed his foot upon a board only to find it instantly give way. His
companion grabbed him before he fell, steadying them both as they
raced toward the ground floor. Before Paul could grab ahold of Tesla
and join the fleeing workmen, a flaming plank crashed against the
doorjamb, blocking his path.

Paul slammed the metal door shut, sealing out the fire. He stepped
back, bumping into Tesla.

"The fire is already on the landing," said Paul. "We've no chance
that way."

Tesla merely stared at Paul.

"There's a fire," said Tesla. The fact was apparently only beginning
to penetrate his brain.

"Do the windows open?" Paul ran to the windows along the far wall of the room. He jerked open a curtain, tearing the fabric from its rods.

Outside, smoke from the floor above spread into the sky.

Tesla stood stock-still. The room was getting hot, the fire above and below turning Tesla's laboratory into a block-wide oven.

"We have to get the windows open," Paul insisted. But neither Paul's words nor his hurry seemed to imprint themselves on Tesla in any way.

Paul grabbed a device from one of the tables and flung it at the window. Whatever the thing was, its long glass tube shattered on contact as its thick metal base crashed through the windowpane. Shards of glass flew in every direction, both out into the night and back toward Paul.

"Mr. Tesla," said Paul, "come this way! We'll have a better chance climbing out the windows than navigating the staircase." He turned to see the inventor still standing near the door. The men made eye contact for a brief moment. For the slightest of seconds, Paul could see the blank emptiness in Tesla's expression. He wasn't afraid. It was, rather, as if he weren't even there at all.

Then the ceiling caved in.

PART II

Reverse Salients

As technological systems expand, reverse salients develop. Reverse salients are components in the system that have fallen behind or are out of phase with the others.

—THOMAS HUGHES, *THE SOCIAL CONSTRUCTION OF TECHNOLOGICAL SYSTEMS*

CHAPTER 26

Powerful Friends

In this business, by the time you realize you're in trouble,
it's too late to save yourself. Unless you're running scared
all the time, you're gone.
                                              —BILL GATES

FOR WEEKS, PAUL Cravath drifted in and out of consciousness. His waking moments were as hazy as his dreams. Only the colors differentiated the two states of mind. One was a bright white sheen, more searing than an incandescent lamp. The other was dark. Black thoughts, red and brimstone. As the days dragged along and his hourly doses of morphine were halved and then quartered, Paul began to differentiate better between waking and sleeping. With a resigned dread, he realized that his black visions of fire were in fact just dreams, and that the real world, the one he woke to, was clean and shining and full of much greater horrors.

The top floor of Bellevue Hospital was easily the whitest place Paul had ever been. The bedsheets were bleached and crisped daily until they were painful to the touch. The coats and tall shirt collars of the doctors who flitted in and out of his private room were as white as the linens. As white as the narrow walls. As white as the fresh gauze wrapped daily around Paul's tender belly.

Tesla was gone. Vanished. Paul could not remember exactly which of his visitors first broke the news to him. Had it been George Westinghouse, whose worried face Paul had seen more than once by his bedside? Had it been Carter? Or Hughes and his wife, who'd left white roses by Paul's bedside early in his stay?

The factory space had been largely unoccupied at such a late hour, and the workmen Paul had seen on the staircase had made it out safely. Paul had apparently fallen amid the burning wood and been dragged to safety by an unknown Samaritan who had deposited him into a horse-drawn ambulance. Had the stranger seen Tesla as well? There was no way to know. If Tesla had not died in the building's collapse, then how could he have fled the scene? The likeliest explanation was that his corpse had been incinerated by the fire. Or crushed by the collapse of the building. And yet no corpses had been found in the rubble.

Paul learned these details from a detective who visited him two weeks into his stay. The afternoon light in his room was quite pleasant, gently falling in from the gray October sky. From his bed, Paul had a view of Twenty-sixth Street. The wire springs of his mattress would squeak whenever he turned to the window, as if chastising him for his desire to flee. Any serious motion at all was exceedingly difficult in those early weeks. The mush poultice, composed of Indian meal and hot water and held tight to him by the gauze, felt strange on his healing ribs. Paul was relatively certain he would have been in quite a bit of pain had it not been for the morphine.

His ribs, nose, and left femur were broken. There had been considerable damage to his organs, though the terms used by the various doctors to describe these injuries were a matter of some dispute. The doctors could not agree on which internal injury was the most severe. But from his morphine-induced haze, he understood the point: He was beat up pretty good. But he would live.

He was sitting up for his conversation with the detective. Sitting had been a victory recently achieved, and not one to be taken lightly. He felt himself in relatively sound shape as he made pleasantries with the policeman, whose high rank was indicated by his attire—a proper coat and tie rather than a uniform.

"So you've no indications as to Mr. Tesla's whereabouts one way or the other?" asked Paul. "Alive, dead, or anywhere in between?"

"Still none," responded the detective. "Mr. Cravath, I'd like to ask you a question, and I hope that it won't offend you."

"In my profession," said Paul, "one can't offend too easily."

"Do you remember having this conversation with me previously?"

"What conversation?"

"This is the third time I've come to visit you, sir," said the detective. "To get your version of the events of September the nineteenth."

Paul became instantly concerned. "I don't . . . I'm terribly sorry, I don't remember."

The detective looked to the bottle of morphine on Paul's bedside table.

"It's to be expected, sir," said the detective. "I don't wish to alarm you, or to cause you any further discomfort. The doctors said you'd be a bit looped for a while. You've seemed more lucid of late, so I thought you'd be ready, but perhaps today is not the day after all for you to receive further visitors."

"Who else wants to see me?"

"My boss. He wants to check on you personally."

"Anything I can do to help."

The detective went out into the hallway. What scared Paul while he waited was not just that he'd forgotten earlier meetings with the detective. Under the influence of the morphine, he was clearly not at his full mental capacities. He would need every ounce of cleverness he could muster if he was to get back to work.

The detective returned to the room followed by a balding man in his sixties. He had the look of a ruffian who'd been tempered by old age. The sort of bulldog who would be forced to do nowadays with bark what he'd more productively done in his younger years with bite. Paul recognized him instantly. When the detective had referred to his boss, Paul hadn't thought he meant the commissioner of the police.

"I'm Fitz Porter. My man tells me you've had a good shaking up, but that you're handling it well."

"I hope this constitutes 'well,'" replied Paul. "I'm afraid that the morphine has left me a bit duller than I'd like."

"Miracle stuff, that," said Porter. "Saved us quite a bit of misery at Bull Run."

Porter had famously led the Union V Corps during the war, long before President Arthur had sent him to the New York Police Department.

Paul had only been a child during the war. His father had followed the news avidly, reading the day's grim casualty numbers from *The Nashville Dispatch*. Since Erastus Cravath was both a committed pacifist and a passionate advocate for Negro rights, the war placed him on uncertain footing. To what depravities should the side of righteousness sink in furtherance of its noble goals? How many men could the Union slaughter and sacrifice in order to free the slaves? His father had not possessed an answer, and so, as far as Paul could tell, Erastus had read the litany of deaths to his family so that they too might share in the moral burden. This had served as a useful reminder over the years: Knowing the difference between right and wrong sometimes did not serve to clarify much of anything. Just because a man is able to draw his line in the sand, it doesn't mean he'll know what to do when his only course of action requires crossing it.

Which is what Erastus Cravath finally did. He enlisted as a chaplain for the Union, spending the final year of the war away from his wife and young son. Never once upon his return did he discuss with his family what he'd seen. Or done.

"I'm flattered that you'd come yourself," said Paul to the commissioner. "This can't be the only fire in the city that requires your attention. Is there any news on Mr. Tesla?"

"If Mr. Tesla is alive, we'll find him," he said calmly. He did not give the impression of a man who lost much sleep on account of missing Serbian scientists. "I'm told by Detective Rummel here that in your earliest conversations, just after the ambulance had brought you to Bellevue, you told him you first saw the fire in the stairwell. Not in Mr. Tesla's laboratory."

"Yes."

"At the time, we thought it likely that the trauma and the morphine had jumbled your memories. We assumed the most likely source of the fire was the laboratory. All that funny equipment. The electrical devices. But we know now that the fire began on the roof. Someone went up there and set it on purpose."

People had murdered one another for a lot less than a billion dollars. Paul thought of Thomas Edison seated behind his office desk, puffing his cigar, plotting the victory that he believed to be inevitable.

"You don't appear surprised at this, Mr. Cravath," said Commissioner Porter as he watched Paul carefully. "Is it the morphine? Or is it easy for you to imagine that someone had it in for your friend?"

Paul didn't know how to answer without divulging too much information about his case.

"The mayor himself," Porter continued, "has asked us to make the matter of this arson our top priority. You have powerful friends, you know. They're looking out for you."

"Please tell Mr. Westinghouse that I'm grateful."

"Mr. . . . Westinghouse?" asked Commissioner Porter, confused.

"George Westinghouse," supplied the detective. "He's Mr. Cravath's client."

Paul felt a sudden chill.

"Thomas Edison called on the mayor himself, to make sure that you were being cared for. And to see that we had our best men on the case. We'll report every development in our investigations back to Mr. Edison directly. We've let him know that we believe someone tried to harm you, and that we will expend every effort in determining who."

Paul looked from the commissioner back to the detective. Both men maintained the same resolute expression. If they'd been tricked, duped, or paid off, they gave no indication of it. "Myself, Detective Rummel here, and the whole department will look after you," the commissioner continued. "And we'll do so with the full weight of Thomas Edison behind us."

CHAPTER 27

Two Walks Along the East River

Whoever lives for the sake of combating an enemy has an
interest in the enemy's staying alive.

—FRIEDRICH NIETZSCHE

PAUL HADN'T SEEN Agnes Huntington since the party at the
Players'. Yet during his slow recovery, he found her frequently
on his mind, in both waking and sleeping states. He made sure
on Carter's first visit to tell him of his new client so that the firm
could handle any correspondence it might receive from W. H. Foster.
Paul's letter was sure to provoke a response. Agnes and her mother
were to be told about the fire and Paul's convalescence. For several
weeks he waited for a sympathy letter that never came.

Then one morning, without warning, she was there by his bedside, immediately insisting to the nurses that he get some fresh air.
She spirited him away on a circuitous stroll through the Bellevue
gardens—though as Paul still required the use of a wheelchair, Agnes
was the only one strolling. There was not a trace of pity in her voice
as she pushed the rattling wheels along the dirt paths.

"Are you enjoying the morphine?" she said as the orange October
leaves rustled in the wind. "One of my costars, she just adores the
stuff. Helps with the throat, after a show."

As Agnes had predicted, Paul found the cold air invigorating after so many days confined to bed. Yet the dull sky was a portent of dread. Manhattan, he felt, had always existed as a bulwark at war with its geography. It rose in stone and concrete as a dam against the sea, a fortress against the coming snow.

"I'm off the morphine now," he said. "Thankfully, I'm on nothing stronger than a little cocaine in the mornings. It helps with the headaches."

"Would you think me sentimental if I say I'm glad you're not dead?"

"I don't know that I'd ever describe you as sentimental."

"Good," said Agnes. "Because I am glad. After all, we still require your services."

Paul smiled. He might even have laughed if the motion hadn't threatened his chest with further pain.

Agnes was easy to like, Paul felt, but at the same time her very charm made her hard to read. The rapier of her wit had been hardened and cooled with practice. Paul found himself wondering—not for the first time—if there was a kernel of truth in the wild rumors Mr. Foster had threatened to spread about her.

He informed her that his office had heard nothing yet from her former employer, and inquired as to whether she had either. She was pleased to say that she hadn't.

"I trust that's a good sign?" she asked.

"For now. I think we should give it more time before declaring victory."

"I should think so, Cravath."

Paul couldn't see the look on her face as she gently pushed his wheelchair, but the way she said it sounded jaded. Whatever Agnes Huntington had seen of the world had taught her to be wary.

"I want to ask you about the fire." She said it plainly, as if propelled by a natural curiosity. "The newspapers all made it sound like an unfortunate accident. Was it?"

"It was indeed unfortunate."

"But was it an *accident*?"

The wheels rattled as they rolled over a few stones along the path.

Paul thought about what it would be like to confide in her, given what he now knew about Edison. It was pleasant to imagine her as his ally. But could he trust her?

Of course he couldn't.

"It was an awful accident, Miss Huntington. One of Tesla's new and untested machines likely started the fire, though there's no way to be sure. We still don't know what happened to him. Have you heard anything from your friend Stanford White?"

"I haven't been out much of late. My mother was put a bit on edge by the near death of our attorney. She's at a peak state of protectiveness. But the Vanderbilts had their yearly seasonal last week, welcoming those who'd decamped for the summer. I glimpsed Stanford there and inquired after Tesla. He pouted—he'd lost a new toy just when he was enjoying it the most. Seemed like he considers Tesla dead." Agnes paused. "God, is that horrible of me? He was your friend."

It would have been hard to describe Tesla as anyone's "friend," exactly. "I felt responsible for him. I still do."

"You're not responsible for his death."

Paul paused before answering. He had to tread carefully. "I'm still not sure he is dead, Miss Huntington."

"Why?"

"I'm alive, aren't I?" The weather was turning. It was time to go inside.

By the time George Westinghouse visited again a week later, Paul had graduated from his rickety wheelchair to a wooden cane. Its squat nub thumped satisfyingly against the dirt as the two men walked in the chill of Bellevue's rear gardens. Just below lay the wind-chopped East River. Paul had almost been weaned off his morning cocaine, but looking at the water still made him slightly dizzy.

Paul wore the brown hospital overcoat that comprised his uniform for outdoor walks. He hadn't worn any of his own clothes in a month. He'd never imagined that he'd find himself missing his few suits so much.

"So you are confident that one of Edison's hatchet men set the fire?" asked Westinghouse.

Paul was relieved to finally be able to confide in his client in person. He and Westinghouse had exchanged cables in the past weeks, after he had achieved lucidity, but he hadn't dared risk revealing his suspicions until they were face-to-face.

"Yes," said Paul. "You know Charles Batchelor. What wouldn't he do for his boss?"

"I'm sorry," said Westinghouse suddenly. Paul was startled to hear the words from his client. He didn't get the impression that Westinghouse said them frequently. Certainly not to a subordinate like Paul. "I led you onto the battlefield. And now you're the one with the war wounds."

"Sir," said Paul as he pressed his cane hard into the dirt and turned to face his companion, "this is not your fault. I chose to go up against Edison. If you're feeling scared, you've every reason to be. If you're feeling uncertain, that only means you understand the complexity of our situation. But if you're feeling guilty, that won't help us a bit. You want to apologize to someone? Apologize to Tesla. He's the innocent in all of this. But in order for you to have such a conversation, we'll need to find him first."

Westinghouse looked away as Paul delivered this speech. He seemed uncomfortable with any display of sentiment. His gesture of apology could not have been easily offered.

"If he is alive, God willing, how will you find him?" asked Westinghouse. "I can call on the Pinkertons."

"No."

"You don't trust them?"

"Do you?"

The Pinkerton Detective Agency was the preeminent investigative force in the United States. And yet the Pinkertons had a reputation for committing their allegiance according to the generosity of their employers. If Edison had been able to exert enough pressure to control the police force, then to do the same to the Pinkertons would be a trifle.

"It's just us, then," replied Westinghouse finally.

"Yes."

"And your partners. They came to me a few weeks back. While you've been incapacitated, someone had to continue our defense on the light-bulb suit."

Paul was well aware. It was only proper for Carter and Hughes to take the reins. Yet it still stung that his injuries had only furthered his demotion.

"Good," replied Paul. "Carter and Hughes can handle the lion's share of legal strategy for a bit. They're quite . . . experienced." Paul gazed out at the East River. He steadied his vision on a pair of boatmen paddling a tiny craft on the icy water. Across the river lay the city of Brooklyn, a vast metropolis of Irish, Germans, Negroes, Jews, Italians, Danes, Finns, and a few well-to-do old families. Brooklyn was the third-largest city in America, and it was largely inhabited by people who had not been born there. Behind Paul, the immense stone construction of Bellevue occupied the entire western skyline. The hospital's oversized American flag with its thirty-eight stars and thirteen stripes flapped in the breeze from the roof of the building. Paul could see more different worlds in one glance than in the entire town in which he'd been raised.

"When do they let you out of here?" asked Westinghouse.

"Two more days, they're saying."

"I want you to be careful. No more nighttime expeditions. This is not worth dying over."

Paul was touched by the concern, and yet he didn't feel the warning was necessary. "What would killing me get anyone? I can see Edison attempting to frighten me off. He tried as much the first time he met me. But actually murdering me? It might delay the case, but it wouldn't eliminate our defense. And frankly, a delay would benefit our side, since he's the one asking for an injunction against your continued production of light bulbs."

Westinghouse appeared unsure about where Paul was headed with this argument.

"Which leaves the only possibility remaining: The arsonist was trying to kill Tesla."

"Why?" asked Westinghouse.

"Because it's the only way to guarantee that he could never help us. Edison knows how difficult it will be to create a new, non-infringing light bulb without Tesla's gifts."

"And you just happened to be there? That's rotten luck, kid."

"I'm not saying it was an accident that I was there."

"How do you mean?"

"How do you think they found Tesla?"

"Christ," said Westinghouse. "He had you followed."

The two men looked around at the churning East River. "As soon as you leave here," said Westinghouse, "you'll likely be followed again."

"The bad news is that we don't know where Tesla is. But hopefully neither does Edison."

"How will either of you find him? Tesla has no family in this country. You said that his one friend, Stanford White, believes he's dead."

"Which means there's only one other person we know about who's been in touch with Tesla since he left your employ. And, helpfully, he and I already have a good bit of history together."

CHAPTER 28

A Frightful Accusation

> No matter how many instances of white swans we have
> observed, that does not justify the inference that all swans
> are white.
> —KARL POPPER

B Y THE TIME Paul stepped into Lemuel Serrell's office two days later, he'd shed his plaster-of-paris cast. His limp wasn't terrible, but it was annoying. He still required the wooden cane. He came to see Tesla's patent attorney hours after being discharged from the hospital, making only a brief trip back to his apartment for fresh clothes. The hospital rags had made him feel weak. Returning to the de rigueur deep-black coat and tall white shirt collar of his professional life, Paul felt instantly stronger.

Serrell was smoking behind his desk when Paul entered. He did not offer greetings as Paul sat. Serrell remained in his chair, a hard expression across his face.

"I'm surprised you've the gall to walk right in here," said Serrell.

"Good morning," said Paul, surprised by the cross tone. "I'm feeling much healed, thank you for asking."

Serrell raised an eyebrow. He was the sort of man who knew the communicative value of a carefully raised eyebrow.

"I'm here to find Tesla. To make sure he's safe."

"You, of all people, want to make sure that Tesla is safe?"

Paul stared at the angry face before him. It took a long moment to realize that Serrell was making a dreadful accusation. "You think that I set the fire in Tesla's lab? Why on earth would I do such a thing?"

"Two dollars and fifty cents per unit is quite a bit of money for your client, Mr. Cravath."

Paul had never before been accused of attempted murder. The sensation was not pleasant.

"Listen to me very carefully, will you?" said Serrell. "I can assure you that Mr. Tesla's demise will not help you in the slightest. His mother is in Serbia. In the event of her son's death, she will receive the entirety of the royalties owed him. I prepared his will myself. So whatever attempts you are making to finish the vile job you started, they are pointless."

"Mr. Serrell," said Paul in what he hoped was a reasonable tone, "do you see my cane? I was with Mr. Tesla when the fire started. I almost died."

"The police have been here. They told me you were with Tesla—which is precisely my point. If you knew where Tesla's laboratory was located, I do believe that makes us the only two men who did. Only one of us had a reason to want Tesla buried."

"What of Thomas Edison?" suggested Paul. "He had more reason to harm Tesla than any of us." Serrell had prepared patent applications for Edison years before. Perhaps their work together had not concluded a decade past.

"Edison?" Serrell smirked. "But that's stupid."

"Why?"

"Because if Thomas Edison had wanted Nikola Tesla dead, then he damn well would be."

Serrell directed Paul's attention to the door. "I'd ask you kindly to leave, though I've little intention of being kind. What convinces me of your culpability in the plot to murder my client is that I believe he's very much alive. And based on my previous dealings with you, I think you're the only one incompetent enough to botch it up."

Paul's injured leg wobbled a bit as he rose, but he remained unflinching. He would not be bested by Lemuel Serrell. Not again.

"I don't know whether you are Edison's knowing accomplice or his unwitting pawn," said Paul. "But I know he's responsible for what happened. And I will not allow him, or you, to frame me for it."

With that, Paul turned and walked out the door. It was only after crossing the threshold that he realized he wasn't even using the cane.

CHAPTER 29

Dead Ends and False Leads

Normal science does not aim for novelties of fact or theory
and, when successful, finds none.

—THOMAS KUHN, *THE STRUCTURE OF SCIENTIFIC REVOLUTIONS*

I N THE WEEK following his confrontation with Lemuel Serrell, Paul
paid visits to the American Institute of Electrical Engineers; the
offices of the journal *Electrical World*, where he spoke to its editor,
Thomas Martin; Westinghouse's laboratory in Pittsburgh, where he
spoke with Fessenden; and the labs of half a dozen smaller New York
outfits that might have employed engineers who'd worked with Tesla
previously. None of these visits—despite Paul's beseeching, despite his
charms, despite his two-dollar bills folded into serious handshakes—
bore fruit.

No one had spoken to Tesla since weeks before the fire. No one
had known, they told him frankly, what in God's name Tesla had ever
been going on about anyhow. And no one had seen him since he'd
fled Westinghouse's operation in August. As far as anyone guessed, he
must have been living in his new laboratory, before it burned down.

Paul tried hotels. He made the run of cheap flophouses on the
Bowery, though he had a hard time picturing the maniacally clean
inventor staying anywhere in which one might hear the rats not only
at night, but at midday. He greased a half month's worth of wages into

the palms of the city's concierges, but it was no use. No giant with a thick Serbian accent and a habit of misplacing verbs had been spotted. Paul considered venturing to the disreputable alehouses and even less reputable gentlemen's clubs—places known to provide some manner of sanctuary to men who preferred not to be found. But then he imagined Tesla attempting to speak with the inhabitants of one of Chelsea's infamous "boardinghouses," and the thought seemed so comical as to be easily disregarded.

By the end of a week's searching, Paul was no closer to finding the vanished genius. His labors had served only to further delay the healing of his hurt left leg. His boots were worn, and his shins pulsed with a dull ache.

He also exchanged brief letters with his second client. Or clients. His correspondence had been entirely with Fannie Huntington, not her daughter. Shortly after Paul's release from Bellevue, Mr. Foster wrote to Fannie directly. As any blackmailer would, he cautioned her against involving lawyers in the matter before them. The more people who became involved, he said, the harder it would be for him to keep the details of this business quiet. He tried to depict Paul's involvement as the Huntingtons' biggest problem.

Paul assured Fannie by post that he was working on the situation. Privately, he didn't know exactly what he was going to do, but he knew he'd better think of something soon. It pained him to think of the precariousness of Agnes's position, and of how little he'd done to help her.

Moreover, there remained the small matter of the billion-dollar patent suit. And the business of defending George Westinghouse's right to manufacture electric lamps was not going well.

Paul's countersuit against Edison was defeated in the U.S. circuit court in Pittsburgh. Judge Bradley ruled that Edison's light bulb had been clearly differentiated from any of its predecessors. As such, Edison had not violated any of the patents that Westinghouse had purchased from Sawyer and Man. Edison's patent remained inviolable. In Paul's absence, his senior partners had appealed. No one had much hope that they would win.

He returned to the offices of Carter, Hughes & Cravath on a Monday as the sky threatened to loose the year's first snow onto the city. As Paul took the steps up from the street and then mounted the iron staircase to the third floor, he felt a curious sensation. Returning to this familiar place felt both strangely comfortable and strangely foreign. He'd worked here for under a year. Yet it felt as if he'd been a child when he first hung his overcoat on this brass rack. He both could not imagine how young he'd been, and at the same time could not fathom ever feeling young again.

He found Carter and Hughes well into a meeting with a short man of serious demeanor. The attorneys and their guest appeared engrossed in a set of contracts. Paul gestured hello through the glass, but none of the three saw him. He returned to his office, to begin, very slowly, to attend to the mountain of papers that had spawned there in his absence.

It was only after the stranger had left that Hughes walked by Paul's office door.

"Welcome home," said Hughes.

Paul asked about their visitor. Hughes smiled with pride before he explained.

In Paul's absence, Carter and Hughes had done what they did best: They'd made deals. Westinghouse's new business plan—the creation of a "network of current" that stretched from coast to coast—required more hands than merely his own to man the decks. It didn't make sense for Westinghouse to ship a whole generator and all the technicians required to set it up to Michigan, for instance; it would be much more efficient for a local shop to build it. Which suggested to Carter and Hughes that perhaps subcontracting out manufacture and installation to a series of smaller, local companies around the country would be prudent. Even Paul had to admit that it was a good plan.

And so Carter and Hughes had begun the process of buying up small manufacturing companies throughout the East and Middle West. To be sure, the Westinghouse Electric Company did not have much of a store of capital on hand. The purchases needed to be strategic, carefully considered. And in many cases they could save money by subcontracting production out to these local entities, rather than buying them outright.

The most substantial of these deals had been made with a Mr. Charles Coffin, the president of the Thomson-Houston Electric Company, based in Lynn, Massachusetts. This was the gentleman who'd been signing contracts just that morning. His company had the capability to manufacture generators from Maine to Connecticut. Mr. Coffin's support would be invaluable.

The Westinghouse team was assembling its players.

Sitting in his office some days later, Paul overheard the arrival of a messenger. The boy told Martha that he had an envelope to be opened only by Mr. Cravath himself. Paul was expecting news of the case or a summons to appear in court. But the contents of the brief telegram were utterly unexpected.

"Mr. Cravath. Please hurry to the new Metropolitan Opera House right away. Will be in my dressing rooms. Have something you'll want to see. Sincerely, Miss Agnes Huntington."

CHAPTER 30

The Metropolitan Opera House

Science seldom proceeds in the straightforward, logical
manner imagined by outsiders.   —JAMES WATSON

I T TOOK PAUL just a minute to hail a carriage, but thirty-four more
to ride it to Thirty-ninth Street. The Metropolitan Opera House
occupied an entire square block. Seven stories tall and almost as
wide, the Met stood above the less formidable sweatshops of the Gar-
ment District. Only five years old, the Yellow Brick Brewery, as people
had nicknamed it, retained a number of the design elements common
to its neighborhood. The building did look more fit for manufacturing
than for high art.

The Met had been founded in 1883 as a great big thumbed nose in
the direction of the Academy of Music, which had occupied a considerably more distinguished space at Union Square. The Academy admitted only the oldest of New York's old money to its velvet seats. Its
eighteen boxes had each been sold off to elite families some fifty years
previous. None would ever be for sale again. Even as the city began
producing enough millionaires to fill another three opera houses, the
Academy's board of directors would not budge. Not even the Rockefellers, the Vanderbilts, or the Morgans were allowed in. So those
three families, and their equally new-moneyed friends, got together
and built their own opera house. The Met had been an instant suc-

cess, and now, five years later, all the finest productions from Europe and Philadelphia came there first when they arrived in New York. The Academy had fallen in '86. Its manager gave a terse statement to the newspapers: "I cannot fight Wall Street."

There was a lesson in all this, Paul thought. America was a place in which the powerful and the popular were doomed to an uneasy alliance. Money, even as old as New York's, was something. But it was no longer quite enough. The fashionable flexed the real strength that made the American muscle bulge. Fashion was popularity. Popularity was people. And it was to the people's ever-shifting tastes that even the wealthiest of this young nation sought to appeal. What's the use in being rich if not a soul admires you for it?

Paul was greeted by the manager of the house, a tall man in a dinner jacket who kept watch over the scattered maids dusting and polishing the ornate fixtures that dotted the walls. As it was morning, the lamps along the corridors were off. But Paul could make out their shape from where he stood. The lamps were electric. And they were Edison's.

Paul explained to the house manager that he was looking for Miss Huntington. It was only after he assured the suspicious manager that he wasn't some devoted fan in search of an autograph, but rather the prima donna's personal attorney, that the man deigned to accept Paul's card.

He soon reappeared, leading Paul into the cavernous theater at the center of the opera house. Their footsteps echoed beneath the domed ceiling. The sensation was eerie. Four thousand empty seats swept across the long floor and up the rear wall. Paul turned to peek at the five tiers of empty boxes that hung from the sides.

To think of the scenes that took place nightly between those chairs. The backstabbing, the social climbing, the bitter family feuds played out at every intermission. The drama among the audience was famously more intense than what was performed upon the stage. Empty in the quiet morning, the house seemed pregnant with the promise of the night's warfare.

The manager led Paul up onto the stage, past the curtains, and finally down a flight of rear stairs to a door on which the name AGNES

HUNTINGTON shone in gold lettering. It would not have shocked Paul if it turned out to have been etched in genuine gold.

The manager knocked twice on the door and then announced Paul's name. It occurred to Paul that he had met two very different Agnes Huntingtons, between her mother's house and the Players' Club. Would he find a third at the Metropolitan Opera?

"They're waiting for you," the manager said before turning away.

Paul stood for a moment, taking a breath.

"They?"

But the manager was already gone.

The door opened with a creak and Paul found the radiant face of Agnes Huntington before him. Her attire was informal, a tastefully casual black dress that extended to the ankles and down her arms, with just a slight touch of white frill at the wrists. She wasn't wearing shoes.

"Mr. Cravath," she said as she ushered him into the dressing room. An enormous mirror covered one wall, lit up by a panel of Edison's bulbs along the edges. The mirror made the room look twice as big as it was. A desk for makeup rested below the mirror, next to which stood a costume rack. The row of hanging clothes was full of bright reds and blues, more saturated and luminous than Paul had ever seen. The light bulbs brought out the deep colors in the silk fabrics.

Beside the dresses were two wooden chairs and a decorated daybed, on which perched a very tall man who was rocking back and forth in his seat, mumbling to himself.

"You already know Mr. Tesla," said Agnes as she shut the door behind them.

CHAPTER 31

Questions Yet Unanswered

Deciding what not to do is as important as deciding what
to do.   —STEVE JOBS

I N AGNES'S TELLING, Nikola Tesla had appeared at the Metropolitan Opera House early that morning. He had approached her as
she'd arrived at the stage door. It had taken her a moment to recognize him as Paul's curious quarry from the Players' Club. But Tesla
had recognized her easily, as if he'd been seeking her out. He had addressed her by name, even though he was filthy and clearly unwell.
He was unable to say more than a few words. She'd had to employ the
house manager in escorting him to her private dressing room.

There sat the prodigal inventor on the opera star's daybed. Paul
was reminded of Tesla's taste for Delmonico's. Strange how this unac-
countable man found himself so often in the lap of luxury.

It was only as Paul approached that he could see just how shaken
Tesla was. He seemed unaware of Paul's presence, mumbling under his
breath. Paul strained to make out words among the sputtered noises
and half syllables.

"Nikola? Can you hear me?"

"He doesn't answer. But whatever questions you might have for
him, I can promise I've got more to ask you."

Tesla's eyes were open, but they were fixed on a faraway point, as if the dressing room wall were a distant horizon. Paul realized that Tesla was wearing the same suit that Paul had last seen him in. The cloth was filthy. Tesla's cotton shirt had once been white, but was now yellow-brown from unspeakable stains. He reeked of pavement, sweat, and horseshit.

It seemed to Paul as if the fence that typically separated Tesla from the outside world had risen and thickened into a full rampart. Normally, one could at least lob a few conversational balls over the wall. But now, nothing landed on the other side. Whatever derangement had overcome him, it had completely severed any ties between the man and the world around him. If Tesla's consciousness was in there—if, as Paul's father would believe, Tesla's soul was present somewhere inside his skull—it was now the sole citizen of an embargoed kingdom.

"Has he said anything at all that might indicate where he's been or how he's survived?"

"Nothing."

"Why on earth has he come to you?" Paul remembered how hypnotized Tesla had been by Agnes's singing at the Players'.

"I have absolutely no idea. The more interesting question is what you're going to do about it."

The situation was one of considerable complexity. "Who else knows that Tesla is here?"

"The house manager who met you in the lobby," said Agnes. "But he has no idea who Tesla is."

"What about your mother?"

"Yes, you have me pegged. Whenever anything noteworthy happens in my life, the first thing I do is tell Mother."

"Miss Huntington. This man is in danger."

Paul could see that her mind was spinning. His problem, he realized, would surely be turned into her opportunity.

"You can rest assured that you were the first and only person to whom I sent word, Cravath. We should take him to a hospital straightaway." She was testing the waters, and he knew it. She wanted to see if Paul was willing to bring Tesla someplace public. It must have been clear from his face that he wasn't. "Unless, of course, there is some reason why you don't want anyone to know that Tesla is here, safe and sound?"

At Bellevue, Paul had felt certain he could not trust Agnes. Nothing about this new encounter had changed his mind. But what choice did he have?

Agnes was a bystander to this game. To the extent that she had any allegiance, it would be determined by the other players involved and what she might get from each of them. She needed Paul—at least for the time being. What Paul could trust, he realized, was not that she would never betray him, but rather that she would only do so when it became in her best interest. Which meant that he had to make sure it never was.

"Someone is trying to kill this man."

"Oh?" she said. "Seems like they're doing a relatively poor job of it."

"I lied to you before. When I said the fire was an accident."

"Did you, now?"

"You assumed as much, didn't you?"

"I do not assume. I consider. And I considered that quite likely. Who has it out for Mr. Tesla?"

The look on Paul's face seemed to confirm her suspicions.

"Do I think Thomas Edison personally came down to Grand Street and lit the kindling?" he said. "No. But I'm sure he was responsible for the fire." Paul filled her in on the details of the case, and of the threat posed by Thomas Edison. She took this in without any sign of surprise or concern.

"You sure know how to pick your enemies." Agnes did not scare easily. Or at least Edison was not the thing that scared her.

"Your cast members. When will they arrive? Will you expect them in this room?"

"They usually trickle in any moment now. We've each got our own room, so no one will demand entry here. But they may come and knock. Gossip, chitchat, what have you."

"I have to get him somewhere safe."

"Where?"

Paul's own apartment was small but serviceable. However, if one of

Edison's men was following his movements, then Tesla would be discovered within hours. Paul's office would not do; his senior partners were untrustworthy. Westinghouse's estate would be too full of loose lips. The staff, the varied visitors moving through the house, the laboratory, the factories and gardens and private rail station—word would be bound to get out. Could Paul bring Tesla to a hotel? He would be at the mercy of a series of strangers. And strangers could be bought.

Paul was no boy's-adventure-book hero. He'd never even read Jules Verne.

"May I make a suggestion?" said Agnes. "You'll need to store Mr. Tesla somewhere that Edison's men won't think to investigate. A place near enough that Tesla can be taken there quickly and big enough that you can keep him there for some time. A place owned by someone who could look after a troubled invalid, and who would never, in a million lifetimes, be under suspicion by Edison or his men."

Her argument was sound. But when she spoke her suggestion aloud, Paul couldn't quite believe it.

"You may keep Mr. Tesla in my home."

". . . Your home?"

"Yes."

"Why would you offer to keep Tesla in your home?"

"How could you possibly refuse?"

Tesla muttered again from the daybed.

"I can keep him there," she said. "I can even get my mother to help. Don't give me that look. She's more amenable than she seems. We'll keep him warm and fed and safe. And then, once he's regained his senses—such as they are—you'll get him to rejoin Westinghouse and create the device you need. The public will purchase Westinghouse's systems rather than Edison's. And then you will, I believe, be the lead litigator for the largest and most influential company in America. You and Westinghouse can buy the Boston Ideals if Mr. Foster threatens me again."

Agnes's bare toes tapped soundlessly against the wood floor. Her presentation had been matter-of-fact, and having concluded it, she did not expect much argument.

"You don't trust me?" said Agnes.

"I trust you a little," said Paul. "You're asking me to trust you a lot."

At any moment, all Agnes would have to do was speak a few ill-considered words at a dinner, and both Tesla's life and Paul's career would be over.

"If you're worried that I'm going to sell you out to Edison, perhaps you should think on it this way: If I want to, I already can."

He blinked. She had a point. Paul found himself both impressed and afraid of her, in equal measure.

"You should be a lawyer," he said.

Taking this as a sign of assent, Agnes went to her clothing rack. She removed a long green coat and a pair of small flat shoes.

"We'll have to get him into new clothes so he won't be recognized. The costume department will have plenty. Then you and I will need to leave separately. If Edison is having you followed, we can't take any chances. A few minutes after you go, I'll take him to a carriage and get him to Gramercy."

"What will you tell your mother?"

"That's my problem," she said as she slipped the soft shoes onto her feet. "I've a performance tonight. Come over after, to check on him. Midnight, on the dot."

"All right."

"Now help him up."

Paul felt nervous about leaving Tesla again. After finally locating him, he was letting him once again out of his sight? And yet he had no other choice.

Paul turned quickly to Agnes. "Thank you," he said. "I promise this affair will not distract unduly from your singing."

"Well, I'll tell you an awful secret about the opera," said Agnes as she rang the bell for a stagehand. "It's the same show every night."

CHAPTER 32

Nightly Terrors at Number 4 Gramercy Park

> Just because something doesn't do what you planned it to
> do doesn't mean it's useless.　　　—THOMAS EDISON

PAUL DECIDED THAT he would not say a word to Westinghouse about the sudden reemergence of Nikola Tesla. Not now.

How could he? Westinghouse was isolated in Pittsburgh and without much experience in high-society subterfuge. He was a blunt boss with little patience for dissembling. If Westinghouse knew, then so might a half dozen top engineers in his lab. Or any of the executives in his manufacturing divisions. All of whom had worked for Westinghouse for years longer than Paul had. Paul trusted Westinghouse with his life. But he could not trust him with this secret. Not yet.

Paul grew angry. Not at himself, for deciding to withhold pertinent information from his client. Not at Tesla, for his mental instability, or at Carter and Hughes, for their small-minded treacheries. Not at Westinghouse, for being so unsuited to secrecy as to require being deceived.

Paul was angry at Thomas Edison. This soul-corroding position in which he found himself was the result of a war that Edison had started.

Thomas Edison was the devil himself. And the real measure of his villainy was the behavior he'd forced on Paul.

That evening Paul paid the first of many nighttime visits to Gramercy. Most nights, after leaving the office, he would descend from the hanging step of his carriage between the hours of eleven and twelve and peer quickly around the park. He would search for signs of anyone watching. But of course in such a vibrant setting it would be impossible to tell. The restaurants and alehouses along Irving Place overflowed with revelers, young men and women promenading gaily beneath the streetlamps even into the winter. The theater at Irving Plaza was only a few blocks down, and if Paul happened to arrive when a show was getting out, he would find the streets flooded with merry music lovers. In all the visits he paid to Agnes's house, he never failed to hear a tune in the air outside it.

Gramercy was not the sort of neighborhood that would take too much notice of a young man paying late-night visits to an actress's darkened home.

On Paul's first visit, Fannie was the one to open the door and bid him to enter. She tilted her neck back to stare him straight in the eyes.

"I don't like this," she informed him.

"Were I in your position, I wouldn't like it either, Mrs. Huntington. If there were any other solution, I can promise you that I wouldn't be here, and neither would my suffering friend."

"My daughter has come too far, in too short a time, to be set back by the blackmail of a dishonest theater manager, the debauched soirees of high-fashion pedophiles, the rantings of a head-sick lunatic, or the schemes of a wily attorney just slightly too clever for his own good. My daughter likes you. I don't. So you may rest assured that I will turn on you, and your friend Tesla, at the very first opportunity you give me to do so."

However Agnes had convinced her mother to allow them to host Tesla, it had worked. Still, she could hardly be called a willing accomplice to their plans. Understandably so. If the wrong eyes caught sight of the small-hour visits a young man was paying to her daughter, there would be hell to pay.

This would be the longest of Paul and Fannie's interactions. He would typically nod a hello in future visits. She would scowl in return. They exchanged little beyond the barest of formalities.

On some nights Agnes would be home upon Paul's arrival, on other nights not. After the first few days, she gave Paul a key so that he might let himself in, but he still felt it impolite to enter without warning. Some proprieties, at least, must be preserved.

Inside, Paul would be greeted by the flickering gas lamps along the smoothly carved vestibule. He'd hang his coat. And, once November had given way to early December, he'd smack the snow from his scuffed leather boots.

Tesla had been given a small bedroom on the second floor that had once been a maid's quarters. He spent most of his time in bed in a pair of Paul's pajamas. When Paul would enter, he would invariably find Tesla under the sheets. Yet the inventor did not seem to sleep much.

He was having visions. That became clear as soon as Paul had been able to coax a few words from Tesla's lips. The words that finally came, as Paul sat by his bedside, were faint.

"A great winged beast," said Tesla.

He said little else that Paul could understand that first night. On the second, he produced a few more words, but no greater meaning.

"A fire," Tesla said. "All I see is fire."

"Yes!" Paul exclaimed. "There was a fire. In your laboratory. But that was months ago. You escaped and you're safe now."

Tesla shook his head defiantly. "No no no no no. With us here. I see a fire engulfing around us all."

On future evenings Tesla would describe further visions. There was talk of horned beetles. Then there were bloody rivers and a solar eclipse of infinite length. Eventually he described an undead army and a colony of ants whose bodies were comprised of particles from distant stars. As the days passed, Tesla's descriptions grew more verbose. He invariably spoke as if these terrible sights were not dreams, but scenes before his waking eyes. They were all as real to him as Paul, Agnes, and Fannie, as palpable as his small bed and the single candle that lit his room.

Paul brought a fresh box of saltines every night. Tesla devoured them ravenously. He seemed so hungry, yet he wouldn't eat anything else. How Tesla hadn't long ago perished from scurvy, Paul could not imagine. As the nights went on, and Paul helped Tesla to his crackers, he attempted to get more information about the nature of Tesla's condition. The inventor knew who Paul was. He had some memory of their history together. By the second week, Tesla even referred to him by name, just as he had with Agnes from the start. However, the names "Edison" and "Westinghouse" seemed to have little effect on him. He either didn't remember who they were, or, in his current state, didn't care.

Yet Tesla's presence had the most unexpected effect on Agnes. She seemed to honestly like having him there. Often Paul would arrive to find her already at Tesla's bedside. Often she'd stay after Paul left.

Tesla seemed to soften her. To smooth the edges in her practiced smiles. When she laughed with Tesla, it was a different laugh than the one she'd boomed at Stanford White's party. Or even than the little ones she offered to Paul. With Tesla, her laugh was warmer. It wasn't comedy, it was companionship.

She seemed to be able to understand Tesla more than Paul ever could. She was more adept at deciphering his tortuous grammar. She was even fascinated by his rambling monologues.

"You like him," Paul said to her one night as they ascended the staircase to Tesla's room. He'd just arrived and his cheeks were still red from the cold. Her quarrel with W. H. Foster still loomed over them, but Paul had already decided that another letter would not do the trick. He would have to come up with something better.

"It surprises you that I like Tesla?"

"He doesn't seem of a piece with most of your circle."

"I've spent a lot of time performing. On the stage, for money, and off the stage, for respect. He's never done so a day in his life. It would never even occur to him. He cares about no one's opinions but his own."

Together they entered Tesla's room. They found him, as usual, mumbling to himself. The winter wind slapped hard against the thick windows, providing a low accompaniment to their quiet conversation.

"Ships," said Tesla. "The particles that are moving, sliding, pressing up against. They are like tiny ships. We must see what they bring. We must trace the waters of their journey."

Paul looked at Agnes. Together they had heard so many of these monologues. Together they would be here the next night and the night after that, to hear so many more.

"Particles, they are ships only, are they not? I will make a machine to push them into the waters. To connect one port with another. I cannot believe no one has thought of it previous. It is obvious when you have seen the boats."

Agnes leaned over the bed, hoping to hear him better.

"It's a coil, Miss Agnes Huntington. The shape is coiled. Can't you see it there? It shines from its wonder."

Paul looked around the cramped bedroom. "There's nothing here," said Paul. "Your mind is conjuring up things that aren't there."

At this, Tesla turned to Paul and, for the first time since his reappearance, matched Paul's gaze with genuine consideration.

"Exactly," said Tesla.

"You're hallucinating, Nikola," said Paul.

"No," replied Tesla with the very first smile that Paul had seen on his face in a long time. "I'm inventing."

CHAPTER 33

Mr. Edison Would Disagree

> When an abnormal man can find such abnormal ways . . .
> to make his name known all over the world . . . [and to]
> accumulate such wealth with such little real knowledge . . .
> I say such a man is a genius—or let us use the more popular
> word—a wizard.
>
> —FRANCIS JEHL, AN ASSISTANT IN EDISON'S LABORATORY, 1913

T HE NEXT TIME Paul entered the Huntington house, he was met with an alarming development.

The man he found by Tesla's bedside was of a solid build. Bald, but wearing a bushy white beard across his cheeks with more than enough hair to make up for the lack up top. He was leaning over Tesla as Paul entered.

"Ah," said the man, looking his way. "You've brought the saltines."

"Who are you?"

Agnes, at the foot of the bed, supplied an answer. "Don't worry, Cravath," she said. "This is Dr. Daniel Touff. He's an alienist."

This proved the occasion of their first quarrel. After the doctor had left, Paul questioned her angrily.

"How could you bring a stranger here without asking me?" He hadn't intended to yell, but he found his voice rising.

"I don't need your permission to determine how to take care of Nikola," she replied calmly.

Agnes had met Dr. Touff months previous at Mrs. Astor's Halloween party. He was known among a certain crowd to be trustworthy. Men in his line of work could not afford to be otherwise.

They were in the sitting room by then. Agnes sat patiently on the sofa while Paul paced about the room. She explained that the alienist was highly fascinated by Tesla's "subconscious," as he described it. Paul asked what the word meant; Agnes admitted she hadn't a clue. She explained that the good doctor thought Tesla seemed to suffer from *démence précoce*—something like a "precocious madness." Paul asked if that meant he was insane. But apparently Dr. Touff didn't think the term applied. This was the thing about these alienists, Agnes said. "They're doing away with 'sane' and 'insane' as categories. They've been working to mess the classifications up a bit. Scientists of the mind, such as they are."

"Did the doctor suggest a treatment?" he asked.

"Rest."

"We've been doing that."

"He pointed out something else as well. Tesla's amnesia—it hasn't extended to certain skills."

"Such as?"

"English, for a start. Has it occurred to you that he hasn't been speaking to us in Serbian this whole time?"

Paul had to admit that was an interesting point.

She continued. "And his facility with mechanics. His speech is peppered with scientific terms, with discussion of machines. Particles, as well as winged beasts."

"His visions . . . his hallucinations," said Paul. "He keeps saying that they're inspiring him to build a new machine. He sees these things, he believes they're real—and that, to him, is inventing."

"A flash of light, like Saint Paul on the road to Damascus."

"He told Westinghouse that he had the idea for his alternating-current motor in a similar fit. This is Tesla's process—he has a series of hallucinatory episodes and then there it is. His device is invented. And he moves on to something else."

Agnes seemed fascinated by this process, if suspicious of its efficacy. "But you haven't 'invented' something until you've built it. If I spend an afternoon staring down at sheet music and imagining how I'm to sing it, it cannot be said that I've performed the piece. I don't actually create the thing until I stand on a stage and move my mouth. My throat gets a bit tired and then there's some applause at the end."

"It's different for him."

"Just saying that you've invented something is not the same as inventing it."

"I think Mr. Westinghouse would agree with you . . ." Paul trailed off.

"Cravath?" said Agnes. "Is something the matter?"

"What if Mr. Edison would not agree with you? What if Edison believes that saying that you've invented something is just as good as inventing it?"

Agnes's expression indicated that she had no idea what Paul was talking about.

"Edison claimed to have invented the incandescent electric light bulb on September sixteenth, 1878," said Paul. "Everyone knows that, because Edison made a grand public declaration of his achievement. He announced it in *The Sun*. He gave private demonstrations to adoring reporters from the *Herald* and *The Times*. He patented the basic design of the device—the base, the circuit, all of that—right away. But he didn't actually file for his patent on the bulb piece itself until a year later, on November fourth, 1879." Paul felt a surge of energy. "Here's what I'm asking. What evidence have we that Edison invented the light bulb when he said that he did?"

"You think he lied?"

"The first patent Edison filed was vague. Or at least that's been my legal argument thus far. Edison filed a vague patent that covered far too wide an area. Only, what if Edison hadn't actually gotten the thing working *at all*? What if he simply *told* everyone he had? Imagine the situation from his perspective. He's working on the lamp. He's got dozens of engineers working twenty-four hours a day. He knows he's close. But he also knows that a number of other inventors are working on the exact same problem. And they're close as well. Hibbard, Swan, and Sawyer . . . they were all almost there."

"So Edison just blurts it out?" said Agnes. "He makes a big show to the press of saying 'That's it, the game is over, I've solved the electric lamp.' And then . . . ?"

"And then," said Paul, "the others give up! The great Thomas Edison just invented the indoor electric lamp. It's cut-and-dried. So they start working on other designs. But there was such a lag between the time that Edison announced his discovery and his patent application a year later, and then another year's lag before products were starting to sell in the marketplace. Westinghouse thought there might be space for another company to get involved. So did Hibbard; so did Swan. But no one ever stopped to think: What evidence was there that Edison actually invented a working bulb?"

"There must have been demonstrations."

"Brief ones. A minute at a time . . . two . . . That's how they're described in all of the articles. A journalist, or an investor, would be led in to see the bulb for a minute. Two at the most, and then ushered straight out. Supposedly this was so that no one could view Edison's design long enough to steal it. But what if the demonstrations were so brief for a different reason?"

"That reason being that the bulbs didn't really work?"

"Stability was the entire issue. No one could build a bulb that didn't explode within minutes and set fire to whatever was nearby. . . . What if Edison's early bulbs, the ones he described on his first patent application, were still exploding?"

"But no one else knew, because they were only seeing it for two minutes at a time."

"Edison had two more years to perfect the thing while everyone else was kicking themselves because they couldn't figure out how he did it."

Paul and Agnes stared at each other for a charged few seconds. She was as tense as Paul. "If I can prove that Edison lied on his patent," he said, "then I don't need to prove that Westinghouse's lamps don't infringe. The case I'm currently waging, the argument I've been making—it would be a moot point. Because instead, we could invalidate Edison's patent. Blow the wicked thing out of the water, from tip to stern."

"And then?"

"Then the Edison General Electric Company and the Westinghouse Electric Company are free to produce and sell two different products, and the public can decide which they prefer. No more lawsuits, no more threats. We will be in the situation that Edison has been dreading since first he learned that Westinghouse would challenge him: a fair fight."

CHAPTER 34

The Empire of Invention

> Innovation comes from people meeting up in the hallways
> or calling each other at ten-thirty at night with a new idea,
> or because they've realized something that shoots a hole in
> how we've been thinking about a problem.   —STEVE JOBS

PAUL HAD TROUBLE sleeping after his late-night epiphany with Agnes. He had walked all the way to East Fiftieth Street alternately hatching his plan of attack and thinking about his unexpected good fortune in having her as a confidante. He reminded himself, not for the first time, that she was his client, not his friend. She would certainly not be anything more. The idea of the brightest star of the New York stage taking up with her attorney was absurd. And yet Paul couldn't help but think about all the invitations she must have passed up in recent weeks to sit with him at Tesla's bedside. She had affection for Tesla, that Paul could see plainly. Was it possible that she had some for him as well?

The next day, Paul began to assemble the materials he would need in order to prove that Edison had perjured himself on his patent application. He quickly became engulfed by both their volume and their variety.

First there were the materials surrounding Patent No. 223,898 itself. The application was a mere three pages. The first page consisted entirely of an ink drawing of the lamp design, with annotations along the borders naming its various components. The second two were a brief handwritten summary of what the lamp did and how it functioned, signed at the bottom by Edison. The whole of the thing was fewer than one thousand words. To think of what legal warfare those few words had birthed. Helen of Troy as a spare pen sketch on two paper sheets.

The documents that surrounded the application were substantially lengthier, however. These included clarifications that Edison had made to the patent office in the years following his claim, as well as correspondence between Edison and the patent office as to the eventual granting of the patent. All of these were dutifully signed and verified. In a race for historical preeminence, the date on which one could prove a man made a claim was at least as important as the claim a man might make.

Then, of course, there were the materials concerning the other relevant patents. There had been dozens of previous patents granted by either the American or European governments for items titled "Incandescent Lamp." Edison had thus far successfully argued that each of these patents was quite distinct from his own, and that he owed none of their inventors a debt. Paul had been working to fully understand their differences, in the hopes of arguing that any might encroach upon Edison's claims.

Then came the interviews, articles, and pamphlets published about Edison's miraculous "invention." If the goal was to prove that no breakthrough had in fact occurred when Edison claimed that it had, Paul would need to collate and organize every claim made by Edison and his associates in the years both leading up to and following the patent. Could Paul show that Edison had contradicted himself somewhere? Could Paul find a statement from one of Edison's engineers that contradicted his boss? Had one of the reporters who'd witnessed a demonstration of the bulb in the winter of '78 noticed a detail, without realizing it, that might do the same?

The body of materials that would need to be combed over in search of evidence was daunting. Paul brought mounds of paper into his firm's offices and stared at them as an experienced climber might regard the distant cliffs of Everest. What man could accomplish the trek alone?

Carter and Hughes already had a legal strategy they favored—a defensive one, arguing that Edison's patent was well and good but that Westinghouse's lamps simply did not infringe on it. Their rivalry with him was such that he strongly doubted he'd be able to convince them to take a more offensive path. He could talk to Westinghouse about the difficulty. But how could Westinghouse help? His men were engineers. Paul was in need of attorneys.

Paul's thoughts turned to the marvel that was Edison's laboratory. He could not help but admire the achievements of Edison's organization. Even Reginald Fessenden had described its ingenuity with reverence. Edison's laboratory had in fact produced more wonders in the span of a decade than any other such place in the course of human history. From the duplex telegraph to the phonograph to the carbon microphone to a hundred other lesser marvels, Edison's achievements were extraordinary.

And yet he had not done it alone, had he? Edison was no solitary inventor slaving endlessly through a thousand orange dawns. The image he had loved to present to the public was just another of his deceptions. Edison was the figurehead of a large organization, just as any industrial-age baron was. Andrew Carnegie ruled an organization that refined more pig iron than any other in the world. Jay Gould produced railroads and John Rockefeller drew oil from the depths of the earth. The genius of each of these men was not in the labors of his own hands, it was in the efficiency of the system he had built.

Edison's kingdom was different from those of the industrial barons. They had built organizations that produced objects. Forests were harvested for trees; mines were dug for coal; factories were built to combine the raw elements of heavy industry. Even the Westinghouse Electric Company had been formed in order to mass-produce industrial machinery for the buying public. But what Edison's headquarters, first in Menlo Park and now along Fifth Avenue, generated first and foremost was something else: ideas. Vanderbilt had built an empire of ships, James Duke one of tobacco, and Henry Clay Frick one of steel. Thomas Edison had built an empire of invention.

Thomas Edison was not, Paul thought, the first man to become rich by inventing something clever. Rather, he was the first man to build a factory for harnessing cleverness. Eli Whitney and Alexander Graham Bell had each made his name by inventing one brilliant thing. Edison had formed a laboratory that had invented many. His genius was not in inventing; rather, it was in inventing a system of invention. Dozens of researchers and engineers and developmental tinkerers labored beneath Edison in a carefully constructed hierarchical organization that he founded and oversaw.

At the top of the pyramid, Edison would identify problems to be solved. He would look for weaknesses in the marketplace and locate areas that might be ripe for a new invention. He would then set a team to determine what technological problems stood between the current state of the industry and a proper solution. Once this team had isolated the relevant issues, a phalanx of under-inventors would tinker and toil on possible solutions until some breakthrough had been made. Then this army would be loosed upon an endless variety of potential refinements, until, by sheer volume of trial and error, an "invention" was produced. And that invention would be patented, mass-produced, and marketed under one name. A name emblazoned on the side of every device that came from that lab. A name whose six letters were rendered in the same font, the same size, on each machine. A name now found on one device or another in the home of any American of means.

E-D-I-S-O-N.

This same name was written so many times on the pages before him. He was taken by a particular jealousy. If only he had an organization around him as Edison did. If only Paul could have a *system* for solving legal problems as Edison had developed one for solving technological ones.

Well, why couldn't he?

CHAPTER 35

Associate Attorneys

No one is rich who cannot afford his own army.

—MARCUS CRASSUS, 54 B.C.

COLUMBIA UNIVERSITY'S HAMILTON Hall was a four-story Gothic Revival structure at the center of the school's Madison Avenue campus. The hall's sharply angled roof peaked just above the leafless oaks that lined the campus's dirt paths. The campus was a fortress of stone in the middle of the city, its gray spires piercing into the blue winter sky.

Paul had long felt that the Columbia campus must have been designed from a place of deep anxiety. Its intricate Gothic facades had been built to give the impression of the Old World, curving stone conveying the European Enlightenment and the storied schools of England and France. Though Columbia was one of the oldest universities in the country, it still had its baby fat. The affliction of insecurity that plagued the Wall Street nouveaux riches was even worse among the midtown academy. Bankers all wanted to be princes. Professors all wanted to be Martin Luther.

Technology had for centuries been the province of London's Royal Society and Paris's Académie des sciences. Before the recent decade, no one would have imagined America to be any forward salient of scientific progress. The United States was of an anti-intellectual bent.

And yet the two most technologically advanced laboratories in the world, as far as Paul could tell, were no longer in Paris's Louvre or London's Burlington House. They were now in Menlo Park, New Jersey, and Pittsburgh, Pennsylvania. They were operated by two self-made men with no formal training at all. And, thought Paul, the third such laboratory might very well be in the small back bedroom of an opera singer's Gramercy house. And it existed entirely within the mind of Nikola Tesla.

Paul entered the fourth-floor auditorium amid a throng of students. He blended easily into the crowd. If Columbia men could be said to look a type—confident, collected, energetically eager—Paul remained of it. He could smell the carefully applied hair grease in the air as he took a seat in the back of the room.

He'd come to observe Professor Theodore Dwight's moot court class. Dwight had been more than amenable to helping out a former student in need. To have the most accomplished young attorney in the city back in his classroom would be an honor for both the professor and the sixty-odd students in his care.

Somewhere in the neighborhood of seventy years of age, Professor Dwight had a pure-white muttonchop beard of exceptional plumage. It matched the wig atop his head, and together they gave him a look of indifferent seriousness: indifference toward the fashions of the day, and seriousness toward the work of his life. Shirt collars changed widths and ties adapted to new knots, but the law maintained a deep immutability.

The subject that afternoon was *Goodyear v. Hancock*, a foundational patent suit from a few decades back concerning the creation of weatherproof rubber. The students had come to get on their feet and litigate the case. Dwight served as judge for the proceedings, while two sets of young men sat on either side of him operating as counsel for the plaintiff and the defendant.

As Paul watched these students engage in their passionate and stakes-less arguing, he took note of four who articulated their points the most clearly. It wasn't that their legal analysis was the most astute; it was that they knew how to lay out their analysis in a concise narrative. They were storytellers.

Afterward Paul stood beside Professor Dwight as he explained his proposal to the four students he'd selected.

"I'm here to offer you employment," said Paul to the young men. "The case you'd be working on is *Edison v. Westinghouse*. Perhaps you've heard of it?"

Their faces told him they had. "I will need assistance in all matters," Paul continued. "Research, drafting briefs, finding and preparing witnesses for deposition. I need a few smart men to assist me."

"So we'd be attorneys at Carter, Hughes, and Cravath?" asked the most energetic of the students, who introduced himself as Beyer.

"Not exactly," answered Paul. "You're still in school, and you'd stay that way while you worked for me, until you graduated."

"Then you're offering us clerkships?" suggested another of the students, Bynes. "All of us?"

"No, what I am proposing is not quite that either."

"If not clerks and not attorneys," said Beyer, "then what are you suggesting we'll be?"

"Somewhere in between," said Paul. "What I'm proposing is both novel and the best opportunity any of you will get to join the race of a law practice at full gallop. Think of your position as that of an . . . 'associate attorney,' how about that? We're going to build a legal factory. Men have arranged themselves into systems that produce every material, mineral, and device under the sun. Why not legal work?"

While all of the students appeared confused, Bynes was the one who spoke for the group.

"Because, and of course without meaning to seem rude or ungrateful, isn't legal work of a categorically different nature than physical work? A brief is not a steel plank."

Dwight smiled, proud of his student for taking part in this Socratic dialogue.

Paul was ready with his reply. "If you can arrange a process for producing one, why not a process to produce the other? And here's the added benefit: I'll be able to instruct you through a full case. After I graduated from this place, I clerked for Mr. Carter, who is now my partner. It was a tricky business upon being promoted to attorney— I'd never handled a client before, and had to rope them in without any experience of having done so. You won't be thrown into such a sea of sharks."

"How are we to get clients, then?" asked one of the students who hadn't yet spoken. Paul had already forgotten the boy's name.

"You'll have mine. Or, to put it more precisely, you'll have exactly one of mine."

"Westinghouse," said Beyer.

"You'll devote yourself to that case and that case alone, under my guidance. And I'll sweeten the pot: You'll be given salaries. Ten dollars a week, which I'll guarantee for one year, at which point you'll have finished school and can come on as full lawyers. Or, if you do subpar work, I'll cut you loose at any point and replace you with other bright young students. But the opportunity is yours to make of what you will, with the only determination of your future success to be the quality of your work."

Beyer, Bynes, and the other two men turned to one another as they considered Paul's offer. The legal profession had existed for hundreds of years as a system of protégés and masters, apprentices and artisans. Law firms still ran themselves like cobbler's shops. What Paul was hoping to do, as he constructed this new phalanx of a legal entity, was to fundamentally alter the shape of the practice.

"What is to be our task?" said Beyer.

"We need to prove that Thomas Edison lied to the public, his investors, and the government of the United States."

". . . Oh," said Beyer. The students' eager hopefulness dissipated.

"Well," offered Paul, "I don't think I ever said it would be easy."

Paul's young associates began immediately. They were to work half days for the few months until they graduated, and then full ones immediately thereafter. He stored them in an inexpensive one-room office on Greenwich Street, just a half mile from Carter, Hughes & Cravath. It was an old building that had been subdivided into as many tiny offices as possible. He had little trouble securing a lease. He paid for the first month's rent by his own check, drawn from his account at First National. He set the boys to find their own furniture, and they quickly brought up a long communal table for them to share from a market in Brooklyn.

"Embezzlement" was not the word he preferred to use to describe his plan for paying for the services of his associates. To be sure, he couldn't very well afford to pay them out of his own pocket indefinitely. He would have to divert funds from the Westinghouse account. But if the attempt to obliterate Edison's light-bulb patent was not a proper expenditure of Westinghouse Electric Company funds, then what on earth would be?

It was the slipperiness of Carter and Hughes that had put him in this position. If they had not betrayed him before, he would not be forced to go behind their backs now. So in those cold weeks of December 1888, while Manhattan bundled itself in layers of New England wool, Paul enveloped his operation in layers of financial obfuscation.

He harbored no illusions about the risk he was taking. He did not imagine that there remained any end to this story that would not involve the brutal dissolution of his law firm. Eventually Carter and Hughes would find out what he was doing. And then they'd fire him. And probably sue him, at that. If Paul's scheme proved successful, they would learn of what he'd done at the moment of his victory. If he was unsuccessful, they'd learn of what he'd done at the bankruptcy filing of the Westinghouse Electric Company. Either way, they would punish him. Win or lose, this would end with Paul out of a job. Either way, he would end up on his own. The only question was whether his next firm would be in Manhattan or on the unheated first floor of his father's house in Tennessee.

CHAPTER 36

Miss Huntington Grants an Interview

> Headlines, in a way, are what mislead you, because bad
> news is a headline, and gradual improvement is not.
>
> —BILL GATES

CHRISTMAS OF 1888 arrived with a cold front that further en-crusted the hardened city. Yet this Christmas managed to com-pare favorably with the previous one, which had fallen just before the worst blizzard anyone had seen in decades. The holiday of '88 was merely freezing.

Tesla spent his Christmas with the ladies Huntington. Paul was not invited to join them. It seemed that Fannie wanted to preserve what-ever private moments she could for the sanctity of her family. Tesla was intruder enough. At least he was a charity case. His presence fit the season. Paul was merely their attorney. He was the help. He could fend for himself.

Paul spent Christmas Day working from his apartment. He dined alone at P. J. Clarke's tavern just down the block on Third Avenue. He'd expected to have the place to himself, but found it even more crowded than usual. He wasn't the only solitary New Yorker who wanted to enjoy his lamb stew and pint of ale in public.

The next day, he trudged through the cold to an appointment on

Park Row, just across from City Hall. He arrived to find the five-story Romanesque building encased in scaffolding. A massive construction project was under way, and the structure seemed to be expanding outward, like an insect bursting from its cracked shell. It seemed an apt metaphor, since Paul did not have great respect for the people who worked inside. They were journalists.

The newspaper he was there to visit was not the largest in the city, nor was it the most prestigious. But *The New York Times* was certainly the most ambitious, and the most self-obsessed with its own comically high-minded ideals.

The plan had been his, though Agnes had taken to it quickly. Fannie had been skeptical, but even she'd had to admit that it was the best idea she'd yet heard from her lawyer. It was risky. But given the nature of their blackmail, what course of action wasn't?

Paul's plan was to use his two clients' respective reputations in each other's service. He thought of this like the symbols common to all of Thomas Edison's products. Each device bore the word "Edison" on it, in the same font, the same size. If a customer liked one, he might be tempted to try another, totally different product, on the logic that it came from the same manufacturer. The very word "Edison" had become a "brand," no less searing and permanent than those imprinted upon the hides of cattle. Edison's circular nameplate even resembled that of a cattleman's iron. This could not have been an accident.

Paul would build his own "brand" as a lawyer. The name Cravath would be at the center of both the cases he was handling, a symbol of impossible difficulties handled with taste and discretion.

There was a reporter at *The Times* by the name of Leopold Drucker. He would be delighted to conduct an interview with Agnes, as the operetta star submitted to them so infrequently. He could be trusted not to print anything that might cast Agnes in an unfavorable light, as so many of these gossip writers loved to do.

"But why," Fannie had asked, "grant an interview in the first place?"

"Because W. H. Foster is blackmailing you with the threat of a public scandal. So rather than wait for him to use the newspapers against you, let's beat him to the punch. Let's use the newspapers against him. He believes that you've much to lose from a public airing? Well, let us make very clear that he does too."

As they had arranged, Paul met Agnes in the lobby of the *Times* building. A secretary pointed them up the stairs to the fourth floor.

"Don't say too much," said Paul. "Just enough."

"I know how to give an interview," said Agnes. "This is not my first. Though if we're successful, I daresay it'll be my most fun."

That Agnes relished an attack on W. H. Foster did not surprise Paul. There was a vengeful side to her, when wronged. It was another trait that he appreciated.

"Mr. Drucker is friendly to our side," Paul said, "but he's not ours completely. This will be a proper interview."

"You paid him," said Agnes boldly. It wasn't a question.

Paul paused before speaking. "Not exactly."

"Edison bought off some men from the *Evening Post,* so you followed suit with some men from *The Times?*"

"Westinghouse has given Mr. Drucker exclusive interviews, exclusive access to reports of coming products. In exchange, Drucker has written generously—and honestly—about those products. It's not a bribe. It's a relationship." Paul emphasized the point: "We haven't stooped to Edison's level."

Agnes raised an eyebrow. "Well," she said, "do you think that might be why you're losing?"

They found Leopold Drucker among the reporters scribbling away at their messy desks. Even the day after Christmas, the newsroom was loud with the clack of typewriters.

Paul watched raptly as Agnes sat for her interview. She was, in a word, excellent. Her performance was no less masterful than any he might imagine of hers onstage. Drucker's secretary transcribed every word she uttered. Agnes spoke at a calm pace, as if this were any other social call. She treated Drucker like an old friend, despite their having met only minutes before. Her tone was light, both funny and refined. She was a small-town girl just delighted at what big-city dreams she now lived. And at the same time, she was a winking doyenne of

THE LAST DAYS OF NIGHT | 181

New York society, elegant in her habits and ladylike in her proprieties.

She spoke of Paris, of London, of her lifelong passion for song. She mentioned her devoted mother, ever at her side. She was a naïf in the rough business of the theater. She let Drucker do the work of asking about the short midwestern tour in which she'd sung—why so quick? Hadn't she liked Chicago?

"Chicago will forever be in my heart," she said. "It is the Paris of the Middle West. There was only a small unpleasantness with a manager on the tour that bade me take my leave of it." When pressed as to the nature of this unpleasantness, she demurred. "You'll have to speak to Mr. Foster about all of that. He runs the troupe I was then singing with. Such lovely people. If you speak to any of the ladies in the troupe, please give them my love? They suffered such an unfortunate time. But yes, Chicago—what a heavenly town!"

Paul had to restrain himself from bursting into applause. Drucker could print that as it was. Only a few words, carefully chosen, had been required to do all the damage she'd wanted. "Ladies." "Unfortunate." "Suffered." "A small unpleasantness." She wasn't smearing Foster's good name. There was nothing libelous in what she'd said. Nothing even that smacked of a grudge. She sounded like she was attempting *not* to sully his reputation. And it was from such a tone that any reader of good judgment might draw her own conclusions about what sort of theater manager had caused an unpleasantness with his female singers. Any speculation as to the nature of this trouble would be left solely to the province of the reader's ample imagination.

As the interview concluded, Mr. Drucker instructed his secretary to submit the transcribed interview to his editor by the evening. The newsroom seemed to silence itself as Agnes strolled out among the clerks and typists. Paul watched as she floated across the room.

"Oh, Cravath," Drucker said to Paul. "There's something came in yesterday that I thought you might want to see. It's down on the second floor—I'll show you. It's a submission from the desk of Harold Brown."

"Surely," said Paul, "*The New York Times* is not going to print an editorial of Brown's." *The Times* had never been a Westinghouse paper, exactly, but neither had it been as sycophantically pro-Edison as its peers.

"It's not an editorial. It's an advertisement. A full page."

"An advertisement for what?"

"For a demonstration," said Drucker. "And dear Lord, does it look like it'll be a show."

CHAPTER 37

A New Year's Grotesque

What is a scientist after all? It is a curious man looking
through a keyhole, the keyhole of nature, trying to know
what is going on.   —JACQUES COUSTEAU

P AUL'S COLLECTION OF Harold Brown's incendiary editorials had
grown considerably over the previous months. The pile rested
on the floor in his office, stacked to a point of structural instability. Almost every major newspaper in America had published one
of the screeds. Their tone was as unyieldingly hyperbolic as the first.
Alternating current had arrived, it had come to murder your children,
and its deliverer was George Westinghouse.

Paul and Westinghouse had tried to educate the public on the science involved, to explain why alternating current was in fact less
dangerous than direct. Westinghouse had personally penned editorials vouching for the safety of his systems. But so far the public had not
been as moved by scientific reasoning as they had been by Brown's
colorful fabrications.

Brown was now taking his campaign a step further. He was set to
launch a traveling road show. He would demonstrate to the public
just how deadly Westinghouse's current would be.

On New Year's Day, 1889, Paul took the train to West Orange,
New Jersey.

He found a crowded lecture hall. He guessed there to be almost a hundred other attendees besides himself, comprised of city safety officials, lighting company representatives, assorted engineers, and a healthy contingent of reporters. Brown's tour was being advertised all along the East Coast. He was to perform in Boston, Philadelphia, Baltimore, Washington. *Edison country,* Paul thought. Though on such trips Brown would have to travel on trains with brakes designed by George Westinghouse.

Harold Brown entered the lecture hall. To Paul's surprise, he looked more like an actuary than a huckster. He was small, mild of demeanor, soft voiced; if he wasn't the man of the hour, he would have disappeared into the crowd. Brown began his lecture by explaining that he had no "financial or commercial interest" in the nationwide debate over A/C versus D/C; his involvement in this scientific dispute was motivated only by his commitment to the truth. He then directed his audience's attention to an animal cage. It was constructed from wood, but strung with copper wires between the bars. Inside, Brown had placed a generously sized black retriever. An assistant attached wires to the animal's legs. One on the front right, the other on the rear left. The unsuspecting retriever did not bark as the copper pressed against its fur. Brown then showed his assembled crowd a direct-current generator. It was of "the type manufactured by Mr. Edison," he explained. With the flick of a switch, Brown sent what he described as three hundred volts through the dog. The animal emitted a small yelp and briefly struggled to shake free. But of course the shackles wouldn't budge.

"You see," Brown intoned, "the direct current hurts no worse than a pinprick."

He then turned the generator to four hundred volts and reapplied the current to the unhappy retriever. The barking grew louder.

Next it was seven hundred volts of D/C. The dog bellowed violently, banging its head against the bars of the cage. The poor thing shook until managing to loose the electrical wire on its front paw. Brown's assistant dutifully reapplied it.

Shouts of protest erupted from the audience. Surely, a few men yelled, this was too much. Paul placed his head in his hands. He had a terrible feeling.

"Even up to seven hundred volts," Brown explained, ignoring his audience's pleas for mercy, "this direct current is quite simply incapable of doing lasting damage to the animal.

"But," he then added, "let us see how alternating current compares." His assistant replaced the D/C generator with a different one, bigger and newer. Brown described it as an alternating-current device, identical to the variety produced by Mr. Westinghouse.

"We return to a humble three hundred volts," he said as he flicked a switch on the new machine and alternating current poured through the dog. It took only seconds of thrashing and an unholy screech before it slumped to the floor of its cage, dead. "Terrible thing," said Brown as he shook his head ruefully. The crowd was too shocked to move. "I am sorry for having to show you such terrors. But if you have concerns, I suggest bringing them up with Mr. Westinghouse. He is the one attempting to string this current up to every thoroughfare in the country. If this is what it does to a dog, imagine what it might do to a child!"

Despite a note of official protest from the American Society for the Prevention of Cruelty to Animals, Brown performed a nearly identical demonstration the following day. A Newfoundland work dog was electrocuted by A/C for a full eight seconds before it died. The next night it was an Irish setter, with identical results.

The following weeks brought a pattern of newspaper coverage of these demonstrations that was almost comical in its predictability and its absurdity. Paul had assumed that the controversy surrounding such grotesqueries would be to his advantage. Surely no one could take seriously the scientific claims of a man who had literally taken to burning animals alive?

Paul found himself in the wrong. Every report went like this: First there was a throat-clearing denunciation from the newspaper editorial board about the moral abomination of animal killing. But then, a breath later, the same paper would reluctantly suggest that if Brown had perhaps gone too far to make his point, that did not invalidate his message. And based on the horrors witnessed, his message was both sound and vitally important.

"While Brown might find a wider audience for his arguments if they were not posed in such an unchristian manner," declared *The Philadelphia Inquirer*, "there can be no denying the dangers he so successfully elucidated by the frying of a Labrador." The controversy itself begat more ink, which in turn brought more attention to Brown's cause. It seemed that in the circus of public opinion, no act was too extreme. Brown's villainy had been successfully painted as Westinghouse's.

"Mr. Paul Cravath," said Tesla as Paul entered his upstairs bedroom two weeks later. "You are looking more pale even than I."

Paul had to smile. Tesla had rarely greeted him by name since the accident. "I'm not getting as much sleep as I might."

Tesla didn't respond. Instead, he turned to the window and stared at the shapes being formed by the ice outside the glass. Geometric paintings in slow-moving frost. Paul spent another twenty minutes trying to re-engage him in conversation, but it was no use. This brief flash of lucidity was all that Paul would get that night.

Yet it indicated improvement. Agnes had even heard Tesla refer to Edison the day before. Names were coming back to him, events too. Paul hoped that soon he might recall how he had survived the fire. And, much more important, that he might regain the creative capacity to invent an original, non-infringing lamp. While production of their A/C generators was going as planned, Westinghouse and Fessenden had reported little progress on development of a new light bulb. It would take, suggested Fessenden, a particular genius to conjure up such a device. Tesla's recovery could not come too soon; Paul could only hope that it would come eventually.

Paul joined Agnes in a late-night glass of port. This had recently become a ritual on his midnight visits, one that he spent all day looking forward to. As a result of his position, not to mention his workload, he was left with few real friends. He had, he realized, only one person with whom he could be fully honest. How lucky, and how fantastic, that it was her.

"Any progress on your friend Harold Brown?" asked Agnes as she sipped from her tiny glass. She'd kept her black silk gloves on, despite their having sat in her drawing room. She was a curious mix, Paul noted, of proprieties adopted and abandoned.

He wondered what it would be like to put down his glass and kiss her. Instead, he talked about his case.

"We haven't found a connection yet to Edison. We can't even find any record they've ever been in the same place at the same time. It's as if Edison is Dr. Jekyll, and Brown Mr. Hyde."

"I've never read that one."

"Neither have I," admitted Paul. "One odd thing my associates did find, though: patent applications, in Brown's name. All rejected."

"Rejected?"

"He submitted his own design of a light bulb, four or five years ago. A few of his own generators. My boys unearthed two dozen of the things."

Agnes considered this, tapping her gloved fingers against her delicate glass. "He's a failed inventor?"

"It appears that way. I asked one of Westinghouse's engineers to look over the rejected applications. He told me they're trash—poorly thought-out mimicry, far from the real thing. The patent office is famously instructed to err on the side of granting too many patents rather than too few, on the logic that it's cleaner for the courts to invalidate them in hindsight than to attempt applying them after the fact. But Brown's ideas were too middling even for them. He wanted to be Thomas Edison, but he couldn't cut it. So instead . . ."

"He gets to pretend to be Edison for the press." Agnes appeared thoughtful, as if allowing the port to percolate through her mind. "*The Sun* ran a profile on him."

"So did the *Boston Herald*. A few others."

"They make mention of his laboratory, in Manhattan."

"On Wall Street no less," said Paul. "He's dressing the part. The stained work pants, the scuffed boots, the Manhattan laboratory."

"Except what does a pretend inventor do in his real lab?"

Paul realized that he didn't have an answer.

CHAPTER 38

A Midnight Theft

> Picasso had a saying—"Good artists copy. Great artists
> steal." And we have always been shameless about stealing
> great ideas.
>
> —STEVE JOBS, MISATTRIBUTING A QUOTE TO PABLO PICASSO

THE CORNER OF Wall Street and William Street was quiet at one in the morning. Four days after his conversation with Agnes, Paul stood there under a great pedestal arc lamp, the lone figure beneath the artificial moonlight. The hours between sunset and sunrise felt different under a mechanical brightness. The area beneath the arcing lamp was the color palette of the Italian Renaissance, while the city beyond it fell into a murky swirl of French Impressionism.

Beneath the brightest public lights that money could buy, Paul contemplated the dirty business on which he reluctantly found himself. Harold Brown's laboratory was on the third floor of 45 Wall Street. The building stood before Paul just at the edge of the illuminated circle that surrounded him.

"You Cravath?" came a voice from behind. Paul turned to find a slim, clean-shaven man approaching. The man was short, dressed in simple work clothes and a warm hat. His hands rested comfortably in the pockets of his coat.

"I think I have a pretty good idea of who you are."

The man shrugged before gesturing to 45 Wall Street. "If your aim is to have a long career in burglary, I suggest starting a little smaller."

"I appreciate the advice," said Paul. "But I'd prefer my career to be as short as possible."

"Suit yourself."

The man was a professional picklock. It had taken some time for Paul to make inquiries, to find a public house where men of murky repute would be likely to congregate. He couldn't very well ask his law school friends if they knew any handy burglars, could he?

It had taken some negotiating and more than one two-dollar bill pressed into the palm of a talkative bartender. Whiskey wasn't Paul's drink of choice, but he made do, given the places he had to inquire.

This man, whose name Paul preferred not to know, had come highly recommended. Tonight Paul would see if his reputation was deserved.

The thief removed from his jacket what appeared to be the tools of his trade. Paul could hear the gentle clink of metal instruments against the lock on the door of Number 45.

Paul watched the street. He hadn't been instructed as to his role in all of this, but manning the lookout seemed the logical thing to do.

Three interminable minutes passed before Paul heard the satisfying click of the tumbler. The two men stepped into a pitch-black marble lobby. There were electrical lamps on the walls—Paul could make out their shapes—but he dared not turn them on.

He had a few candles ready in his coat pocket. He lit two with a match, and handed one to the thief. The light was underwhelming. They couldn't see more than ten feet in front of them.

Paul found his way to a staircase. He'd spent an afternoon idly walking through the area at midday. He knew where Harold Brown's office was. It didn't take long to make it up to the third floor, and to Brown's door.

Wordlessly the thief took his cue and reapplied his tools to this inner door. There were two locks to tackle. The look on his face was relaxed. He'd done this many times before, Paul reasoned. This night, for him, was not out of the ordinary.

Sometimes it took a criminal to catch a criminal. And Thomas Edison—along with his compatriot Harold Brown—was most certainly a criminal.

Had Paul become one himself? He had to admit that it had been a strange path from Columbia Law School to breaking and entering.

Paul looked across the dark third-floor hallway. He listened carefully for any sounds on the staircase. But all he could hear was the soft scraping of the thief's work.

The lower of the two locks submitted quickly. It took less than a minute of effort. So far, this was going well.

"Can't do it," whispered the thief suddenly.

"What?" said Paul.

"Your top lock here. Can't open it."

"You've barely tried."

"It's the model . . . too heavy. I ain't got the tools."

"You're a professional."

The thief shrugged again. His professionalism was not something he seemed to feel he needed to defend.

"What am I supposed to do?"

"Damned if I know. But whatever it is, I'd be quick about it. Someone will see our lights soon enough."

He wasn't wrong. Windows looking out onto Wall Street were evenly placed down the hallway. Paul had seen the streetlamps when he'd passed the windows. Which meant that someone looking up would be able to see them, faint as their candles were.

"How strong is the door?" asked Paul. "Can we kick it down?"

The thief pondered the door.

"Probably not, I'd say. But maybe. If you land a good blow or two right about there"—and here he gestured to a middle section of the wooden door—"you might get a chunk free. Something you could climb through. Though I doubt it. And what you're talking about would be dreadful loud."

"But you're saying it's possible."

"I'm saying it's stupid."

Paul took a moment to consider his options. It was not a long moment.

"Sometimes those are pretty much synonymous."

Paul took three steps backward. He pointed at the middle of the door, then looked to the thief for confirmation. The thief nodded. Paul took a breath. Once he started breaking down this door, there would be no going back. And yet . . . Well, he'd passed the point of going back long ago, hadn't he?

With all the strength he had, he launched his right foot at the locked door to Harold Brown's office.

CHAPTER 39

Inventions Already Invented

> If a cluttered desk is a sign of a cluttered mind, of what,
> then, is an empty desk a sign?   —ALBERT EINSTEIN

P AUL'S KICK CREATED a three-foot hole in the door. His body ricocheted back. There was a searing pain from his foot to his forehead. His leg, he quickly realized, was caught in the half-broken door. His body hung strangely on the outside.

He pulled his foot free slowly, painfully. His pants tore on the sharp wood. He could feel the shards dig into his skin; he couldn't see blood, but he felt confident it was there.

"You're strong, for a fancy man," said the thief.

"My foot . . . ," said Paul. "Can you . . . ?"

The thief regarded Paul's limp leg and then the hole in the door.

"You want me to have a go at the rest of it?" he said.

"Yes," answered Paul.

"I have a better idea." The thief stuck his hand through the hole in the door and found the top lock on the inside. He flicked the bolt, and the door swung open.

"Thanks." Paul had little time to waste. The crash had made quite a noise. Someone was bound to have heard it.

The supposed laboratory resembled Paul's office more than it did Westinghouse's. The front area contained a few desks for secretaries.

Tables for correspondence. There appeared to be two private offices in the rear. Paul moved to them instantly. On the left, there seemed to be the only space that could really be devoted to any sort of scientific exploration. It was a small room, full of devices, with a worktable at the center. But the devices looked to have been laid around the room haphazardly. Paul had been in enough electrical laboratories to recognize them as a few different kinds of generators, lamps, and some basic motors. It was a room full of inventions that had already been invented.

This was not a space for discovery; it was a space for dissection. Brown took other people's devices and toyed with them. He did not create his own.

"What is all that stuff?" asked the thief, peering over Paul's shoulder.

"Not much," answered Paul before moving to the other rear office. This looked more promising. It contained a simple cherry desk, a tall chair at which to sit, and two filing cabinets. This would be where Brown conducted his real business: manipulating the public.

Paul set his candle on the desk as he looked through Brown's papers. It was no surprise that almost all were letters. Paul flipped through the documents on the desktop and in the drawers beneath, finding little that he would describe as being scientific. There were no schematics, no diagrams, no plans. Only letters to editors, letters back to Brown, letters from city commissioners and concerned citizens and journalists and curious mayors and from . . .

Thomas Edison.

There was Edison's letterhead. Paul instinctively skipped straight to the bottom. Edison's signature. He was holding a letter from Edison to Brown. Proof of their conspiracy.

It was only when Paul started to read the letter's contents that whatever elation he had felt at the letter's existence quickly dissipated.

CHAPTER 40

The Chair

> Expectations are a form of first-class truth: If people believe
> it, it's true.
> —BILL GATES

"**H**AROLD BROWN HAS designed something he calls an electrical chair," said Paul.

George Westinghouse frowned. "How can you make a chair out of electrical current? That is nonsense."

"The chair isn't made of electricity—it *transmits* electricity to whoever is sitting in it."

"Why in God's name would you ever want to do that? It'd kill you."

"Exactly."

The men were speaking aboard Westinghouse's private rail car, the *Glen Eyre*. The empty acres of Pennsylvania countryside sped by. The recent snow had left the landscape a dull white, an even plain stretching into the distance.

He explained to Westinghouse that what he'd found in Brown's office was a series of letters between Brown and Edison that confirmed their conspiracy.

It appeared that, in secret, Harold Brown had petitioned the New York State Legislature to consider alternate methods of execution for those whom the state had sentenced to death. The noose was ancient technology. Perhaps, Brown had suggested, a more scientific method of execution could be used. And did he have a method in mind? He did. It was this "electrical chair." A convicted criminal would be strapped to a chair made of wood, with metallic contacts attached to his forehead and lower back. These contacts would then be hooked up to an electrical generator. When the generator was turned on, the convict would be dead instantly. This, Brown had argued, would be much more humane than the noose. Not to mention the firing squad.

Brown had even taken the trouble of specifying the type of generator that would be best for such a device. It ran on A/C. And it was manufactured by the Westinghouse Electric Company.

That company's namesake took this news poorly. Edison and Brown were working to make his alternating current the official current of execution. The state-sponsored current of death. Westinghouse's A/C systems were selling briskly, and the initial installations in Great Barrington, Massachusetts, and Oregon City Falls, Oregon, had gone well. But who in the world would want to install the same technology in their home that the New York State Legislature had chosen to install in their prisons?

"But Edison doesn't support the death penalty. He's campaigned against the thing. Publicly. I've read his sanctimonious editorials."

"That was before he recognized that the death penalty could be put to his own advantage."

Westinghouse stared out the window at the wintry fields. "You almost have to respect the ingenuity."

"'Almost' being the operative word."

"And I suppose no one cares that it wouldn't even work? My system, properly constructed, would do a poor job of killing someone."

Paul's expression made perfectly clear that the public was uninterested in this kind of logic.

"So how do we respond?" asked Westinghouse.

"I've sent word to Albany. In two weeks I'll argue before the New York State Legislature that the use of an electrical chair in executions would constitute cruel and unusual punishment."

"You're not making the argument that D/C should be the official current of executions?"

"I don't want to ask the state senators to be scientists. I'm asking them to be humanitarians."

"What happens if you lose?" asked Westinghouse. "If they do use my equipment to build this electrical chair? How can we possibly compete under those circumstances?"

"We can't."

"So what do we do?"

Paul looked out at the clean white expanse. A city was just coming into view along the horizon.

"We hope that for the next few years, no one in New York commits any murders."

"Or," added Westinghouse ruefully, "at least that they don't get caught."

Typically, Paul's trips to Pittsburgh were brief—ten hours in transit for a meeting with his client, then an overnight trip back. But this time, Westinghouse asked if he'd like to stay the night. They were having friends for dinner on the following evening, and Marguerite had wondered why Paul never came by the house anymore. She'd invited him to attend, if he was free. The guest apartments were all made up.

Dinner was for only eleven this time. The salad dressing had a familiar taste. The other guests were not scientists, but rather Pittsburgh gentry. Paul found himself seated next to a young woman who'd clearly mastered all there was to learn at western Pennsylvania's finest finishing schools. She was well versed in discussing her favorite breeds of dog, charity work, and the fashions of the day.

Paul did not give himself much credit for not making a fool of himself this time on an impolitic subject. It wasn't hard—no impolitic subjects were brought up. It was a well-socialized crowd.

Paul recalled his last aborted dinner at the Westinghouse estate, and Tesla's sudden exit before it began. He still hadn't told Westinghouse that Tesla was alive. The deceit gave a bitter taste to his strawberry galette. He was glad there was Bordeaux to absolve his well-intentioned sins.

"You didn't like Stephanie much," observed Marguerite as Paul joined her in the kitchen after dinner. All the other guests had retired to the billiard room.

"Pardon?"

"Paul," said Marguerite, "you're not stupid. That's why George likes you. And that's why we wanted you to make Stephanie's acquaintance."

Paul was so flattered to have been described as being liked by George Westinghouse that it took him far too long to realize that Stephanie was the name of the politely effervescent iron heiress sitting beside him at dinner.

"Oh," said Paul. "I didn't realize . . ."

Marguerite gave a disappointed sigh as she poured sweet dessert wines for the guests. "It's only that you're a very eligible young man. You know that. And you're not *that* young, are you?"

"I'm twenty-seven."

Marguerite smiled as if to say this was not quite as young as he might like to believe it was.

"And I have my eye on someone," he explained. He'd never said it out loud before. Having formed the words from mere air, he felt instantly embarrassed.

"Oh!" said Marguerite, clearly encouraged. "Might I have made her acquaintance?"

"I don't think so." Paul was clearly not going to provide her with a name, and she was far too clever to ask.

She lifted a tray on which were balanced eleven glasses of Vouvray.

"Well," she said as she led Paul out of the kitchen. "If you don't want to tell me who it is, I hope at least that you're not so mum to the young lady in question."

CHAPTER 41

The Mystery of the Filaments

> If you really look closely, most overnight successes took a
> long time.
> —STEVE JOBS

T HE "WAR OF the currents," as the press had begun to call it, had
opened along so many simultaneous fronts that Paul was having trouble keeping them straight. It was difficult to remember
which battles were even winnable and which were simply on their
way to being lost as slowly as possible.

First there was *Edison v. Westinghouse* itself—the main event—and
the 312 assorted lawsuits that came with it. If Paul's associates were
successful in their quest to prove that Edison had lied on his patent
application, every single one of these suits would be moot. But until
then, they were unenviable drudgery. Edison's plan to bury Paul underneath a mausoleum of paperwork had been a savvy one. Even
though Westinghouse's adoption of alternating current gave him a
clear advantage in the majority of these suits, Carter, Hughes & Cravath had to compose 312 sets of briefs, attend 312 sets of court appearances, prepare 312 "motions to continue"—that is, requests to
delay the trial. Thankfully for Paul, Carter and Hughes had taken the
lead here after Paul's hospitalization. He'd been bitter about their insistence on doing so at the time, but now it allowed Paul to focus on
other fronts.

The second of which was Paul's argument before the New York State Legislature that electricity should not be used in executions. These arguments were to be made in person to members of the state legislature in Albany. Paul journeyed there to dine with different state senators. They all appreciated the steaks to which he treated them, the cigars he shared, the offers of similar hospitality on their next visits to Manhattan. Whether he'd won their votes or not, that was a different matter. Edison's pocketbook had done more to ensure a friendly governmental environment than might a hundred of Paul's filets mignons.

While the two sides fought both in court and in the realm of public opinion, the electrification of America continued. Edison sold D/C units to the mansions of Boston, Chicago, and Detroit while Westinghouse sold A/C systems to Telluride, Colorado, and Redlands, California.

In New York, Tesla was remembering more and more. Paul would sit up late at the inventor's bedside, watching him scribble his way through notebook after notebook. It seemed that the inner workings of what he'd designed for Westinghouse, for Edison, and on his own were returning to his command. Paul was encouraged to hear him curse both Westinghouse and Edison at the mention of their names. He had no idea if the inventor's scribbles would ever comprise a new and non-infringing light bulb, but if they did, that would constitute by far the best path to victory.

It was on such a visit that Paul had an opportunity to speak to Fannie. There was a proposal he'd been building up the nerve to make ever since his conversation with Marguerite Westinghouse. The chance presented itself on a Saturday night in early February. Agnes had gone out with her castmates after the show, which meant that Paul found a moment alone with her mother.

Despite the hour, she made them tea. Paul felt this was a peace offering. Their press gambit against W. H. Foster had gone well—the Huntingtons hadn't heard from him since Agnes's interview had run in The Times. Paul found himself in Fannie's good graces, at least for the moment.

"I must thank you, Mrs. Huntington," he said. "I know what you've done for me, and for Mr. Tesla, these past months."

She inspected some fading flowers on the table between them. "Your help with my daughter's situation has been appreciated," she said.

"We've had a mutually beneficial partnership."

She rearranged her flowers by dim candlelight. Paul waited awkwardly for a few moments. "Mrs. Huntington. There is another humble request I'd like to make of you."

"I can see that," she said.

She was, once again, no fool. "I was hoping to take Agnes on a walk. Perhaps this Sunday. The gardens, I'd thought. Prospect Park, out in Brooklyn. They've actually got some winter orchids that are still in season. Lovely. Quite lovely. Before I asked her, I wanted to have your blessing."

Despite Agnes's rather modern disposition, he had decided that in courting her he should pursue a distinctly old-fashioned path. She was very much a New Woman, as they called them in the papers. Having seen the champagne-doused society company in which Agnes secretly traveled, Paul had decided to distinguish himself by way of a formal courtship. A walk through the gardens had been selected to appeal to both of the ladies Huntington.

Fannie Huntington looked at him as if she were for the first time picturing the aquatic life of a distant planet.

"Mr. Cravath," said Fannie slowly, "I believe Agnes already has plans on Sunday afternoon."

Paul didn't get it at first. "Well. Perhaps next week, then."

"With Henry La Barre Jayne."

"Oh," said Paul.

"Of the Philadelphia Jaynes," Fannie added unnecessarily.

"Yes."

"It's not their first afternoon outing together."

"No, no, of course not." Paul wanted to flee. Of course Agnes Huntington would be courted by American royalty. How foolish had he been to think that of all the offers she must receive, she would favor his? That she hadn't mentioned any gentleman callers to Paul only accentuated the extent of his stupidity. She'd been immersed in a social world so far from his that such matters never even occurred to her while in his company. She had not judged Paul wanting; she had found him too insignificant to judge.

Henry Jayne was the latest in a long line of shipping heirs whose family fortune had recently been extended to real estate. The Jaynes owned half of Philadelphia and had recently begun snapping up wide swaths of Manhattan as well. Henry Jayne, who was only a few years older than Paul, managed his family's foothold in New York. The quarterlies all agreed that he was the most philanthropically inclined of his siblings, and the standard-bearer of the family's fine-art holdings to boot.

"Are they to marry?" Paul asked. It was only after the words had come out that he realized how impolite they were. It was shame speaking. He wished he'd kept his mouth shut.

"Well, I most certainly can't say," snapped Fannie. "But I will say that Mr. Jayne is quite an interesting young man. Completed his studies in Leipzig. Speaks five languages."

"How fascinating."

"My daughter's company is in high demand, Mr. Cravath. Will she marry Mr. Jayne? I'm not sure. Her gifts, not to mention her grace, have afforded my daughter a rare opportunity. It is her intention not to waste it. And it is my earthly duty to make sure she doesn't."

She crossed her arms before her small frame.

"Mrs. Huntington," said Paul, "I wish you both the very best. I'm proud to be your and your daughter's attorney. It is a position I cherish, and one that I hope to maintain for a very long time."

This emphasis on Paul's position seemed to satisfy Fannie. Her goodbye was peaceable.

Paul found his way to the front door as quickly as he could. He'd made an ass of himself.

But he gave a start as he opened the door. Agnes stood on the stoop, fishing in her handbag for her key.

"Cravath!" she said with a smile, pleased by the magic of the opening door. "Perfect timing, as always."

Agnes looked a little tipsy. She was in good spirits, clearly happy from her night out. Had she been with castmates? Or with Mr. Jayne? He realized how little he knew of her activities when they were apart. He couldn't imagine being in Tesla's room with her ever again.

He moved aside so that she could come in from the cold.

"Will you join me for a nightcap?" she asked. "You will never believe the night I've had. Did you know that swans bite? They bite hard; it's horrible. You'll love this story."

But Paul did not remove his hand from the door. "I'm sorry, Miss Huntington," he said. "I must be off. Good evening."

Before she could remove her coat and place it on the brass rack, Paul had already walked out and shut the door behind him.

He descended the steps quickly, walking determinedly into the night.

He did not look back to see if her face was in the window. Instead, he kept his eyes on the black leather of his shoes. He wished for sleep to come quickly, for his dreams to pass unremembered, and for the dawn to greet him soon.

He needed to get back to work.

Paul's four associate attorneys were waiting for him when he entered their ramshackle offices on Greenwich Street the next morning. It was time for their weekly appointment. They appeared to have slept there the night before. The men's shirt collars were loosened, their ties undone. The single room smelled of sweat and dried coffee. For once, he envied them.

With flair, one of them handed Paul a folder full of papers.

"Why don't you summarize it for me, Mr. Beyer?" asked Paul as he opened the folder.

The associate exchanged a look with his fellows.

"What?" said Paul.

"It's only . . . well . . . I'm Bynes."

Paul looked up. He could have sworn that Beyer was the one with the mustache.

"Apologies. What do you have to show me?" asked Paul.

"Well, sir," said whichever one of them it was. "I think we've got him."

The associate gestured to the top document within the folder. "That is an interview with Thomas Edison in *The New York Sun* from October twentieth, 1878. In it, he clearly states that his new electrical lamp consists of a glass bulb, hollowed out into a vacuum, with a platinum filament inside. The filament is the part that glows."

"I know what a filament is," said Paul.

"Well, Edison's patent, granted January twenty-seventh, 1880, refers to a glass bulb, hollowed out into a vacuum, with a *cotton* filament inside. He changed the filament."

Paul realized what this meant. "He told the press he was using one kind of filament. But by the time he filed for the patent, he was already using a different kind. He hadn't gotten the lamp to work as early as he'd claimed."

"Yes," said the boy.

"But," added one of the associates who Paul was certain was neither Beyer nor Bynes, "that's not even the best part. All that proves is that Edison lied to the press."

"Which is not a crime," said the one with the mustache.

"Right," said the fourth of the associates. "So then what if we can show that Edison lied on the patent itself?"

"That would be something, Mr. . . . ?"

"I'm Beyer," said the boy.

Paul had a hard time believing that to be the case, but it could not have mattered to him less.

Beyer continued. "The bulbs that have been coming out of Edison General Electric plants use *bamboo* filaments." He showed Paul a sketch of the device in question. There was no mistaking the material that composed the filament, even to a layman's eyes.

"First he told the press it was platinum," said Paul. "Then he told the patent office it was cotton. But it's actually bamboo."

"Yes."

"He was just making things up. He didn't actually get the bulb working with bamboo till *after* the patent was granted."

This was the moment Paul had been waiting for. The four associates tried to hide their proud smiles behind professionally blank expressions. They'd done well, and they knew it. But they seemed to feel that convincing Paul of their competence required masking their youthful exuberance. Watching these boys pretend to be older than they were made Paul feel even older himself.

"What will you do now?" asked the mustached associate, who was probably Bynes.

Paul did not try to hide his smile. "I think it's time that we took the deposition of Mr. Thomas Edison."

CHAPTER 42

The Deposition of Thomas Edison

Everybody steals in science and industry. I've stolen a lot
myself. But I know how to steal. They don't know how to
steal.
—THOMAS EDISON

OR OVER A year, the name Edison had haunted Paul's days. He
had met Thomas Edison only once, and yet the inventor was
ever present in his thoughts. His daily life was a groove in the
invisible orbit around Edison's solar mass. Practically every slip of
paper that crossed Paul's desk bore Edison's name. Edison's presence
dominated the work of Paul's waking hours and often his sleeping
ones. He had spent many times more hours dreaming of Edison than
speaking to him.

Paul arrived early for the deposition. At barely seven in the morning, he entered Grosvenor Lowrey's Broad Street law offices. The
wallpapered rooms crackled with activity. Assistants, apprentices,
secretaries, and errand boys flitted about in preparation, bursting with
energy. As Paul waited, the whole office primped itself for the great
man's arrival. The brass was polished with vinegar, the wood rubbed
with alcohol and wax, and every stray paper was tucked into a drawer
or filing cabinet.

When Edison finally arrived, late, Paul was instantly struck by the
change in his appearance. He'd aged in the past year. His hair had

gone almost completely gray. He'd grown plumper around the middle. His clothes had been applied haphazardly.

He was, in short, a human being. And that seemed strangest of all. The devil himself could barely knot his own bow tie.

Edison sat at the long table as if this deposition was but one of the many chores to which he would be forced to attend that morning. No doubt it was. He whispered a few words to Lowrey, his attorney, who took the seat to his left. To Edison's right sat the court secretary, here to transcribe his every word.

"All right," said Edison. "Let's get this over with."

"Good morning," said Paul, fastidiously laying out his papers on the table.

"And you are?"

Paul stopped. Edison smiled. The inventor was taunting him. Trying to rattle him before the questioning had even begun. Edison's act was terribly good. He would feign a discombobulated indifference to these worldly affairs before lashing out at just the right moment.

"I am Paul Cravath, attorney for Mr. George Westinghouse."

The court secretary dutifully typed as the men spoke.

"Grosvenor Lowrey, attorney for Mr. Thomas Edison."

"And I am Thomas Alva Edison."

"Please state your place of birth, for the record," said the court secretary.

"Ohio. But I grew up in Port Huron, Michigan."

"And the place where you currently reside?"

"I have an estate in West Orange, New Jersey. I have my offices at sixty-five Fifth Avenue, New York City."

The secretary nodded. "It is March eleventh, 1889," she informed the room. "Mr. Cravath, you may begin."

Paul had been practicing his questions for days.

"What was the first thing you invented, Mr. Edison?"

Edison laughed. "It was a . . . well, it's called an automatic repeater."

"And when was this?"

"Is George Westinghouse planning on claiming that he invented that now too?"

"What year was it?"

"Eighteen sixty-five. I'd been a butcher boy before that, selling candy on the rails. Left home with a single bag to my name. Rode the line for a few years. I learned the trains well. Found odd jobs, here and there. Things that needed fixing, repairing. I've always had a way with machines."

"So it would appear."

"I became friendly with the Western Union men at the stations. Now, they had some fun devices, didn't they? I started to do what it is that I've always done. I tinkered. I asked a lot of questions. Some the men could answer, some they could not. If not, then I was required to develop my own answers. There were things they would discuss— I would overhear their conversations. *If only we could loop messages automatically. If only we had a device to relay the signals.* But then they wouldn't do a thing about it. They would just move along, drown their complaints in their beer. So I did what it is that I have done ever since: I recognized a problem, and then I set about solving it. There was use for a small machine that might automatically relay telegraph messages? Fantastic. I spent a few months fiddling until I'd built one that worked."

"And then," said Paul, "you sold the design to Gold and Stock. For two hundred dollars."

"You know this story?"

"You've recited it many times to the press."

"It's a good story."

"It's a very simple one," said Paul. "But your tales of invention always are, aren't they?"

"This is what your kind—and let the record reflect that by 'your' I am referring to Mr. Cravath and by 'kind' I am referring to idiots— can never wrap your brains around. It genuinely is simple. I identify the gap in existing technology and then I plug it. With these hands right here. Oh. I just realized. You were trying to get a rise out of me, weren't you?"

"If Mr. Cravath is being argumentative," offered Lowrey, "I can instruct the court—"

"No, no, Grosvenor," said Edison. "Mr. Cravath and I are just having a bit of fun with each other, aren't we?"

Paul agreed, silently. He had expected some sparring. He would have been disappointed without it.

"This process you've described," said Paul. "Your plugging. You've applied it ever since?"

"After the repeater, Western Union made me a deal. I invented a number of things for them. And then I came to New York, where I opened up my own shop. A place to tinker."

"You were a teenage vagabond. Riding the rails. And by twenty-two, you'd made it to New York."

"And by thirty I was a millionaire. People seem to find some value in my tinkerings, it would seem. From the telegraph to the telephone to the phonograph to the light bulb. They were all problems, out there for the solving. I did so, and have—no thanks to your efforts—been comfortably compensated for it."

"You invented the telephone?" asked Paul.

"Yes."

"Funny. I thought Alexander Graham Bell did that."

"It's a lie," said Edison, "but so far the courts have failed to recognize the truth of what happened. I invented the telephone, not him. I had the idea; I crafted the device. He just got his application to the patent office before I did."

"Whoever files first holds the patent."

"Says the lawyer. To which the inventor at this table says, 'Why?' Why should it be so? It wasn't always."

"That's true. The courts have not always held that the first to file gets the patent. But they do now."

"Men like you have reduced my profession to a game of paperwork. It's tedious, and it's absurd."

"You weren't first to the telephone," said Paul, "but here you are claiming the invention was yours. What about the light bulb?"

"Much to your chagrin, the courts have steadfastly upheld my claim on that."

"We're working on it."

"I was first to the light bulb."

"Were you, though? Surely the 'problem,' as you put it, had been around for decades. A thousand engineers had tried to create indoor electrical lamps."

"But only I succeeded."

"What about Sawyer and Man?"

"What about them?"

"Their patent on incandescent light—which my client licensed—predates yours by a few years."

"I suppose so," said Edison indifferently. "But their device wasn't complete. It didn't work. Their patent was quite broad. It was a suggestion of the thing, not the thing itself."

"For instance," offered Paul, "the Sawyer and Man patent did not specify a type of filament?"

Edison's face lit up. "Oh my! That's very technical coming from you. Yes. The Sawyer and Man patent suggests, among its vagaries, that there should be some sort of carbonized filament. A thin thread in the center, which emits light when it gets hot. But it doesn't go further on that point, or on many others."

"And then on your patent claim, you did specify a filament, didn't you?"

"I most certainly did."

"And what was that filament?"

Edison gestured to the papers on the table. "You must have the claim among that pile of documents before you."

"I want you to tell me. For the record." Paul nodded toward the typist.

"You will be disappointed, then," said Edison. "I'm not sure I remember."

"Then I'll help. Your application says it was a cotton filament."

"All right."

Paul selected one of the papers from his neat piles. "Was it?"

"Was it what?"

"Was it a cotton filament that, after decades of trying, finally made the lamp work?"

"Yes."

"Are you sure? Because you told the *New York Herald* that it was made of platinum."

"As you said earlier, Mr. Cravath, I give many interviews."

"Is there cotton in the bulbs that you currently ship to your customers?"

"What are you getting at?"

"It isn't bamboo?"

Lowrey spoke quickly. "Don't answer that."

"I'm happy to," said Edison.

"Don't," insisted Lowrey.

Edison turned his wrath away from Paul and toward his own attorney. "I said that I'll answer, Grosvenor. Don't give me that goddamned look." He turned his attention back to Paul. "It's all three."

"All three?"

Edison shook his head. "You have never understood what it is that I do."

"So tell me."

Edison leaned forward, resting his elbows on the table. "I create things, Mr. Cravath. Things that did not exist before. Someone like you will never understand what it is to bring something new into the dull world."

"Didn't your staff do that? All the engineers in your lab. The army of technicians who do the actual work of experimentation at EGE."

"Yes," said Edison. "That's my point exactly. I hired those engineers. I set them to their task. I defined the scope of their inquiry and then set the method by which they might inquire. For a century scientists had failed to build an indoor electrical lamp. Until me. How did I do it? That's what you want to hear? It was this: I surveyed all the designs that had been tried before. I saw what had gotten close; I saw what had fallen short of the mark. I found the cracks and I set my men to paving them. This is what science is, Mr. Cravath. This is what discovery is. It's not a flash of color. It's not a moment of divine inspiration. It is not the hand of God reaching down to press the pointed finger. It's work. It's drudgery. It is trying ten thousand different shapes of bulb. Then trying ten thousand different air fillings. Then, yes, ten thousand different filaments. It is realizing that those are the three components that matter and then trying ten thousand times ten thousand times ten thousand combinations until one of them works. And then selling it to a public who never thought such a thing was possible. It is this last part that you are really accusing me of. And of that, I will confess. I am guilty as sin. Yes, Mr. Cravath, I sold the light bulb. Americans did not have them. Then they did. Then they bought them by the trainload, and is there any part of you that doubts you owe all of that to me? Is there any part of you that believes that without me Americans would have electrical light inside their homes? Of course not. You want the light but you don't want to know how I made it. You privilege the effect, but you're horrified that someone had actually to cause it. I invented the goddamned light bulb. I gestated it in the minds of the public. You whine to me about filaments. Platinum, cotton, bamboo? There were ten thousand more. My patent covers all of them. George Westinghouse can twiddle with his idle details. He so loves his details, doesn't he? This precise shape of bulb, this precise angle of wiring. That's all well and good. But knowing the steps is hardly any good if you've failed to make it to the dance. I hired the band; I booked the hall. I advertised the show. And you hate me because my name is on the poster. Well, I say this: The light bulb is mine. If the word 'invention' is to maintain even a semblance of rational sense, then it must be said that the light bulb was my idea. It was my invention. And it is my patent. Every bulb. Every vacuum. Every one of your piddling filaments. And to the mute ingratitude with which you've repaid me, I will say only one last thing."

Edison leaned back in his chair before he loosed his final words.

"You're welcome."

CHAPTER 43

Fail, Fail, and Fail Again

Sometimes we stare so long at a door that is closing that we
see too late the one that is open.

—ALEXANDER GRAHAM BELL

I T CAME AS little surprise when, two months later, a New York federal court ruled against the Westinghouse Electric Company in the
central light-bulb suit. Paul had been prepared for this defeat since
Edison's deposition. The argument Edison had made to Paul was repeated by Lowrey in court. It was undeniably effective.

Thomas Edison had not patented the *perfect* light bulb, agreed the
judge. He'd patented the *field* of light bulbs. That he'd later improved
on his design, and that Westinghouse had potentially improved on it
even further, was beside the point. Westinghouse's bulbs infringed on
Edison's patent, even if Edison's exact patent was for a device that
didn't work as intended. Paul's strategy had been to narrow the scope
of Edison's patent to a nonexistent, nonfunctioning device; in response, Edison had succeeded in broadening the scope of his patent to
include practically anything that lit up.

In court, Hughes had done almost all the arguing for the Westinghouse side. Carter had supplied the gaps. Paul had barely gotten a
word on the record. He wanted to attribute the loss to his partners'
stodgy techniques. But he knew in his heart that it wasn't their fault.

Edison's genius extended not only to science, but apparently to litigation as well.

Spring had sprinkled Manhattan with bunchberry, violet, and rose mallow as Paul and his partners drearily descended the steps of the lower Manhattan courthouse. They would appeal. Paul had already begun to prepare the paperwork. The New York court would not be the end of *Edison v. Westinghouse*. The federal court of appeals would be next. And if that failed . . . there were higher courts still, and Paul could only hope to fall from ever-taller heights.

To further blacken Paul's mood, the light-bulb suit was not even the only battle he lost that month. Paul also found himself on the wrong side of the New York State Legislature in Albany. The electrical chair was approved for use by the people's elected representatives. Now Paul would have to take this battle to the courts as well, arguing that this state law was invalid on constitutional grounds. Electrocution, Paul would argue, constituted the very definition of "cruel and unusual punishment" forbidden by the Constitution.

He would have to make this argument quickly, because soon enough some New Yorker was bound to be sentenced to death by Westinghouse's alternating current.

Paul's failures did not end there. He was soon summoned to the Huntingtons' sitting room.

He could hear Tesla pacing the floor above them. He had barely visited the house since his mortifying conversation with Fannie. His work had given him ample excuses, so his evening visits had grown infrequent and brief. Surely Fannie had told Agnes about their attorney's unfortunate offer. He could not bear to be alone with Agnes, for fear that she might bring it up. His best hope was for his infatuation to be forgotten by all involved. No doubt outings with Mr. Henry Jayne would be enough to occupy Agnes's attention.

Sitting across from Paul in her typical finery, Agnes wore the same uncracked Mona Lisa look that she wore whenever her mother was present. At one point Paul had imagined he understood some of what lay behind that smile. Now he was certain that he did not.

"Since my daughter's interview," said Fannie, "which you so helpfully arranged, we've heard no more from that vile Mr. Foster. You have, we believe, succeeded. We are quite grateful." Paul looked to Agnes for reaction. He found none.

"Thank you," he replied. "It has been my pleasure, I assure you."

"I'm sure you'll understand, then, when I suggest that your friend upstairs should therefore take his leave of this house."

Paul had expected this from Fannie eventually. But now? "Mr. Tesla has nowhere else to go," he said. "If I could depend on your hospitality just a little longer . . ."

"We cannot have him here any longer. I trust you to understand."

Agnes turned away. This was not her plan, he could tell that much. Nor was it her wish. But she wasn't prepared to go against her mother.

Fannie went on. "The thrust of the matter is that we're having some people for dinner in four days' time. Thursday evening. The Jayne family." Paul thought he saw the hint of a smile as she spoke. "We haven't been able to receive guests since Mr. Tesla took up residence here. I'd ask you to see to it that he's departed by then. I wish it could be helped."

If the parents of Henry La Barre Jayne were visiting the Huntingtons' considerably more humble home for dinner, then they were vetting Agnes. Agnes must have done quite well in the courtship thus far. And so the real subject of their visit would be Fannie. She was the one up for judgment. A potential marriage into a family of fortune and stature could not be allowed to be jeopardized by the presence of Nikola Tesla.

"I understand" was all that Paul could say in response.

"We are very sorry about this," said Agnes. This was the first she'd spoken since Paul had arrived. "I'm so very sorry."

"I will see that my friend is removed from your hospitality by Thursday," said Paul. He rose to his feet, buttoning his black jacket in what he hoped appeared to be a gesture of professionalism. "Your patience has been appreciated. And I hope that I might continue to represent you."

He had started for the doorway when Agnes spoke again. "Where will you take him?"

Paul had no immediate answer to her question. Could any other corner of New York be safe from Edison's grasp? He could check Tesla into a mountain sanitarium somewhere . . . except that sanitariums required nurses and groundskeepers and window cleaners.

What Paul needed to do was to remove Tesla to a place where money could not reach. A place where Edison's connections would do him no good. A place where the lights still flickered from melting wicks.

"Miss Huntington," said Paul as he arrived upon an unpleasant solution, "have no fear. Mr. Tesla will be perfectly safe. I've another place I can keep him."

CHAPTER 44

The Prodigal Cravath Returns

I believe it is worthwhile trying to discover more about the world, even if this only teaches us how little we know. It might do us good to remember from time to time that, while differing widely in the various little bits we know, in our infinite ignorance we are all equal.   —KARL POPPER

A GNES INSISTED THAT she accompany Paul and Tesla to Nashville. The forcefulness of her demand came as a surprise, both to Paul and to Fannie. Paul knew that Agnes had come to care greatly for Tesla. He'd spent too many nights with them in the attic room to doubt that. But he had not realized just how much of a fight she would put up to remain alongside him.

Paul would not have thought that Agnes could ever convince her mother to acquiesce to the trip. Yet somehow she did. Whatever backstage dramas went on in the Huntington house, the two women's negotiations were hidden from him. Whatever Agnes said to her mother was unknown. Whatever Fannie would extract in return was unimaginable. But ultimately Fannie relented. Dinner with the Jaynes was postponed for a week and an understudy given a chance to shine at the Met. All so that Agnes could make certain that Tesla arrived safely in Tennessee.

Had Fannie softened her grip? Or had Agnes hardened her rebellion? Perhaps the warm thoughts of a Jayne courtship had relaxed Fannie's worry. Perhaps Agnes had grown bolder in her demands for a life outside a polished glass case.

The journey to Nashville took two separate railroad lines and a transfer through Cincinnati. The travelers employed three first-class sleeping quarters. Agnes consumed herself with practicalities. Seats, meals, tickets, departure times. Tesla was quiet and rarely left the sleeping car. This had been his first journey outside in months, and it clearly overwhelmed him. That first night, Paul heard Agnes sing him to sleep through the wall of the car. He realized that he had only ever heard her sing before at the Players' Club. Tesla had evidently become a frequent private audience. As Paul turned his ear to the wall and strained to better hear the sound, he knew that Tesla was a lucky man.

Paul spent much of the trip worried about how Agnes would react to Nashville. He imagined that she would recoil from the Cravaths' humble three-story. He couldn't even fathom what she'd make of his father. But during their meals together, she mostly discussed Tesla. The slow process of his recovery, a recent update from her alienist. She left little doubt as to on whose behalf she had undertaken this journey.

Paul's offer of a Sunday walk went unmentioned over the two-day trip. So did the name Henry Jayne. She was kind enough not to rub it in Paul's face. He was appreciative. Between the crowd in the dining car and the time spent caring for Tesla, they were rarely alone. He had blessedly little opportunity to further embarrass himself in front of his client. He enjoyed her company so much that he was almost able to forget that this was likely the last time he ever would.

It was dawn when a terrific scream of brakes announced the arrival of the Louisville Railroad's Train No. 5 at the Nashville depot. The conductors roused yawning passengers from their seats. Paul hopped the single step from the train onto the platform. His eyes took a moment to adjust to the golden Tennessee light, the bloom of a late-spring day that was just promising to begin.

Behind him, Agnes led Tesla out into the sunshine. She looked bleary-eyed; he was awake, if typically catatonic.

As Paul exited the station, he could see a familiar figure standing tall beneath the willows.

"My son," said Erastus Cravath, extending his hand.

A firm handshake was Erastus's preferred greeting. It always had been.

Paul turned to introduce his companions, but his father beat him to the punch.

"And you," said Erastus, "must be Miss Huntington." He bowed politely. She returned the gesture with unpretentious grace.

"Your son has told me so much about you, sir. It's an honor to finally meet you."

"Oh, my dear, you mustn't listen to too much of what Paul tells you. He does so like to exaggerate."

"Father," interrupted Paul, "this is Nikola Tesla."

"My, you're tall. And it's a great pleasure to make your acquaintance as well." He extended a hand, but the inventor merely stared off into the distance. He seemed largely unaware that there were human beings around him. Or that one of them, Paul's father, was attempting to say hello.

"You are unwell, my friend," he said. "I understand. Let us see if we cannot get you better."

He gestured to Big Annie, the family horse that Paul had named in his childhood. She was tied to a post beside the family's carriage, which was older than she was.

Paul and his father didn't speak much during the hour-long ride back to the house. Instead, Paul pointed out various sights to his guests. Though Paul had been born in Ohio, the family had moved to Nashville when he was five. His sister, Bessie, had been born soon thereafter. Bessie was off and married now to a respectable husband in Clarksville. She wrote to him occasionally. He didn't always have the time to respond.

Nashville had grown since Paul had last ridden up the Cumberland River. The noisy docks now teemed with young workingmen, a generation of laborers who'd been able to trade farm tools for barrel lifts.

Erastus and Ruth Cravath lived in a three-story farmhouse northwest of the town center. It was quite a hike from the university, but

Paul's mother appreciated the separation from her husband's working life. The Cravaths had selected the farmhouse for its spiritual simplicity, not its practical comforts. They had never made any proper attempt at farming. They kept no livestock in the adjacent barn, save their few horses for transportation. They grew no crops. With Paul in New York and Erastus traveling so much to raise funds, there was no one around the house that could be counted upon for field labor. The barren acres surrounding the house stretched to the horizon.

The slanted wooden roof had worn since Paul had last laid eyes on it. The whole house seemed to have fallen into a state of comfortable dishabille. Neither Erastus nor Ruth would demand thicker windows or sturdier front steps until one of those parts had completely broken. In Paul's childhood, no one wanted for anything they truly needed, but no one had anything they might merely want.

The house was the color of Tennessee dirt.

"Hello, Mother," Paul said as he pushed open the squeaky screen door. "I'm home."

CHAPTER 45

All Happy Families . . .

> Technology is nothing. What's important is that you have a
> faith in people, that they're basically good and smart, and if
> you give them tools, they'll do wonderful things with them.
>
> —STEVE JOBS

IT TOOK A long day for Paul and Agnes to explain their rather unique predicament to Erastus and Ruth Cravath. In letters, Paul had described the basic events of the past eighteen months: Tesla, Westinghouse, Edison. He'd told them about his difficulties in court and the looming disaster surrounding the electrical chair. None of this information was new. But the fact that Paul and Agnes had conspired to house Tesla in secret, to keep him safe from Edison without even Westinghouse knowing . . . this was not a fit subject for a letter home. Ruth and the reverend both took it well. They seemed more concerned for Tesla's safety than anything else. Erastus's faith prized nothing so much as a man in need.

Ruth suggested that Tesla might take the bedroom that had belonged to Bessie. It hadn't yet been cleared of her childhood detritus. But Erastus hoped that Tesla wouldn't mind the clutter.

"It's a kind thing you're doing," said Agnes to Ruth.

Ruth shrugged. "It's a kind thing you've already done."

"He might be here for . . . a little while," said Paul.

"It would be our pleasure, my son," said Erastus. He turned to Tesla, who sat straight-backed on the sofa. "Would you like me to show you to your room?"

Tesla stared straight ahead, his eyes fixed on a point midway up the white wall. The activity of the past days seemed to have caused his recovery to regress.

"The universe wears coats. The universe wears shirts. The universe shall be unbuttoned."

Everyone stared at Tesla for a moment. "We'll get him well," said Ruth.

Later that night, after his parents had retired to bed, Paul came out onto the back porch to find Agnes sneaking a cigarette. It startled him for a moment to see her there, on the porch of his childhood home. The moon lit her curly hair better than any light bulb ever could.

"Miss Huntington," he whispered.

She looked as if she'd been caught committing a crime.

"Sorry. I know your father hates smoke."

"I won't tell if you won't."

He sat next to her on the porch. The old wood creaked under his weight. "I know how much you've done for Nikola. Thank you."

"Ah. Well." She took an inhale. "It's not as if he has anyone else."

She gazed out at the night sky. She puffed a plume of smoke into the air and watched it disintegrate between the stars. A colony of crickets hummed from the faraway weeds.

"Have you ever met someone so alone?" she said suddenly.

"He's the emperor of his own private kingdom."

"He's its only inhabitant."

"Yes."

"So that makes him its slave as well."

She seemed reflective. Almost philosophical. She'd been that way since they'd arrived. He wasn't sure what had brought about the change in her demeanor. On previous occasions on which Paul had seen Agnes delivered from her mother's peering gaze, she'd been fiery and playful. Now she was wistful.

All Paul's worries on the train about how she would take to Nashville had proved unnecessary. She'd made herself very much at home. She'd been friendly with his parents. She'd insisted on helping Ruth make up Tesla's bed. Agnes settled into what had once been Paul's childhood bedroom like a long-lost cousin.

She took another puff of her fading cigarette. "Nikola Tesla arrived in Manhattan with, what, a few nickels in his pocket? He was homeless. He had no job, no connections, no family or friends to rely on. Do you know what he had?" She gestured to her skull. "His mind. It was his very otherworldliness that made him what he is. He did not become the most famous inventor this side of Thomas Edison by playing the game so well—he did it by refusing to play at all. And as someone who's played awfully well myself, I respect him for it. I'd very much like to live in a world that doesn't see people like him eaten alive."

"And Henry La Barre Jayne?" asked Paul. "Would he agree?"

He'd never said the name aloud to her before. His voice sounded petulant, even to himself.

"You apparently have a lot of opinions about someone you know nothing about."

"That was mean."

"It was."

Paul had avoided this conversation for two days on the train. He'd avoided it many times in New York. But the intimacy of having Agnes in his parents' house made him feel unable to preserve such polite silence any longer.

"I've spent my life coming in second place to men with last names like Jayne. You'd think I'd be used to it by now."

"Second place?"

Paul searched her face. Her mother had apparently not told her about his invitation to a Sunday walk among the flowers. Was this a generous act on Fannie's part? It had saved Paul some measure of embarrassment, without his knowing. Yet he no longer had anything to lose by honesty.

"I asked your mother if I might take you walking," he confessed. "She informed me of the time you've spent in the company of Mr. Jayne."

"That sounds like the kind of thing I'd expect from my mother."

"I'm sorry for insulting him," said Paul. "It wasn't fair of me."

"I'm sorry that my mother embarrassed you," said Agnes in turn. "She is . . . complicated. As is the situation."

Paul looked at her curiously. He wasn't sure what she meant.

She appeared to be in the midst of making a very difficult decision. Paul stayed quiet. If she was going to say something to him, something difficult, he would let her make that decision on her own.

"Look," she said at last. "There's a lot about all of this—my mother, Henry Jayne—that you don't know. And . . . well, I want to tell you."

"All right," said Paul.

"But I'm afraid to."

Of all the emotions she'd expressed to him, fear had never been among them. Edison had not frightened her, nor had Stanford White, nor had the danger of keeping Tesla in her home. What was scaring her?

"You can trust me," said Paul. "If nothing else . . . I'm your lawyer."

She smiled for a moment. "I lied to you."

"About what?" He watched her struggle to find the words. "Miss Huntington?"

"That's just the thing," she said at last. "My name isn't Agnes Huntington."

CHAPTER 46

But Each Unhappy Family . . .

The history of science, like the history of all human ideas, is
a history of irresponsible dreams.   —KARL POPPER

SHE HAD BEEN born Agnes Gouge in Kalamazoo, Michigan. Her
mother, Fannie, was not then the high-society maven Paul had
met; she was a maid. Agnes's father had sailed deep-water.
Once, when she was eight, she'd received a letter from him. The post-
mark was Oslo. He'd sketched the serene harbor for her, and inquired
as to her health. He'd left no address at which to reach him. And
she'd never heard from him again.

She'd always loved to sing. The upstairs neighbors would bang
their boots against the ceiling, but she didn't care. Neither did her
mother.

When Agnes was fourteen, Fannie moved them to Boston, where
she scrubbed floors and polished china plates for the Endicotts while
Agnes auditioned for the Bijou. The parts went to local girls whose
parents knew the manager. Agnes got a job sweeping stages at the
Howard Athenaeum, but it wasn't what she'd imagined. She did not
find herself amid a tight-knit group of artists. There was no creative
camaraderie in which to conspire. She was the sweeping girl, the
singers were the singers, and the stagehands were sauced. It was as

much a bordello as a theater. Though a bordello might at least have been profitable.

Boston wasn't working. Fannie had seen her daughter's tears, had felt the pain of her unrealized ambitions from the moment they left Michigan. She knew how much Agnes wanted this, and she also knew that the daughters of housemaids didn't become *prime donne*. Fannie had to watch her precocious, inquisitive, curious daughter learn cynicism. That was what she could not stand.

Agnes had no idea how long her mother had been planning it when it happened. Whether it was a spur-of-the-moment decision or whether her mother had set the whole affair up months before.

One day, when she was seventeen, Agnes came home to find a dress lying across her bed. The dress was of a color that Agnes had never before seen. It was green, bright but somehow still subtle. The shade of orchid leaves, lady's mantle, saxifrage. The shade of a far-away ocean. She gasped when she saw it, when her eyes caught the glimmer of afternoon light from the dirty, square window. At the top of the dress, resting delicately over the silk, was a string of diamonds.

Agnes stepped closer. She reached out to touch the fabric, but pulled her hand back. She was afraid to press her grease-stained fingertips against such a cloth. This dress, these jewels, did not belong to anyone she knew. Or anyone she might know. They were a princess's evening wear.

"Do you like it?" Agnes turned to see Fannie in the doorway, smoking a thin cigarette.

"What is it?"

"It's a dress," said Fannie. "And it's yours."

"You . . ." Agnes couldn't believe what she was going to say. "You . . . stole it?"

"It comes from the dressing room of Miss Endicott. So do the jewels. The girl is about your age—a little younger. It might be a little wide around the bust, but we can take it in."

"You stole a dress from Mary Endicott?" Agnes was dumbfounded, terrified. The family would discover the loss, and her mother had been polishing their silver for just long enough to be the first likely suspect. The police would be at their door within days.

That's when her mother explained. They were going to leave Boston and they were going to do it that very night. They would take a coach steamer to Paris, packing the dress in their valise. Agnes would board the steamer in her normal clothes, and she would disembark in green silk. She would leave Boston Harbor as a sweeping girl . . . and she would arrive in Paris the daughter of new California money.

"Miss Agnes Huntington," her mother had said. "Doesn't that sound nice?"

"I don't know who that is," Agnes had protested.

"Exactly. No one does. But soon enough, everyone will."

With only an impossibly expensive dress and a string of gems, the teenage Agnes would be reborn in Paris. There, she could be anyone she wanted. There were enough moneyed Huntingtons roaming the world that no one would be sure from which line she'd descended, and if she worked her manners, no one would be rude enough to ask. Agnes was beautiful, her mother had explained. She was radiant. She was funny. She was both smart and clever, which were never quite the same thing, and she was enormously talented. The only thing holding her back in America was her family.

"But what about you?"

Fannie would be there as well. Waiting in the wings. Silent and unseen, Fannie would be backstage, awaiting her daughter's triumph.

The police wouldn't be able to find her in Paris—they'd never look that far afield. But they would most certainly be looking. The Endicotts were not a family to be trifled with. So forever, even if their deceit were to be successful, Fannie would have to stay in her daughter's shadow.

"I'm afraid."

"I know," her mother had answered. "But I love you. And that's why we're going to do this."

Fannie had moved close and kissed Agnes once on her forehead. And then Fannie had packed both of their bags while Agnes puttered and paced, too shocked to argue or do anything but what she'd been asked.

They boarded the Cunard Line steamer bound for Europe that very evening.

And that was the last anyone had ever seen of Agnes or Fannie Gouge.

In steerage, Agnes kept the dress hidden for the duration of the trip, clutching her bag even while she slept. Only on that final morning had her mother removed the green cloth from its cover. The other women in their steerage cabin were incredulous. Agnes and Fannie said nothing.

Agnes had heard of a café from some men on the boat, gentlemen from the first-class cabin whom she passed as they smoked on the communal deck. It sounded, from the snatches of description she'd been able to overhear, like a good place for introductions. On her second day in Paris, she left the cheap women's boardinghouse Fannie had found and asked for directions.

Agnes sat with her café au lait along the Boulevard Saint-Marcel wearing a high-society evening gown and matching necklace at eleven in the morning. But after twenty minutes, she was approached by a tall man with slick black hair and an old wool coat. He was actually quite handsome.

He addressed her in French, which of course she did not speak.

"Pardon," she said. "Would you like to try that in English?"

"You're a touch overdressed for the morning."

She looked him up and down. "I should say you'd be better off with a bit of dressing up yourself."

The man laughed at her insult and helped himself to the seat opposite.

There was a party the following night. There was always a party, she would learn. He invited her, and when she accepted, he asked where he might claim her on the evening in question.

"Why, right here, of course!" she answered. "Won't you want a cup before a long night out? Unless," she added, "you don't think it's going to be a very long night."

He assured her that it was. And when he came to pick her up in his two-horse carriage the next evening, she found that he wasn't wrong.

If he noticed that she was wearing the same green dress as on the day before, he made no comment about it. She would come to learn that his sort never did.

It took her only three more parties before she found someone to buy her another dress. His name was Coulter, and he was friendly with Monsieur Jacques Doucet himself. Surely she'd appreciate a little something from his shop? Her collection of gowns grew in direct proportion with her collection of gentleman admirers. A silk baron, a minor aristocrat of the old order, a German banker who found himself frequently in Paris at the House of Lazard. None needed any prompting to send her a little something.

Her mother was her only female companion in that first year. The women of Paris society were competitive, and they could smell a rat, even when their brothers and husbands and fathers could not. But what were they to do except to exclude Agnes from their teas? To gossip about her incessantly? To keep her name on their lips in snide and disparaging tones?

She returned nightly to her mother, who'd given her everything and who'd received nothing, yet, in return.

If the social intrigue stung on occasion, the pain was easily balmed by the singing. Agnes made her debut during a party at Thomas Hentsch's mansion. The crowd was more than receptive and her name was passed around. First she sang at parties, and then an offer came to sing at the Théâtre du Châtelet. When she closed her eyes mid-song, when she felt the air in her throat and the rapt audience before her, it was everything she'd ever imagined. If she could ignore the circumstances of her arrival, she was at home.

People said that Agnes could bring even the most stoic of audiences to tears with her voice. If that was true, it was because she knew of what she sang.

After a year the Huntingtons decamped for London. Agnes used the reputation she'd built up in Paris to arrive fully formed across the Channel. And this time, her mother "arrived" to meet her from California. They had enough money, at this point, for even Fannie to acquire the accoutrements of society. The West End theater owners clamored to book Agnes before she'd even arrived. She and Fannie passed a few successful years there. The Earl of Harewood had taken a fancy to her. She'd taken a lovely sail with the Duke of Fife. And then back to Paris, where she was hailed as a returning champion.

After touring Europe, Agnes returned to Boston at the age of twenty-one as the toast of the Continent. She was welcomed with open arms into the opera houses and parlor rooms of the Back Bay, rooms that she would never have been able to enter before. And she went unrecognized. As did Fannie. Who would even remember a poor, sad sweeping girl named Agnes Gouge? Agnes Huntington was the toast of the European elite to which all American classes aspired. A certain green dress and its accompanying diamonds had long been sold off. Fannie stayed away from the parties, away from the opening nights. She stayed very far away from the Endicotts. Her face went unseen in Boston society, even as her name was mentioned frequently in connection with Agnes's.

They'd gotten away with it. The life that Agnes had won became so full that she believed it herself. She had not succumbed to cynicism; she had grown into the woman she'd dreamed. The talent of Agnes Huntington, the things that made her a star of the stage and a belle of the ball, were wholly real. No one else had made her who she was. And though she'd lied to get there, it was not the lies that echoed from the walls of the Metropolitan Opera House every night. It was the truth. The lie had only granted her a fair shot. She owed nothing to anyone except for one person, and that was a debt she would repay every day. Was Fannie difficult, controlling, omnipresent? Of course. Did Agnes relish the occasional night out? The infrequent tipsy moment, where she might be free of the perfect caution her mother expected of her? Well, of course. But if she resented her mother's wrath on occasion, that did not mean that she didn't love her. Fannie had given her everything.

"Why are you telling me all this?"

"Because I haven't told anyone else," she said. "And I thought . . . I wanted you to know why this is so important. Why I have to . . ."

"That's why your mother wants you married into the Jaynes. She's worried that one day this will all catch up to you. That someone will recognize Agnes Gouge in the face of Agnes Huntington."

She held his gaze.

"And that's why you hired me in the first place. It wasn't just about Foster making up stories. You could have handled that yourselves. You were worried he might start digging into your past. If your identity was exposed, all of this—everything you've done—would be for nothing."

Her smile was sad.

"Unless you have some manner of protection," concluded Paul. "Agnes Huntington is susceptible to accusation. But Agnes Jayne is not." Paul had to admire the brilliance of their plan. "No one would dare confront you. Even if the Endicotts found you, they wouldn't possibly suggest anything. They'd be eaten alive by the Jaynes."

"To go up against the Jaynes," she said, "would be like going up against Thomas Edison. Only a fool would attempt it."

"A fool like me?"

"Or like our eccentric friend in there."

Paul knew more than ever that he could never marry her. She deserved a peace that he could never afford. Did she care for him? Is that why she'd made her confession? He didn't know. Could she? He hoped so. But because he knew he cared for her, he let those hopes recede into the starlit night.

Paul reached out and took her hand. He hadn't decided to do it, it just happened. Their fingers intertwined suddenly. He wasn't sure if he'd wrapped his fingers around hers or if it was the other way around. Her skin felt warm.

"Sometimes I hate it so much," she said. "Always having to pretend."

Paul gripped her fingers tighter. "This is America," he said. "We're all pretending."

He looked up at the clear night sky. His eyes naturally traced the constellations among the bright stars. Dipper, Orion, Cassiopeia. He'd been spotting their hidden shapes from this very place since he was a boy. Yet the irony of constellations was that their shapes were but narratives imposed by an active mind. The brightest design among the heavens was in truth only what you imagined it to be. Glance across the stars differently, and the figures they formed were suddenly different as well. Blink once and you could draw the lines between them into anything you chose.

He leaned in and kissed her.

CHAPTER 47

The Morning After

> I do not think you can name many great inventions that
> have been made by married men.   —NIKOLA TESLA

T HE NEXT MORNING was a strange one. Paul woke late, having
slept fitfully on the downstairs couch. When he lifted his head
from the stiff pillows, he could already smell the coffee boiling
in its tin pot. By the time he'd dressed and made his way to the
kitchen, he found Agnes and Erastus engaged in conversation. The
mood was casual, familial. Paul attempted to read Agnes. He thought
of her lips, her fingers, the feeling of her body pressed against his as
they held each other close. When she looked at him in the kitchen,
did her mind race to such scenes too? In her smile he found no clues.
She said her hello, smiled warmly, and then turned back to Erastus's
discussion of Tesla. Erastus had ideas about the peculiar nature of
Tesla's mind. Teresa of Ávila had suffered similar hallucinations.
Might Tesla be blessed with a divine sight, as she had been?

They passed the morning in conversation with Paul's parents until
heading off to catch their noon train. After they had said farewell to
Tesla and Ruth, Erastus took Paul and Agnes to the station in silence
before offering his typically formal goodbye.

Paul spent a few cents on newspapers and a baked bun as they
waited on the platform. He needed to say something about the previ-

ous night, but he didn't know what. Or how. Should he apologize? Should he admit to having been ungentlemanly, given that she was soon to be engaged? Or should he tell her, one time, just so that the words might be loosed into the air, that he was in love with her?

"Miss Huntington," said Paul, fumbling. "I mean Agnes—"

"He's proud of you, you know," she said.

"What?" he asked.

"Your father is terribly proud of you, whether you realize it or not."

Clearly, his family had made some sort of impression on her. Perhaps, Paul thought, in the absence of her own family, she looked longingly to his.

Paul scoffed. "I find that hard to believe."

"You think that he's cold."

"I think that when he is reminded I exist, I am a terrible disappointment to him."

"How often has he come to see you in New York?"

Paul considered. "Once. On Fisk business."

"Or maybe that's how he put it to you."

"Why wouldn't he just tell me he wanted to see me?"

"God. You're so . . . manlike. Listen. Did you ever think that perhaps he doesn't think you're proud of *him*?"

The suggestion was absurd. "What in the world are you talking about?"

"You were the one who left, Paul. Not him. Imagine how he felt about that."

"What did he think I was going to do?"

"Teach at Fisk, preach in Nashville. He thinks you were the one who rejected him, and it's your approval for which he is wanting."

"That makes no sense at all. How could he think that?"

"Because," said Agnes as if it were the most obvious thing in the world, "the two of you are pretty much exactly alike."

Paul was quiet. No one had ever compared him to his father before.

"You should tell him," she said.

"That I'm proud of him?"

"That you respect him. That he's a good man, and an admirable one, and that you've always known that. That he's your family, and New York is just the place you've chosen to live."

Paul thought about this. How could Agnes, who'd met the man only the day before, know his father better than he did?

"I'll try."

This seemed enough for her.

"And . . . about last night," she said. "There's nothing you need to say. Nothing I expect you to do. This is where we are. This is who we are. I wish things were different, and I know you do too."

"I'm sorry that I kissed you."

"I'm not."

And then they both looked down. The feeling was too great to handle politely.

Paul looked at the newspaper stand beside him. A small headline, below the middle fold, instantly grabbed his attention.

Paul turned to the signboard that announced the schedule of arrivals and departures.

"I'm so sorry," he said. "I have to go. There's a train in five minutes." His mind was a jumble.

Agnes looked confused. "The Number Five doesn't leave for almost an hour."

"I'm going to Buffalo." He grabbed the newspaper and obliviously overpaid the boy behind the counter. "Look. There's been a murder. The article says that a Mr. William Kemmler, of Buffalo, has just been convicted of butchering his wife with an axe."

Agnes frowned as she read. "So?"

"So if he is sentenced to death, then he'll be executed with an A/C-powered electrical chair."

She looked up at him, knowing full well what this would mean for Paul. And for Tesla. "Go," she said.

He stood. "I'm so sorry," he said. "I wanted to . . . I should say . . ."

She waved him off. "Go."

"Goodbye, Miss Huntington," he said as he grabbed his luggage. His formality felt instantly ridiculous. "You'll be all right getting back to the city on your own?"

"I think I can manage just fine, Mr. Cravath."

He ran across the station.

CHAPTER 48

The Hatchet Man in Buffalo

We can't blame the technology when we make mistakes.

—TIM BERNERS-LEE

"I F IT PLEASE the court," said Paul in his most lawyerly baritone, "the use of an electrical device for performing an execution is not—"

"And I object again, Your Honor," said Harold Brown. "You have already ruled on the issue of this technology's fitness for use in capital punishment, and Mr. Cravath is attempting to re-litigate—"

"And you see, sir, not only am I not 're-litigating' but that's not even what 're-litigate' means. I would again like to object to Mr. Brown conducting this hearing without a proper lawyer present—"

"Both of you, be quiet," barked Judge Day, already annoyed at how the day had been progressing.

Paul had at first been surprised that Edison hadn't arranged for one of his real attorneys to handle this motion and had instead allowed Brown to run the show himself. It was certainly a show. Though Paul realized that that was perhaps the point. To the public, Edison still remained removed from Brown and the grim business of the electrical chair. The only thing was that Brown wasn't an attorney at all. Arguing with him was like arguing with a half-informed child. The legal community had discussed requiring that prospective lawyers pass a proficiency exam, but such proposals remained purely talk. One did not need to take any sort of test to practice law in New York. Brown had gotten a friendly firm to attest that he'd spent some time apprenticing with a local attorney, and that was enough for Judge Day. Harold Brown had every right to sit at the desk opposite Paul's and argue that William Kemmler should be executed by means of A/C.

"Mr. Cravath," said the judge, "I'm not going to waste time hearing arguments on this issue again."

"It is not my intention to rehash any of those arguments."

"So then, what *is* your intention?" asked the judge.

"Simply to point out that even if New York State has the right to electrocute a man with alternating current, the state lacks the equipment to do so."

The judge looked bewildered. This was not a line of argument that he'd anticipated. "How do you mean?"

"It's quite simple. The only company producing A/C electrical generators in New York State is the Westinghouse Electric Company. And my client has never sold a generator to the State of New York. Furthermore, my client has no intention of doing so. I would suggest that if you're keen on killing him with electricity, the state has no choice but to employ direct current."

"That is absurd!" yelled Brown. "Direct current is far too low voltage, it cannot possibly be—"

"Quiet," interrupted Judge Day once again. "Mr. Cravath has made an excellent point. But I will interrogate further: Cannot the state simply purchase a Westinghouse generator from one of the many citizens of New York who own one? I cannot imagine Mr. Brown here would have a hard time finding someone willing to sell."

"Yes, yes, Your Honor," said Paul. "I'm sure that Mr. Brown could browbeat a man into selling his firstborn. I'm sure he could get someone to sell him—or the state—an A/C generator. The problem is only that in such eventuality the seller has no legal right to sell, and the buyer no legal right to make use of his purchase."

Paul took a sheaf of papers from his desk and approached the judge's bench. "If it please the court, these are the bill of sale and licensing deals that the Westinghouse Electric Company makes with each purchaser of one of its A/C generators. Mostly these are small towns or neighborhoods. Occasionally a wealthy individual with a lot of ground to cover. This is what makes A/C so valuable—it covers many multiples the distance of D/C. But I digress. As you'll see, the standard language of this contract clearly states that the purchaser of one of these devices is forbidden from selling the device to a third party. We've aimed, from the very beginning, to make sure that Westinghouse devices have not gotten into the wrong hands. But as it prevents third-party resale, it thus also means that if anyone were to sell their A/C unit to the State of New York without the Westinghouse Electric Company's written approval—which I can assure you they won't receive—they'd be doing so in violation of their license to operate the unit in question. Which means that the state would possess the unit illegally, and would not be legally permitted to turn it on."

Judge Day read over the documents he'd been given. The language was clear-cut and ironclad. Carter and Hughes had written them. If Brown knew enough legal terminology to understand the contract, he'd quickly see that he'd lost.

Paul returned to his desk with a sense of satisfaction. His work with Westinghouse had not produced a great deal of successes in the legal realm; it was nice, for once, to have a victory.

"I've only one thing to add," said Harold Brown. "To clarify the situation that Mr. Cravath has described."

"Yes?" asked Judge Day.

"What if I was already in possession of one of Mr. Westinghouse's A/C units? A unit that I did have the legal right to sell to our friends in the state legislature?"

"My client has never sold you an A/C unit, I can promise you that. Any document you produce that might show such a thing would be a forgery."

"I agree with you, sir. The Westinghouse Electric Company has never, and will never, sell either my agents or me a licensed A/C system."

"All right."

"But the same cannot be said for all of Mr. Westinghouse's licensees."

While Paul had recuperated at Bellevue, Carter and Hughes had helped Westinghouse to license local manufacturers to build and distribute his electrical systems. Those local shops were their own corporations, which paid royalties to Westinghouse on the equipment they sold. They were also supposed to use the sales contracts that Westinghouse provided them—the contracts that Carter and Hughes had drawn up. If one had crafted its own language, it would have had to do so *specifically* for the purpose of double-crossing Westinghouse. This would have to have been planned ages ago, a Trojan horse in Westinghouse operations.

A small, round man stood up from the gallery. All eyes in the courtroom turned to see him walk down the center aisle and up to Harold Brown's desk.

"If it please the court," said Charles Coffin as he stood beside Brown. "I am the president of the Thomson-Houston Electric Company. I am a licensee for the Westinghouse Electric Company, and I have the right to sell generators to whomever I choose."

Paul turned to face the man he'd last seen in his own offices on the day he'd returned from Bellevue.

"This is a bill of sale," said Coffin, "for one A/C generator from my company to Harold Brown. It grants him the right to resell this device to whomever he chooses, on whatever terms he chooses. And the paperwork was drawn up by my people. Not by Mr. Cravath or his partners."

Coffin winked at Paul, who couldn't believe what he was seeing. His face flushed with anger. Thomson-Houston depended on Westinghouse for the entirety of its business—for its very survival. At this betrayal, Westinghouse would cut all ties to Coffin's company. What was Coffin thinking? Unless . . .

Coffin was realigning his company. He was switching sides.

"I am quite certain, Your Honor," said Paul, "that as soon as next week the Thomson-Houston Electric Company will announce that it's switching from A/C to D/C. And that it's partnering with Edison. I have no doubt that Mr. Coffin will be well compensated for this betrayal."

"I don't believe my dealings with Edison General Electric have a thing to do with today's proceedings. And of course my business is no longer any of yours."

It didn't take long for Judge Day to go over the documents, or to rule that they did in fact promise exactly what Coffin and Brown said they promised. A few minutes later Paul had lost, yet again.

"It was a good try," said Harold Brown as they all left the courtroom. "But not quite good enough."

"I will make it my mission to see that neither of you gets away with this," said Paul.

"Really?" said Coffin with a smile. "How?"

Paul opened his mouth to speak, but found himself without a suitable retort. He didn't have a move to make.

"Oh," added Brown. "And you may consider that payback for my office door. Did you really have to kick the goddamned thing down?"

CHAPTER 49

The Execution of William Kemmler

> Sometimes when you innovate, you make mistakes. It is
> best to admit them quickly, and get on with improving your
> other innovations.   —STEVE JOBS

O N AUGUST 6, 1889, William Kemmler was to be executed
upon a "chair" designed by Harold Brown. The chair would be
wired up to an A/C generator. The generator had been theorized by Nikola Tesla, perfected and integrated into a functional system by George Westinghouse, and then manufactured by Charles
Coffin. It would soon send over a thousand volts of alternating current into William Kemmler.

Brown had the gall to arrange invitations for both Westinghouse
and Paul. Westinghouse threw out the letter. Edison would not attend
either, of course. He'd made a few public comments about the brou-
haha in Buffalo, but he remained steadfastly "uninvolved." Reporters
who wrote about the "controversy" surrounding the debate between
D/C and A/C asked him whether he thought Westinghouse's current
would get the job done. Edison answered that Westinghouse's current
was a dreadful thing, and was fit for little else besides murder.

Which left Paul to attend the execution alone. He felt that someone on his side should be there. Paul had seen grisly scenes before.

He'd even seen a death by electricity, in the air above Broadway a year ago. He wasn't one to shy from the grotesque. If this was to be the end, Paul had no intention of covering his eyes.

Paul arrived at the New York State prison in Auburn at 6:00 A.M. A crowd had already gathered outside the gates. Reporters awaited the first news they could fire away to their editors. Citizens hoped for a glimpse of the dead killer. Paul muscled his way through the commotion. He was recognized by a few of the reporters. He didn't want to talk to anyone. Especially the press.

Inside the prison gates, Paul was led to a basement newly renovated for the proceedings. The walls had been painted, the windows polished, a fresh set of chairs brought in for the viewing gallery. Paul noticed two gas lamps along the walls. He almost laughed. They didn't need lighting. The morning sunshine poured into the clean basement from two tall windows. Thirty or so guests took their seats. There was little chitchat. Most of the men were physicians, come to see for themselves what the strange current did to human flesh. Two reporters had been granted attendance; the prison warden had personally selected them. A few criminal lawyers, the district attorney, and Kemmler's court-appointed defense lawyer represented the legal community. Judge Day was there. And so was Harold Brown.

"Good morning, Counselor," he said to Paul.

Paul took a chair a few rows behind Brown, at the back of the audience. This was not a performance at which one wanted orchestra seats.

It was near six-thirty when a pair of prison guards led the condemned man into the sunny basement. Paul realized that he'd never even seen Kemmler before. He didn't look like an axe murderer. Or not like what Paul might imagine an axe murderer to be. He was small, with a close-cropped beard and narrow eyes. He looked thin, as if the prison food had not been to his liking. His hair was dark, and his three-piece suit was a perfect summer gray.

The chair itself was quite simple. Just a tall-backed oak chair, of a dark and average color. The seat was lined with leather. Leather too were the straps across the arms.

"Gentlemen," said Kemmler to the assembled, "I wish you all good luck. I know where I am headed, and I know that it is a good place. I can only hope the same will be true of you."

Kemmler removed his jacket. He folded it gingerly and placed it on an unused chair.

He took the chair at the center of the room. "Now, there's no rush. So take your time, and make sure you do the job right."

The two guards placed electrodes on Kemmler's back. To do so, they had to cut holes in his white shirt. He sighed as they did. The electrodes were attached to long wires that swept up toward the ceiling and ran into the wall.

The A/C generator required to power the electric chair was big, and it was loud, and so a decision had been made to keep it in a distant room. When it was time to turn the crank, the warden was to use a bell to send a signal to the men operating the generator.

The guards used the leather straps to bind Kemmler's body. First his legs, then his stomach, then his forearms and biceps. A headpiece was fit atop his skull. It was of the same matching leather, except for a wet sponge that fit into Kemmler's mouth. After the sponge held down his tongue, the headpiece would hold his jaw tight. He wouldn't be able to scream.

"All right, then," said the warden as he stepped back. Paul looked to Brown, who had the face of a child on Christmas morning and was tapping his shoes on the wooden floor.

Paul already felt ill. His stomach was churning even before the horror began.

But he would not shut his eyes. He was going to take in every detail. If he could accumulate enough precious and terrible facts, just maybe they would get him through.

Without any more preamble, the warden rang the bell. The ding was sharp and clear. The warden repeated it a few times so that there could be no ambiguity. It was time for Kemmler to die.

Suddenly the prisoner's body shivered. The switch had clearly been thrown in the adjacent room, and one thousand volts of A/C raced through him. His muscles tightened. His hands fluttered in the air, trying to escape his bonds. As Westinghouse had shown Paul in the lab, the A/C did not make the body inert. Kemmler's muscles were not permanently clenched. He would have been able to get up if only the leather straps were not holding him tight.

Westinghouse's A/C system would have been perfectly safe had not Brown and Coffin conspired to make a version of it specifically designed to kill.

Paul saw Kemmler's right-hand index finger curl up into itself. His nails convulsed against his palm so violently that he drew blood from his own hand.

And that was it. The current ran through Kemmler for seventeen seconds before the warden again rang the bell, and the men in the generator room turned off their machine. All of the assembled took a breath. It was done.

Paul looked to Brown, who seemed ready to applaud.

Paul stood. Some summer air would be helpful. But just as he got to his feet, he heard a strange noise. It was faint. It was coming from the direction of the electric chair. Everyone else seemed to hear it too. All heads turned to look. The noise was coming from William Kemmler.

Blood continued to drip from his hands. His head rocked side to side. His chest moved up and down, the air seeping back into his lungs. He was mumbling. Trying to say something through the charred sponge.

"Oh dear God," someone said. Horror spread across each man's face as he realized that Kemmler was still alive. Paul saw a white froth coming out of the man's mouth. He was trying to breathe. What unimaginable state must his inner organs be in?

The warden quickly took control of the situation. He bade the men to again be seated, and rang his bell furiously. They would try again.

The current again zapped through Kemmler. But this second attempt proved no more successful than the first. The prisoner heaved against his restraints, every muscle in his body tensing and releasing and tensing again. The sponge in his mouth began to fry, like blackening chicken in an iron pan. Paul saw the faintest whiff of smoke rise from his hair to the ceiling. William Kemmler was burning alive.

But he still didn't die. Not this second time, to the embarrassment of the warden and to the great horror of the witnesses. Nor did he die on the third try either.

By the fourth attempt, the protests from the guests had grown forceful. "My God, man," said one of the physicians. "You must make this stop. This is torture." It was impossible to disagree. Even the reporters had joined in, pleading with the warden to end this barbarism. But this was the law. The warden's duty was to follow its letter. He had instructions from the office of the governor himself. He intended to carry them out.

Harold Brown got up and approached the warden. They shared a brief whispered conversation. It seemed as if Brown was offering to consult. He was ever eager to play the role of inventor. But the warden shook his head and quickly sent Brown back to his seat. This was an affair of the state.

The current again entered Kemmler's body. The prisoner raged against the leather straps with such force that his skin began ripping off. His mouth and eyes grew black from char. Blood no longer dripped from his hand, but rather poured in a bright gush. Dark smoke rose from his head.

And then, quite suddenly, blue fire shot from Kemmler's mouth. Paul watched as the same blue hellfire he'd seen above that street in Manhattan incinerated Kemmler's skull, lit his hair on fire, and then washed across his body. It stripped the skin from his bones.

The guests jumped to their feet as the blood flew across the basement. Paul was among the men sprinting for the door.

In the prison yard, the first thing Paul did was vomit. Without food in his stomach, what came up was just a bitter clot of bile. He knelt in the dirt, spitting the taste from his lips.

Paul looked up at his fellow witnesses. He wasn't the only one being sick. The physicians, more accustomed to gore, had lit cigarettes. They were talking animatedly, trying to figure out what they had just witnessed. They'd never seen a body do that before. Their personal horror was tinged with professional curiosity.

The reporters were scribbling in their notebooks. Paul realized that within minutes they would file reports of what they'd witnessed, a scene they would paint for the many newspapers across the country. The Westinghouse system of alternating current had just proven itself to be a spectacularly poor instrument of murder. If Edison and Brown had wanted to demonstrate the stubborn safety of alternating current, they could have done no better job.

Paul still felt ill. But for the first time in a long while, he also felt like his side had won something.

Paul turned to see Brown exiting quickly through the prison gates. He thought he could make out dark stains on Brown's linen jacket. And on his hands as well.

CHAPTER 50

When London Trembles . . .
New York Quakes

An investment in knowledge pays the best interest.

—BENJAMIN FRANKLIN

EORGE WESTINGHOUSE WAS in his shirtsleeves when Paul burst through the double doors of his private study. Paul felt a little bashful about his excitement, considering the previous day's events. And yet an unrepentant axe murderer had been punished, and his death had exposed to the public the extent of Edison's lies about alternating current. No one could now believe that alternating current was particularly lethal. The question was already being asked in the papers: Had Brown been simply mistaken? Or had he been lying? And if the latter, why?

Paul had not often been able to relay such good news to his client.

"Mr. Cravath?" Westinghouse checked his pocket watch.

"Sir, I telegrammed. The news from Buffalo—surely you've seen it?"

Proudly, Paul removed the day's *New York Times* from his coat pocket. He slapped the paper down on Westinghouse's desk.

The headline blared in forty-eight-point type across the top of the thin broadsheet: ELECTRICAL ATROCITY IN BUFFALO—IS EDISON TO BLAME?

"The papers are all looking into Edison," said Paul. "They all are reporting that Brown was a fraud and someone had to have put him up to it."

Westinghouse said nothing. He looked down at the newspaper, taking it into his hands and giving the headlines a long, hard stare.

"This is good," said Westinghouse.

"Yes, this is good," said Paul. This wasn't quite the reaction he had hoped for. "Your current is too safe to be of any use in executions. They could barely kill a man with the stuff when they tried. Every newspaper in the country is reporting the story in the same terms: A/C is *too* safe. The scandal is no longer about the worrisome dangers of your current—it's about your current's worrisome safety."

"We'll sell more units."

"We'll sell *a lot* more units." Paul was perplexed by his client's muted response. Sales of A/C systems had been slowing of late. This was just the thing to reinvigorate buyers. This should have been a long-awaited moment of triumph. But Westinghouse looked as if the two men were at a wake.

"We'll need to," said Westinghouse as he set the paper down and sat back in his chair. "We're bankrupt." He said it so abruptly that Paul wasn't quite sure what he meant.

"What?"

"Well, not quite yet. But soon. Very soon."

"I don't understand . . ." Sales had slowed, but they hadn't slowed enough for that.

"Perhaps you've been reading the wrong papers," suggested Westinghouse as he took a folded paper from under some letters on the other side of his desk. He placed the thin newspaper down on top of Paul's *New York Times*. It was *The Wall Street Journal*.

WHEN LONDON TREMBLES . . . NEW YORK QUAKES. The subheading was less sensationalistic and more descriptive: "Rumors Spread Across Atlantic of Baring Bros. Collapse." The second subhead then added helpfully: "Banking House Among World's Oldest May Fall on Argentine Bond Loss—What Does This Mean for U.S.?"

"It is the damned Argentines," said Westinghouse. "Everyone thought it was a solid bet at the time."

Paul took *The Journal* from the desk and quickly scanned the left-hand column. From what he could gather, the reporting was nothing more than hearsay. Unidentified and unsourced rumors. Certain "suggestions" had "grown louder" in recent days. And these suggestions were that the Baring Brothers bank in London might soon crash. Since this was an institution that had withstood 120 years of financial turmoil, if Baring Brothers had a problem, it was likely not alone. "If the Bank of England itself were to be questioned," the article said, "it could not carry a more severe shock." There was more technical information about the nature of the Argentine deal—a South American recession, a bubble in Brazil, a ripple on one continent that would become a tidal wave when it reached another.

"How does this spell our bankruptcy?" asked Paul. "The Barings don't own this company."

"But how many of our creditors are now soon to be theirs?"

Paul began to understand the problem.

"Your creditors are going to demand repayment of their loans sooner than anticipated."

"A lot sooner than anticipated," replied Westinghouse as he gestured toward a letter on his desk. "That's from A. J. Cassart. He would like his loans repaid by this coming Friday."

"Christ . . . It's Tuesday."

"Did you read that in the paper too?"

"How much?"

"Hard to say. But this letter will not be the last of its kind that I receive this week. I have been going over our numbers. . . . It's no secret that we operate at a loss. Under normal circumstances, this is not a problem. Most growing businesses employ the same tactics."

"How much debt are we in?"

"*You*, Mr. Cravath, are not in any debt at all. *I* am in debt for approximately three million dollars."

"And what are the assets of the company?"

"All told? Approximately two and a half million."

Paul began to pace the room, considering the problem. "So we'll need to raise at least five hundred thousand in capital in order to convince your creditors not to seize the company."

"I'm glad to see you've been practicing your mathematics."

Paul stopped pacing by the ceiling-high bookshelves on the far side of the room. He turned to face Westinghouse.

"It's not *you* who is in debt. It is your company. So that's the first thing. It's not on you alone."

"You're mistaken," said Westinghouse.

"What are you talking about?"

"I've put up this house and everything in it as collateral. It might not be worth a full half a million, but it's no tenement."

Paul knew George Westinghouse had always taken the affairs of his company quite personally. It was named after him, and he treated the corporation as an extension of his own corpus. But it was one thing to do so emotionally; it was another to endanger the roof over his wife's head.

Seeing the expression on Paul's face, Westinghouse smiled with a stubborn naïveté.

"You think this is a grave mistake," suggested Westinghouse.

"Sir, it's your family," said Paul.

"Am I in for one of your speeches? They're quite good, kid, I'll give you that. But if your aim is to convince me to simply let my company fall without placing every ounce of weight I have underneath it as support, well . . . not even *you* are that eloquent."

Paul knew his argument would lose. The first thing he had learned about persuading others was how to determine when—and of what— they were capable of being persuaded. On that day, he knew Westinghouse would not be moved. And so he also knew that the only way to save his client was to stave off this bankruptcy himself.

CHAPTER 51

Apologetic Millionaires

You have to learn the rules of the game. And then you have
to play better than anyone else.　　—ALBERT EINSTEIN

OVER THE NEXT few weeks, Paul and Westinghouse took turns
making penitent pilgrimages to the most moneyed of the New
York moneymen. The stations of their cross were formed by
Wall Street, Union Square, and Madison Square. Not a millionaire
was spared their devotionals. Westinghouse forswore his company's
sins. The financial promiscuity would come to an end. The firm's gov-
ernance was pledged to frugality. In their pleas, the men asked for
more than mere blessings. They asked for absolution.

Research into newer and more elaborate products would be halted,
with a focus fixed solely upon improving the manufacture and cost-
effectiveness of existing devices. They were without the bottomless
war chest that J. P. Morgan provided Edison, and so their culture was
naturally quite different. They did not aim to be some manner of pie-
in-the-sky idea factory. Westinghouse *worked*. The company would
continue to make things, and they would be the highest-quality electrical products in the world. That had always been their goal, and it
always would be.

Even the program to develop a new light bulb far afield of Edison's
would be abandoned. They could not continue to afford the man-

power on a task that had, after a year, borne no progress at all. Westinghouse's engineers were good, but they were expensive, and not one of them was Nikola Tesla. The immediate survival of the company was at stake.

They would need only a moderate injection of capital to keep things going through the coming winter. The few hundreds of thousands of dollars they required to maintain operations were small beer compared to the fortunes to be generated by electric light.

But every time Paul and Westinghouse concluded their practiced supplications, they were reminded by the apologetic millionaires across from them that this all depended on a victory over Edison. From the safety of their glazed oak desks, the bankers were quick to suggest that if direct current became the standard of the day, then the Westinghouse Electric Company would play little part in the prosperity. The problem was not with the frugality or operational efficiency of the company—it was with the fragility of its very existence. Who would profit from providing expensive medicine to a man whose illness was already terminal?

They did experience moments of success. Fresh investments were secured from Hugh Garden, A. T. Rowand, and William Scott, extending the company's life by a few frenzied weeks. Carter and Hughes lent their extensive connections to the cause, producing a much-needed $130,000 just a week into the crisis; it bought them another month. Paul was able to scrape together a few days of survival here and there through his Columbia network. These were the terms in which they now measured—not in dollars and cents, but in weeks, days, even hours. A million dollars could buy a year. A thousand dollars barely afforded a day.

By a unanimous vote, the firm of Carter, Hughes & Cravath decided to defer their legal fees until after the crisis was over. To be sure, the dues owed them continued to mount. They dutifully recorded their labors in the leather-bound ledger they kept for such a purpose, scribbling every meeting, every letter, every late evening beneath the office gas lamps. The right-hand column of their book filled with imaginary dollars. Who knew if they would ever be paid? As the firm—as Paul—built a theoretical fortune, the men remained all too aware that these paper riches might never become real. Paul continued to manage his "associate attorneys" in secret in the hopes that they might uncover another hole in Edison's patent. Paul paid them from a combination of his own rapidly depleting savings and whatever scraps he could surreptitiously borrow from the firm's meager accounts. No day ended with a promise of the next.

One September day Agnes Huntington strode into his office. Four months had passed since their goodbye in Nashville. She hadn't made an appointment.

He hadn't written to her. He hadn't known what to say. Seeing her in front of him, he still didn't. He knew her secret. She knew his heart. They were in this way intertwined by the impossibility of their predicament.

"Miss Huntington." Once again the name felt foolish on his lips after what had passed between them. But what else was he to call her?

"Good morning, Paul," she said as she shut the door behind her.

"It's good to see you," he said. He was telling the truth. "Will you take a seat?"

The humid September air wafted in through the open windows. It had rained only that morning, and the breeze was damp.

"How is Nikola?" she asked.

He told her what he knew. He'd instructed his father not to use the inventor's name in letters, since they couldn't be sure if anyone was reading Paul's mail. Erastus was to speak only of the Tennessee sunflowers in their garden. As his father described the sunflowers, Paul would know that what he was really describing was Tesla. The old man hadn't liked this subterfuge, but he understood its necessity. His most recent letter had said that the flowers were blooming nicely. Not as tall as he'd hoped, but they were showing their color.

Agnes complimented Paul on handling this with typical cleverness. Paul was proud to be clever in her eyes. Between them, they'd spent a lot of time in the company of geniuses over the past year. Clever would do just fine.

"And how is Mr. Jayne?" Paul asked. He still wasn't sure just why she'd come to see him. But this was the figurative elephant in the room. He couldn't go without mentioning it.

"He's invited me to journey with him to Paris next month. Three weeks of traveling and sightseeing through France. I haven't been since last I sang there. His family—well, they have their house in the city, in Paris. And a summer cottage farther south. Near Lyon."

Of course they did. "Are you to be married?" The question was difficult to voice. But he had to know.

She swallowed. "Paul . . . I . . ." She stopped herself. When she tried again, her voice was lighter. "I believe the purpose of the trip is so that he might propose."

"Of course."

"He'll offer me his grandmother's ring in Paris, I'd imagine. Then we can celebrate through the countryside for a few weeks, before returning to Manhattan and Philadelphia to tell our respective families what they assuredly already know."

"And you'll accept his proposal?"

"Paul . . ."

"What does he think of your performing at the Met? Surely he'll want you to stop?"

"Henry is a good man," she said. "You think I must be compromising myself for his money. Well, let me tell you, he's a better man than most, and any woman would be lucky to have him. Just because he comes from money doesn't make him callow. And if you knew how much I've wanted to stop singing professionally, or how many times I've almost quit . . . It is not the constant jockeying for position and stature that I love. I can *sing* for anyone. Henry doesn't have such a poor voice himself." Her voice was firm. But her eyes were wet.

"I understand," he said. "I respect your decision."

"You haven't written me."

"Nor you me. I've been trying to win this suit—or at least not to lose it."

"So we're both playing games. You cannot blame me for winning mine just because you're losing yours."

They were silent for a moment. Paul wondered if she too felt like a pawn on someone else's board.

"I didn't come to tell you that," said Agnes finally. "I came about your case. About Westinghouse. I know you've been to every investor below Fourteenth Street, trying to scrounge up funds. And I know it's not going well."

"How do you—" Paul didn't need to finish the sentence before he realized the answer. "Jayne."

"Of course he knows that you're my attorney. And he told me about your troubles. That every banker in town knows of them. But he told me something . . . well, something that not every banker in town knows. He told me why you're having such a hard time."

"Why is that?"

"J. P. Morgan."

"Morgan owns sixty percent of Edison General Electric," said Paul. "Personally."

"Yes," she said, "but think of what else he owns."

His mind raced to see the implications of her suggestion. In addition to his controlling shares in EGE, Morgan possessed a piece of nearly half the companies listed on the New York Stock Exchange. This was the very reason that Westinghouse had hired Paul in the first place.

"Morgan's people have been visiting all of our prospective investors ahead of me. Morgan has been threatening them. 'Invest even a dollar in Westinghouse's company, and you'll be punished.'"

"It's smarter than that. Morgan didn't threaten them—he made them better offers. If they had capital that they were looking to invest during the crisis, he let them know they would be safer putting it into one of *his* companies. The Northern Pacific Railway. A few others. He offered them favorable terms. Much better than anything you could have given them."

"He exploited their greed. Not their fear." Paul could not deny the ingenuity. "But how did he know who I was going to see? How did he get to them first?"

"I don't know. He's J. P. Morgan. At this game, he's the best in the world." What she left unsaid was that this was precisely why Morgan and Edison would win in the end. Their kind always did. Manhattan would reward its own. And it would, at long last, cast Paul away. Far from Washington Square, far from Wall Street, far from Broadway, and very far from Agnes.

From the depth of Paul's sadness came an iron resolve. "We've found a few investors. I will find more. I won't give up."

Agnes smiled. "I know you won't," she said. "From the moment I first met you, I knew you never would."

And with that, it was time for her to go. He would need to begin looking for investors far outside New York. Would it make a difference? He didn't know. But at least she'd given him a better path to go down.

They lingered for a moment at the doorway. He reached out to take her hand. But the instant he felt her fingers touch his, he knew he couldn't bear it.

She pulled her hand away first. Was this just as difficult for her as it was for him?

She turned, leaving without another word.

It took Paul a moment before he was able to return to his desk.

CHAPTER 52

End Times

> I'm convinced that about half of what separates the success-
> ful entrepreneurs from the unsuccessful ones is pure
> perseverance. —STEVE JOBS

A S THE HUMID summer of 1889 cooled into fall, the tectonic plates beneath the global banking system began to shift. The rumor of the Baring Brothers' disastrous speculation into Argentinian bonds hardened into admitted fact, and the debt that Edward Baring had built up over the years was revealed to be ever more precarious. A panic set in. The flowing pools of capital that streamed the very lifeblood of finance were poisoned. In September the Bank of England stepped in to secure the Barings' losses in the hopes of averting a worldwide depression. But by October even the Bank of England's backing appeared insufficient. The British government lacked the capital necessary to bail out Sir Edward. Fortunately, Lord Rothschild added his family's muscle to the cause. He scolded the Chancellor of the Exchequer as if he were an immature child.

But thankfully, as the November winds swept across the East Coast and stiffened the collars of its bankers, New York held firm against London's downward pull. Wall Street was buoyed by a record summer of wheat production. Exports reached unprecedented highs.

Even so, by the first frost of December, the three-card monte that

Paul had been playing as he shuffled Westinghouse's debts from investor to investor was revealing itself for the cheap trick that it had been.
Doors that had opened to them in August were now closed. As fewer
and fewer investments seemed safe, money had tightened. What little
of it trickled across Manhattan would not make it all the way to Pittsburgh. And what larger pools might be available were closed off by
the dam that was J. P. Morgan.

The safety of alternating current was becoming more and more an
accepted fact, and ever-larger municipalities were choosing Westinghouse generators over Edison's. But what precious revenue was generated by the wiring of Elmira, New York, and even Baltimore, Maryland,
did not come close to covering the company's expenses. The A/C
royalties they continued paying to Tesla's attorney, in the inventor's
absence, only widened the gulf between the company and profitability. Financial schemes they had once mocked soon appeared necessary. The Westinghouse coffers leaked their last dimes, and in the face
of corporate penury Paul felt the unavoidable word slowly forming on
his lips.

Hughes said it first. Not in the dim evening of one of their emer-
gency conferences, but on a crisp morning as he first walked in the
door. There was no preamble; there was no explanatory broaching of
the subject. He just said it.

"We must start to plan for the bankruptcy."

Before Paul even knew what he was doing, he was saying it too.
"I've been looking over the procedures," replied Paul instantly. "The
'74 revisions to the '67 Bankruptcy Act are a bit Byzantine, but I
know my way around them by now." It was as if they'd skipped over
the agony of making a terrible decision and jumped straight to the
mechanics of carrying it out.

They spent all that morning developing a plan of action. The
Westinghouse Electric Company's debts were numerous and their
creditors varied. Of paramount importance was maintaining the distinction between Westinghouse's highly profitable rail business and
his exceedingly unprofitable electrical endeavors. Westinghouse's air
brakes would generate a healthy revenue for decades; the goal was to
see that this could be leveraged into some manner of support for

Westinghouse's other holdings. They sought to arrange things such that he might hold on to his home.

It took less than a week to lay out the basic structure of the operation. It was an unemotional ordeal. The carving up of the Westinghouse corpse was performed with a clinical disassociation. Paul could devote himself to the complexity of the task and thus ignore its larger implications.

Hughes's wife—Carter's daughter—was due to give birth to her first child before the new year. Paul's senior partners would move on to new cases, established careers, and full lives. What would happen to Paul was far less certain.

It was a bright and clear Tuesday morning when Paul and his partners finished. The tired men surveyed the delicate paper stacks before them. New York was waking up, Paul thought, as they were finally ready to put Westinghouse to bed. Paul cradled the warm china cup in his hands, taking small sips of black coffee. Carter smoked. Hughes stared out the window as if somewhere in the bricks of the neighboring buildings was a place he'd rather be.

"Well then," said Carter as he rested his cigar on the table. "Who's going to tell him?"

CHAPTER 53

The Second-Most Mysterious Telegram That Paul Had Ever Received

Many of life's failures are people who did not realize how
close they were to success when they gave up.

—THOMAS EDISON

I
T WAS A long train ride to Pittsburgh. He'd made this trip many times over the past year and a half, but this journey felt infinitely longer. The gray Pennsylvania prairie stretched on endlessly. Paul felt that he was being delivered, ever so slowly, to the gallows. And what he felt as he approached the gilded noose, more than anything else, was shame.

He kept imagining Westinghouse's face. Westinghouse had done everything right. He'd made the big gambles, and he'd gambled correctly: first on electrical light, then again on alternating current. He'd identified a future market, he'd identified the technological problems that would need solving in order to serve this market, and he'd then designed and manufactured the best product in the world to fill this niche. What more could one ask of a businessman?

One could ask for a better attorney. If Carter had been in charge from the beginning, would they still be in this position? Could Hughes have negotiated their way out of it if he'd been given a chance? Could anyone? Why had George Westinghouse done something so foolish as to entrust the future of his company to *Paul*?

Paul had been called a prodigy when he'd signed Westinghouse as his client, but he had not felt like one. And only now, as he came to the end of his brief career as a lawyer, was he aware of the extent of his previous accomplishments. Now that it no longer mattered, he realized what a marvel his early work had been. He'd made it far. How many people could claim that?

And how many people had squandered such promise?

Paul entered the Westinghouse estate's central mansion wearily. The butler took his coat, his hat, his worn gloves. Mr. Westinghouse was in the study. Paul made his way slowly through the house. This would likely be his last time here. Westinghouse would remain cordial, to be sure. Marguerite might even extend the occasional invitation to dinner. But Paul knew that he wouldn't be able to bear attending. His shame was so deep that he could not imagine ever being able to look George Westinghouse in the eye again.

Paul paused in the study's doorway. Westinghouse was seated at his enormous desk. He was absorbed in diagrams of some sort. Mechanical designs that, most likely, would never come into being.

Paul waited there for a long moment. He took the longest breath of his life before he opened his mouth.

"Mr. Westinghouse," said Paul. "We need to talk."

Westinghouse didn't look up. "Yes, yes," he said, still focused on his diagrams. "Take a seat, kid."

Paul didn't feel like sitting. He stood there another moment, marshaling his strength.

There was a loud knock at the door.

"Come in!" called out Westinghouse.

The butler entered. "Pardon, sir. But there's a telegram just arrived. Marked 'urgent.'"

"Fine, fine," said Westinghouse. "Bring it here."

"It's for Mr. Cravath."

Carter and Hughes wouldn't have interrupted him at such a moment. They'd wanted to be as far away from this meeting as possible. Who even knew he was there?

Paul took the telegram from the butler and peeled open its wax seal.

This was easily the second-most mysterious telegram he'd ever received.

"The Tennessee sunflowers have bloomed," the message read. "They are the most beautiful sight. You must see them for yourself. Please come to Nashville posthaste."

It was signed "A.G."

CHAPTER 54

Teatime at the Cravath Household

> At the heart of science is an essential balance between two
> seemingly contradictory attitudes—an openness to new
> ideas, no matter how bizarre or counterintuitive they may
> be, and the most ruthless skeptical scrutiny of all ideas, old
> and new. This is how deep truths are winnowed from deep
> nonsense.
> —CARL SAGAN

"**W**HERE'S TESLA?" WERE the first words that Paul spoke to
Agnes, improbably seated in his parents' Nashville kitchen.
Ruth Cravath was heating the kettle for tea while Erastus
puttered about, making sure Agnes had everything she required. She
had evidently been here a few days.

Paul could not help but notice the bright diamond on Agnes's ring
finger. He tried not to stare. It probably cost more than the entire
house in which they were seated, though that wasn't saying much. At
least he would not have to ask whether her trip to France with Henry
La Barre Jayne had gone according to plan.

"Paul," cautioned Erastus, "that's not a very friendly way to greet
our guest."

"Where is Mr. Tesla, Father?"

"He's usually back by dinnertime."

"Usually?"

Agnes was more sympathetic to Paul's understandable confusion. "A week ago I received a letter from Wilhelm Roentgen."

The name meant nothing to him. "All right."

"He's a professor at the University of Würzburg."

"Fascinating."

"Paul," said Ruth, "would you like some tea?"

"Mother," said Paul, growing frustrated. "Please give me a moment with my friend." At the word "friend," Ruth raised an eyebrow.

"Mr. Roentgen informed me that he'd been receiving letters from one Nikola Tesla. Weekly."

"Who let Tesla send letters?" Paul looked accusingly at his father.

"Nikola wanted to send letters to a scientist in Germany," said Erastus. "I did not think this would endanger him."

"Damn it," said Paul. "That is *precisely* what will endanger him."

"Your language," castigated Erastus.

"So that is what brought me here," said Agnes. "Because Roentgen wrote to me to say that he'd been having the most enlivening correspondence with Tesla, and hoped to meet with him on an upcoming visit to America. But Tesla had said that wouldn't be possible unless I'd given permission. Which Roentgen asked for."

"Why you?" asked Paul.

Agnes stared at him. "Because," she said calmly, "he trusts me."

For whatever reason, she was the one whom Tesla had gone to after the fire. It was in her house that he'd made a temporary home. Agnes had little family; Tesla had none. Together, they'd made the most unexpected of siblings.

"If he'd been writing to Roentgen, perhaps he was writing to others. The community of scientists is small, as you've taken pains to make me aware. I'd taken the season off from performing anyway, given my . . . other voyages. I came here to make sure he hadn't been found."

Across the room Paul's parents seemed perfectly comfortable with all that was happening.

"So he's safe," said Paul.

"You should see it. What he's done. It's magical."

"What's he done?"

Her face crinkled. "It's very difficult to explain."

"Is it a new light bulb?" asked Paul eagerly. "A completely original A/C lamp? That's what he'd been working on."

"Perhaps," interjected Ruth, "the simplest way to clear this up would be a visit to Mr. Tesla's laboratory. After tea."

"His *laboratory*?" sputtered Paul. "Where is Mr. Tesla's laboratory?"

There passed a moment of silence. The only sound was the clatter of four cups being set, by Ruth, against their saucers.

Agnes turned to Erastus. "You should tell him," she said to Paul's father. "It was your idea."

> The most beautiful thing we can experience is the mysteri-
> ous. . . . He to whom this emotion is a stranger, who can no
> longer pause to wonder and stand rapt in awe, is as good as
> dead.   —ALBERT EINSTEIN

"How could you build him a laboratory?" Paul asked his father as their carriage wound down the dirt road toward Fisk University. The horses kicked up clouds of dust, coating the air in a dull beige sheen.

"He built the laboratory himself," said Erastus. "I just gave him some unused space in the basement."

"I've never seen anything like it," supplied Agnes from the carriage's back seat. "What he's built there."

"Once again, I'll ask without expectation of being answered: What is it that he's built there?"

"Oh, son," said Erastus, "I'm not much for the natural sciences. You'll have to ask him yourself."

Agnes shrugged. "I never even got a handle on the whole A/C-versus-D/C issue, and the man lived in my maid's room for months."

Paul fidgeted in his seat as the Fisk campus came into view. Though only a quarter century old, the school had blossomed from a lecture hall for freedmen on an abandoned army barracks into a thousand-student institution. A half dozen stone buildings, all designed in the Gothic style. Paul had been four years old when his father helped to found Fisk. He had little memory of those days, but the story had lived on at his family's dinner table. The first class had consisted entirely of former slaves: men as young as seven and as old as seventy, few of whom had much experience with a book, much less any sort of formal education. With the support of the Freedmen's Bureau and the American Missionary Association, the school had thrived. It had recently educated its first second-generation applicant, the teenage son of a former cotton picker from a West Tennessee plantation.

Paul entered the basement laboratory of Jubilee Hall to find a vibrant Nikola Tesla huddling in a semicircle with five Negro students. The men's backs were to the door, so none saw the entry of Paul's group. Tesla and his students were too deeply engaged in something happening on a wide metal table in front of them to notice that anyone had come in.

"Move the plate," Tesla commanded one of the students. "One additional foot. Yes. *Stop*."

Tesla fiddled with a device on the table, while another eager assistant moved to what Paul thought might be a generator on a nearby tabletop.

"You just say the word," said this student assistant. All the students were in suits of either brown or light gray. Not a button had been loosened on their collars. Not a roll was to be found upon their shirtsleeves. They had apparently inherited their teacher's obsession with neatness.

"Robert," said Tesla without looking up from his device, "climb aboard the table."

The students exchanged confused glances.

"Pardon, sir?" replied the tallest of them.

"Mr. Robert Miles," said Tesla. "Lift your corpse aboard this table."

"You want me to stand on the table?" said Robert.

"No," said Tesla. "You will not stand. I want for your laying yourself in front of the tube."

Though this did little to clarify matters, Robert moved as instructed. He had clearly been studying with Tesla for some time and knew better than to question one of his teacher's demands, no matter how odd.

Robert heaved himself onto the table and lay down with his feet pointing toward Tesla, his head aimed toward a silvery plate that rested on the tabletop, reflecting slices of light across the room.

"Revolve," said Tesla. Robert, after performing a quick Tesla-to-English translation, turned his body ninety degrees. His long legs hung off the wide end of the table, and his head drooped out of Paul's sight over the other side.

"Like this?" asked Robert.

"Just as so," answered Tesla. "Now please raise your right leg."

Robert strained to balance his leg in the air as Tesla adjusted something on the device before him.

"Mr. Jason Barnes," said Tesla into the air. "Current now, please."

A student by the generator turned two metal knobs. The machine began to hum.

"And here you will have it," said Tesla proudly as he turned something on the device before him. The student near the silver plate watched it closely. Robert did his best to remain perfectly still on the table. The whole of the room seemed to breathe in with a nervous anticipation as long, tense seconds followed Tesla's proclamation.

Nothing whatsoever happened.

Ten seconds of awkward silence lengthened into twenty.

Neither Tesla nor his students did so much as look up from the table. Paul was quite confused.

"Aha!" Tesla declared. He stood suddenly, the full length of his frame rearing up over the huddle of men around him. "Mr. Robert Miles, you may disembark."

Robert hopped off the table. The students all stared at the silver plate. To Paul's surprise, it was now growing black.

"You will all be patient for a moment," said Tesla. "The salts are having their reaction."

It was only then that Tesla noticed his visitors.

"Mr. Paul Cravath," said Tesla with a smile. "It is pleasing to visage you."

"And you too," replied Paul. On the faraway shores of Tesla's mind, visitors came and went. As to how they arrived or departed, Tesla seemed neither to know nor to care.

"What is it that you've created here?" said Paul. He did not recognize the device on the table. But if it either was—or prefigured—the device that Westinghouse needed, Paul felt certain he would not be able to resist physically embracing Tesla whether the inventor liked it or not.

"In scant seconds, you shall see. Come, come, come!"

Tesla motioned for Paul and company to join him and his students across the makeshift laboratory. The assembled devices and machines were less gargantuan than those destroyed in his burned-down New York lab, and yet their variety seemed at least as impressive. Glass objects of every shape that Paul might imagine lined one wall, mushroom bulbs and fat circles and long, delicate spears. Each was perfectly clear, hand polished into dustless radiance. Another wall held what seemed to be electrical components: the wound copper coils, spidery antennas, and precisely weighted gears that formed the backbone of all of Tesla's work. With these tools, Tesla harnessed the mysterious liquid of electrical energy and built from it . . . something. The alternating-current motor had been only the first act of his performance; the giant coil of lightning Paul had seen in New York had been the second. Would an entirely new form of light bulb be the third? Would there be any end to the wonders that Nikola Tesla might conjure into the world?

"Come regard, Misters Cravath and Miss Agnes Huntington," said Tesla. "I call it a shadowgraph."

Tesla directed his guests' attention to the once-silver plate. It was now mostly pitch black, with ghostly silver forms tracing through its center. It took Paul a moment to make out the shape etched in silver: It was a bone.

"Is that . . . ?" asked Agnes, coming to the same realization.

"It's my femur," said Robert. "It's inside my leg."

"Nikola," said Erastus, "did you just take a photograph of the inside of this man's leg?"

"No, no," replied Tesla. "Not a photograph; it is a shadowgraph. It records density of matter, not brightness of illuminations. On the shadowgraph, that which is of greatest density is lightest. That which is of none is dark."

"It strips away the skin," said Agnes, "and reveals an image of the bone underneath?"

"Precisely," said Tesla.

Quietly, in secret, from an impromptu subterranean laboratory in the Tennessee plains, Tesla had teamed with the precocious sons of southern freedmen to engineer wonders stranger than anything Edison and his well-heeled peers might have dreamed. Paul had once thought that Thomas Edison was the most American man of his generation. But looking around the worktable before him at Tesla and his students carefully considering their darkening plate, Paul saw another America. This one had been born in an impoverished Serbian village and a West Tennessee cotton field. Where the first America was brilliant, the second was ingenious. What the first America did not invent, the second would tinker into being. What Wall Street would not fund, a Nashville basement would build. This was what men like Edison and Morgan feared. With checkbooks such as theirs, with the ability to buy and sell a place like Fisk with a single pen scribble, they still slept badly in their Fifth Avenue redoubts. They used their lawyers to batter down places just such as this. They had their patents, their carefully worded claims to preeminence. Tesla and his students had only their inventiveness. Paul saw on the faces of Robert and Jason and their peers that what these men did was not for money, it was not for class or some abstract social achievement. These men built things because they were *smart*. They were eager and they were precocious and they were curious. Paul wanted always to live in an America in which Thomas Edison would fear a smart kid in a basement whose father had harvested enough cotton that his son might harvest volts.

"Does it hurt?" Erastus asked Robert.

The student instinctively looked toward his leg and wiggled it. "I don't think so?"

"You are quite well," said Tesla. "So you witness the machine's operation. Mr. Wilhelm Roentgen shall be pleasing."

"This is what I've come to discuss with you," said Paul. "You've grown healthy again. Your memory has returned, and so has your genius. I cannot tell you how happy I am to see it. This machine . . . or any of the others along the walls . . . is it an incandescent lamp?"

Tesla looked at Paul as if *he* were the one whose speech was largely indecipherable. "Why is it that they would be lamps?"

"A light bulb designed to make the most use of A/C," offered Paul. "Something that would clearly in no way infringe on Edison's patent. This is what Westinghouse needs to survive the lawsuit. That's what you were working with his team to build. Can the device that you've created here help them in that regard?"

Tesla came the closest to laughing that Paul had ever seen him.

"Oh, Mr. Paul Cravath. I have told you. Who is caring about light bulbs? We have them already. Now *this*, which I have built—Mr. Wilhelm Roentgen calls it an 'X-ray,' though I am liking my 'shadowgraph' more aptly. I have sent him my designs so that he may build these machines. This is a new thing. This is a wonder."

"What the hell is anyone supposed to do with this X-ray?" said Paul.

If any man alive could save Paul's career, his livelihood, it was Tesla. And yet he wouldn't. Or couldn't. Perhaps for him there wasn't even a difference. Paul cared about Tesla. Would Tesla ever care about him in return? He wasn't sure. Tesla was unwilling to engage his mind in anything but his own daydreams, not even to save his only friends in the world.

Tesla noticed the defeated look on Paul's face. "What is it that is the matter, Mr. Paul Cravath?"

"Paul is losing his lawsuit, Nikola," said Agnes. "He's worried that Thomas Edison is going to win."

Tesla nodded sympathetically. "I have sadness about this also."

Paul realized that there was a lot that had happened of which Tesla was unaware. He started talking fast. Maybe this would be his one chance to impress upon Tesla the importance of his work on A/C. Paul told the assembled everything, sparing no grisly detail of the past year. Damn confidentiality. His client had nothing to hide. The students took their seats, rapt with attention. It was quite a tale.

Paul watched Erastus's face when he got to Westinghouse's looming bankruptcy. There was little reaction. Erastus did not give Paul the sympathy he'd imagined, but neither did he present Paul with the pity he'd feared.

His sorry tale completed, Paul stood gloomily in the center of the room. What was there for anyone to say?

"Hmm," said Robert. Paul turned, surprised to hear his voice.

"Robert," said Erastus, "if you've something to add, you should add it." Robert looked to his college president, then to Paul, then to Tesla.

"Well, it's only . . ." Robert fidgeted. "Mr. Tesla says that there are two types of problems out there. On the one hand, you've got problems that people have been struggling over, solving or not solving, forever. Known problems. But then on the other hand, you've got problems that no one ever even thought to tackle—new problems. Uncharted ground, right? Unknown problems."

"It is eloquently more so when I say it," added Tesla, "but Mr. Robert Miles is correct." He nodded at his student appreciatively. Somehow, thought Paul, Nikola Tesla had ended up being a surprisingly good instructor.

"And so?" said Paul.

"And so, sir, I don't mean to tell you your business, but when we're faced with a problem, Mr. Tesla has us, first and foremost, categorize it. We have to determine if it's known or unknown. Have you done that with yours?"

"I suppose," said Paul, "that defeating Edison is an unknown problem, since no one has ever . . ."

Paul stopped himself. "No, wait," he continued. "Edison has been beaten before. He told me so himself when I deposed him."

"Well," explained Robert, "if it's that type of problem that you're trying to solve, then your first step should probably be to go to someone who's solved it already."

"There is exactly one person who's gone up against Thomas Edison and won," said Paul. "And you're suggesting that he might have some interesting advice to share?"

Agnes smiled. She had already realized whom Paul meant.

"Your epiphany is pleasing," said Tesla.

"Well," said Erastus impatiently, "who is it?"

Paul told them. He couldn't believe he hadn't thought of this earlier.

"How do you think you might reach him?" asked Erastus.

"I imagine I'll give him a ring on a telephone," said Paul. "After all, he did invent the thing."

CHAPTER 56

At the Foot of Beinn Bhreagh

That's been one of my mantras—focus and simplicity.
Simple can be harder than complex. You have to work hard
to get your thinking clean, to make it simple. But it's worth
it in the end, because once you get there, you can move
mountains.   —STEVE JOBS

I T TURNED OUT that Alexander Graham Bell did not own a telephone.

Fourteen years earlier, Bell had patented an "apparatus for transmitting vocal or other sounds telegraphically." A dozen other inventors, chief among them Thomas Edison, had been working on similar designs for a telegraph that could transmit the human voice itself. The uses and applications were tantalizingly lucrative. But Bell had beaten all his rivals, filing his patent mere hours before a nearly identical claim from Elisha Gray, and weeks ahead of another, from Edison. The lawsuits that resulted were still ongoing, and yet thus far Bell had won them resoundingly. His telephone patent was ironclad.

The invention, easily among the most significant in the world, had positioned him to be the most important inventor of his age. However, to the great shock of the scientific community, Bell had opted not to build the devices himself, nor to bring them to the market. Instead, he appointed a distant relative to manage the company that bore his name. Bell and his wife controlled more shares of the Bell Telephone Company than anyone else, and yet he steadfastly refused to have any involvement in its operation. Once his shares were comfortably generating millions per year in revenue, Bell had taken his family and moved to a remote Canadian peninsula.

Alexander Graham Bell had beaten Thomas Edison at his own game, and then vanished.

Paul and Agnes spent a week traveling from the dusty fields of Nashville to the quiet harbor of Bell's frozen lake. Before they left, Agnes sent Henry Jayne a note to say that she was taking a last-minute trip with her mother. She sent her mother a note to say that she was staying another week in Nashville. Paul pointed out that Fannie would be sure to send a sternly worded reply, but Agnes only shrugged. She wouldn't be there to receive it.

"What can she do? She'll yell when I get home. There will be a great row. She'll lock me up till the very day of my wedding, I'm sure. But at least, before all of that, I will have done this."

They passed the 1,800-mile trip to Canada pleasantly. Happily, even. He finally brought himself to ask about her engagement, but they skipped through the painful details as quickly as possible. The wedding would not take place until the following July. It would take some time to organize. Everyone in New York, not to mention Philadelphia, would be in attendance. Everyone, Paul assumed, but himself.

That unpleasantness concluded, Paul and Agnes then had six days on a train together. The train became its own world—a glowing filament enclosed in a vacuum. Removed from the society of New York, they had only to be themselves. Paul wasn't a young lawyer on the make. Agnes was not the star chanteuse of the Metropolitan Opera. They were just a good strong boy from Tennessee and a whip-smart wit from Kalamazoo. In the midst of all that was happening, it was actually . . . fun.

They made friends with a newlywed couple just across the border. When the bride gestured to Agnes's ring and asked about their coming nuptials, Paul realized that this trip was almost like a honeymoon. Before he could correct their assumption, Agnes answered, "September!" To Paul's surprise he found himself joining in her lie. Together they concocted an entire story of their lives—names, dates, a fictional romance that was soon to culminate in an imagined wedding. "Alice Boone" and "Peter Sheldon" were Tennessee mining heirs off to visit distant Canadian relatives. The foursome played bridge till all hours of the night.

The irony was not lost on Paul that he felt most himself here, on the train, at play under a false name. Agnes seemed to feel the same way. Agnes Gouge was pretending to be Agnes Huntington pretending to be Alice Boone. Paul was pretending to be someone who was permitted to love her. They were the king and queen of the first-class dining car.

But a proper honeymoon this was not. Each night they returned to their separate sleeping cars. Paul was not an adulterer, he assured himself. They shared not one stolen kiss as their train skirted the snowy Gulf of Maine. Not even their fingertips touched over six days. The only occasion on which Paul felt the soft warmth of her skin took place within the safety of his dreams.

These were vivid.

Westinghouse had made the introduction to Bell via telegram, having known him casually from years of engineering conferences. Bell had replied that he did not often receive visitors, remote as his home was. He would thus be delighted to receive some intelligent company for lunch. Paul guessed that this was easily the longest distance he would ever travel for salmon sandwiches and a pot of tea.

Bell and his wife, Mabel, lived on a six-hundred-acre estate on the island of Cape Breton, in Nova Scotia. Nestled within the indigo rim of Bras d'Or Lake, the estate occupied its own private peninsula. Mr. Bell and Mabel had named the place Beinn Bhreagh. It was Gaelic for "beautiful mountain," in reference to the rising slopes just across the harbor, in the shadow of which rested their secluded kingdom. Paul and Agnes's carriage climbed a lush hill, leaving the sky-blue lake and the red-rock formations of the bay behind them. The shape of Bell's home suddenly came into view. To describe the structure as "palatial" would have been not understatement but misidentification. It resembled a small city more than any sort of house.

The Bell compound was a series of interlocking buildings, stretching out from a three-story mansion in the center to nearby sheds, cabins, boathouses, warehouses, laboratories, and servants' cottages. Through the thick woods, paths had been carved to connect most of these structures to one another. Some buildings were even linked by covered passageways for pedestrian travel in the snowy winter. The style of the estate stood in some contrast to its size, for its dark-wood rustic design gave the impression that the whole thing had blossomed from the great forest around it. Alexander and Mabel Bell waited outside to greet their arriving guests. A row of servants claimed the travelers' valises, scurrying their bags into the house as Paul and Agnes shook the hands of their hosts.

"Good Lord," said Mr. Bell. "George said you were young, but he did not say you were still in your swaddling clothes."

Bell was large, almost as tall as Paul. While only forty-two years of age, Bell was possessed of a face that made him look much older. His white muttonchop beard, four inches in length, completed the effect. Yet the man—easily richer than any of the other inventors Paul had met—wore loose work pants tucked into his faded boots. His vest did not match his coat, and instead of a proper tie he wore a simple kerchief around his neck. Mabel wore her gray hair tied back into a schoolgirl's bun. Her beige coat had been designed for warmth, not for fashion, and her plain linen dress did not appear to have been sewn within the past decade.

"You must be the famed Miss Huntington," said Bell, kissing her outstretched hand. "I regret never having seen you on the stage, but now we must make an effort to get to New York more often."

"I'm flattered," replied Agnes. "But if you can dig up a piano, I'll spare you the train fare."

There followed an hour of pleasant introductions as Paul and Agnes sipped tea in one of the mansion's many sitting rooms. Mabel talked about their time on the lake, how their children had learned to sail and how lovely it was for the family to take picnics in the wooded hills. Every Christmas Day the children were allowed to toboggan down the cape and across the solid ice. Mabel watched them each year with her heart pounding. Mr. Bell described the laboratory he'd built just yards down the dirt path, eagerly promising to give his guests a tour after lunch. He'd been working on hydrofoils, gasoline-powered ships that glided just above the surface of the water. He'd begun work on a flying machine as well, a winged device that threatened to carry its occupant as far as a few hundred feet through the air. He'd exchanged a few encouraging letters with a pair of bicycle designers from Ohio at work on something similar. Bell's own work wasn't as far along, but early tests were promising.

Sure enough, an old rosewood piano made its appearance. Agnes sang "You'll Miss Lots of Fun When You're Married." Mabel accompanied her on the piano. The older woman lost her fingerings a few times, the chords shifting into accidental minors. Agnes covered the mistakes with a smile and a higher harmony, her musicianship skilled enough to make up for her partner's lack thereof. There was much laughter in the sun-dappled drawing room.

Paul waited until everyone's cup had been drained of its tea before broaching the subject of their visit.

"The elegance of your home, Mr. Bell, certainly befits the only man alive who can claim to have bested Thomas Edison."

"I will take my cue to check on the salmon," said Mabel as she stood.

"No, no," said Paul. "Please. You needn't leave. It's only that we've found ourselves in dire straits, and we've come to you for guidance."

"Well then, I hope you find what you've come for," replied Mabel. "But for my part, I did not move to Canada so that I could spend another minute of my life talking about Thomas Edison."

Bell watched her go, a loving smile on his face as his wife shut the wooden door behind her.

"She exaggerates," said Bell as he was left alone with Paul and Agnes. "She unfortunately still has to spend more than a few minutes of her life talking about Edison, though I try to leave her out of it."

"How do you mean?" asked Agnes.

"How many times do you two think I've been sued by the Wizard of Menlo Park?" he asked.

"Mr. Westinghouse has been sued three hundred twelve times by Edison," answered Paul. "I cannot imagine you faced a lesser on-slaught."

"My lawyers summarized it for me in a letter," said Bell. "In the past decade and a half, between Edison, Elisha Gray, and their friends at Western Union, I've been sued more than six hundred times over that silly telephone business."

Paul and Agnes were dutifully impressed by the insanity of this figure.

"Have you ever tried one?" asked Bell.

"One what?" said Paul.

"A telephone, of course."

"I haven't yet."

"I have," said Agnes. "It was thrilling."

"It wears off quickly," said Bell. "Horrid things. Infernally loud. As soon as you wire one up, the damned bell never stops ringing. That's why I won't keep one around. All that fuss over something so annoy-ing. Do you know I keep a place in Washington, just for the lawsuits? The Supreme Court sits in the fall, so the lawyers like me to spend a few months down there every year, to testify in person as Edison and his cronies rake my name through the mud."

"Washington is lovely in the autumn," suggested Agnes.

"I practically never leave the courthouse when I'm there. I make my yearly pilgrimage, raise my right hand, tell everyone the same bor-ing story of that first telephone call. 'Mr. Watson, come here.' Like many future telephone conversations, it was rather less interesting than one might hope. I tell my story, and the court rules again and again that my patent is valid. Edison and his boys go back to New York to skulk around until they find another reason to sue me."

"You've won every single one of those six hundred suits," said Paul. "It's remarkable."

"It helps that I did actually invent the thing," said Bell. "Not that that always makes a difference. But this is what inventing has become in America, thanks to you lawyers. Courtrooms are the new laborato-ries."

"And you prefer the older kind."

"If you've come here for advice, my friend, then you're welcome to the very best advice I have: Get out while you still can."

This was not what Paul had come to hear. Bell might be old and comfortable with retirement, but he was not.

"The Westinghouse Electric Company is soon to declare bankruptcy," confessed Paul. "Edison is going to win the light-bulb suits. You can't be saying that in my position you'd just as well let him."

"No," said Bell. "I'm saying that in your position, I'd have let Edison win a long time ago."

Bell stood, stretching his legs with a stroll to the tall windows. He gazed out at the maple trees for a moment before he spoke again. "What is it that you think you're fighting for?"

"We're fighting for the future of this nation," said Paul.

"You're not," said Bell softly. "You're fighting for money. Or honor, which is worse."

"What are *you* fighting for?" asked Agnes. "You haven't let Edison steal your patent."

Bell turned to Agnes.

"What do you think, Miss Huntington? Why do I go to Washington each fall?"

She seemed to find something in his eyes. Something silent and tender passed between them at a pitch that Paul could not hear.

Agnes smiled. "You do it for her. For Mabel."

"And my girls," said Bell. "But I control no company. I file for no other patents. Defending the royalty I have is enough trouble for one life. You want to make a fortune, Mr. Cravath? You already have. You're George Westinghouse's attorney, not even thirty. And you've a woman by your side, who let me add is as lovely and charming and smart as any man of your generation might hope to marry. It doesn't seem so bad."

Paul reddened in the face. He thought about correcting Bell, but to his surprise saw Agnes quickly motion him to be still.

"In my laboratory here," said Bell, "I can work on any problem I choose. I can tinker all day on any device that strikes my fancy. I am free of the terrors of public opinion that so torture Thomas Edison. I am free of the dull pains of manufacturing that so weigh down George

Westinghouse. That is winning. To sit in the dark and *create* things. That's how we all started. Yet somehow we all forgot that when we allowed our days to become consumed by bickering over which of us first ran which current through which wire. Who cares?"

He turned to Paul as he continued. "The future you're fighting for, it belongs to the moneymen. Not the inventors. Leave the former to their well-appointed hell. And tell the latter to join me here, where only genius matters, and only wonder thrives."

Alexander Graham Bell was, in this speech, as decent a man as Paul had met in years.

"You are one of the smartest men in the world, Mr. Bell. Don't tell me you think I'm going to stop."

Bell gave a laugh. "No, Mr. Cravath," he said. "I don't." He gazed again at the thick maple trees stretching for miles outside his window. He seemed lost in a series of thoughts that Paul was sure he would never understand.

"You really hate him, don't you?" asked Bell.

"You don't?"

"I pity him. . . . You will not understand why I am doing this today, and you will not understand why I am doing this tomorrow. But when you do . . . well, just please remember that I warned you. I'm going to tell you what you want to know. I'm going to tell you how to defeat Thomas Edison. And I think you're going to be successful. But please remember this. I'm not going to do it for you; I'm going to do it for him."

CHAPTER 57

The Reverse Salient

We often miss opportunity because it's dressed in overalls
and looks like work.   —THOMAS EDISON

"I DIDN'T BEAT EDISON," continued Bell. "The silly fool beat himself. I was just clever enough to let him do it."

"What do you mean?"

"The most dangerous enemy that Thomas Edison will ever face is Thomas Edison. And even after all this time, he still hasn't learned his lesson."

"You're being terribly cryptic."

"Have you ever picked up one of those papers—*The Wall Street Journal?*"

"Yes," answered Paul.

"Rubbish things, but a friend was here last week, brought a stack along. All the information you need to know to beat Edison is in one of those."

"Edison's stock price? It's at an all-time high. I don't understand how that helps us."

"Edison's stock is valued highly," said Agnes, "because everyone believes that he's going to defeat Westinghouse."

"Go on," said Bell.

"And that is the primary source of its value," suggested Agnes.

Bell smiled. "Honestly," he said to Paul, "your fiancée has a much better head for business than you do."

Paul did his best to ignore this comment. "You're suggesting that we spread rumors? To depress the value of his stock?"

"You've no need to *lie*. The truth is damning enough."

"And the truth is . . . ?"

"All right," said Bell. "You asked how I beat him. It was exceptionally simple. I invented the damned thing before he did. I was quick. He was late. That's the thing that kills him, even to this day. It wasn't that I was a better inventor than he was. It was that he was so obsessed with solving a different problem that he didn't even notice the answer to the telephone problem was lying right at his feet. He was consumed with telegraphs; he'd been working on them for a decade, even then. He'd done some early work on the telephone but felt it was a distraction. Why would he waste time on some silly talking box when his telegraph lines were getting finer and finer? He actually had the idea for the 'phone at the same time as I did, you know. It's not a secret. And this is what will haunt that poor man until his dying day—he had the idea at the same time, but I patented it. And the law is the law. Do you know, I think that's why he's been so rough with Westinghouse? He must have vowed never to make such a mistake again."

"I already showed that he lied on his patent application for the incandescent lamp," said Paul. "It did no good."

"No," said Agnes. "That's not the point that Mr. Bell is trying to make."

"Correct," said Bell.

"He's saying," said Agnes, "that Edison is an obsessive. Like someone else I know. And this is Edison's weakness. He becomes so fixated on one line of attack that he becomes completely oblivious to another one."

"Clever girl," said Bell.

"A reverse salient?" asked Agnes. Bell laughed approvingly.

"What?" Paul was confused.

"Sometimes an army will intentionally create a reverse salient in its forward line," she said. "A point of such obvious weakness that its enemy cannot help but take advantage. Do you know much about military history?"

"How do *you* know much about military history?" asked Paul.

"I was once friendly with a general. In London. Anyhow. What is the obvious weakness of Westinghouse's? What is his reverse salient that has so consumed Edison?"

Paul struggled not to let his thoughts stray to this general in Agnes's past.

"I would think," said Bell, "that Mr. Cravath would know the singular obsession of Thomas Edison better than just about anyone else in the world."

"The lawsuit!" exclaimed Agnes. "Paul, you've been saying for months that this lawsuit is costing Westinghouse a fortune."

"Yes . . ."

"Do you think it's costing Edison any less?"

As Paul finally understood the point that Bell and Agnes had been making, he began to smile.

"Edison is so focused on winning the patent war," he said, "that he's forgotten that he also needs to win the corporate war. The Edison General Electric Company . . . it's not actually profitable. He's running the thing into the red to beat Westinghouse. Undercutting his prices so severely that he's barely eking out a profit. Throwing a fortune away on legal fees, a fortune that I cannot imagine that *his* attorneys have so graciously deferred."

"You're deferring your legal fees?" said Bell. "Remind me to hire you the next time Edison sues me."

"Sooner or later Edison's shareholders will notice their lack of profit," said Paul, "and they will not be pleased."

"The question you need to ask yourself," said Bell, "is: Who is the largest shareholder in EGE? Besides Edison himself?"

Paul and Agnes both knew the answer.

"Sixty percent," she said very quietly. "It's hard to get much larger than that."

Paul remained silent as he put the pieces together.

"I get the impression that a plan is forming," suggested Bell. The old man couldn't help but tease his youthful guests.

Paul stood suddenly. "I know how we're going to win," he said.

"You look . . . amused," she said.

"Well, it is rather funny," he replied. "It turns out that, quite fortuitously, you might be the only person in the whole world who can help me do it."

PART III
Solutions

Contrary to popular myth, technology does not result from a series of searches for the "one best solution" to a problem. . . . Instead . . . practitioners of technology [confront] insolvable issues, [make] mistakes, and [cause] controversies and failures. [They] create new problems as they solve old ones.

—THOMAS HUGHES, *AMERICAN GENESIS*

CHAPTER 58

The Metropolitan Opera House Ball

> You can't connect the dots looking forward; you can only
> connect them looking backwards. So you have to trust that
> the dots will somehow connect in your future. You have to
> trust in something—your gut, destiny, life, karma, what-
> ever. This approach has never let me down, and it has made
> all the difference in my life.
> —STEVE JOBS

I T COULD BE fairly said that the New Year's ball at the Metropolitan Opera House was the second-most exclusive party in the world. Credit would need to be given to the first, Mrs. Jacob Astor's summer gala. That preeminent party was limited to four hundred guests, who crammed into the Astors' Newport estate for one sweaty, well-sauced evening each July. Mrs. Astor composed the list of attendees herself and, in a colorful flourish, would stamp by hand each invitation as it went out. New York society would spend their Junes nervously checking their mail tables for the telltale stamp upon the incoming envelopes. The names and qualifications of the guests were duly reported in *The Times* and *The World*. *Harper's* typically documented the event with a page-wide pencil sketch of city glamour at its most impossibly dense.

New Year's at the Met was more than twice as populous, which made the party necessarily half as glamorous. The guest list topped one thousand, and included more than the usual stock of stiff gentry. Also invited were crude politicians, European dancers in for the season, and young women of such beauty that one would never know they possessed only a simple West Side mansion and a generous uncle along Union Square. For one night, artists and railroad tycoons and English dukes all mingled effervescently. The notables of New York bounced against one another like the fizzy bubbles in the champagne flutes. Not coincidentally, Mrs. Astor was also a principal organizer of this second-place gala. This was due less to her personal investment in the Met and more to her simple dictate that no party of any great significance should take place in Manhattan without her involvement. Her monopoly on the New York social scene was more thorough than her husband's was on American coal.

But while the Met's yearly party lagged behind Mrs. Astor's ball in exclusivity, it more than made up for this shortcoming by the ingenuity of its fashions. Whereas the July party stood as a symbol of black-on-white formality, New Year's was a rainbow atop a bright pile of gold. The men were of course white-tied and black-tailed in the appropriate manner, but the women were permitted—encouraged—to show what could be done with a yard of silk and a carefully stitched bit of muslin. Diamonds were hung across every limb a woman could bare.

Paul knew all of this merely from newspapers and magazines. He was left to imagine the scene inside the party, however, as he stood shivering in the alley behind Thirty-ninth Street at quarter to eleven in the evening. There was little more than an hour left of 1889; he could hear the party from the street. Paul was very cold.

He'd been waiting in the alley for almost an hour, during which time Agnes was the only thing standing between himself and hypothermia. She was also the only thing standing between the Westinghouse Electric Company and bankruptcy. Paul needed to get into that party. He would wait for her as long as it took, whether or not his toes blackened from frost.

With a sudden screech, the metal door swung open and Agnes appeared in the orange light. She effortlessly wore a dress of shocking yellow, elegant and tasteful yet more delicately stitched than it might at first appear.

"Lord, it's freezing out here," she said. "Hurry up and get in."

She yanked the door shut behind them and led Paul through the winding maze of corridors. He hadn't been back to the Met in a year, since Tesla's arrival in Agnes's dressing room. He still hadn't ever been to a performance.

"Is he here?" asked Paul when it no longer pained him to move his lips.

"Yes," replied Agnes. "But there's a problem. He has a friend with him."

"Who?"

"Thomas Edison."

Paul stopped. "Damn it."

"I know."

"Was Edison on the guest list?"

"Who knows? If I had been able to get a copy, I'd have had a shot at getting your name on it. Clearly we've had to make do with other means. My guess is that Thomas Edison was permitted to use the front door."

This was going to make Paul's plan for the evening considerably more difficult. "Are they together?"

"Not every moment. Edison has a lot of admirers. He has rounds to make, handshakes and tall tales. You'll have to find a minute when they're separated to make your move."

There was no chance of turning back.

Paul followed Agnes toward the glittering ball in search of his target.

All the seats had been removed from the auditorium, allowing the thousand guests to spread freely across the floor of the great domed room. Strings of electric lights hung from the balconies, stretching toward the stage in blinking spiderwebs. From the stage, a forty-person orchestra played a spirited waltz. The dancers swayed forward and back, the waves of motion splashing against the solid rocks of conversation that dotted the floor.

Paul was a small trawler sailing into the rough seas of this crowd. Stepping slowly into the gala, he was practically knocked off his feet by a drunken couple who spun wildly through their dance.

"Careful," counseled Agnes. "We can't have you making a scene."

Paul watched Agnes glide across the floor. She was a bird in flight over the choppy ocean. But Agnes was no gull, he thought as she smiled, putting up bulwarks against the curious glances being cast in her direction. She was a hawk.

"Over there," said Paul, turning his head away.

Only fifty feet away was Thomas Edison, chatting amiably with acquaintances. He looked strangely younger in his tuxedo, the white bow tie askew below his chin. He was the only member of his circle without a drink in his hand.

"Do you know how to waltz?" asked Agnes.

"What?"

She took his right hand with her left and held it at the level of her waist before grasping his left hand with her right. Then she spun.

It took Paul a few moments to realize that she was leading him onto the dance floor in a three-count twirl. He tried to remember the last time he'd danced a waltz. Her perfume washed over him and for a moment it was as if he were back with her at his parents' house on a warm Tennessee night.

"Steady," whispered Agnes. "Just follow me."

They spun across the dance floor, orbiting the other dancers. The room was a constellation of the very latest fashions. At first he clomped against the glazed wood floor. But as she tugged at his hands she gave shape to his movements.

"Slow," she whispered. "Quick-quick, slow. There it is, yes."

Paul struggled to fight the dizziness.

She'd already told him that he needn't worry about the presence of Henry Jayne, who was in Philadelphia with a sick relative. For an affianced couple, they spent little time together. Was that how it was done among the rich? He didn't think he could bear to be in the same room with the man. And he certainly didn't want to have such a meeting take place with his hand softly touching Agnes's hip.

He felt her warm and even breath on his neck. He felt the muscles along her back tense and release with the rhythm of their dance. Paul knew that he wasn't only doing this for Westinghouse. He didn't need to win only to punish Edison. He needed Agnes to see that he was as worthy as Henry Jayne.

"Edison is thirty feet behind you," she whispered. "While our man is ten feet over there. Come on."

Agnes pressed at Paul's hands, urging him through the crush of partygoers. They approached a circle of five chattering men in perfect white collars and long black tails. None was under the age of fifty, and all boasted the comfortable waistlines of lives well lived. At the center, Paul caught the eye of a large man, the only one of the lot without a beard. Instead, a thick brown mustache provided a striking contrast of color across his face. The hair parted across his head was a chalk white. His cheeks looked as if they had never once been forced into a smile.

It was J. P. Morgan, the man he had come to see.

CHAPTER 59

A Secret Meeting with the Richest Man in America

Capitalism has worked very well. Anyone who wants to
move to North Korea is welcome.   —BILL GATES

T HE SONG CAME to a stop with a long and satisfying bow stroke
from the violins. The guests clapped absentmindedly, their gra-
ciousness as instinctive as a cough.

Agnes was studying Morgan's circle. "They look relatively drunk,"
she whispered conspiratorially. "Wait here." She pulled free of Paul's
grip. Before he could ask any questions, she had stepped away and
dived into the middle of the group.

"Mr. Routledge!" she cooed to one of Morgan's associates. "How
was Brussels?"

Paul watched as Agnes maneuvered herself into the men's conversation. They were rabbits to her fox. Paul heard their sudden laughter,
saw their jockeying for position as each tried to impress the beautiful
woman shimmying gaily before them. Paul stood mutely to the side of
their conversation, uninvited and straining to listen surreptitiously.

In under a minute, Agnes had slipped her body into their circle in
such a way that Morgan was cut off from the center. It was so subtle
as to be not at all rude, and yet Morgan's isolation was unmistakable.

Paul understood then what she was doing. If he had been impressed before, he was now doubly so. Morgan was not accustomed to being ignored. Paul began to sense boredom in the old man's stance.

Morgan stepped back from the group with a glass of Scotch in his hand. He walked across the dance floor, Paul following close behind. Morgan received a series of nods and smiles from the people he passed, but none seemed to interest him. He walked into the rear hallway and through the door of the gentlemen's lounge.

Paul waited ten seconds before following him in.

The lounge was long. Marble countertops lined one side and a row of toilet stalls, likely stocked with the new chain-pull design, lined the other. On the far wall, a chaise provided a comfortable perch for the weary. When Paul entered, Morgan was reclining onto the chaise, still clutching his glass.

Two other men stood by the mirrors. They fixed their loosened neckties as Morgan relaxed on the back chaise. He closed his eyes as if enjoying this brief and singular moment of peace.

Paul stood at the mirror, purposefully pulled his own tie out of place, and then feigned difficulty at righting it. He examined the part in his hair, making sure no strand had fallen astray.

The two strangers seemed to feel that whatever conversation they'd been having before J. P. Morgan walked in would best be continued elsewhere. They exited, a backslap sealing their conspiracy. The door closed behind them. Paul had his chance.

Paul quickly moved to the door and flipped the bolt.

He had just locked himself into the men's lounge, alone with J. P. Morgan.

Morgan heard the metal bolt snap into place and looked up at Paul.

It would be scant minutes before either Morgan's absence aroused unwanted interest outside or the locked door attracted a passing servant's concern. Paul had very little time.

"If you're planning to rob me," said Morgan, still seated, "I should inform you that my pockets are empty."

His utter nonchalance indicated that he was afraid of very little in this world. What private fears he might harbor certainly did not include strangers in white bow ties who made vaguely threatening advances at costume galas. The look of Paul, locked door or no, did not appear to concern Morgan in the slightest.

"My name is Paul Cravath."

"That's nice," said Morgan.

"I am a partner at Carter, Hughes, and Cravath."

"Your parents must be so proud."

"I am the lead attorney for George Westinghouse in his lawsuits against Thomas Edison."

"Oh, pity. Perhaps they're not so proud." Morgan stood. "Your name did sound familiar. I'm going to leave now."

He took a step toward the door. Paul stepped forward as well, making clear that he was putting his own body between Morgan and the exit.

"I have a proposition for you," said Paul.

"I have an office," said Morgan.

"It's confidential."

"Oh my."

"Thomas Edison is costing you money."

"You're costing me money. There's business to attend to out there."

Morgan stepped again in the direction of the door. Again Paul made clear that he would not be moving aside.

"I used to keep a pistol on me, you know," said Morgan. "I am going to give my security boys quite an earful about convincing me not to carry it."

"The war between Thomas Edison and George Westinghouse is going to drive them both broke."

"And?"

"And as you own sixty percent of the stock in the Edison General Electric Company, I propose that this is an even bigger problem for you than it is for me."

"I might suggest that your biggest problem right now is what my friends are going to do to you when I get out of here."

"You and I have the same problem. And I propose that we work together to fix it."

Morgan didn't say a word.

"Edison and Westinghouse are dueling to the death over their respective slices of a pie that is only this big." Paul formed a small circle with his fingers. "But working together, we could take equal shares of a pie that is *this* big." Paul expanded his circle threefold. "A partnership between the two companies—a licensing arrangement—would eliminate the burden for consumers of having to choose which of our incompatible products they wanted. A/C, D/C . . . it wouldn't matter. You could sell our current. We could sell your bulbs. Everyone wins. Let's stop putting the future of these companies in the hands of the courts. Let's stop leaving it to the vagaries of newspaper opinion and the shifting winds of the free market. Let's put the important decisions back in the boardroom where they belong."

Morgan slipped his hands into his pockets. He pursed his lips.

"Competition," argued Paul, "does no one any good. A friendly monopoly, on the other hand . . ."

Morgan smiled. Paul was speaking in his native language.

"You've got some hustle in you."

"It takes one to know one."

"I'm not much of a hustler, Mr. Cravath. Whatever you've been told about me, I think the reality is far less dramatic than people like to say. You know who's a great hustler? Thomas. Or your friend Mr. Westinghouse. I'm just a simple businessman."

"The most successful one in the world."

"It's the thing about businessmen. There is nothing of which we despair so much as a free market."

It was Paul's turn to smile.

"Off the top of my head," said Morgan, "I can think up a half dozen critical difficulties with this scheme. But the most clearly insurmountable is a simple one."

"What?"

"Thomas Edison." He took a thoughtful sip of his Scotch. "I don't know what you've told Westinghouse, or even what you might, with that silvery tongue, be able to convince him of. But I can assure you that Thomas will never go along with this plan."

"I know," said Paul.

"He *despises* Westinghouse."

"I know."

"So long as Thomas Edison is at the head of the Edison General Electric Company, it will engage in no partnership with your client."

Paul moved a step closer to Morgan, placing his hand boldly on the industrial baron's left shoulder. "But whoever said Edison has to remain at the head of his company?"

CHAPTER 60

Bury a Penny

I just invent a thing, then wait until man comes around to
needing what I've invented. —BUCKMINSTER FULLER

"WOULD YOU LIKE to know the easiest way to make a billion dollars?" asked J. P. Morgan the next day. They were standing among the Cypriot antique collection at the Metropolitan Museum of Art.

"I'd love to," replied Paul. The two men gazed at the rows of ancient pottery before them.

"Take a penny. Bury it in the ground for a thousand years. Then dig." Morgan gestured to the faded brown vases, intricately etched plates, and darkly stained pitchers that lined the walls of the hall. The Cypriot wing was vacant save for these relics. The voices of the two men echoed through the room.

The museum was under construction. Scaffolding covered its Fifth Avenue facade.

"Do you know Luigi di Cesnola?" Morgan asked.

"I'm afraid I don't," said Paul.

"Sardinian, but he came here in the fifties. Fought in the war. Ours, not theirs. Well, theirs too, I think, at some point earlier. But he made his name in ours. After which he sailed back to Cyprus, took care to amass this collection, and then sold it back here for . . .

298 | GRAHAM MOORE

well, Mr. Cravath, what do you think the museum board gave him for it?"

"I couldn't possibly say."

"They gave him *the museum*. They made him the director. And the Metropolitan Museum of Art now has an antiquities collection that's starting to give London worry."

"It sounds like a smart deal."

"Bury a single penny, and in enough time, you'll have yourself a fortune. That is my point. It only gets hard if you want to get it done a bit faster."

Paul looked around. They were still alone, and their secret meeting remained, so far as he could tell, unobserved.

"You may speak freely here, Mr. Cravath. We have the wing to ourselves for the afternoon. Luigi is a good friend."

Paul knew that he should not be surprised by anything Morgan was capable of. Nothing in New York was beyond Morgan's grasp. Paul was certain that even as Morgan had entertained this talk of a partnership, the older man was in no sense his ally. He would turn against Paul in a second flat if it ever became in his financial interest to do so. One doesn't lie down with a lion and get to act surprised if one finds oneself devoured.

Paul knew that there was a sizable chance that after their meeting at the ball, Morgan had rushed immediately to Edison with the sordid details of Paul's proposition. What mitigated his fears was the comforting reminder of Morgan's immense greed. While what motivated Tesla, Edison, and Westinghouse would always remain somewhat uncertain, what motivated Morgan was no mystery. No one amassed as much money as he had by accident. And it was unclear if anyone in the history of the world had ever before amassed that much money.

Money was a far more predictable motivator than legacy, or fame, or love, or whatever else might rouse a man from his bedsheets. An artist—or an inventor—was a far more dangerous partner than a businessman. The latter's betrayals could be planned for, even depended upon.

"You've examined my proposal," said Paul. "You have the authority to stage a coup, so to speak, at EGE. You can depose Edison and put your own man in charge. Someone sympathetic to our cause."

"I know what I can do, Mr. Cravath. I have lawyers too. They're quite a bit more experienced than you are."

"And yet I'll wager they told you that everything I said was absolutely correct."

"They did indeed."

"And your accountants, I am sure, have analyzed the profits and losses of EGE as well."

"Two cents," said Morgan. "That is EGE's profit per share. It's not a loss, but it's not much in the way of benefit either."

"So you see that I'm right. If you can depose Edison from inside, I can handle things on Westinghouse's end."

"This seems terribly simple from your perspective, does it?"

"Yes," said Paul. "It is mercilessly simple. But that doesn't mean it's going to be easy."

"Do you trust me?"

Paul was startled at the question. "Of course not," he replied honestly. If he intended on negotiating toe-to-toe with the most powerful businessman of the age, then he would do so without insulting either of their intelligences by pretending that they were friends.

"I don't trust you either," said Morgan. "Which is why I'm going to tell you a secret. A very expensive secret. And your response to this secret is going to give me quite a bit of information as to how far I need to go in *dis*trusting you."

"What is it?"

"This is going to be a bit more complicated than you think it is."

"Why?"

"There's a spy inside the Westinghouse Electric Company."

Paul stared blankly. It could not be true. Westinghouse had chosen his team personally. His engineers, his factory foremen, even his lawyers.

"Edison has a spy in Westinghouse's senior leadership. He's been reporting back all of Westinghouse's plans—corporate strategy, the laboratory reports, even the designs of those Pennsylvania factories—to

Edison. He's been doing it for more than a year. You idiots kept getting beat and you couldn't figure out why. Well—this is why."

Paul felt sick, but he could not show weakness.

"How can you be sure Edison has a spy?"

"Because," replied Morgan, "I was the one who put him there."

Paul looked Morgan dead in his calm, unblinking eyes. In confessing this secret, he seemed to feel neither pleasure nor relief.

"Your plan is going to be significantly more complicated than you realize, Mr. Cravath, because if Westinghouse tells his senior staff about it, then our spy will tell Edison."

"Who is it?" asked Paul. "Who is the spy?"

"You bury a penny," said J. P. Morgan, his words echoing among the ancient pottery, "and in a thousand years you'll have a fortune. But if you want to get to the fortune a bit faster . . . you need to bury something a whole lot bigger than a penny."

CHAPTER 61

A Fox in the Chicken Coop

Is the sudden transformation of all the relevant scientific characters [in your book] from petty people to great and selfless men because they see together a beautiful corner of nature unveiled and forget themselves in the presence of the wonder? Or is it because our writer suddenly sees all his characters in a new and generous light because he has achieved success and confidence in his work, and himself?

—RICHARD FEYNMAN, FROM A LETTER TO
JAMES WATSON, CONCERNING THE LATTER'S MANUSCRIPT
OF HIS MEMOIR *THE DOUBLE HELIX*

"REGINALD FESSENDEN?"

Paul's mind raced to make sense of what Morgan had told him. Paul had not only spent hours by Fessenden's side over the past year, but had even recruited the man himself. It had been Paul's sales pitch that won Fessenden to their side, after he'd been fired by Edison. . . . "You're lying," said Paul.

"Frequently. But not, as it happens, today."

"Prove it."

Morgan sighed. "You hired Fessenden yourself, eighteen months ago. You did so at a meeting at his Indiana office, after coming to believe that Edison fired him. You read about the firing in the papers, and went to find a bitter ex-Edison employee who might be bought off. You contacted Fessenden for information about Edison's patent filing, only . . . Well, tell me: Did he actually give you any information that would help you take down Edison's patent?"

Paul replayed his first meeting with Fessenden in Indiana.

"Of course he didn't," said Morgan. "Your next question is going to be about why Fessenden sent you in the direction of what's his name, Tesla. Because Edison thought it would be a waste of your time. Fessenden had to appear to be helpful, while telling you something that wouldn't actually help at all. And so we figured we'd make use of that loony Serbian nut. Thomas got a copy of his engineering society lecture long before he delivered it; told me it was ridiculous. Which gave me the idea of sending you after him in the first place. That you managed to actually get some use out of that man—that was unexpected. It didn't make Thomas happy, I can tell you."

Paul felt suddenly naked, his thoughts and plans and seemingly clever moves over the past years now revealed to be but a pathetic sham. Edison had been outplaying them from the very start.

"You believed you were hiring an apostate. What you were actually hiring was a Trojan horse. Fessenden took the job with your client specifically so that he could gain access to the latest Westinghouse technology. Bit of an irony, really, since Westinghouse thought he was getting access to Edison's."

"But," Paul countered, "Edison never made use of alternating current. If Fessenden has been leaking Westinghouse's designs—and you already had Tesla's lecture—Edison must have seen that it was superior to his own direct-current work. If what you're telling me is true, then how is it that Edison never created an A/C device?"

"Ah," said Morgan. "That's just the thing: Edison disagreed with your supposition. He saw the full reports. I did too, for that matter, not that I paid much mind to the technical gibberish. Edison thought he knew better. His advocacy of direct current—perhaps a mistaken one, as it turns out—did not come from a place of subterfuge. He genuinely believed, after surveying all of his own research and all of yours as well, that his system was the better one."

"He wasn't dishonest, but instead merely incompetent?"

"I would more charitably suggest that he simply followed the available evidence to a different conclusion. Scientists. You ask one hundred of them a simple question, you get one hundred different answers. They're a necessary annoyance in the industrial business, I suppose."

"This was all your idea," said Paul. "Fessenden. Tesla. The whole ruse."

"Of course it was. Thomas isn't nearly devious enough to come up with something like this on his own."

"This past autumn, when you were blocking our attempts to find new investors—this is how you knew who we were going to before we got there. This is how you were able to contact them first."

Morgan looked pleased. "I'd been wondering if you'd figured that out."

Paul had been in over his head from the moment he'd taken on the Westinghouse case. He'd been drowning in water even deeper than he'd known.

Paul was clever. Tesla, Edison, and Westinghouse were geniuses. What was Morgan? Paul felt himself in the presence of something else entirely.

"Is this the part where you pretend to be so much more noble than I am?" asked Morgan. "I'd rather not bother, if it's all the same to you."

"I didn't illegally place a spy in your company, Mr. Morgan."

Morgan spent a long moment looking Paul up and down. "Do you know what awaits you at the end of this, Mr. Cravath? I have a notion that you're going to gain all of the riches that you desire. Congratulations, in advance. But have you considered what you might have to give up in return?"

"What's that?"

"The illusion that you ever deserved it."

Morgan gazed thoughtfully at a bronze statue. It depicted a warrior, spear in hand, galloping on horseback into a great and long-forgotten war.

"Poor people all think they deserve to be rich," he continued. "Rich people live every day with the uneasy knowledge that we do not."

Morgan spoke as if they were the same class of men. As if Morgan were Paul's own reflection in a darkened mirror.

"Westinghouse is likely with Fessenden at this very moment," said Paul.

"I'm sure."

"I must speak with him. If he tells Fessenden about our plan . . ."

Paul prepared to run off to the nearest Western Union office, before he had a better idea.

"Mr. Morgan," said Paul as he turned to face him. "I'll ask you for one more favor."

"Yes."

"Could you find me a telephone?"

CHAPTER 62

Whether or Not It's True

The good thing about science is that it's true whether or not
you believe in it.　　　　　　　　　—NEIL DEGRASSE TYSON

A
S IT HAPPENED, Luigi di Cesnola kept a telephone in his private office on the museum's third floor. As the device had been a gift from Morgan, Cesnola was more than happy to let the banker's young friend make use of it while he and Morgan smoked in the corridor outside. Paul listened nervously to the odd ringing noises emanating from the black earpiece he held up to his ear.

A laboratory assistant finally picked up on the other end of the line. Paul demanded to speak urgently to George Westinghouse.

"Paul?" came the scratchy but recognizable voice of George Westinghouse through the earpiece. It felt more like he was speaking with a ghost than with another human being. There was Westinghouse's incorporeal voice, right there, pressed against Paul's right ear. The personhood of Westinghouse had been reduced to a voice in the ether.

"Are you completely alone?" said Paul.

"Did you meet with Morgan? Did he go for it?"

"Is anyone with you in the laboratory at the moment? Next to you, while we're speaking? That assistant I just spoke with?"

"What are you talking about?"

"Please. Are you alone?"

"Yes."

Paul could tell even this far away that Westinghouse was dismayed at the tenor of this conversation. But it couldn't be helped.

"Then listen close."

Paul explained as plainly as he could what Morgan had told him. Westinghouse was shocked at first and then incredulous. The lead engineer on all of his electrical projects had been working in secret for their enemy? Was Paul suggesting that he was some sort of fool?

"I'll have the police here within the hour," said Westinghouse. His disbelief and embarrassment had given way to a righteous anger. "False representation, intellectual theft, broken employment contracts, simple fraud—I will see him shackled before sundown."

"That was my initial reaction as well," said Paul calmly into the receiver. "Then I thought better of it."

"Why?"

"Where is Fessenden now?"

"The lab, I should assume. Gathering up every detail of my work on—"

"Can you keep him there? And keep him out of the meetings you'll need to have in the coming days concerning Edison?"

"Why would I do that? He should be arrested."

"Think it through, sir. If you arrest Fessenden, what happens?"

There was silence on the line as Westinghouse went through the same series of thoughts that Paul had run through only a few minutes before.

". . . Edison will know that we discovered his spy," said Westinghouse.

"Yes."

"He'll assume that one of his own people ratted him out."

"Yes."

"And then he'll go looking for a rotten apple inside his own barrel."

"Which," said Paul, "is exactly what we do not want him doing."

"So what else would you propose?"

"Can you give Fessenden a task? Some sort of project—it can be a waste of time, I don't care what it is—to keep him busy?"

"I'm sure I can come up with something," said Westinghouse.

"Do that. Meanwhile, we might be able to get some real use out of Fessenden yet."

"How?"

"Anything we tell him will leak back to Edison."

"Yes."

"Whether or not it's true."

Westinghouse could not see the grin on Paul's face as these last words were spoken. And yet as Paul listened patiently to the quiet clicks and hisses of the telephone wire, he hoped that far away, in an oak-lined office in the countryside near Pittsburgh, Westinghouse was grinning too.

CHAPTER 63

Brief Vignettes as the Stage Is Set for the Final Performance

Before anything else, preparation is the key to success.

—ALEXANDER GRAHAM BELL

GEORGE WESTINGHOUSE LISTENED carefully to Paul's plan before informing his attorney that he would not play a part in it.

"You're asking me to tell the whole of my management team that you've found Nikola Tesla?" asked Westinghouse incredulously.

"Yes," said Paul. "Tell them Tesla has been hiding out in Chicago."

"What—why—" Westinghouse sputtered. "Why Chicago?"

"Because it's far away."

Paul could hear the huffing from the other end of the line.

"Our aim is to distract Edison's attention, is it not?" continued Paul. "Very well. Edison knows that he's likely put you out of business unless you can come up with an original light bulb. Or unless Tesla can. So if we leak to Edison that Tesla has been working on just such a thing in secret, from a laboratory in Chicago, he'll be distracted."

Westinghouse did not answer.

"It's the perfect wild-goose chase," added Paul.

"I will not lie to my entire staff."

"I'm sorry. But we can't have Fessenden growing suspicious. If you tell only him, he might catch on that something is afoot. The story needs to pervade the conversation of your employees."

"Edison will realize soon enough that Tesla is not in Chicago," said Westinghouse. "And that he has not designed any new light bulbs."

"Yes. But by then it won't matter." Paul heard a creak coming from the direction of the doorway. He turned to see J. P. Morgan framed in a wispy gray stream of cigar smoke. Having concluded his conversation with Luigi di Cesnola, Morgan was ready for Paul to be finished as well. They had a lot of work in store for them. And J. P. Morgan did not look like a man who was accustomed to being kept waiting.

"No one will believe that Tesla has a secret laboratory in Chicago," came Westinghouse's voice through the telephone. "No one will even believe that he's still alive."

Paul had been dreading the conversation that he was about to have for a very long time. He felt lucky only that he did not have to see the look on his client's face as he confessed his deception.

"Nikola Tesla is not in Chicago," said Paul. "But he is very much alive."

As Paul kept talking, the pale smoke from Morgan's cigar drifted across the museum office.

The next evening, Paul caught Agnes as she exited the rear door of the Metropolitan Opera House. Theatergoers poured from the Met onto Thirty-ninth Street, the din of their commotion a background rattle. An hour to midnight, and Manhattan glowed with lights both new and old.

"There you are!" exclaimed Agnes. Her expression shifted from startled to worried. "I went by your office looking for you."

"I've been busy."

"Is Morgan on board? Is it working?"

"I need you to go back to Tennessee," said Paul.

"Excuse me?"

"I'm sorry. We are in a terrible rush."

"A rush to do what?"

"I need you to collect Nikola and bring him here."

Agnes gave Paul a long and searching look. They had been waiting for this moment for a very long time. Now that it had arrived, it came without fanfare or celebration. The hour felt grave. The night sky glittered.

"Why now?" she asked.

"Because I believe Thomas Edison is about to try to kill him."

"And you want me with Tesla when he does?"

"Of course not," said Paul. "This time, I want Edison to look for him in the wrong place."

Paul told her about his confession to his client, and their move to make use of Fessenden's betrayal.

"I cannot imagine that your talk with Westinghouse was easy," she said.

"It wasn't."

"Are you all right?"

Paul had no idea how he felt anymore. He had only to press forward.

"He'll forgive you," she said. But Paul was not of a mind to be comforted.

"Eventually" was all he said in response. "It doesn't matter now."

There was no time, at the moment, for sentiment. Not even with Agnes.

"Where would you like me to take Tesla?" she asked.

Paul looked up at the bustle of Manhattan. "Bring him home."

"Mr. Cravath," said Walter Carter as Paul walked into his office the next morning. "Where in the world have you been? We have a bankruptcy to attend to."

Paul had cabled his partners from Nashville, suggesting that there was one last resource he sought to exploit before declaring Westinghouse's bankruptcy. They had heard nothing from him since, save for admonitions to continue waiting.

"I need a favor," Paul said.

"We need to know what is happening. I wrote to Westinghouse, who said that he is aware of whatever it is you're up to. This is unconscionable, young man."

"I'm sorry, but this maneuver must remain a secret. Soon enough you'll know why. At the moment, Westinghouse and I need you to sue someone."

Carter looked at Paul for a long moment. "What in the world are you talking about?"

"Fetch Hughes. There's a lawsuit we need you to bring, and we need you to do it right away. Do this, and you'll no longer need to attend to Westinghouse's bankruptcy. Instead you may attend to his victory."

"Oh yes?" said Carter. "And whom exactly would you like me to sue?"

"I actually don't care. Anyone. As long as his attorney is Lemuel Serrell."

Paul told him what he needed to know. And nothing more.

By noon Paul was waiting anxiously at the Western Union offices on the southern tip of Broadway. He focused his nervousness by pacing along the seams of the black-and-white marble blocks beneath his feet.

Finally the boy behind the counter tapped at the copper bars that shielded him from the general public. He gestured to Paul, who came near.

"We've a message for a Jonathan Springborn," said the boy.

"Thank you," said Paul as he took hold of the narrow slip of paper that the boy handed to him.

The message was from "Morgan," no first name or initials listed. And it was very short.

"Received urgent message from TE. Tesla alive. In Chicago. Full weight of EGE and Pinkertons sent to locate. Please advise."

Paul's plan was working. So far.

"I'd like to wire a message back to this sender," said Paul to the boy, who dutifully took out his pen.

"Train to Chicago takes thirty-six hours, stop," said Paul. "Then thirty-six back. Stop. We have three days to finish. Stop."

"Seven cents," said the boy after he quickly tallied up the words.

"It's worth a lot more than that," said Paul as he fished in his pocket for the coins.

Later that afternoon, Paul took the Saugus Line to Lynn, Massachusetts. It wasn't a long trip to the small town, nestled near the coast just ten miles north of Boston. He emerged from his train to find the central square covered with a thick layer of snow. Paul's carriage cut lines through the snow as it carried him to the largest of the great factories that ringed the village.

Eight separate four-story structures extended for what looked like an acre in each direction. Smoke plumed from stone stacks above each one. Paul found the executive offices in the largest of the buildings.

THOMSON-HOUSTON ELECTRIC COMPANY was etched in wide type above the doorway.

A series of secretaries passed him back through the hallways, until finally he reached a rear office.

Inside, Charles Coffin leaned against his desk. He'd been waiting for Paul's arrival all morning, and gave no pretense of having been busy with other affairs.

"Mr. Cravath," said Coffin. "I had rather suspected I'd never see you again."

"I had rather hoped for the same."

Coffin smiled. "You really dislike me, don't you?"

"You betrayed me and you betrayed Westinghouse and you did so against all of your better technical and scientific judgment. What do you think?"

"That no one likes a sore loser."

Doing business with this man made Paul furious. But Coffin's duplicity had become the very quality that Paul now required.

"You've agreed to meet me," said Paul. "So I take it you've spoken with Mr. Morgan."

"I received a letter," replied Coffin. "It beseeched me to hear you out."

"I can't quite imagine Mr. Morgan doing much 'beseeching.' But I'm glad you've acquiesced nonetheless."

"He said you had a business proposal for me. And that this proposal should stay far from the ears of Thomas Edison. Under normal circumstances, of course, I would have told you to go to hell. But if you've involved Morgan, whatever you're doing must be quite serious."

"I've come to ask you a very simple question: How would you like to be the new head of EGE?"

Coffin tried very hard not to show how stunned he was. He looked down at his polished shoes.

"That's quite an offer," said Coffin.

Paul shrugged nonchalantly. Morgan was wearing off on him.

"And what about Thomas Edison?"

"He's outlasted his usefulness."

"To whom?"

"To Morgan, for one," said Paul. "And perhaps to the world as well."

Paul paced the soft carpets as he continued. "You are running quite a little company here, aren't you? Thomson-Houston has a profit ratio triple that of EGE and quadruple that of Westinghouse. Morgan has noticed. So have I. Edison and Westinghouse, they're scientists. But you, Mr. Coffin, have proven yourself to be a businessman. A shrewd one."

"And what would be the play of a shrewd businessman in this situation?"

"He'd know in which direction the wind was blowing. And he'd arrange his sails accordingly."

Coffin smiled. It felt as if they were bonded together by their mutual antipathy.

"How would this work?" Coffin asked.

"You agree to sell Thomson-Houston to EGE."

"You want me to sell my company to Edison?"

"I want you to sell your company to Morgan. Just as Morgan convinces the other EGE investors to fire Edison."

"Then Morgan owns both companies."

"Yes," said Paul. "At which point he can combine them and install you as the new president."

"Why would he want me to . . ." Coffin trailed off. Paul waited silently as Coffin figured it out.

"Oh my," said Coffin. "As the head of this new conglomerate, I would have free rein to do things such as, for instance, negotiate a licensing deal between Westinghouse and EGE? A deal of which Edison would never approve?"

"I knew you were the right man for the job."

"Why me? You could get anyone to be Morgan's stooge. He'll own a majority share in the thing no matter who its president would be."

"True," answered Paul. "But you'd actually be good at the job." Paul had no need to admire the talents that Coffin possessed. He had only to harness them.

"What Morgan wants above all else," continued Paul, "is returns. No more feuds, no more personal vendettas. When you're in charge, you'll make the deal with Westinghouse because you know it makes financial sense. It's good business. And you, sir, are a filthy bastard whom I do not trust so far as I can throw you. Which means I can trust you to always do what is good business."

Coffin tapped his fingertips against the desk. He was being offered the position of president of the largest lighting company in America. When all these deals were concluded, Coffin would be among the most powerful industrial executives in the world. His fingers danced gentle rhythms against the wood.

"And then what of Edison?" Coffin asked at last. "What becomes of him?"

"Retirement," said Paul with finality.

Coffin nodded. This was evidently the answer he'd hoped for. He paused again.

"Really, man," said Paul. "How long do you have to think about whether you'd like to be the president of Edison General Electric?"

"Oh, I'm not interested in that job."

"Are you kidding?" asked Paul.

"I'm not interested in running a company with the name 'Edison' in its title. I would forever be drowned by the impossible legacy."

"You are turning down the most powerful position in the field of electricity because you're worried that the public won't regard you as the same haloed saint that they mistakenly thought Edison to be?"

"I never said I was turning it down," said Coffin.

Paul could see the implications in his smile.

"Oh dear Lord," said Paul. "You have demands?"

"Only one. If you were to remove Edison's name from the company masthead, well, then I would not have to stare at the damned thing every day when I came in to work."

"I cannot believe that a man in your position, after what I have just offered you, is bargaining."

"A word of advice, Mr. Cravath?"

"I have so longed for advice from you."

"The moment you stop bargaining is the last in which you're ever given a thing."

"Fine," said Paul. "I'll tell Morgan. Call the thing whatever you like. I'm sure you could call it Aunt Sally's Electrical Shop and he'd be happy as long as it makes a nickel more in profit than its current iteration."

"Thank you," said Coffin as he plucked a pen from its cradle and started to doodle a few words on paper. He was testing out names. Titles. Legacies.

"If we are agreed," said Paul, "then the company is yours. And I will take my leave."

He turned to the door. Coffin did not even look up, his attention focused on the scribbled names before him.

"Hmm," uttered Coffin as Paul's hand was on the brass knob. "Let's make it simple. Just lop off the first word. The one I dislike."

"All right."

"'General Electric.' It has a rather nice ring to it, doesn't it?"

CHAPTER 64

Nikola Tesla Returns to Manhattan

Intellectual property has the shelf life of a banana.

—BILL GATES

TWO DAYS LATER, Nikola Tesla stepped out of a carriage onto lower Fifth Avenue. Paul was there to greet him. George Westinghouse stood by Paul's side.

Paul had too much on his mind to notice the morning cold.

Westinghouse appeared pained at the sight of the long-lost inventor. Or perhaps he was simply overwhelmed. Paul could not pretend to know how deeply he'd hurt Westinghouse with his subterfuge, or how profoundly Tesla moved him by descending, alive, from a two-horse hansom.

Agnes followed Tesla out of the carriage. She handed a few coins to the driver before catching Paul's gaze. She'd gotten Tesla back to New York precisely on time, precisely as planned. She had been as good as her word, and her word was better than most. Perhaps better than anyone's. It occurred to Paul that this woman who lived with a borrowed name and an imagined history was the most trustworthy person he knew.

Paul introduced Agnes to Westinghouse. Strange to think that the two most important people in his life had never met. Neither seemed to know what to say to the other. If only they knew how intricately their lives had been bound together.

Tesla surprised them all by taking Westinghouse's hand. "Hello, Mr. George Westinghouse," he said. "I thank you for your welcoming."

Westinghouse smiled. "I am glad to see that you are well."

"What is this?" said Tesla, gesturing to the edifice behind Westinghouse.

"Would you like to see?" replied Paul. The building at 33-35 South Fifth Avenue was a four-story stone behemoth, just below Washington Square Park. They could see the arch two blocks to the north. This was some of the most coveted real estate in the city.

Westinghouse removed a key from his coat pocket and unlocked the building's heavy front door. He led the group up the winding copper staircase to the fourth floor, where he opened a steel door.

"Welcome to your new laboratory," said Westinghouse as he ushered Tesla inside.

The laboratory was a wide-open space stretching two hundred feet in either direction. It took up the entire floor, and it was of brand-new construction. It smelled of fresh masonry. Metal cabinets lined the walls, holding what appeared to be all manner of electrical components. Spools of fresh wire—zinc, steel, silver—lay in untouched bundles. Masses of rubber had been piled in uncut sheets. One cabinet appeared to be full of glass plates. The one next to it was fully stocked with tubs of what Paul imagined was silver nitrate. The photographic tools had been stocked along with the electrical.

"This, Mr. Tesla, is the most finely appointed lab in the country," proclaimed Westinghouse proudly. He handed the keys to Tesla, who regarded them as if they were something to be dissected.

"You are giving to me a laboratory?" asked Tesla, his face expressionless. "I do not understand."

"We're not giving you a thing," replied Paul. "You paid for this yourself."

Tesla looked up at him.

"When you disappeared," Paul continued, "your attorney, Mr. Serrell, didn't know what was to be done with the $2.50 per unit you continued to earn in royalties from our sales. I told him that the Westinghouse Electric Company was more than happy to keep writing checks, but we were not sure who would deposit them. To whom could we even make them out?"

"And it has amounted to quite a bit of money," added Westinghouse.

"So we agreed, with your attorney, that your royalties should go into a trust until your return. If you reappeared, you could claim it all. And if you did not . . ." Paul trailed off. Left unsaid was that for over a year he had known that Tesla was very much alive.

Tesla appeared immune to any implication of unpleasantness.

Tesla began to stroll through the lab. He inspected the cabinets one by one, taking stock of their contents. He turned back to face Paul.

"I would have chosen copper, not your zinc," he said. "But yes, this is well."

"We assumed you'd want a laboratory as soon as you'd returned," said Paul.

"I have done much work in Tennessee," replied Tesla as he continued his survey. "I will continue it here."

"We hope so," said Westinghouse.

Tesla took two glass plates from a cabinet and laid them on a table. He looked up.

"Screws?" he asked.

Westinghouse pointed to a cabinet in the back.

They watched as Tesla went instantly to work. He found a screwdriver near the screws and a circular saw for recutting the glass plates. He began, without a moment of emotional reflection or even consideration for the other human beings around him, to build.

"Well," said Agnes. "Looks as if he's of a mind to get right down to it."

"Do you think he likes it?" said Paul.

"I think for him any moment he is not creating is a moment spent thinking about things to create."

Westinghouse stared silently at Tesla. They were both most at home in their laboratories, and yet they could not be more different in their attitudes. Tesla was happiest when he was working. Westinghouse was happiest when he'd finished. Edison would be happiest only when he'd won.

Paul was on the cusp of making sure that he would not.

"Mr. Tesla," called out Paul over the clatter. "There's another matter we'd like to discuss with you."

Tesla obligingly set down his tools.

"I have so much to do," he said. "What is it that would be helping?"

Agnes looked at Paul. He had kept her in the dark as to this final part of the plan. He hated doing so, but there was no alternative. She wasn't going to like it.

"The Westinghouse Electric Company is a few days away from declaring bankruptcy," said Paul plainly.

"I am apologetic to listen to that," said Tesla, as if he was struggling to discern the proper response.

"But we are in the process of securing a licensing arrangement with Edison's company. Which, if we are successful, will no longer have Edison at the helm."

Tesla's brow perked up. This alone among human affairs seemed to possess some interest for him.

"And yet if we go bankrupt," continued Paul, "it will all be for nothing. And the cause of our bankruptcy, the reason that Mr. Westinghouse's corporation stands on such unsound financial footing, is me."

Paul stepped toward Tesla, his hands at his sides to suggest a subtle supplication.

"The $2.50-per-unit royalty that I negotiated on behalf of the Westinghouse Electric Company, that we have been paying into your trust and that has purchased this laboratory, is not sustainable."

"Paul, what are you talking about?" asked Agnes.

He ignored her. "What I am asking you to do, Nikola, is to sign away this royalty. To give it up, for the common good."

"The common good?" exclaimed Agnes. "What on earth is happening right now? Paul, come with me." She motioned to the hallway outside so that they might have a private conversation.

"Let me finish," he asked of Agnes.

"Nikola," said Paul, "these royalty payments are soon to cease one way or another. Either we go bankrupt and you stop receiving them, or you give us this technology as a gift. And then we beat Edison."

"You ask that I choose this second path," said Tesla.

"If you give us your alternating-current patents, we can beat Edison. And we can make A/C the national standard. If you do not, then, well . . ."

"Edison will win," said Westinghouse.

"It cannot be so simple as that," said Agnes.

Paul motioned for Agnes to wait. "If Edison wins, the entire national electrical network will be built on direct current. If you allow Westinghouse to go under, you will doom America to D/C. To Edison. To a century of technological backwardness."

Tesla's face darkened. This was a serious and terrible consequence that he had not previously imagined.

"Paul," said Agnes, "I will not allow you to cheat Nikola out of his royalty payments."

"I am not cheating anyone out of anything. I am laying the case out plainly and in full view. He may make his own decision."

"Where is Mr. Tesla's attorney? I will get him down here this second."

"Mr. Serrell is unfortunately not available right now. He's in Washington. Working on another matter."

"You got rid of Tesla's lawyer so you could cheat him alone?"

"I am not 'cheating' anyone."

"None of my new devices shall function on the direct current. . . ." Tesla was contemplating the dire future this posed for his work.

"If you do not do as I'm asking," said Paul, "the national grid of the United States will be based on D/C. There will be accidents. People will die. This nation will be doomed to a medieval century. And the future you've seen in your visions will never take shape in America."

Tesla stared into a hazy distance, as if he could literally see all his planned machines evaporating into the air. These marvelous creations were there before him, hallucinations of chrome and wire. But they were vanishing.

"I care not at all about your money. But you must not let the direct current devour my world. I want only to build. You know this about myself."

"Nikola," said Agnes, "listen to me. Giving Westinghouse all of your money is not the way to protect your work."

"Miss Agnes Huntington, I cannot invent that which I must invent within the world that Mr. Paul Cravath describes."

"We can stop that world from becoming reality," said Paul. "If you renounce the royalty, we can survive. We can continue making alternating-current systems. We can depose Edison from the head of his company, make a deal with the new leader, and live on. Both D/C and A/C can percolate through the country. The range of possible devices will be even greater."

"Then you must do this, Mr. Paul Cravath. And I will help you. Not for your benefit, and not for Mr. George Westinghouse's benefit, and neither for to see Mr. Thomas Edison's fall. But rather for the future of these sciences. I have seen wonders in my mind. The invisible rays that can see through skin. A machine that can take the photograph of your thoughts. I shall build that too. These wonders must come true."

George Westinghouse had the good sense not to have said a word during this exchange. He let his lawyer do his talking for him. But now he removed a thin collection of papers from his pocket. He laid them gently on one of the laboratory tables, and then took out a pen. He placed it gingerly beside the papers.

"You've only to sign this," said Westinghouse quietly. He did not meet Tesla's eyes.

Agnes's face curdled with disgust. "Nikola," she said, "do not make this deal. I know that it seems like only money to you right now, but what source of income will you have if you give away your royalties? You will watch in penury as your peers grow rich."

Tesla smiled at her sympathetically. "My ideas for the alternating current are old. If in the future I want for money, I shall have so many more ideas from which to farm fortune." He came toward the table that bore the contract and took the pen in his hand.

Agnes gave Paul a look of such violence as he had never seen before. He had known this was coming. He'd even reasoned that her anger would be a relief. What would it matter, he'd thought, if she blamed him for doing what needed to be done? She would never have to love him as if he were her fiancé. Wouldn't they both be better off if she didn't? She was soon to be married, and with any luck her hatred would only help them to forget each other.

And yet now that he was confronted with her withering gaze, the sting was so much worse than he'd imagined.

She turned her glare to Westinghouse. "You're a co-conspirator in this villainy?"

Westinghouse said nothing. He did not appear to feel a need to justify his actions to some singer.

"Goddamn you both," said Agnes. She marched angrily from the lab. She slammed the door behind her.

Paul wanted to follow. He had to explain. Surely she could understand the occasional need for well-intentioned deception. But he couldn't leave until the job was finished.

In a few moments, Tesla scribbled his name at the bottom of the page. He had given over his patents freely and without compensation. They were now George Westinghouse's to do with as he chose.

"Go forth," said Tesla as he set down the pen. "And create my future."

Paul took a deep breath. It was done.

He ran to the door.

CHAPTER 65

Men and Women

In those days when the comparatively recent discovery of
electricity and other kindred mysteries of Nature seemed to
open paths into the region of miracle, it was not unusual for
the love of science to rival the love of woman in its depth
and absorbing energy.   —NATHANIEL HAWTHORNE

PAUL CAUGHT UP with Agnes at the corner of South Fifth Avenue and Houston Street. She had her hand in the air to hail a passing cab. He'd thought he could bear the deathly chill of her anger, but now that he'd felt it, he was overwhelmed. He had to fix this. To argue his case.

"You are *despicable*," she cried as she caught sight of him.

"Agnes," pleaded Paul. "Come back inside. Just talk with me for a moment."

"You thought me cheap because I chose a kind man who happens to be rich. Well, let me tell you: Henry Jayne is a better man than you in every way."

She was trying to hurt him, and she was succeeding.

Paul attempted to take her arm. She batted away his advances.

"You just stole crumbs from the pockets of an innocent man who is too confused to know what you've done. That is fraud. You are a criminal." Her hot words puffed into the winter air.

324 | GRAHAM MOORE

"Please let me explain."

"What happened to you?"

She searched his face as if she was trying to read his soul but found nothing there.

"You were the one who told me to do whatever it took to win. And you were the one who believed, more than anyone else, that I could."

"Not this, Paul."

"Tesla will be fine," he said. "Look at what I've done for him." He gestured to the building behind them.

"You manipulated him."

"I told him the truth!"

"You've been planning this the entire time, haven't you?" she said. "Since Bell's?"

"Yes."

"And then you lied to me about it."

"It's more complicated than that."

"You did not do this for me. You didn't do this for Westinghouse, or anyone else. Your need to beat Edison is so great, your own ego so consuming and cancerous, that it has devoured whatever was good in you to begin with. You are no better than Edison; you are worse."

Comparing him to Edison was too much. He had no way of explaining to her that in a way, he'd done this all out of love for her. To show her that he was worthy of receiving her love in return. She would never get to witness his daily adorations. At least she could witness the unimaginable success that his adoration had inspired.

"I had imagined," suggested Paul, "that you of all people would be more forgiving about the occasional need to craft the truth in the service of a greater good."

"What I told you in confidence you now fling back at me to conceal your own immorality? Is nothing sacred to you?"

"I only mean that we have all done things of which we aren't proud."

She slapped him cleanly across the cheek. Pedestrians turned to stare. Paul's face flushed.

And yet he felt the hot flush of indignation as well. Could she really not see this from his side? Could she not see how his actions were so much like her own? He had acted in the best interests of everyone involved. He was undeserving of her rebuke.

"You're behaving like a child," he said. The words sounded, when they came out, even more condescending than he'd intended. "You cannot have spent as many evenings as you have champagne-drunk in high-society parlors and still be this ignorant about how the world really works."

Tears swelled in Agnes's eyes. She let them spill and refused to brush them with her coat sleeve. She kept her pained face pointing directly at Paul's, forcing him to feel her hurt.

"Do you know," she said through her tears, "that I once considered breaking off my engagement for you? Because I thought you understood me. I thought you just might be the only person who did. I almost fell for it. But I've come across your type before. The cynical young social climber who infects the metropolises on either side of the ocean. Your kind mistakes cleverness for wisdom. Your kind mistakes high-class trappings for genuine class. You take such pride in being so very smart, and do you know what the saddest part is? You're actually not stupid, Mr. Cravath. You're just not nearly as smart as you think you are. Good luck. You'll need it. I sincerely hope that you win this, I really do. Because I know something you don't. I know that winning will not make you a great man. It will reveal that you're not much of a man at all."

And with that, she turned and walked away, leaving Paul alone on Fifth Avenue.

CHAPTER 66

The Current War Comes to an End

> We are called to be the architects of the future, not its
> victims.   —BUCKMINSTER FULLER

PAUL FORCED HIMSELF to put Agnes's condemnation out of his mind. He spent the evening with his associates, proofreading again and again the documents that would conclude the coming deal. The coup had been arranged, and the licensing arrangement had been negotiated. All that remained was the paperwork.

He was exhausted. He had barely slept since New Year's. His associates had gotten even less sleep than he had. From their warren on Greenwich Street, they marked up the ever-changing contracts relentlessly. No one trusted Morgan, and no one had any confidence that what he'd verbally agreed to would be reflected in the contracts delivered by his attorneys. It took constant vigilance to see that nothing devious had been snuck into a stray subparagraph. To everyone's surprise, nothing had. Either Morgan had been uncharacteristically honest, or else he'd simply decided the deal was beneficial enough as it was. Whether he'd been restrained by honesty or moderation, Paul would never know.

The afternoon of January 17, a weary Paul entered through the front door of 3 Broad Street. He had been fortified with three cups of coffee to defend against his two hours of sleep. There was a caffeinated twitch in his fingers as he marched to Morgan's private office. There was no longer any need for subterfuge; if Edison found out, it was far too late for him to do anything about it.

Paul had come to Morgan's office to preside over the final signing of the contracts. It was not a crowded room. Only Westinghouse, Morgan, and a few of Morgan's attorneys were present for the end of the current war. Westinghouse and Morgan were both wealthy enough to assume a comfortable familiarity with each other, despite having only met on brief occasions over the years. Neither had ever been the object of the other's animosity. Now they were partners.

The tall windows let in light from Wall Street, while on Morgan's great maple desk lay a single unlit electric lamp. It was a generation behind the present technology. It had been the first indoor electric lamp commercially sold in America. Not just this model, but this exact lamp. When Thomas Edison had finally finished his first working device, all those years ago, he'd sold the thing to Morgan. At a price that he alone could afford. And now it rested here, an unused symbol of a well-known history.

Morgan's office housed many other treasures, from Old Kingdom Egypt to ancient Mesopotamia. The world's first light bulb was but the latest addition to a few millennia's worth of riches.

Morgan signed his name. Charles Coffin's signature had been affixed in Massachusetts at dawn. And the war was over.

"Congratulations," said Morgan to the room. Westinghouse stepped back from the desk hesitantly, as if he couldn't quite believe it. There was a dissociative discrepancy between the magnitude of the event and the smallness of the moment. Every man present knew its importance, knew that what they had done would reverberate for generations. And yet here they were, a few men of middle age—and one much younger—standing silently in a smoky office. Gabriel's trumpet went unblown.

Westinghouse turned to Paul, his thumbs tucked into his vest pockets. He nodded solemnly. "You did it" was all that he said, but in his eyes a great deal more was communicated. Paul nodded back. There was so much that could be said, too much. And so nothing would be.

"*We* did it, sir."

Paul felt a strange sensation: He wished that his father were there. Erastus would never understand what Paul had just done. But he hoped that somehow his father would still be proud.

With an unexpected creak, the office door opened.

The man who stood in Morgan's doorway was tall. His gray hair was strewn haphazardly around his scalp. He wore a suit and vest but no tie. The top few buttons of his white cotton shirt were loose and his gray vest was askew. On his haggard chin was stubble. His face was ashen.

It was Thomas Edison.

CHAPTER 67

The Fall of Thomas Edison

> I think if we ever reach the point where we think we
> thoroughly understand who we are and where we come
> from, we will have failed.   —CARL SAGAN

EDISON'S LIPS QUIVERED as he looked across the room at the men who had just taken his company out from underneath him.

"Thomas," said Morgan, seizing authority, "I hope you're not here to make a scene." He came around from behind his desk as if to create a barricade between Edison and the newly signed contracts. But Edison paid no mind to the paperwork. He devoted the weight of his ruined stare to the men who'd done the deed.

"So it's true," he said.

"It's business," replied Morgan. "I'm sorry to be the one to remind you that it always was."

Paul braced himself for Edison's uncontainable ferocity. He looked instinctively behind Edison's shoulder for the sight of Charles Batchelor with a firearm. But the office door revealed only a placid office outside.

To Paul's great surprise, no well of rage burst forth from Edison. There was no anger in his face, no muscular tension in his posture. Instead, he appeared deflated. He looked as if he were held up only by some thin rod running through the center of his body. He'd been beaten, and he knew it.

"Please," Edison said quietly, "just tell me the part about the name isn't true."

It took Paul a moment to figure out what Edison was referring to.

"Blame Coffin for that," answered Morgan. "He was the one who wanted your name off the thing."

"You took my name off the company I built from nothing."

"Charles Coffin took your name off the company I own."

"It is my *name*." He stepped toward Morgan as his plea became more direct. "I'll make you a deal for anything I have left. But please. Don't take away my name."

Edison was about to lose unfathomable millions of dollars, and the part that tortured him was that Edison General Electric would now be plain old General Electric?

"I'm sorry, Thomas," said Morgan. "You have nothing else that I want."

"George," said Edison, turning to address his enemy as his peer. "You understand this. These men"—he gestured to Morgan and the lawyers—"they don't. They've never built anything. They've never bent down and with their own two hands molded something that did not exist before. Something that no one even believed *could* exist before. Tell them to leave my name in place. Our war? You win. Do you hear me? I will say publicly that you win." He bowed his head formally, the salutation of a losing general to a victorious one. "The country can run on A/C. You want everyone to know that your devices are better? So be it. Maybe they are. But do not let them say that mine did not exist."

Westinghouse's expression was sympathetic.

"They won't, Thomas," he said. "General Electric is not going away. It's going to grow. If anything, this will burnish your legacy, not banish it. Everyone will know it was yours. I promise you."

Paul was horrified. Edison deserved many things, but sympathy was not among them. This was the man who'd hurt them both so much.

"I hope they forget about you by the morning," said Paul. A bitterness had been festering inside him for two years, and now at last it could be released. "You lied. You cheated. You stole. You spied. You tried to kill Tesla. You almost killed me. You bought off the police. You bribed a state legislature. You paid off a judge. You promoted a horrific instrument of death in an attempt to convince the public of something that was not true. You would knowingly install an electrical system across the cities of the United States that would kill thousands per year. And those are just the crimes I know about. You deserve a punishment far worse than this."

The room was silent as Paul finished. He'd given everything to beat Edison. He'd committed his own sins to prove that Edison's had been greater. He'd pushed away the one person he'd grown to love. Now he had only his anger.

It felt good.

"Paul," cautioned Westinghouse, "enough."

"I've done things that I should not have," said Edison. "I won't deny it. But not everything you've accused me of is true."

Paul wanted to rebut this, but Westinghouse interrupted:

"I'm sorry, Thomas. But you won't be forgotten. Your name will live on. I give you my word."

To Paul's great shock, both men reached out and clasped hands.

"Thank you, George. And for what I've done I'm sorry as well."

"You can start again. Like the old days—just you, a hot iron, and a dusty laboratory."

Edison gave a tight, rueful laugh. "My God. I can't even remember."

"It's not as if you'll be a pauper," said Morgan. "You can hire a staff. You'll own stock worth a hair over two million dollars."

At this, Edison shrugged. He turned back to Westinghouse and they exchanged a look.

"Businessmen," said Edison. It was Westinghouse's turn to laugh.

With that, Edison turned to go. There were no goodbyes, no acknowledgment that this might very well be the last time he would see any of these men again. However tired Paul felt, Edison looked twice that. He slunk out of the room.

Westinghouse shut the door and the room was quiet. The victors were left alone to their silent spoils.

After a few moments, Paul was the first to speak.

"I don't understand. How could you apologize to him? After everything he's done."

Westinghouse's thoughts seemed further removed from Paul than ever before.

"I know you don't understand," said Westinghouse. He placed a hand on Paul's shoulder. "One day, you will."

CHAPTER 68

Revelry

> When you have exhausted all possibilities, remember
> this—you haven't.   —THOMAS EDISON

VICTORY FELT STRANGE.

After brief, formal goodbyes with Westinghouse and the attorneys, Paul left Morgan's office in a disoriented state. Out of instinct he began to wander up Wall Street in the direction of his office until he realized that Carter and Hughes would be there. They would be in the mood for a fight, as they would soon learn of Paul's various deceptions. Tesla's survival, the associate attorneys, the coup to dethrone Edison . . . it was an impressive list. Either they would be firing Paul or he would be quitting, depending upon one's perspective. Carter would do a lot of yelling, Hughes would do a bit of scolding, and Paul would have to sit quietly until they eventually let him negotiate something—the formal terms of the separation. It was likely that others would need to become involved: lawyers hiring lawyers hiring lawyers, the snake litigating with its own tail. The process would be occasionally enraging and mostly tedious.

Paul slowed his steps. He was suddenly placeless. He didn't know if he wanted to sleep, to eat, to celebrate, or simply to sit quietly in a dark room and stare at the wallpaper. For a moment it occurred to him that he might visit his associates in their stuffy, sweat-smelling office. The diligent boys deserved a drink. He would finally figure out which one was Bynes. And yet it wouldn't be much of a celebration. The associates were not his friends; they were his employees. They were so like Paul in their aspirations that a celebration in their company seemed dreary. They would all have new positions in his new firm soon enough. Tonight they could wait.

Paul thought of the friends on whom he might call. Friendly faces from law school whose company he had long appreciated. But he hadn't seen any of them in months. This meant that a dinner would be spent catching up. There would be a ritual recitation of their respective affairs: trials, suits, parties, new women in their social milieu. Paul imagined a few hours, two bottles of champagne, and a fleet of baked oysters as he recited the litany of events that had been taking up his time. It would be a history lesson, not a conversation. What Paul wanted was a compatriot, but what he would get would be a congregation.

He thought of Agnes. He was still angry with her. Still indignant over her refusal to understand his decisions. Time would vindicate his actions, he felt assured. She would not need to forgive him; he would need to forgive her.

She would be married soon enough. He hadn't been able to win her hand as a poor man. To become a rich one, he'd had to drive her away. The irony offended him. As did her throwing in his face the suggestion that he might once have had a chance to be with her. She was wrong. Men like Henry Jayne would always have an advantage. Jayne had been spared the burden of difficult choices. He'd never had to dig into the dirt for his fortune. He had been blessed with the luxury of his pricey innocence. Agnes told Paul to win, and then was aghast at what it took to do so.

It was this train of lonely thoughts that led Paul to a dim alehouse along the Bowery. He had not intended on going anywhere so seedy, but he found himself beckoned by the noise from the thoroughfare. The density of the din made him feel appreciated, at home in the buoyant laughter of strangers.

Paul drank three tin mugs of Brooklyn's newest batch of lager. All around were the shouts of men who'd come to work their mouths as their calloused hands were given a rest. The men could tell that Paul didn't belong, but they left him alone. It was as if they could tell that he was fit only for solitude.

Cheers, he thought as he tasted his bitter brew. *To great success.*

The alcohol swirled pleasantly around his brain as a man slid onto an adjacent stool. Paul didn't look up at first. Not until he heard the man call for a glass of gin. He spoke with a voice that Paul had heard only once, a very long time before.

"What in hell are you doing here?" said Paul.

Charles Batchelor paid for his gin with two silver coins. "Mr. Cravath, I'd like to make you a proposition."

Paul nearly knocked over his lager. He felt an implicit threat of violence. And yet, as he watched Edison's right-hand man grimace at the poor-quality gin, Paul realized that Batchelor had not shown up for a fight. He had not even come to threaten one.

"Are you all right?" said Batchelor. "You've gone pale."

"Did you follow me here?"

"Do you think I typically pass my evenings in places like this?"

"Why?"

"Because you have a problem. With which I believe I can be of help. I will also humbly admit that I too have a problem. And together we might come to agree that the solution to your problem and the solution to mine are in fact one and the same."

"I beat you," said Paul. "I beat Edison. I can assure you that you will never in your life receive an ounce of my help."

Batchelor rolled his eyes. He seemed to find Paul's earnest anger rather quaint. "Come off it, will you? We're both professionals. This is business. Let's act like it." Batchelor set his glass on the pockmarked bar top, twirling the rim with his fingers. "Charles Coffin, your newly installed president of General Electric, is as crooked as an old screw. You know this. He's dishonest, unpredictable, and eventually he's going to betray you. You need to install an experienced number two at the company, someone Morgan can trust to keep the ship afloat. Someone who won't sell off the cargo mid-voyage the first time somebody makes an offer. I've been a vice president at EGE for years, and I know how to run it better than anyone."

He spun his fingers again, the gin in his glass swaying like the waves in a summer storm. "I've gotten too far in this business to start again. I'm not following Thomas back to New Jersey, tail between my legs. I've tended to his particular lunacy for long enough. It's time I tried another's. Put in a good word for me? Tell Morgan to keep me on as Coffin's vice president, and you may both count on my assistance."

While many thoughts rattled through Paul's mind, the most prominent was a fervent wish that he were not three beers into his evening. Wooziness combined with exhaustion made clear thinking difficult. Was Batchelor trying to lure him into some sort of trap? Had Edison put him up to a late-play revenge?

Except that injury to Paul no longer served Edison. Nor would it serve Batchelor. The war had ended, and Batchelor's speech only made any sense if it was genuine. Yet the notion that Edison's man was coming to him with outstretched palms was too bizarre to comprehend. Paul wanted one night—just one brief and drunken respite—in which to relish his well-earned anger. He'd be strategizing for the next war soon enough.

"Go home," said Paul. "Come and see me in a few weeks, and we'll see what I can do."

Batchelor seemed unperturbed by Paul's reticence. "You're celebrating. I can see that. It's rude of me to disturb your . . . revelry." Batchelor looked around the alehouse. The sound of the workmen seemed to grow louder. Paul stared at his nearly empty mug. His loneliness was none of Batchelor's concern.

"One point of caution, though," continued Batchelor. "If we don't help each other, then I'll have to assume that you'd like us to hurt each other. I do not want this. But it must be noted that I can hurt you a lot worse than you can hurt me."

"What are you talking about?"

"This war of ours . . . there has been no shortage of casualties. I know where the bodies are buried. On my side, yes. But also on yours."

The accusation was bracing. But still, the break-in at Brown's, the lies of omission to his partners, the subterfuge surrounding Tesla, the eventual betrayal of his eccentric friend—they were still a pittance in comparison with those weighing on the other side of the scales. Paul wore his sins on his sleeve. "I've had to do some things of which I am not proud. But I'm not the one who electrocuted William Kemmler, who set fire to Tesla's lab, who spread lies in every newspaper in America."

Batchelor frowned. It seemed he was trying to gauge something in Paul. "I'd been curious about this for a while, I have to say. Thomas and I actually debated it on more than one occasion. I guess you've given me my answer." He looked Paul dead in the eyes. Paul did not flinch. "Christ. You really don't know."

"Know what?"

"Who set that fire at Tesla's laboratory."

"You did."

"No, we didn't," said Batchelor calmly. "George Westinghouse did."

CHAPTER 69

The Good Guys and the Bad Guys

> Whenever a theory appears to you as the only possible one,
> take this as a sign that you have neither understood the
> theory nor the problem which it was intended to solve.
>
> —KARL POPPER

"THAT'S NOT TRUE," said Paul.

"The night of the fire," said Batchelor, "Westinghouse told you to take Tesla to dinner at Delmonico's. Only you didn't go. He suggested it because he wanted you both out of the lab. Did you or did you not share the address Tesla gave you with Westinghouse? He wasn't trying to kill Tesla—only to shake him up, to bring him back into the fold. But the fire was much worse than he'd planned. You were hurt, Tesla vanished. His man didn't know you were still in the building when he set the flame. For Christ's sake, who do you think pulled you out of the fire? Who do you think saved Tesla?"

"The police said it was a stranger . . ."

Batchelor looked at Paul as if he were the greatest idiot on the earth. "You think some Good Samaritan dove into the flaming wreckage and saved your life? This is New York. It was my man. I'd had him following you for a month. The Pinkertons are plenty tough. He ran into the building when he saw the flames. By the time he got inside, you'd collapsed. He got Tesla to help get you out of the building, but while he was trying to revive you the lunatic ran away. The terror of it all threw the poor man's brain out of sorts. Westinghouse's plan had the opposite effect of the one he'd intended. Fortunately for us."

Paul struggled to conjure some bit of proof that might show that Batchelor was lying.

"Don't make that face," Batchelor continued. "You've never been good at playing the doe-eyed naïf. In the end, you did Westinghouse's dirty work for him. You were the one who talked Tesla out of the royalty. You did more to doom Tesla with a compelling speech and a scrawl upon the dotted line than Westinghouse did with arson."

Paul felt as if he were looking into a kaleidoscope. As if all the colors in the known universe had been rearranged. "Even if what you're saying is true . . . how can you know? How could *you* know what *Westinghouse* told me that night?"

"Surely by now you know the answer to that," said Batchelor. "Reginald Fessenden told us."

The heavy air caught in Paul's throat. The bitter irony was that Edison had known more about the secret operations of Westinghouse than Paul did.

All this time, Paul had thought he knew who the villain in this story was.

Now he realized that it was him.

"Speaking of which," continued Batchelor, "would you go easy on the kid? Fessenden? He's a good boy. We conscripted him into conspiracy. I was his damned press-gang. Pittsburgh has been hell on him. Miserable place. Worse than Indiana."

Paul was out of argument. What he had achieved was worse than losing. He'd won, and now he knew that he shouldn't have. He couldn't defend Westinghouse anymore. He could not even defend himself.

Westinghouse could go to hell. So could Edison. Coffin. Morgan. Batchelor. The lot of them be damned. Paul already was. There remained only one person in this blood-speckled tragedy who deserved more than brimstone.

"I'll make you a deal," said Paul.

Batchelor nodded. "Much appreciated." He stood, stretching his legs. He'd gotten what he'd come for.

"You haven't heard what *I* want yet."

"Pardon?"

"You want to make a deal? Let's make a deal. But first you should hear *my* offer."

"You're still negotiating?"

"Yes," said Paul. "The moment you stop is the moment you're never given another thing."

Batchelor sat again.

"We'll keep this all a secret," offered Paul. "What my side has done. What your side has done. You have mud to fling at Westinghouse? I have mud to fling at Edison. I know about his connection to Harold Brown. I trust you're not eager for him to make another appearance."

Batchelor shook his head ruefully. "I told Thomas—told him a hundred times—not to do business with that man. This was always Thomas's problem, I suppose. Poor management."

"Brown's off hiding from the mess he created?"

"Banished would be a better way of putting it. He's far from New York, and we've made it very clear that his appearance within a thousand miles of here would not be healthy for him."

"I'll happily do you the service of not finding him. You want Fessenden to join Edison in New Jersey? I'll see that it's done. Westinghouse wants him jailed, but I'll find some pretense to let him loose. You want to stay on at GE? Easy. But in exchange, there is one more thing I'll need you to do for me."

Batchelor waited expectantly.

There were many grand prizes Paul might demand for keeping his fetid secrets. And yet the only thing he really wanted would be inconceivably small to Batchelor.

"We're all going to burn," said Paul, "and we all deserve to. You. Me. Edison. Westinghouse. Brown. But together we might have a chance of seeing that one good thing comes of this unholy mess."

"Oh?"

"There is one person who we can assure is granted the justice that we've so thoroughly deprived each other."

"And who, Mr. Cravath, is that?"

CHAPTER 70

All Men Get the Things They Love

> Let's go invent tomorrow instead of worrying about what
> happened yesterday. —STEVE JOBS

GNES WASN'T AT home when Paul presented himself on her doorstep the following afternoon. He rang the bell a dozen times, but there was no response. Not even the maid came to answer the door. Number 4 was the stillest house along Gramercy.

Paul next went to the Metropolitan Opera House. The house manager was awkward. Miss Huntington was not in attendance. Paul asked when she might arrive.

"She won't."

Miss Huntington had given the Metropolitan board just a few days' notice, he explained. She'd said that the city no longer suited her. She'd left no sign of where she might be headed.

This information was repeated by everyone of whom he inquired over the following days. No one had seen Agnes. Her house was being put up for sale. Even Stanford White told Paul, by way of letter, that he'd heard the news of Agnes's sudden departure, but hadn't any idea where she'd replanted her flag. Though if Paul did find her, would he please bring her back?

Three sleepless nights later, Paul read in the society pages a most curious item: The chanteuse Agnes Huntington's engagement to Henry La Barre Jayne had been called off. DID HE JILT "PAUL JONES"? read the titillating headline in *The Washington Post*, referring to Agnes by her most famous role. Paul's further inquiries confirmed that the Jayne clan had departed en masse for Philadelphia. This was a blow for their beloved son, but it was survivable.

It seemed that Agnes had simultaneously turned her back on both the city of her dreams and the safe perch of a marriage into wealth and stature. What she had once craved she had apparently renounced. And now she was somewhere else, searching for something else.

It didn't take Paul long to figure out where she'd gone.

The Chicago Railway didn't even stop in Kalamazoo, but the Michigan Central did, after a transfer in Toledo. Kalamazoo wasn't a place someone went to be noticed; it was a place someone went to escape.

Paul arrived on a bright winter day. His hired carriage took him to a two-story wooden house at the center of the snowy town. It hadn't been hard to find the address. Property was not bought and sold too frequently, so just a few conversations with locals gave him the information he needed.

Fannie was at the door when he arrived at the brown-slatted house. She clearly wasn't happy to see Paul ascending the steps of her new home. But she allowed him a cup of tea and the few minutes he required to deliver some news. As for the request that accompanied his explanation, she admitted it wasn't hers to grant.

When Agnes came downstairs, she gave little reaction at the sight of Paul.

"What stubborn need for abuse brought you here?"

"Now, now," interrupted Fannie. "He's not quite as foolish as I used to think."

And with that, Fannie took her leave.

Agnes leaned against the kitchen cabinets, wrapping her orange cotton dress tightly around herself.

"This is the most chipper I've seen my mother since we left New York."

"I read about you and Henry Jayne."

"Did you travel here to file a report for the society page?"

"Miss Huntington," said Paul, "I've spent most of the time since I met you making a lot of pretty terrible decisions, and I'd like to make a good one for a change. So here it is: I've come here to tell you that I'm in love with you."

She didn't even blink.

"I'm sorry for taking advantage of Tesla. I betrayed his trust."

"Then I don't think that I'm the one who needs your apology."

"But I'm going to make it up to you. Listen: These giants in whose shadows we've played our games? They're terrible. Those great men and their great obsessions. I want no more of them. What I want is you."

Agnes scoffed.

"I thought that winning was enough," said Paul. "It wasn't. I thought that success . . . well, I thought that success would mean something. It doesn't. Because success is in the eye of the beholder. And the only eyes I care to be witnessed by belong to you."

"You were always good at speeches."

Paul took in the humble kitchen. "You've gone into hiding."

"I've gone into reality."

"You couldn't do it in the end. The pretend name. The pretend life. The pretend you for the whole rest of your years. You thought you could. But it wasn't worth it."

She looked to the floor. It was hard to tell if she was more upset with Paul in that moment or herself. "Nikola described something to me once. Refraction, he called it. The way light is broken up into component colors when it passes through a prism. I felt like a refraction of a person. So many different shades that layer to create the illusion of a solid thing. I was only what was reflected back in others. A demure princess for my mother. A full-throated mimic on the stage. A smiling wit for my fiancé. All parts to be played. I thought it was worth it, until I saw . . ."

"Until you saw what it did to me."

She looked up at him. "If I stayed, I would have been no better than you."

The remark stung.

"So you came back here. You'll sing at a local theater somewhere. If anyone recognizes Agnes Gouge, no one will care. If anyone recognizes Agnes Huntington, no one will believe it." Her plan was sound. But Paul had done everything he could to see that it might be rendered unnecessary. "What if you can keep New York, without pretending?"

"With you as my new Jayne?" she asked incredulously. "I read that you won your war. But that doesn't give you as much power as you think."

"It doesn't give me much at all. But I'm not the one who's going to give you New York."

Her brow furrowed.

"Thomas Edison is."

For the first time since he'd arrived, he had surprised her.

"What I have here is a letter," he said, removing it from his coat pocket. "It's from a Sergeant Kroes, of the Boston police."

Her expression made clear that she could not possibly guess where this was going.

"In it," continued Paul, "the good sergeant informs my friend Charles Batchelor that there are no records of a theft occurring at the Endicott house in 1881. That the police do not have—nor have they ever had—such a record. And that he spoke to the Endicott family, who have assured him that no such theft ever occurred."

Paul watched as she struggled to process what he was telling her. So massive were the implications of his words that she could not immediately wrap her mind around them.

"But that's impossible," she said.

Paul smiled. "Your mother is safe. So are you."

"How did you—"

"It is my understanding that Charles Batchelor—trusted employee of Thomas Edison and J. P. Morgan—made very clear to the Endicott family, and to the Boston police, that his employers had taken an interest in the crime. And that it would be in everyone's interest, for reasons left unspoken, if the incident had never occurred."

"The family agreed to forget about it because Charles Batchelor told them to?"

"The names 'Edison' and 'Morgan' are quite powerful ones, even in Boston."

She appeared as if a decade of tension was being released from her body. Paul could almost see her shoulders start to relax.

"You're free now," he said. "You can be Agnes Gouge. You can be Agnes Huntington. Or you can even go become Agnes Jayne if you want. But you don't need his name to protect you. You have your own. And your mother has hers."

Agnes said nothing. She held herself still against the cabinets.

"What was required of me to do all this was an act of dishonesty. But look at what it has allowed. The lives of everyone involved are better off for it. I sinned in the service of a better America. If you return with me to New York, we can spend the rest of our lives making up for it."

"Not everyone involved is better off, Paul."

"Tesla is not so hard up as you might think. Not only does he have a new laboratory, but he has a new company as well."

"How can he afford to found a new company?"

"Because believe it or not, he has acquired his first investor. And the man has awfully deep pockets . . . J. P. Morgan. I'm negotiating the deal myself."

She gave a start. It couldn't be denied that whatever else he was, Paul was a very good lawyer.

"We can do anything now," he said. "We can be anyone. We can give a fortune to charity. We can found civic institutions to outlast us both. We can make New York a place where the next boy from Nashville and the next girl from Kalamazoo are welcomed with open arms. We can look after Tesla and make sure that he's always cared for. We can do all of this and so much more. But if I cannot do this at your side, then there's no point.

"If you would consider returning to New York," he continued, "I have a humble request: Don't marry Henry Jayne. Marry me instead."

He took a step closer. "Do you know that in our adventures we came to know three men who in their own ways each changed the world? And do you know what I can't stop thinking about? *Why* did they do it? What made them fight, strive, connive so hard for so long?"

She raised an eyebrow. "That's what you want to talk about right now?"

"Just hear me out," pleaded Paul. "What did they love? The three of them? Edison loved the audience. For him, it was the performance. It was the crowd. He remains the most famous inventor in the world. I'll bet he'll stay that way for generations. He wanted the applause. That's what he was fighting for. Now, Westinghouse . . . Westinghouse was different. He loved the products themselves. And he made them better than anyone. He is the ultimate craftsman, isn't he? He didn't want to sell the most light bulbs. He wanted to make the *best* light bulbs. If they were too expensive, if they were too late into production, he didn't care. They had to be the best. The most useful, the most current technology. And he did, didn't he? It's his products that won out. He wanted to perfect the light bulb and he did it. Then there's Tesla. He was the third leg in this tripod. He didn't care a bit about Edison's public, or Westinghouse's products. No, Tesla cared only for the ideas themselves. Their promulgation did not matter. Tesla was his own audience, and his ideas were his product, for consumption by himself alone. He had the idea, then he was done. Once he knew he'd solved a problem, he moved on. He knew that he'd made A/C work; he knew that he'd made the bulbs work. Actually building the things was irrelevant. That was someone else's problem.

"And look: They all got what they wanted. Because they wanted such different things. I've been trying so hard, all this time, to understand them, and what I understand now is that I never will. Because I'm not like them."

"You wanted to win," said Agnes.

"Yes. And I did. It was the same as losing. Edison gets the audience. Westinghouse gets the excellence. Tesla gets the ideas. But all I really want is you."

She smiled. In the years to come, Paul would see many of these smiles. He would come to know well their shapes, their shadings, their infinite variety of splendors. And yet of all the million smiles that she would show him, it would be this particular one, grinned on that particular afternoon, that would forever be his favorite.

"You're getting better at the speeches," she said.

CHAPTER 71

Postwar

The game of science is, in principle, without end. He who
decides one day that scientific statements do not call for
any further test, and that they can be regarded as finally
verified, retires from the game.
—KARL POPPER

P AUL MARRIED AGNES Huntington in a ceremony at St. Thomas
Church. They moved to an apartment on Fifty-eighth Street,
one block from Central Park. Agnes soon stopped singing professionally, but never stopped singing at home. Sometimes Paul imagined that her voice had seeped so deeply into the apartment's bright
wood that the walls would reverberate ever on with the sound of her
arias. Their daughter, Vera, was born in 1895. She looked the spitting
image of her mother. Fannie Huntington lived close by.

Together, Paul and Agnes participated in the founding of the
Council on Foreign Relations, and Paul became one of its officers.
Paul served as corporate counsel for the Metropolitan Opera, and
then the chairman of its board. In time, he would be a director of the
Philharmonic, a trustee of the Juilliard School of Music, the chair-
man of the board of Fisk University, the president of the Italy Amer-
ica Society, and an official of the India Society of America. Paul and
Agnes became among the greatest of Manhattan's philanthropists.

And yet the name of Nikola Tesla would always haunt their marriage. Paul's sins against the man would be recalled whenever they struggled both to do well and to do good, and whenever they fought behind closed doors.

In the years that followed, the Westinghouse Electric Company's system became the national standard for generating and harnessing electrical power. By way of its licensing arrangement with the newly christened General Electric, Westinghouse provided the power to light the country from coast to coast using alternating current. At the same time, GE itself switched standards and sold many times more bulbs. Under Charles Coffin its profitability tripled. Both companies grew to be among the largest in the world.

Paul remained the lead counsel for the Westinghouse Electric Company for a while, until he was able to transition the company into hiring an in-house counsel. Paul chose the young man himself and remained on retainer as a consultant. It was time for him to move on.

Paul and Westinghouse remained cordial business associates, if not close ones. Paul never asked him about the fire. There was nothing Paul could do about it, and nothing, even if Westinghouse did admit it, that he could prove. No one would benefit from an argument. Their relationship cooled, but never froze. Westinghouse was not the father that Paul wanted. He had his own. Erastus Cravath even visited New York every now and again to see his granddaughter.

To be sure, those years saw their share of intrigue. J. P. Morgan attempted a hostile takeover of Westinghouse, failed, and then tried it again. The effective monopoly created by the licensing partnership didn't suit his balance sheets quite so well as would a literal one. But Westinghouse, with Paul at his side, saw these attacks coming. Morgan was kept at bay, and the Westinghouse Electric Company remained free of outside ownership. Paul became known for his cunning, not merely on the lawyerly blocks of Broadway, but on Wall Street as well.

Paul founded a new firm with his associates. His success as Westinghouse's chief counsel served as no small advertisement to future clients. He soon had dozens. Most were household names. Paul eventually took over William Seward's old firm, originally founded decades before its name partner had successfully negotiated the Alaska

Purchase. Paul soon brought on Hoyt Moore, an expert in the new field of taxation law, which was becoming more important to the firm's larger corporate clients. Eventually, Paul would promote his own protégé to a partnership: Bob Swaine, a bright young man only a few years out from Harvard Law. (No one's perfect.) Moreover, the pyramidal structure he had developed to handle the light-bulb suit proved useful on other cases as well. He wrote of his "Cravath system" in various journals. Its method was that each suit was overseen by a partner at the firm, below which a team of associates handled the daily drudgery of legal work. The associates ascended through a hierarchy of their own, based on the length of time they'd been with the firm—first years, second years, and so forth, on and on up the totem pole until one day, if they were quite lucky, they might become partners themselves. The system rivaled Westinghouse's factories for efficiency of production.

Paul had turned the practice of law from a craft into an industry. As attorneys from Washington to San Francisco had learned of his system, they'd begun adopting his methods. If only, he thought, one were able to patent the practice of law as one might patent the devices the law protected.

Even Nikola Tesla prospered on and off. While Tesla saw not a cent of income from his work on alternating current, the enterprise he founded with J. P. Morgan's money did not go bankrupt until 1903. His personal wealth, while nothing compared to Edison's or Westinghouse's, was enough for him to take a room at the Waldorf Astoria. It was a short walk from there to Delmonico's, where Tesla would dine every single night, without fail. The manager gave him his own table, which they set each evening especially for him.

The writer Robert Underwood Johnson and his wife, Katharine, made it their sworn mission to find Tesla a suitable mate. Though the couple introduced him to all the most eligible women in New York, and some even took a fancy to the tall, commanding genius, he never reciprocated their affections.

Paul saw him around the city a few times, at dinner and a number of parties. Agnes made sure to attend every event at which she knew he'd be present. She kept close watch over him at first, but over time they grew distant. The fame that she had given up openly delighted him. For a time his name was spread almost as wide as Edison's. Journalists lined up to profile him. He became one of the city's great characters—a mysterious and eccentric sage. A ganglier oracle at Delphi. Paul and Agnes watched as Tesla enjoyed the show. His black suits, Agnes pointed out, were always immaculate. Ever alone in his own world, Tesla had learned to pause and occasionally savor the delicacies of this one.

Paul would never know it, but Nikola Tesla would outlive them all. He died quite penniless in 1943, having had to trade the Waldorf Astoria for a single-occupancy hotel.

Tesla never did invent the non-infringing light bulb that Paul had once so desperately needed; Westinghouse's engineering team did. Under Westinghouse's leadership, they worked methodically to modify the old Sawyer and Man patent. Instead of a single piece of glass surrounding the filament, they used two. Called the "double-stopper lamp," it was mass-produced in Westinghouse's own air-brake factory just in time to light the World's Columbian Exposition of 1893. The courts instantly and unequivocally ruled that this light bulb was fundamentally different from Edison's. Arguably the most lucrative invention of the entire current war did not arrive in any grand spark of individual genius, but rather flowed from a simple, painstakingly achieved modification to a decade-old British design performed over three years by a team of organized experts. Westinghouse held the patent on the double-stopper lamp, but no one person could quite claim to have "invented" it.

And then, of course, there was perhaps the greatest irony of the age: the curious and unexpected fate of U.S. Letters Patent No. 223,898.

Paul and his associates pursued the case vigorously. So did Morgan and Coffin, who could use the victory to bludgeon a number of smaller electrical companies into either bankruptcy or more-profitable licensing arrangements. Westinghouse, flush from success, was happy to spend the legal fees in order to defend his good name. For Paul, it was all a matter of pride. This was the largest patent-infringement case in the world. The attorney who litigated it successfully would secure a place in history.

And so it was that Paul found himself arguing before the Supreme Court of the United States. He argued brilliantly, defending himself against Justice Fuller's quick barbs. He did his work well, and it was a sight to behold. It was the capstone to any lawyer's career.

A few weeks later Paul found out the result. He lost.

And no one much cared.

Edison v. Westinghouse had become an undead lawsuit. It had lived on far past the point that either of its named litigants cared about its result. By the time Edison's patent was upheld in court, it was soon to expire. Westinghouse's double-stopper lamps were already on the market, so he was forbidden from manufacturing a bulb that he'd already stopped making. The few minor electrical companies that had continued using designs similar to Edison's, in the hopes of a Westinghouse victory, were duly sent out of business. In some quiet, smoky room somewhere, Morgan crossed another victory off a long list.

It was, Paul realized, the fate of lawyers that they might lose the case but win the war.

In the rest of Paul Cravath's life, he would see Thomas Edison on only one more occasion.

CHAPTER 72

Niagara Falls, 1896

My model for business is the Beatles. They were four guys who kept each other's . . . negative tendencies in check. They balanced each other and the total was greater than the sum of the parts. That's how I see business: Great things in business are never done by one person. They're done by a team of people.   —STEVE JOBS

O N THE DAY that he would last see Thomas Edison, Paul watched 100 million gallons of white water pour over the great lip of Niagara Falls. A twenty-nine-ton turbine used the raw force of those tumbling gallons to spin a generator that converted it into enough alternating current to power tens of thousands of household light bulbs.

Paul was there for a gala reception to mark the opening of the largest electrical-power generator in the world. It had been built by Westinghouse, designed based on Tesla's ideas, and would power lamps across the East Coast that had been manufactured by Edison's former company, GE. The unveiling was a ceremony of a size as unprecedented as the plant itself. Every figure of any prominence in the American electrical community was in attendance.

Which meant, so Paul realized as he stood at the falls, that Thomas Edison, George Westinghouse, and Nikola Tesla would for one evening all be in the same place. To Paul's amazement, this had never happened before. He knew that it would almost certainly never happen again.

It was after the dull, formal ceremony that Paul stood in the open air, sipping from a flute of champagne as he watched the churning waters. It was nice to be reminded that of all the fantastic things he'd seen in his life, of all the man-made inventions he'd witnessed, none held the power that Niagara did. Or rather that even Westinghouse's perfect current depended upon nature for its power. The God of Paul's father still powered the devices of Paul's client.

From the corner of his eye, Paul saw Edison leaning against the railing over the water. To Paul's surprise, Westinghouse was with him. As was Tesla. They were talking.

Paul didn't know whether to approach the group, but Edison caught a glimpse of him and waved him over.

"Mr. Cravath," said Edison. "I didn't know if you'd be here."

Paul nodded. What was there to say to this man whose life had once so dominated his own?

"Mr. Bell sends his greetings," said Edison.

". . . Excuse me?"

"Mr. Bell says hello. I was at dinner with him in Nova Scotia just the other month. He told me the story of your visit."

Paul was startled. "He said he was helping me for your sake."

Edison nodded. "It worked. I'll have to have you down to my new laboratory sometime. I've been working on motion pictures."

Paul's face made clear he had no clue as to what the phrase "motion pictures" might refer.

"You should see, Mr. Paul Cravath," added Tesla. "Many photographs all in a row. It creates an appearance of a real thing moving."

"How have you seen it?" asked Paul.

"My laboratory on Fifth Avenue, New York, has gotten crowded. I broke some items." Tesla shook his head sadly. "I am clumsy, it is possible, with my things. Mr. Thomas Edison offered a space for working to myself. While some unnecessaries were cleaned away."

"It's actually quite nice to have Nikola around," said Edison. "It's been a pleasure to bounce ideas off him, see what he thinks of the new cameras. My boys are very much in awe. I've built the camera lab next to Tesla's; Black Maria, I call it. A 'motion picture' studio. It's fun. All in all, these years have been . . . well, they've been the happiest of my life. So whatever part you played in that, Mr. Cravath, I just wanted to say . . . you didn't do so badly."

Paul stared. After a long moment of silence, he laughed. Of all the things he'd imagined that Thomas Edison might ever say to him, he'd never imagined that.

He extended his hand, and Edison shook it.

All four men turned their attention to Niagara. Together they gazed out at the froth. The wet spray rose up from the waterfall, a mist rising up to the heavens. The effect was hypnotizing. As they stared, Paul noticed that Tesla's eyes went elsewhere. To somewhere that none of the others could see.

"Wonder," said Edison.

Paul turned. "What's that?"

"Wonder," said Edison again. "I fear it's soon out."

"It won't ever go out," said Westinghouse.

"Wonder?" asked Paul, not quite following along.

"Our age of invention," explained Edison. "These days of hand-crafted miracles . . . they won't last much longer. Does that ever worry any of you? Light bulbs. Electricity. It seems likely that ours will be the last generation to ever gaze, wide-eyed, at something truly novel. That our kind will be the last to ever stare in disbelief at a man-made thing that could not possibly exist. We made wonders, boys. I only wonder how many of them are left to make."

"The study of science," said Tesla, "it is not ever to end."

Edison nodded. "That's true. But it won't be like this. It will be more . . . technical. Inside the magic box, not outside it. A light bulb is intuitive; an X-ray is practically alchemy. The machines are becoming so infernally complicated that barely a soul can even conceptualize how they work. And moreover, they won't need to in order to use the things. From here we can only build incrementally. Improvements. Not revolutions. No new colors, only new hues. Do you remember the first time you saw a light bulb at work?"

"I practically fainted," said Westinghouse. "I didn't think it was possible. That was barely fifteen years ago."

"Exactly," said Edison. "And when was the last time you saw any-thing that made you feel that way?"

"I always saw it," said Tesla. The men turned to him. "The electri-cal bulbs. I have seen them always." He tapped his fingertips twice against the side of his head. "Here."

Westinghouse and Edison both laughed.

"We know," said Westinghouse. "And we're grateful for it."

Edison asked, "Have you met that young fellow—what's his name . . . Ford?"

"I gave him his first job," said Westinghouse.

"I must have given him his second," said Edison. "He's probably younger than Mr. Cravath here. It's depressing. I like Henry Ford, I honestly do. But he's not . . . well, he's just cut of a newer cloth, that's all. So damned professional. Everything done to perfection. His ca-reer planned out from the start. He knows exactly where he's going: what sort of company he wants to start, how to run it, what they'll work on. Can you imagine? In our day all you had was a few stray strips of wire and—if you were really lucky—enough pennies for a stamp to mail a sketch to the patent office. Ford has a goddamned *business plan*."

"A professional inventor," said Westinghouse.

"A professional scientist," said Edison. "Darwin never made a cent off what he did. Neither did Newton. Hooke. The whole of the Royal Society lot—they simply found things out. Invented things because they could. Not because there was money in it. We got wealthy doing what they did for fun."

"And now a whole generation is setting out to grow rich from their idle fiddling."

"And so there will be little fiddling that remains purely idle."

The irony in Edison's speech made Paul smile, but he kept his amusement to himself. This newfangled marriage of business and sci-ence that would birth technology was precisely what Edison himself had created. It was his greatest invention. And, like all progeny, it was now going to leave its maker behind.

Paul watched the three inventors fall into silence as they stared out at the churning falls.

The current war already felt like an exotic and arcane quarrel. Like a strange dream whose plot had faded in the morning light. Their machinations would soon be forgotten. But the world it had led to, the one in which he now lived, was permanent.

Who had invented the light bulb? That was the question that had started the whole story off.

It was all of them. Only together could they have birthed the system that was now the bone and sinew of these United States. No one man could have done it. In order to produce such a wonder, Paul realized, the world required men like each of them. Visionaries like Tesla. Craftsmen like Westinghouse. Salesmen like Edison.

And what of Paul? Perhaps the world needed men like him too. Mere mortals to clean up the messes of giants. Clever men to witness and record the affairs of brilliant ones. Perhaps if Tesla had invented the light bulb, and Westinghouse had too, and so had Edison, well then, Paul had a claim to it himself. Maybe Paul was more of an inventor than he'd thought.

He smiled very briefly at the notion.

The men said their goodbyes. One by one, the inventors drained their glasses as they drifted back from the misty precipice.

Paul was the last of them to leave. He watched as the sun began to set across the water. The river glowed the day's last rainbow of golden yellow and shimmering orange. He turned away, descending the stairwell into the darkening shadow of a country that was just becoming America.

As a work of historical fiction, this novel is intended as a dramatization of history, not a recording of it. Nothing you've read here should be understood as verifiable fact. However, the bulk of the events depicted in this book did happen and every major character did exist. Much of the dialogue comes either from the historical personages' own mouths or from the tips of their prodigious pens. Yet many of these events have been reordered and characters appear in places they may not have. I've frequently invented situations that very well could have happened but were certainly not documented. This book is a Gordian knot of verifiable truth, educated supposition, dramatic rendering, and total guesswork. What I'd like to do in this note is to help untangle it for you.

Additional material, including a chronology of actual events, can be found on my website: mrgrahammoore.com.

Almost all of the events that historians generally describe as forming the "current war" took place between 1888 and 1896. I have compressed the narrative into only two years, from 1888 to 1890. As you'll see, even though most of the major scenes depicted did occur in one way or another, I've fudged their chronology. What was often simultaneous in real life becomes sequential in this book. I've frequently taken multiple events or multiple historical characters and amalgamated them. This is to help the reader's tracking of the many story lines and to give narrative shape to the messily discrete events of history.

Empires of Light: Edison, Tesla, Westinghouse, and the Race to Electrify the World, by Jill Jonnes, is for my money the most delightful nonfiction account of the current war. It contains brilliantly sketched portraits of

Thomas Edison, George Westinghouse, and Nikola Tesla, as well as thoughtful insights into their rivalries and antipathies.

When I first discovered that a twenty-six-year-old attorney, only eighteen months out of law school, was at the center of the current war before going on to found one of America's most preeminent law firms, I immediately wanted to learn everything I could about him. I was shocked to find that there is no proper biography of Paul Cravath. It was this absence of scholarly history that inspired me to write this book, and it was the paucity of material available that dictated it should be a novel.

The basic biographical information about Paul Cravath and his family contained in the novel is true. My descriptions of Paul and his life come from the few sources we have: *The Cravath Firm and Its Predecessors 1819–1948* (Robert Swaine, privately printed), a *New Yorker* profile of him from when he became chairman of the board of the Metropolitan Opera in 1932 ("Public Man," *The New Yorker*, January 2, 1932), an entry in *The National Cyclopædia of American Biography* (Volume 11, 1902), his and Agnes's wedding announcement ("Marriage of Agnes Huntington," *Chicago Tribune*, November 16, 1892), the Oberlin student newspaper, and of course his court filings.

My depiction of Thomas Edison is largely based on *The Wizard of Menlo Park: How Thomas Alva Edison Invented the Modern World*, by Randall Stross. It's a wonderful and highly engaging biography of Edison, and it supplied a lot of Edison's personality and biography in this book. Edison's voice is drawn from his letters and journals, which are kept at Rutgers University. Edison wrote in his diary most every day of his life, and through it one gets a fascinating glimpse of his inner thoughts. The majority of the Edison Papers at Rutgers are online, as of this writing.

There is no definitive biography of George Westinghouse, but that's a book that I would very much love to read one day.

All personal and biographical description of Nikola Tesla contained here is accurate. Margaret Cheney's *Tesla: Man Out of Time* was an extremely helpful resource, as was Tesla's own autobiography, *My Inventions: The Autobiography of Nikola Tesla*. It's as singular a reading experience as you'd expect.

Many historical accounts of Nikola Tesla mention his impenetrable accent and the difficulties faced by those struggling to decipher his speech. In real life, however, his grammar was impeccable, if elaborate. It was only his thick accent that made him so hard for Americans to under-stand. This left me with a problem: How to convey Tesla's accent on the page? I could transliterate his Serbian accent, but that seemed inelegant to read. ("Meeesterr Crahvahth . . .")

But as I read through Tesla's autobiography, a solution presented itself. Tesla wrote in long, winding, grammatically adventurous sentences. His English was fluent, but it was almost archaic, even for the 1880s. Every sentence reads as if it's about to fall in on itself from the grammatical circumlocutions and unexpected word choices. What I've done here is to use his writing style as a model for his speaking style, while upending the grammar so he's even harder to understand. This makes his sentences as confusing to read as they would be to hear.

When it comes to Agnes Huntington, the historical record is shock-ingly blank. All information that we have about her comes from an ar-ticle about her career and marriage in *The Illustrated American* (December 3, 1892); her entry in *The Dramatic Peerage* from 1892; her entry in *Woman's Who's Who of America* (1914–1915); an interview she gave about her legal troubles with W. H. Foster ("Agnes Huntington's Story," *The New York Times*, December 14, 1886); her entry in *Lippincott's Magazine of Literature, Science and Education* (Volume 49, 1892); a review of her per-formance in *Paul Jones* ("Paul Jones in New-York," *The New York Times*, September 21, 1890); the 1870 U.S. Census of Kalamazoo; gossip reports of her engagement to Henry Jayne (*Town Topics*, November 3, 1892; "Did He Jilt 'Paul Jones,'" *The Washington Post*, October 30, 1892; "De-nied by Miss Huntington," *The New York Times*, October 30, 1892).

From those sources, I can confidently assert the following: Agnes Huntington was born in Kalamazoo, Michigan, but never found renown (or even mention!) in society until her first appearance singing in Lon-don. She made a name for herself in Europe, accompanied always by her mother, who seemed oddly silent about their family background. As far as I can tell, even though Agnes and Fannie have the last name Hun-tington, they were not related to the famous Huntington family, either its California branch or its East Coast one. Agnes had some sort of murky legal squabble with the manager of the Boston Ideals. She had many gentleman admirers of very high status on both sides of the pond. She was engaged to Henry Jayne for a time, but he broke it off in 1892. She later married Paul Cravath, an up-and-coming New York lawyer who at that point in their lives would have been of considerably lower social status.

Everything else about Agnes's story in this novel is imagined (the stolen dress, the borrowed name, etc.). The manner in which she meets Paul—hiring him as her attorney—is also imagined, though the case for which she hires him is real. (In reality her lawyer was named Abram Dittenhoefer.) In compressing the timeline of events, however, I've moved this legal case from 1886 to 1888. In real life it would have been resolved before Paul became Westinghouse's attorney.

It is my belief—though I can't prove it—that the historical Agnes Huntington was hiding something about her past. Something tells me her real story is even more fantastic than the one I've created for her in these pages.

Chapter 1: The opening scene of the burning workman is based on two real public immolations: one on May 11, 1888 ("A Wireman's Recklessness," *The New York Times*, May 12, 1888) and another on October 11, 1889 ("Met Death in the Wires," *The New York Times*, October 12, 1889). Paul was likely not present for either of these, but as the first took place mere blocks from his office, placing him on the scene seemed reasonable enough.

Chapter 7: Reginald Fessenden did work for Edison before he went to work for Westinghouse, with a stop at Purdue in between, though the timeline has been simplified here. Fessenden was not actually Edison's mole within the Westinghouse operation. The real mole was of lower status—a humble draftsman, arrested in 1893.

Chapters 15–16: Tesla did go to work for Westinghouse outside Pittsburgh in 1888, in exchange for a license on his alternating-current patents. The fundamental shift in strategy on Westinghouse's side in going from a "house by house" electrical system to a "network" electrical system is discussed in Thomas P. Hughes's fascinating *Networks of Power: Electrification in Western Society, 1880–1930*. However, in reality this shift was not as sudden as I've rendered it. Westinghouse had been interested in A/C technology for a few years before Tesla's demonstration—which is real, though Westinghouse was not present for it. Westinghouse acquired a portfolio of A/C patents to develop as early as 1886; he just hadn't gotten the technology to work yet.

Chapter 21: The crisis concerning royalty structures that confronted Westinghouse and his attorneys following Tesla's sudden departure is real, though the timeline has been compressed and we don't know whether the negotiating error was Paul's.

Chapter 25: Both the mysterious fire in Tesla's laboratory as well as Tesla's ensuing mental breakdown and amnesia did occur. They just took place at different times, and in a different order, than the sequence presented here.

In 1892, Tesla's long hours of work in his lab, on the concept of "wireless telephones," sent him into a mental breakdown. He passed out and woke with no memories of his life at all, save scattered images of his infancy. He spent months in bed, struggling to regain his memories. It was some time before he was finally able to invent again.

This episode recalled other moments of mental illness in Tesla's life. According to his autobiography, he experienced frequent hallucinations, both visual and auditory. He wrote: "[These hallucinations] usually occurred when I found myself in a dangerous or distressing situation, or when I was greatly exhilarated. In some instances I have seen all the air around me filled with tongues of living flame." These visions, however, gave him insight into the machines he began to design. Thomas Hughes and others have explored whether Tesla might have been diagnosed with schizophrenia were he alive today; to my mind, it seems likely that he would have been. Tesla figuratively saw the world in ways that no one else did in part because Tesla *literally* saw the world in ways that no one else did.

Three years after this breakdown and recovery, on March 13, 1895, a fire engulfed Tesla's lab. Tesla was not present when this fire broke out—he discovered it the next morning, at which point he became inconsolable as to the destruction of his machines.

Chapter 34: Paul's big idea that he could construct an industrial system for the law—just as Westinghouse had for manufacturing and Edison had for inventions—is very much accurate. I think it's fair to say that Paul Cravath invented the modern law firm, in exactly the same way that Edison, Westinghouse, and Tesla invented the light bulb.

However, Paul is generally credited with inventing his "Cravath system" in the early 1900s. I've moved this idea to 1888–90, so that it might fit within this narrative. Whether Paul was in fact inspired by Edison and Westinghouse when he had this idea is impossible to say, but seeing as he did implement these ideas after his experience with those two inventors, it seemed to me likely that he was.

Chapter 36: Agnes's interview with *The New York Times* is real, though I've combined two *Times* pieces—"Agnes Huntington's Story," December 14, 1886, and "Paul Jones in New-York," September 21, 1890—into one.

Chapter 37: Harold Brown's character and backstory are largely accurate and are discussed in Jill Jonnes's *Empires of Light* as well as in Tom McNichol's *AC/DC: The Savage Tale of the First Standards War*, Mark Essig's *Edison and the Electric Chair*, and Richard Moran's *Executioner's Current*.

The timeline of Brown's campaign to promote the electric chair has been compressed—I depict the flurry of activity over the chair as happening in early 1889, but it actually happened at the end of 1887. The description of Brown's horrifying animal electrocutions is accurate. Brown's dialogue in these scenes is partially verbatim, though I've trimmed some parts and elaborated upon others for a more conversational tone. If anything, I have probably minimized the physical horrors he committed on these poor animals. In reality, he quickly progressed from dogs to horses to—seriously—an elephant.

Chapters 38–39: Someone really did break in to Harold Brown's office in August 1889. After the burglary, stolen letters proving a connection between Edison and Brown were leaked to *The New York Sun*.

Did Paul do it? Most historians feel that *someone* on Westinghouse's side did. If so, it stands to reason that Paul at least knew about it and kept the secret. So while this scene is invented, Paul's moral culpability in the events thereof is certainly plausible.

Chapter 41: What Paul refers to as the "lie" on Edison's patent application—that is, the *discrepancy* between the filament specified and the filament that his company would come to use—is accurate. However, I've simplified the progression of Edison's filament experiments, and whether or not this constitutes deceit rather depends on one's perspective about the nature of invention.

Edison's undeniable fraud about when he'd gotten the bulb to work, on the other hand, has been depicted fairly. Edison's habit of exaggerating to the loyal press—or in this case flat-out lying to them—was a recurring theme throughout his career.

Chapter 48: The courtroom scene of Paul arguing against A/C use in a New York State execution is a dramatization of a real case. The murder is real, but I've moved it from March 1889 to May 1889.

Westinghouse was in fact betrayed by Charles Coffin in the manner described, a treachery that took his team by surprise. One of Westinghouse's lawyers really did go to Buffalo to try this case in court, though it was not Paul, and Harold Brown was not present.

Chapter 49: The description of the execution of William Kemmler is accurate and comes from contemporaneous newspaper accounts, such as "Far Worse Than Hanging," *The New York Times*, August 7, 1890.

Also, while the electrocution itself is described accurately, neither Paul nor Harold Brown was in fact there to witness it.

Chapters 50–52: The financial crisis that followed the Baring Brothers collapse is real, though I've moved it from November 1890 to September 1889. The tactics by which Paul and Westinghouse attempted to weather the crisis have been rendered accurately. That Edison and Morgan then used their considerable Wall Street muscle to drive Westinghouse further toward bankruptcy is true, though it's hard to know exactly what backroom deals were being made during the financial crisis.

Chapter 55: All descriptions of Fisk University are accurate, as are descriptions of the Cravath family's involvement therein. (Based on *The Cravath Firm and Its Predecessors 1819–1948*, by Robert Swaine, and *Thy Loyal Children Make Their Way: Fisk University since 1866*, by Reavis Mitchell, Jr.)

All description of the work on X-rays that Tesla conducts there is based on real work that Tesla did in 1895, though not, of course, at Fisk. The specific characters of the Fisk students are invented.

Chapters 56–57: The scene of Alexander Graham Bell is imagined, though Bell's history and personality have been rendered as accurately as possible. All of the backstory on Bell depicted here is real—if simplified—and is based on *Reluctant Genius: Alexander Graham Bell and the Passion for Invention*, by Charlotte Gray.

In this book's final chapters, Paul Cravath hatches and implements a multifaceted plan to win the current war. This plan involves organizing a secret coup within Edison General Electric, backed by J. P. Morgan, to depose Edison as the company's head and replace him with Charles Coffin. Then Nikola Tesla is talked into signing away his royalties on Westinghouse's A/C systems. The current war is ended, with Westinghouse victorious and Edison tragically excommunicated from the company he founded.

All of these events occurred. However, the timeline of events has been compressed from a few years to just a few months, and Paul has been depicted as the mastermind behind the whole thing. In reality, we don't know what his role was.

It is unlikely that Paul was present at the swindling of Tesla. Jonnes describes Westinghouse visiting Tesla alone and delivering the arguments Paul makes in this novel. Tesla seemed, in his own writing, proud of his decision to give away the royalty. He really did believe what Westinghouse told him.

Chapter 72: Paul, Westinghouse, and Tesla did attend an event at the Niagara Falls power plant on July 19, 1896. However, I've combined some details of this event with a subsequent one at which only Tesla was present, in January 1897.

Edison was not at either of these ceremonies. However, Tesla had taken refuge in Edison's West Orange laboratory after the fire at his lab. The two men had become friends. And then on Tesla's way to Niagara Falls he actually stopped by Westinghouse's home outside Pittsburgh. Tesla spent many hours in the warm company of both Westinghouse and Edison in those days, some of which Paul, as counsel to Westinghouse, was present to witness.

GRAHAM MOORE
Los Angeles
February 5, 2016

WRITING THIS BOOK would simply not have been possible, much less advisable, without the essential care and guidance of:

Jennifer Joel, my literary agent and creative partner

Noah Eaker, my editor and loyal adversary

Susan Kamil, my publisher and champion

Keya Vakil, my research assistant and partner in crime

Tom Drumm, my manager and unwavering voice of calm

I'd like to give my deepest thanks as well to the generous friends who read (oh so many) early drafts and offered their invaluable suggestions: Ben Epstein, Susanna Fogel, Alice Boone, Nora Grossman, Ido Ostrowsky, and Suzanne Joskow.

The initial idea for this story came about during a long conversation on a road trip through Pennsylvania with Helen and Dan Estabrook. I'm indebted to both for their enthusiasm as well as their safe driving.

All of my thoughts about the nature of invention and technological innovation were generated, explored, and honed during a thousand lunches and late-night chats with Avinash Karnani, Matt Wallaert, Samantha Culp, and my (little) brother Evan Moore.

While titling this book, I was fortunate enough to receive assistance (and commiseration) from Sam Wasson and Mary Laws.

Many thanks to the copyeditors who taught me more about English grammar than I ever learned in school: Dennis Ambrose, Benjamin Dreyer, Deb Dwyer, and Kathy Lord.

I'm immensely grateful to the legal historians Christopher Beauchamp, of Brooklyn Law School, and Adam Mossoff, of George Mason University, for each spending many thankless hours on the phone explaining the history of patent law to me. One couldn't imagine better teachers; I find myself jealous of their very lucky law students. Any legal errors in this book are my fault alone.

I'm further indebted to the following experts, who were gracious enough to lend me their respective expertise in filling in the countless historical and scientific details contained in the narrative:

Christopher T. Baer at the Hagley Museum and Library

John Balow and Madeleine Cohen at the New York Public Library

Kurt Bell at the Pennsylvania State Archives, Pennsylvania Historical and Museum Commission

Nathan Brewer and Robert Coburn at the IEEE History Center at Stevens Institute of Technology

Mike Dowell at the Louisville & Nashville Railroad Historical Society Archives

C. Allen Parker, Deborah Farone, and Diane O'Donnell at Cravath, Swaine & Moore

Jennifer Fauxsmith at the Massachusetts Archives

Mark Horenstein, professor of applied electromagnetics at Boston University

Paul Israel, director and general editor of the Thomas A. Edison Papers, Rutgers University

Deborah May at the Nashville Library

John Pennino at the Metropolitan Opera

Henry Scannell at the Boston Public Library

Nicholas Zmijewski at the Railroad Museum of Pennsylvania

And finally, thank you to my family, for letting me do this with my life.

GRAHAM MOORE is the *New York Times* bestselling author of *The Sherlockian*, and the Academy Award–winning screenwriter of *The Imitation Game*, which also won a Writers Guild of America Award for best adapted screenplay. Moore was born in Chicago, received a BA in religious history from Columbia University in 2003, and now lives in Los Angeles.

MrGrahamMoore.com

Facebook.com/GrahamMooreWriter

@MrGrahamMoore

This book was set in Goudy Old Style, a typeface designed by Frederic William Goudy (1865–1947). Goudy began his career as a bookkeeper, but devoted the rest of his life to the pursuit of "recognized quality" in a printing type.

Goudy Old Style was produced in 1914 and was an instant bestseller for the foundry. It has generous curves and smooth, even color. It is regarded as one of Goudy's finest achievements.